BEFORE DAWN

THE AFTER DARK SERIES
BOOK TWO

DEAN ALAN CONRAD

eBook ISBN: 979-8-9904560-2-0

Print Edition ISBN: 979-8-9904560-3-7

Acknowledgments

I am indebted to my son Spencer and daughter-in-law Jennifer for their artistic talents in designing the cover artwork for After Dark and Before Dawn. I can't wait to see how the cover turns out for The Reluctant Vampire, the third and final book in the Ater Dark Series. Also, thank you to my daughter Meredith for tirelessly helping promote my books.

As always, thank you to my editor, Gail Delaney.

CHAPTER ONE

The knock at Del Hatch's front door surprised him.

There was a time when salesmen went door-to-door, but that was a bygone era. Hardly no one knocked anymore. Even though he was new to the neighborhood, the formalities of meeting new neighbors were over. Casseroles had been consumed and the Pyrex dishes cleaned and returned to their owners with thank you notes placed inside the covers. Plates of cakes and cookies were the first to disappear. Del had a sweet tooth. Some names were still tricky in his mind, but he knew who had kids and dogs. He heard them enough. School buses jolted him out of bed in the morning.

The knock came again and a third time. There might be trouble and Del had said, after all, "If you ever need anything..." Each rap, after a brief pause, got louder. Del stood from the table where he was at work on the daily newspaper Sudoku, walked through the kitchen, dining room, and living room to the front door. Beveled and wavy old glass distorted the images outside. Del would have to open the door to see who it was. At least he could tell there were three people waiting and one was a tall Black man.

The vampire hunters were outside on the stoop. Overboard

George was about to knock a fourth time when Del opened the door. The intruders would surely get the message Del was annoyed. He didn't like to be interrupted when he worked on a Sudoku. There was a gasp of surprise and recognition. Del grasped Overboard George's hand and pulled him into the home. They hugged and hooted. Then held each other at arm's length to get a better look.

"I don't believe it!" Del shouted. "George. I thought you were…"

"Dead?"

"Well, if not then at least off the grid."

"That's where I been," Overboard George said, with a beaming smile. "Well off the grid, but now I'm back. I hope we're not intruding."

"You? Never. I was planning a trip. Out Washington state."

The women George was with stood grinning, apparently embarrassed.

"Good for you, Del. We're a little pressed for time, so I'll get to the point. I need a gun."

Del raised a hand and scratched his chin. Looked at Overboard George. "What caliber?"

"Large. We need to kill a vampire."

"I thought…" Del started. He pursed his lips as Overboard George interrupted.

"The bullets are supposed to slow her down."

"*Her*? Now you got my interest."

"Then we'll stake her and finish the job."

Del looked to the women who nodded in agreement.

"She's fast as the devil and mean as a bitch. By the way, I'm Old Harriet."

"And I'm OG's girl. My name is Mad Maggie."

Del Hatch closed his eyes and cocked his head as if he were memorizing the women's names. Then he stared at Old Harriet's lopsided beehive hairdo for a moment. "It's nice to meet you. I have just the thing you need. Come on in. I'll put coffee on."

"No time," Overboard George said. "We're losing sunlight."

Del smiled and looked at the sky for a moment. "Yes. Of course. Vampires. Let's go."

Del twisted his mouth and raised an eyebrow, then ushered the group into his reloading room off the kitchen. He pulled out a World War II-era Browning Automatic Rifle, better known as a BAR, from one of several gun safes, opened the action, and handed it to Overboard George.

"It's a beauty," George said, with a smile, hefting the rifle, sniffing the gun oil. He worked the action himself and dry-fired the empty gun.

"I know a little of its history," Del said. "This one was used in Europe against the Nazis. How'd you like to lug this around all day? Plus tripod? Plus ammo? Weighs about twenty pounds."

"No thanks."

Del was tall and lean and wore a khaki jumpsuit that zippered up the front. It looked custom-made. His pant legs were bloused inside highly polished laced-up boots. "I'm ready when you folks are. I expect we want to do this in the daylight. I do have night-vision goggles, but not enough for us all." He loaded his pockets with extra twenty-round clips for the rifle. Del smiled and added, "If I shoot that vampire with more than one clip, there won't be anything left to stake. This baby can shoot up to 650 rounds per minute. It's a fearsome weapon. Has a distinctive sound. The Nazis hated it."

"If you don't get her with one clip, you'll never load the second," Old Harriet said.

"She's that fast?" Del asked. He stared again at Old Harriet.

"Faster," Old Harriet said, with an emphatic nod of her frizzy head and its teetering pile of hair.

Del looked at Overboard George, who smiled. "She's right. If you're lucky, all you see is a blur, and hope she's going the other way. We want to hit her while she's standing still."

"Then I won't miss. I'll fire from the hip. Aim in front of her. Spray so many bullets a mosquito wouldn't get through."

"She might be naked, Del, so stay focused," Mad Maggie said, with a smile. "Don't go all googly-eyed if you see her tits. After she feeds, they stand straight out like a teenager's, but she's older than your great, great, great, great grandmother. You might be able to add a couple more *greats* till you reach her true age."

"Don't worry about me," Del said. "I've seen plenty of tits. All shapes, sizes, and colors. Isn't that right, George? I understand the mission."

"We already killed two of the undead this morning. She's the last to go," Old Harriet said.

Since his retirement from the Navy, Del Hatch was more comfortable carrying a camera tracking Bigfoot around inhospitable territories, appearing on Sasquatch-oriented television shows and documentaries as a survivalist and expert cryptid tracker, than pointing a BAR loaded with .30-06-caliber armor-piercing bullets at anything other than targets.

The group piled into Del's SUV and roared off to After Dark. Del was an old Navy buddy George knew from what seemed like a previous life before George became a heroin addict and homeless. The two worked aboard the same ship, in the same radio room. They palled around together on shore leave and knew how to get out of trouble when they got in it, even if it meant losing some skin on their knuckles. They shared a lot of laughs until George went AWOL. Then they lost touch.

From the back seat, Old Harriet chirped, "I find it strange that you turned over a gun like this to us."

"Well, if George says he wants to kill a vampire, I believe there must be such a thing, even if I never saw a vampire," Del said, scrutinizing Old Harriet in the rearview mirror. He smiled. "Hell, I never saw a Bigfoot, either, but I believe they exist. I plan on seeing one of them someday and taking his photo."

"What if the Bigfoot in front of your camera is a *she?*" Old Harriet said.

Del Hatch grinned. "I don't discriminate."

***

OVERBOARD GEORGE ENTERED After Dark's basement tentatively, one step at a time from the trap door hidden in a grassy lot near the historic restaurant and bar, careful to remain in the sunlight that shined down the stairwell, where he knew he would be safe from Eva the ancient vampiress. Overboard George never thought he'd return to this foul-smelling place, but now here he was. His converted potato gun was primed and ready to fire a wooden stake at anything that moved. Other than the three vampire fighters with him, there shouldn't be anything *living* left in the large, high-ceilinged dank basement. Mad Maggie and Old Harriet carried similar weapons. In addition, Maggie had a machete strapped to her hip. It had become her weapon of choice.

This was the third trip to the basement for Overboard George. The first time he was captured by mutated vampires, dog-like creatures who brought in the homeless — mostly junkies — to be exsanguinated after their blood cleared and was free of drugs. Mad Maggie followed a day later. She wasn't a user. She was just crazy. She was on the lam too, after killing her mother's abusive boyfriend years earlier. Old Harriet, with her beehive hairdo, was another junkie who joined the group to kill vampires. She had nothing better to do. Now, only one of the undead remained in this colony.

The square of sunlight on the concrete floor that had kept them safe during the previous attack hours earlier was smaller, less intense now as the day progressed, making a thin, oblong, creepy-looking window shape, the kind you might see in an old Universal Pictures movie. It was hardly big enough to protect them all from the vampire they hoped and dreaded was still there. The vampire they intended to kill. *Really* kill this time. They panned their weapons across the basement, including the ceiling. *You never knew where you might find the undead. They always liked to attach themselves to ceilings in movies,* Overboard George thought. *Especially one as crafty as this ancient female.* Her strength was incredible, and she was able to outrun their potato gun stakes. That's where Del Hatch's BAR came in. He'd knock the wind out of the beast and allow the others to stake her.

Most of the overhead fluorescent bulbs had been smashed since they had retreated from the basement that morning. The remaining ones flickered and hummed, casting dim light and deep Shadows. The switch for the ultraviolet ceiling lights had been pulled from the wall. Those lights, as lethal to a vampire as direct sunlight, controlled the Whistlers and could cook both them and the vampires in a matter of seconds. Now those lethal lights were useless. The smell of death was heavy in the damp air. The door to the vampires' secret crypt hung open. Del Hatch checked it. As expected, the crypt was empty. A line of abandoned caskets lay on the floor. In the distance, in the main basement, the feeding room door was open, too. That is where Eva fled and locked herself inside to escape the vampire hunters during the first raid. She must be somewhere in the basement. After all, she should be trapped inside while there was still daylight.

The attack on After Dark basement was hardly a success, George thought, as he moved forward. The vampire fighter known as New Girl was dead, her neck torn out, her body crushed against the basement stone wall, flung there by the male vampire Gerrard. Her body still lay in a heap to George's right. Still, Lisa Van der Meer, pregnant with Jimmy Young's baby, and Jimmy himself had been rescued from their basement cells. The couple had returned to the safety of Lisa's apartment, where they awaited the outcome of this latest foray. The cruel vampiress, who planned to sacrifice Lisa's infant at the moment of birth, had escaped in a blur, outrunning their wooden stakes, and fleeing to the feeding room, where an unknown number of victims had been drained of blood. The vampiress's brother Gerrard, who had once dined with Napoleon, was staked, and so was Charles Van der Meer, Lisa's father, recently turned into a vampire. Both were reduced to piles of ashes that slowly scattered across the floor by the outside air currents that rushed down the exterior stairwell. The stakes that killed them still lay on the floor, Gerrard's near the steps. Charles's was in the crypt, where he was staked before he registered his first kill as a new vampire.

The Whistlers, the foul, mutated vampires who caught the homeless and conveyed them to the basement to be used as food, were cornered in their pen, reduced to noxious, putrid puddles, all killed by volleys of stakes from the potato guns. The basement was eerily quiet. Occasionally there was a crack when a vampire hunter shifted weight or took a step over the lightbulb glass that littered the floor. Somewhere in the darkness water dripped, steady and constant, almost like a heartbeat.

Bo Bentwood, another vampire fighter, had disappeared as the attack started. His whereabouts were unknown. The vampiress had a special liking for Bo, and some fighters believed he was under her control. Others thought he had chickened out on the first attack at the last minute and fled back to the safety of his university frat house. Regardless, the vampire fighters believed Bo was already dead or left with a grimly short life expectancy.

They moved ahead cautiously, keeping a wary eye on the oblong stretch of sunlight and the distance between them and their only escape route. As if in a child's game, the splash of sunlight on the dusty floor was their base, a

safe zone regulated by the ever-moving sun and interrupted occasionally by late afternoon clouds. Overboard George led the group. His mouth was dry. It was difficult to swallow. Mad Maggie shuffled her feet along the concrete floor, to avoid stepping on glass. It wasn't like the vampiress wouldn't know they returned to the lair.

She knew they were coming the first time. In her own nervousness, Old Harriet scratched her head under her dilapidated beehive hairdo.

The vampiress's reign of terror was almost over. The homeless on the street would have one less problem to think about. When junkies disappeared, leaving behind their scant possessions, friends never knew whether they would return. Were they taken by the Whistlers, dead from an overdose, reclaimed by their families in a surprise intervention, entered rehab, or simply moved away to another street, another city? Life on the street was not much different from life a hundred or two hundred years ago. People might disappear unexpectedly. Anyone who moved any distance probably would never be seen again. The modern homeless often had problems remembering time and places, keeping appointments, recalling the names of friends on the street. It didn't take long for a person to become forgotten.

The vampire hunters moved slowly across the floor, ever watchful. Their breath was deep. They shared glances often to bolster their nerve. It was important to know they were all still there. Even a grimace, registered as a smile, helped. As they approached the feeding room door, Del moved in front. He pointed the rifle toward the door indicating he would spray the room with bullets if anything moved. He motioned for Mad Maggie to check behind the feeding room door, first, a place where the vampire might hide.

Mad Maggie faced the heavy door and sidestepped along its wooden front, her stake gun ready to fire. She reached the edge of the door, took a look back at George—who raised his weapon, nodded—and jumped to the side. The space behind the door was empty. The vampire hunters released a collective sigh.

DEL APPROACHED the feeding room door, stopped for a moment, turned his head to nod at the others. He motioned for them to move to his left away from the rifle's receiver, which would spew a stream of spent shells when he fired. Del took a deep breath and jumped into the opening. The room was empty. Somehow, the vampiress had fled the basement in full sunlight.

"Maybe she went upstairs, but the restaurant's open, has been for hours," Overboard George said, scratching his head. "There might be another passage underground for her to escape, or a vault where she can wait until dark. Fan out. Check the walls. Look for anything suspicious."

The vampire fighters separated. They tapped on the stones, looking for hollow-sounding voids, secret latches, unusual drafts. They ran their fingers over the dusty mortar in the rock walls. Del kept a nervous eye on the high ceiling, checked between the beams. They rummaged through the vast stack of moldy, foul-smelling clothing that was stripped off victims after they were captured. Del and Old Harriet stood a few feet away, trained their weapons on the pile, while George and Maggie dug through it, a possible hiding place they didn't want to ignore.

"These look like your shorts," Mad Maggie said, waving a pair of red pants over her head. "Want 'em back?"

"Here's my shirt, too. All torn up." George added, lifting the shirt on the barrel of his potato gun. He examined the shredded, blood-stained T-shirt for a moment, dropped it on the floor, and kicked it away. "I don't want the shorts, either. You can toss them. They were part of a life I don't want to go back to, even though right now I'd give anything for a fix. I just wish I could turn off that desire for dope. It's a hunger that won't give up."

"One day at a time, Brother," Del said. He winked at George. "You can do it. You were a leader back in the day. You're a leader again."

Overboard George acknowledged the compliment with a smile.

The sun was setting when they finished their investigation of the basement. All the walls were solid. Overboard George and Del hauled New Girl's slight body up the steps and laid her on the ground outside, on her back, with her arms at her sides. Her face was bloodied and swollen where it struck the wall. Half her small neck was gone where the vampire Gerrard bit her. Finally, they closed the ground-level door and sat on the grass.

"There's your vampire escape route," Del said, pointing at barely visible tire tracks that led across the grass to the street. "I'd say it was a van."

"I wouldn't have noticed them," Overboard George said. "The tires left hardly a trace."

"A van without windows in the back," Maggie chimed in. "Somebody threw a cape over her head to avoid the sun. That's how it works. That's how they move vampires during the day when they don't have a casket to put them in."

"So, she has help. Someone, maybe more than one, like Chaz was," Overboard George said, slowly, looking skyward for a moment. "Or Bo."

"Bo? I say he was under her will," Mad Maggie said. "He probably told her all about our raid."

Overboard George swiveled his head toward Mad Maggie. "Possibly. There's no doubt that they were ready for us. Never liked that kid. Too much white privilege. Fancy car. Never had to work for anything. Spoiled rotten. Supposedly having sex with that vampire. I think he's just the kind to get into something dark like that. Maybe even enjoyed it."

Del Hatch whistled. "Sex with a vampire? Somebody dead? That's strange." He twisted his mouth and shivered.

Mad Maggie took New Girl's hand. Rigor Mortis was setting in. They were silent for a while. Tears rolled down Mad Maggie's cheeks.

"Remember how she could run?" Mad Maggie said. "Never saw anybody so fast. Not quite vampire speed, though."

"She made a toga from a sheet she stole off somebody's wash line," Overboard George told Del with a grin. His eyes filled with tears. "She was fast all right, even in a toga and those shoes she swiped that were too big."

"What do we do with her, George?" Maggie asked.

"We'll contact Jimmy. He knows the police. He can let them know she's here."

"I didn't even know her name," Mad Maggie said.

"Me neither. I never thought to ask," George said. He turned to Mad Maggie. "I never thought we'd lose her. She liked being called New Girl. She probably had something to hide, just like the rest of us."

"What will the police think?"

"They'll think she was hit by a truck," Del said, "and crawled up here on the grass."

"Just another dead junkie," Overboard George said. "I hope to hell somebody knew her, so she can have a proper burial. So her family finds out what happened. That she's gone."

"They'll never know," Old Harriet said. "It's better the family doesn't know she was murdered. Who would believe in vampires? The other thing is they'll never know she was a hero. Escaped from the vampires and fought the undead. Got herself sober for a little while. That should go on her tombstone, if the truth ever comes out, if she ever gets a real stone. I wouldn't mind finding its location and visiting someday."

CHAPTER TWO

Following the attack on After Dark and the vampire fighters left the scene, Lazlo backed the van, jumping the curb, across the lot to the hidden door in the ground. Lazlo and Kazmer entered the vampire lair, announced their presence outside the feeding room, and ushered the vampiress covered in blankets up the steps and into a new casket in the van. The brothers took off for the abandoned warehouse, from which *she* would call Bo to join her.

Lazlo and Kazmer drove west, taking turns behind the wheel. They moved always below the speed limit. The van had magnetic signs on the sides, precisely placed, *All Plumbing Supplies, Inc.* Behind the vehicle's front seats were stashed stolen license plates in a box and lying flat on the floor other magnetic signs—*Ric's Auto Parts, BJ Electronics, LLC, and Red Cap Roofing, We've Got You Covered.* None had telephone numbers or website addresses.

When the brothers stopped to gas up, eat, or use a bathroom, one always remained inside the van in the driver's seat, a .9mm pistol on his lap, the engine running. The cargo in the casket, Eva the vampiress and Bo, was never left alone. The men slept in turns inside the van in secluded spots not visible from the highway. The back roads they traveled, with their twists and hills, couldn't shake the casket, but the action inside, the muffled cries, the sheer panic, sometimes did. Bo Bentwood was still Eva's prisoner. The brothers traded glances and smiled.

"Someday, my brudder, we will have such fun," Lazlo said. "The undead have many powers. Very strong. And they are good lovers." Lazlo raised an eyebrow and smiled.

"Maybe we will have two women in each of our caskets," Kazmer said, smiling at the thought. "Unlimited strength. We can trade the girls we get."

"You were always the dreamer, my brudder," Lazlo laughed.

Typically, just before twilight the brothers scouted a hiding place for the night where they could pull off the road far enough that traffic headlights would not find them after dark. Then they drove to the nearest town, gassed up for the next day, and found food for themselves and Bo. A full tank of gasoline was essential, especially if they found it necessary to run from the authorities.

A lone hitchhiker or runaway on a lonely stretch of road was always a bonus the vampiress appreciated after the exertions with her pet. Offered drugs or booze before a promised ride, the brothers returned with their hapless quarry to the hiding place for the night and opened the casket.

The vampiress could spring out immediately—no need to stretch her dead muscles or pause for a cup of coffee to wake—to catch the helpless prey. There were times she exsanguinated the victim immediately, gulping a gallon of blood in a minute; or she could sip at her leisure, taking an hour or more to drain the captive. There also were times she tortured the hostage, hissing, sneering, scratching, showing her fangs, feeding off the victim's terror.

On one such occasion, a fifteen-year-old runaway girl was promised beer and a tent to spend the night, before a ride in the morning to the state line and a truck stop where the men would buy her breakfast and find her another lift. She believed the brothers with their unruly dark hair, heavy brows, and crooked noses. She found their accents amusing. Their soft voices were more reassuring than her brutish stepfather. The last thing she expected was to be stripped and tortured for hours while the vampiress sucked her blood.

Meanwhile, Bo, still naked, wearing his neck collar and now ankle shackles that hindered his mobility, sat on the casket lid between the brothers, eating from a bucket of fried chicken. All three ate silently and flicked fleshless bones into the dust outside the van as each piece was consumed. Even Bo was now hardened to death.

He finished off a slice of lemon meringue pie and shuffled into the woods to take a dump while the brothers smoked hand-rolled cigarettes on the van bumper, their picks and shovels at their sides. For Bo, escape was impossible without clothes, without shoes. The grass was long, its blades sharp. He knew the vampiress could bring him back to her with a thought, no matter where he hid. Bo was powerless to resist Eva's demand to meet her at the empty warehouse. Her demands for sex resulted in an instant erection. If he tried to escape, a severe beating would surely follow. She showed little mercy. He was already weak from daily bloodletting. He couldn't get far without collapsing. Still, Bo studied Eva's actions, the brothers' schedules, in the event a chance would present itself to get away. He pretended to be weaker than he was. Every movement was accompanied by a groan or sigh as if it were painful to do anything. The teenager, meanwhile, shrieked in muffled cries, and the vampiress chortled from within the woods. One life was ending. Another life—if you could call it a life—was extended.

Soon there was silence. The vampiress emerged from a copse of birches—she moved silently—into the clearing that served as their camp. She was naked, too, and her torso was smeared with the teenager's blood. The brothers averted their eyes. Bo noticed scratches on her torso were already healing. The teenager had been a fighter. She wiped a forearm over her bloody mouth and approached the trio.

The vampiress began, "You will locate her..." pointing into the woods.

"We will find her, mistress," Lazlo said. "It is early. We will bury her deep. This is good soil for graves. The ground is soft. Come, Kazmer." The brothers stabbed out their cigarettes, crushed and scattered the remaining tobacco, and picked up their tools.

"What would Bo and I do without you brothers?" the vampiress said. Blood dripped down her chin.

"It is an honor to please you, mistress," Lazlo said. "We are your humble servants."

"Such loyalty. Your rewards will be great. So I say it," the vampiress said, smiling at the brothers as they walked toward the woods.

Bo stood outside the van. The vampire sat on the van's tail. "Come to me, Bo. I want your company." She patted the van's floor beside her.

Bo was obedient. He couldn't resist, even though he wanted to run from the clearing toward the highway and scream for help. He shuddered when his arm grazed her cold, hard flesh. "Are you cold, little rabbit? You shiver. Certainly, you do not fear me, but your heart thunders away. You will wear out that little muscle."

"The night feels chilly when you have no clothes."

She smiled at Bo and ran her fingers through his hair. "Your poor mistress has no clothes either," she said.

"You don't mind it."

"No, I don't mind the temperature. But I enjoy your body heat, little rabbit. My clothes were left behind in the city. I will need a new wardrobe and modern attire. You and I are starting, as they say, a new chapter. When we get to our destination perhaps you can help me select new clothing. Things you would like to see a sweetheart wear on a date. I look forward to going to a movie with you.

I'm not familiar with the fancies of modern life. I will buy you popcorn loaded with butter. I, perhaps, will eat an usher." The vampiress clapped her hands and laughed.

"I will need clothes to go to a movie," Bo said.

"If you remain a good pet, you shall have new clothes, little rabbit. Nice clothes. Inside the movie theater, when it is dark, you will fondle me, and we will kiss like lovers. We will be the envy of everyone. What a couple we will make."

Bo shuddered again.

"Go to the grave and get warm, little rabbit. I will join you soon. Today you will have a night off. I pleasured myself on the girl's corpse and drank all her blood. I can't hold anymore."

The vampire burped up a mouthful of blood that hit the ground with a splat. She wiped her bloody mouth with a forearm and sent Bo to the casket.

The vampiress sat on the van's tail, head raised, sniffing the air. Eventually, the brothers returned with their picks and shovels, their shoes caked with dirt.

"We found a good grave, mistress, and buried the young one deep. She won't be disturbed. She will sleep silently through eternity."

"Excellent, my children. Excellent! Come, receive my blessing."

The brothers approached the vampiress and bowed. She kissed each gently on the top of his head. "You have had a strenuous day, my children. Rest tonight. Who knows what will happen tomorrow? I will sit up and guard our little party. It's a lovely night. It reminds me of so long ago."

The brothers backed away and placed their tools inside the van. They looked at Bo inside the casket. He stared back. Kazmer frowned at Lazlo and the brothers climbed into the cab to sleep.

In this way, the van meandered through the countryside, covered state after state, avoided turnpikes, interstates, and cities where there might be traffic cameras, sometimes taking routes that temporarily increased the distance to the vampire colony that was their destination. The brothers were ever watchful, avoided any potential conflict, preferred higher-priced gasoline at stations where fewer cars stopped, and ordered food at diners with empty parking lots. At some point almost every day the brothers pulled well off the highway, sealed light from the van's interior, and let Bo out of the casket for a breather. He would shuffle around outside the van, use the wild facilities when necessary, and then ride with the boys after they hit the road again.

One night, after all four had eaten, the vampiress asked Lazlo, "Tell me more about this new colony. I didn't have much of a choice in its selection. We had to move fast after we knew the junkers would attack us." It was already dark. The brothers lounged on the van's tail, smoking their reeking, hand-rolled ciga-rettes, with only the moon for illumination. Bo sat on the casket lid to avoid the smoke and the vampire's stench.

If only the boys would leave the van keys in the ignition, Bo thought. He wondered whether he could sneak to the driver's seat, start the engine, and burn out before they caught him. His Charger might do it. That was a car that could move. The brothers always parked the van to allow for fast getaways. Was the vampiress fast enough to run down the vehicle after it hit the asphalt? Was there a distance beyond which she could no longer control him with her mind? Could he operate the gas pedal and brake barefoot with the leg shackles in place? What would happen to him if he crashed the van? If they caught him? There was no way to tell. He knew what a moot point was. After all, he was a senior in college. The ignition key was missing anyway.

"I am familiar with this new colony, mistress," Lazlo began as if he shared a sudden familiarity with the vampiress. Meanwhile,

Kazmer sat silently, smoking, occasionally inspecting the end of his unraveling cigarette, spitting loose bits of tobacco on the ground. "I hope you will like it. It is larger than what you were accustomed to and quite...elaborate. There is an old, mostly abandoned cemetery, all overgrown, very quiet, with practically no visitors. I believe cemeteries should be quiet for the repose of the dead. I don't like to see a noisy highway built next to an old cemetery. So it is sometimes in this country. People might not think the traffic, the noise, the vibrations, matter because only the dead are interred. *They* no longer matter."

"That is one thing that is beyond our control, Lazlo. I appreciate your concern. You are a caring human. A kind spirit."

"Thank you, mistress." The brothers bowed to the vampiress. "We will enter the colony through a mausoleum inside the cemetery set against a hill. It is one of many such mausoleums in a row, but only one leads to the colony. There is a tunnel at the back of *our* mausoleum that goes into the hill. The tunnel leads to a large vault inside the hill with crypts dug into the earth. The tunnel continues on the other side of the vault to an abandoned home on top of the hill. The house was condemned by the city years ago for being unfit for...habitation, I think they call it. However, the colony has arrangements with certain city officials who make sure the house is not torn down. In fact, it has heat and running water. Again, special arrangements keep everything running and very quiet. The windows and doors are boarded over. No sunlight shines in. No light shines out from the inside. You will see. The colony's members are all much younger than you, mistress, in vampire years. Much younger. Some of them like that rock music, even after their deaths. It will be different. Just as there are more vampires, there will be more servants, too, which will be for your benefit as well. Some vampires rest inside the house. Some prefer the vault."

Lazlo hesitated a moment. "When you go out in the modern

world, it is important to be clean and wear clean clothes when you mix with humans. They will...recoil if they smell the grave on your person."

"How interesting. Everyone smelled during the so-called Middle Ages," the vampiress said, smiling at the brothers. "Alive or dead. There wasn't much difference." She craned her neck toward Bo and raised an index finger, with its sharp, claw-like nail, to her pouting lower lip. "Bo, be honest. I couldn't tell you when I last washed. Do I stink?"

"Yes," Bo said, without hesitation, without emotion, returning her gaze from hollow eyes with dark circles. "You stink. I stink. We all stink. What do you expect when you ride in a traveling graveyard."

Kazmer grunted.

She turned back to Lazlo. "How do we...remedy that?"

"*Remedy*, mistress?"

"Fix."

"Oh yes. Fix. I see, *remedy*. Not medicine. The house has a bathroom with tubs and showers. I think you will enjoy a shower."

"Like rain?"

"Yes, mistress. With warm water and soap," Lazlo said. "It is refreshing."

"Mmmm," she said, turning back to Bo. "Bo, it will be your job to refresh me. And I will refresh you." She licked her lips with her long, pointed tongue.

"I'll need a sandblaster," Bo said, glumly, lowering his head.

Kazmer grunted.

"What is that?" the vampiress asked.

Lazlo gave Bo a stern look, then returned his gaze to the vampiress. "It is a special washing device, mistress. One I don't think we need and *won't* mention again." He shot Bo another glance. "It would make noise that could bring attention."

"We can't have that, can we, Bo?" the vampiress said, smiling, narrowing her eyes to two slits.

Bo said nothing.

"The only noise we will hear will come from you, Bo, your screams of ecstasy. You do have fun. What a pity you, a virgin, can't remember our couplings. So is life with a vampire."

CHAPTER THREE

The white van rolled down Fifth Street, almost too slow, as if the driver was looking for an address or parking spot.

Finally, almost painfully, the van pulled to the side, avoiding rubbing the tires against the curb. Lazlo and Kazmer sat for a few minutes, scanning their surroundings through the windows and with the mirrors. Satisfied they weren't followed, even noticed, they slipped into the cool, autumn night, pulled up their hoods, and hurried silently toward After Dark. The baseball season was over. The home team ended a disappointing second in the division, with a record only slightly better than last year's dismal finish—not good enough for a wild card berth in the playoffs—despite the acquisition of several marquis players, two of whom finished the season on the disabled list. In the city, attention had turned to football. There was always a new season, a new hope for the fan base. And yet, little hope remained for the homeless with their poor health, mental problems, and addictions. The city seemed to care more about professional football than those who lived and died on the streets.

This was the brothers' second visit to the East Coast. They had delivered the vampiress and Bo to the vampire colony on the West Coast and immediately returned east. Eva the vampiress had more work for the brothers to complete. The trip east had been fast. Mostly interstate highways. After all, *Denn die todten rieden schnell.*

The dead travel fast.

The brothers entered After Dark, stopped side-by-side, and scanned the restaurant, each looking in opposite directions. Half the tables were empty and only a few people sat at the bar. As if their surveillances were timed by shared clocks, they turned to each other and nodded.

"The dead reside here, my brudder," Lazlo said. "I can feel them." He pointed toward the statues purloined from the old cemetery that was under part of the nearby stadium's outfield.

"Kazmer said, "I feel it too. The air is heavy with their presence."

They walked to the bar and sat down.

"Menus, please," Lazlo, the older brother, said in his European accent when the bartender approached. The young man in a white shirt and black vest, red garters on his sleeves, smiled and handed the men menus.

"And something to drink?"

"Two Coca-Cola," Lazlo said. "Large."

"And for your friend?" The bartender grinned and stroked his light beard.

Lazlo didn't smile. "One Coca-Cola for me and one Coca-Cola for him," Lazlo said, jerking his thumb toward Kazmer. "Large."

The bartender flushed. "Of course. I'll be back for your orders."

"You can take them now," Lazlo said. "Two double cheeseburgers. Do you have sweet potato fries?"

"Of course. They do cost more."

"That is not a problem," Kazmer said. "We have cash."

"Two orders of sweet potato fries?"

The brothers nodded.

And onion rings," Kazmer said, holding up a manicured index finger.

"One order?"

The men nodded.

"Very good. Coming right up, gentlemen."

The brothers sat scanning the bar. Occasionally, one or the other leaned in to talk in a European dialect that would be recognized by only a few modern scholars of ancient languages.

When the bartender returned with their food, he refilled their drinks. "The sign on the door outside says kitchen help wanted," Lazlo said.

"You'd have to talk to Bart, the building superintendent," the bartender said. "He runs everything here. We lost our best cook and his brother, a dishwasher. ODs. Both of them. It was a shame. I can give you applications."

Kazmer bit into his cheeseburger. Grease ran down his chin. He nodded approvingly at the burger's taste. The younger brother had administered the lethal fentanyl doses to Jose, the cook, and Miguel, his brother, a dishwasher. Both knew people were held in the basement, but they had never seen them and thought they were slaves on their way to another destination. Although they had never been to the basement, the kitchen workers saved food for the unknown captives.

"Is Bart here now?" Lazlo inquired.

"In the morning."

Kazmer grunted.

Bart was the vampires' caretaker, was careful to keep his identity hidden. He had escaped justice in the recent attack on the After Dark basement.

"How is the bus service here?" Lazlo said.

"Good. It runs until 3 am, but you have to get on at the stadium." The bartender pointed toward the wall behind the brothers. "That's the end of the line. That's what I use. You're better off getting a monthly pass. It's cheaper."

"Good to know," Kazmer said, raising a french fry to his mouth. "I like your ring."

"Thanks," the bartender said, waving a pinky finger. "It was my grandfather's. He gave it to me when I was fifteen. If I ever have a son, I'll leave it to him."

"Someday," Kazmer said, smiling, before biting his cheeseburger again.

The bartender grinned at the brothers and turned his attention to two young women at the end of the bar. He inclined his head toward them as he talked and they sniggered, then looked at the brothers and laughed more. Lazlo and Kazmer traded sullen glances. The brothers ate their meals in silence. Suddenly, Kazmer poked Lazlo sharply in the ribs. Lisa Van der Meer, obviously pregnant, approached the bar, walked behind it and looked over the liquor bottles, tapped her pencil against them as if playing a tune. The bartender returned and gave her a list. Lisa scanned the list, smiled, thanked the bartender, and retreated through a door marked "Employees Only."

The bartender returned to the brothers with their bill. "Is that your baby?" Kazmer said, pointing toward the door Lisa disappeared through.

"No, man, not mine." The young man shook his head. "She's the bar manager and my boss."

"She a nice boss?" Kazmer said.

"The best. I hope she stays on after the baby is born."

"Where we come from bosses are mean," Lazlo said. "That's why we work on our own."

The brothers paid their bill in cash and left a generous tip. They exited After Dark and walked past the van to the stadium's bus stop, where they slipped on latex gloves and sat in silence, hidden from the street among holly bushes that retained their leaves.

"It's too bad the baseball season is over. We could go to a game," Lazlo said. "I like baseball."

Kazmer grunted.

"It would be our first game."

"We don't know the rules," Kazmer said. "We might draw attention."

"We buy a hat and look like everybody else. Then we cheer when they cheer. You will see, my brudder. When do we have fun? We will learn the rules...how do they say...on the fly."

"When did we ever have fun," Kazmer said. "Getting too cold now to sit outside. I don't like the city. I don't like the cold. Too many junkies. Too dirty. Too much smell. Too many eyes on you all the time."

"Today, it is like that everywhere, my brudder. When we become Nosferatu, maybe the future will be better."

"We will see, eventually. I hope so."

They sat in silence for a while. "What if he is not alone tonight?" Kazmer said.

"We will follow him. See where he gets off," Lazlo said calmly. "Then we will wait for him there tomorrow if it is a good place. If not, we will find a good place, even if we wait until another day. We have several important jobs to finish for our mistress before we return across the country. Another road trip, as the Americans say."

Kazmer grunted. Then smiled. "Road trip. Again."

Within a few minutes, a thin white man approached the bus stop and dropped onto the end of a bench inside the bus stop's plexiglass enclosure. Kazmer poked Lazlo. Lazlo nodded. "I see him. A dope fiend, I think."

In short order, the man produced an elastic band, rolled up his sweatshirt sleeve, and tied off his arm above the elbow, using his teeth and free hand. He tore open a pack of powder, transferred it carefully to an old spoon, along with a little water from a bottle, and heated the spoon over a cigarette lighter's flame. He held a syringe in his mouth while the powder turned to liquid, used his teeth to pull back the plunger, and loaded the dope into the syringe. The junkie concentrated on his fix, never bothering to check his surroundings. He was intent. His breathing was shallow. The brothers watched him with interest. With the needle poised upright, he flicked the syringe with a finger and pushed the plunger to squeeze out air bubbles. The brothers remained in their hiding place. The man licked his lips as he rested the tied-off arm on his thigh, and slapped the pale skin inside below the elastic band. Finding a vein to his liking, he inserted the needle in the vein, wincing slightly as he pulled a small amount of blood into the needle to ensure he had hit the vein properly, and pushed the dope into his arm. His mouth grew slack, and he slumped against the end of the enclosure.

"Now what?" Kazmer said.

"Nothing. You could sit next to him for an hour and he wouldn't remember you were there. Look. Here comes our friend. Remember, this must look like a robbery. We want to take his cell phone, money, jewelry, credit cards. We leave the wallet on the ground."

The bartender approached the bus stop, noticed the junkie, and stood outside the enclosure, leaning against it. He immediately lit a cigarette, opened his cell phone, and swiped a finger across the front.

Lazlo and Kazmer looked at each other and nodded. Both knew what to do. This was not their first murder. It would not be their last. Eva could not be traced to the West Coast. This bartender could not identify the brothers. The men separated. Walked in opposite directions. Lazlo skirted around a high shrub and stepped to the sidewalk.

The bartender recoiled.

"Look who it is! From After Hours." Lazlo smiled.

"After Dark"

"Yes. After Dark."

"What are you doing here?" the bartender demanded.

"Was taking a leak." Lazlo jabbed his thumb toward the bushes. "We thought we would look at the bus stop. Maybe see Bart in the morning about jobs. My brudder is cook, you know. Went to cooking school in Europe. A very good school. You like crepes? Soufflés? You should see him handle a knife. He can carve anything."

The bartender seemed wary. He moved away from the enclosure and bench as if preparing a pathway to escape. The junkie remained immobile on his seat, still crumpled against the enclosure's interior. Lazlo stood relaxed and smiled.

"Where's your friend?" The bartender's voice cracked.

"My brudder? Making number two." Lazlo held up two fingers. "I told him not to use so much hot sauce on his food. You want to go see?" Lazlo laughed and pinched his nostrils, then waved his other hand in front of his nose."

The bartender seemed to relax. He shook his head. "No, thanks. I'll wait out here. Give your brother some privacy."

Lazlo smiled at the man and nodded. "Everyone in America likes privacy."

Meanwhile, Kazmer approached the bartender silently from behind. He pulled a length of thin wire with wooden handles from his hoodie pocket and uncoiled it. By the time the bartender sensed someone behind him, Kazmer slipped the wire over the man's head and, with amazing speed, pulled it tight. The bartender choked, struggled, flailed his arms, kicked his legs. Kazmer drug away the struggling man, and pulled him behind a high piece of ornamental grass as the wire sawed back and forth, cut through the flesh, severing the carotids and windpipe. The man's lungs exhausted a last breath and a splash of blood. Kazmer pushed the body forward, expertly avoiding the blood splatter. He wiped the wire clean on the man's underarm, then coiled it and returned it to his hoodie pocket. The younger brother dug through the man's pockets, retrieving a money clip that contained a credit card and driver's license. Kazmer dropped the driver's license and pulled a small gold crucifix from the bartender's neck. Somehow, the garrote missed the fine chain. A signet ring on the right pinky was removed roughly, breaking the finger. Kazmer knew the man's cell phone lay on the sidewalk, dropped during the attack. Kazmer inspected the ring briefly and smiled.

Kazmer stepped from the ornamental grass. His brother waited, smoking the bartender's dropped cigarette. Each nodded. Lazlo held up the cell phone. The younger brother displayed the loot taken from the bartender.

"Look at all the cash," Lazlo said. "He had a good job."

"I like big tippers," Kazmer said, cracking a smile. He showed his brother the crucifix and ring. "These things will look nice in our jewelry box."

"See? You worry too much, my brudder. All is well. Now, we must make another stop before the night is over."

"Let me have a puff," Kazmer said.

Lazlo handed over the rest of the cigarette. "Remember..."

"I know. No traces left behind." Kazmer inhaled deeply, consuming the rest of the cigarette. He knocked off the ash, ground the filter between his thick fingers, and transferred the small pile to a pocket, along with the stripped-off latex gloves.

CHAPTER FOUR

The brothers, with grim faces, left the bus stop and walked down Fifth Street toward the white van. Before they turned their backs on the enclosure with the sleeping junkie, they noticed a bus in the distance crawling toward the last stop on the line. They passed dippers and junkies on the sidewalk. A breeze stirred trash in the gutter.

"A terrible way to become," Lazlo told his brother. "Look at that. They have no control over their lives. They are slaves to this dope."

Kazmer grunted in agreement.

"Not us. We are in control."

Kazmer grunted again.

At one point on their return to the van, Lazlo said, "I didn't think we walked so far. Not really far, but longer than I imagined."

"Not really far," Kazmer mumbled.

A young black man approached the brothers, sliding out of the bushes near the park entrance. "Hey man, can you spare a few bucks for a brother who's hungry?"

The brothers stopped a moment, stared at the man, and separated a step on the sidewalk. Lazlo fingered the coiled wire in his hoodie pocket. The brothers remained silent.

"Got ya, man. Maybe another time." The black man returned to the park, making one final turn to look at the men before he melted into the trees.

The brothers continued onward silently. As they approached the van, they stopped and lit hand-rolled cigarettes, which they kept in an old, flat metal box. They stood in place, smoking, checking the surroundings. Satisfied there were no cameras or human eyes watching them, the brothers climbed into the van. With Lazlo behind the wheel, they continued down Fifth Street, turned right on Chestnut, and drove two more blocks. Lazlo had traced the route often with a thick, crooked finger over a city map. They passed Bart's three-story apartment building and pulled around the corner. Carefully and silently, they followed the building's exterior, staying close to trees and hedges, within Shadows, virtually invisible, until they reached the main entrance. There they entered a vestibule with mostly glass walls, found Bart's name among the residents, and rang his doorbell on the second floor.

The brothers stood motionless in front of the vestibule security door. In a moment an annoyed voice crackled over the intercom. "Who is it?"

"It's Lazlo and my brudder." Lazlo was equally gruff. "We have news from the coast. Let us in."

"Oh yes, boys. Of course. Pull the door when you hear the buzzer."

The door buzzed and the brothers entered the building, careful to leave no fingerprints. They walked slowly, making sure no residents stepped into the hall to see who was admitted at such a late hour. They were halfway to the second floor when Bart met them on the stairs. He reached to pump Lazlo's hand, but Lazlo raised a finger to his lip indicating quiet. He swirled his other hand around his head, indicating his news was confidential. Bart winked at the brothers and ushered them up the steps and down the hall to his apartment. Bart entered first followed by Kazmer. Lazlo remained in the hall a moment to ensure there were no prying eyes.

After the door was closed and locked, Bart was effusive, waving his arms like a windmill. He signaled the brothers to take seats and offered his visitors drinks. He smiled and sweated in his silk paisley smoking jacket and monogrammed carpet slippers.

"You have a nice apartment, Bart," Kazmer said.

"Thank you. I have mostly antique furniture, some from all over the world. Quite valuable, I might add."

"How's the neighborhood?" Lazlo said.

"The best. There's a park down the street with a playground. Puts the park near the stadium to shame. No riffraff. No junkies. Very little crime. Almost none. Are you sure you won't take a drink? I have everything you can imagine. I order it through After Dark."

Kazmer grunted.

"If I knew you were coming, I could have had food delivered. A feast. I'm not much of an eater myself, but you boys, I imagine, have big appetites."

"We ate already," Lazlo said.

"I don't know exactly what you do for the colony, but I'm sure it's important and you work hard. Have a good work ethic."

Kazmer grunted.

"I hope your building is secure, with all the valuable furniture you have," Lazlo said.

"I have to admit right now it's not secure at all," Bart said, waving his arms again. "We had cameras inside, closed circuit, the same kind we have at After Dark, but a few residents, the trouble-makers, wanted cameras outside, too. The building association decided to put in new cameras. Everywhere! Had the old system ripped out. But, get this, the new system had a bad motherboard."

"Mother fuckers," Kazmer interrupted.

"Exactly. We're waiting for a replacement. Could take another week. Coming from who knows where."

Lazlo shook his head. "Always it has to be delayed."

"Is your news from the coast about me?" Bart swallowed hard and grimaced.

Lazlo smiled. "It is about you. News from our mistress."

"Are they finally getting me out of this God-forsaken place?"

"You could say that," Lazlo said.

Kazmer grunted.

"It's about time," Bart said. "You know, this job at After Dark was to last only a few months, not a few years. I feel I deserve—"

"Your time has come," Lazlo said. "The mistress has acknowledged your loyalty." He smiled again at Bart. Kazmer remained silent on the sofa.

Bart swallowed. He pursed his lips, drew in a great breath, and let out the air slowly. Then he smiled at the brothers. "We must celebrate. Boys, you must have a drink with me. It's the very least—"

"I like champagne," Kazmer said. He grinned. "Ice cold champagne."

"Of course! I have it all," Bart shouted. "And it's ice cold. Just the way you like it."

Lazlo raised a finger to his lips again.

"Sorry," Bart mouthed silently. He grinned and then ran toward the kitchen on his short legs, spun in a wide circle, and returned to the men. "I have very old champagne glasses. They were my mother's. We'll toast with them."

Kazmer grinned. "I like champagne."

"Who doesn't?" Bart held his hands over his head and danced to the kitchen in his slippers. The brothers followed him. Bart pulled out a champagne bottle from his refrigerator. He handed it to Kazmer, who in turn gave it to Lazlo. Lazlo peeled off the outer foil and untwisted the wire that secured the cork. He placed a thumb over the cork while he inspected the label.

"Good stuff?" Lazlo said as he took hold of the mushroom-shaped cork with his large fingers. He looked at Bart.

"Very good stuff," Bart laughed. "From After Dark." He floated to the sink in his monogrammed slippers and reached overhead for the cabinet handle. He rose on his toes and stretched for a tray of slim, long-stemmed glasses inside.

Kazmer stepped behind Bart. "I like champagne, you know. Hand them down to me, Bart. I'll be careful with your mother's glasses."

Bart stretched. "I don't use these glasses very often. That's why I keep them up here. That way they're out of the way and safe."

"I understand," Kazmer said. "How do you say it? Keepsakes."

The champagne cork exploded with a pop. Bart dropped his hands with a jerk as Lazlo inspected the cork held in his meaty fingers. Bart patted his paisley smoking jacket, rubbing the front and sides. "Oh fuck! I thought I was shot!"

The brothers laughed. Bart laughed more. "I thought I was fucking shot. Oh, you guys gave me the shock of my life. First, I get good news, then I am shot. You never know what vampires are thinking." Bart grabbed the sink and steadied himself for a moment while he recovered from the shock.

Lazlo set down the champagne bottle on the counter near the kitchen sink. He slapped Bart on the shoulder. "Let me get those glasses, Bart," Lazlo said. "I'm taller."

"No, no. I want to get them, especially after the scare of my life." Bart called. "I can use a good stretch. I'll reach them. You'll see." He glided to the cabinet again, rose on his toes, and reached for the glasses. Kazmer moved behind him and pulled a long stiletto knife from a pocket inside his hoodie.

Bart was sweating. Grunted with the exertion of reaching for the glasses. "Exactly what was the mistress's message?" Bart said, in halting words, gritting his teeth, straining to reach inside the cabinet.

"She said, 'Bart, you have betrayed me.'"

The blade gleamed in the light from the ceiling. The glint

caught Bart's eye as he pulled out the glasses and looked over his shoulder.

Kazmer's thick fingers gripped the knife handle and thrust the blade into the paisley smoking jacket so it separated ribs and punctured the left lung. He twisted the blade, slicing the lung, and causing a hemorrhage. Kazmer pushed harder, piercing Bart's heart. Kazmer knew the feeling. Felt the blade's trajectory, and guided it with skill to the target. Bart looked at the brothers in disbelief. His mother's fine glasses slid from their tray and smashed on the floor. He coughed up a mouthful of blood. Kazmer held his smoking jacket collar and let him fall noiselessly.

Kazmer grunted.

"Too bad about the glasses," Lazlo said. "They were beautiful. They would have looked nice in our kitchen."

"We still have the champagne," Kazmer said. "The good stuff."

"I liked Bart's jacket," Lazlo said.

"It would never fit us," Kazmer said. "Still, I tried to hit a seam, but Bart stretched. I missed it. Now the jacket has a hole in the side."

"Even though it was too small to wear, the jacket would have looked nice in our closet. To look at when we visit our apartment and open the door. The important thing is you hit his heart, my brudder. We have enough clothes in our apartment that don't fit."

Kazmer wiped the knife blade clean on Bart's back. The men pulled up their hoods, grabbed the open champagne bottle, and quietly left the building. As they sneaked along the building's exterior, Lazlo said. "We have one more job, my brudder, before we return to the coast. It will have to wait until tomorrow. We are making excellent time."

CHAPTER FIVE

OVERBOARD GEORGE GOT THE CALL FROM JIMMY YOUNG early. Bart had been killed in his apartment the night before. Stabbed through the heart. It appeared nothing was taken. A champagne bottle cork was found in the kitchen. Some glasses were smashed in an apparent struggle. Bart had few friends, and even fewer visitors, his neighbors told police. The neighbors also told Jimmy and Lisa Van der Meer.

The couple had headed to Bart's with plans to force him to tell them about the vampiress's whereabouts. After Bart drugged them with laced soft drinks, the couple could not remember the incident and how they got to the basement and interred in the cells underneath After Dark. It was foggy in their minds. Still, they remembered the fight between their friends and the vampires and knew Bart had to know about the undead in the basement.

They arrived at Bart's apartment building just after the police pulled out. They saw the taillights of what they thought was the last squad car turn the corner at the park as they drove up. Residents were huddled outside in small groups, sending members back and forth, each trying to outdo the others on the information they learned or at least imagined.

Overboard George would gather the vampire hunters at Old Harriet's sweet box later in the afternoon for an emergency meeting.

Lisa had been to Bart's apartment once, as far as his apartment's front door, to pick up her first After Dark paycheck. She got a brief look at the apartment's clutter-free interior before he stuffed an envelope in her hand and closed the door in her face. Lisa felt it was like a final paycheck rather than her first. She would have quit there if she didn't need a job in what was then a new city to her. Now she was back at the door with Jimmy. The hall was quiet, except for the noise of a television game show down the hall.

Jimmy inspected the apartment doorknob. A loose-mouthed tenant with a lopsided wig perched on his head had told them outside that the security cameras inside the building were out. Lisa handed him a pair of latex gloves. As expected, the door was locked. The door had several strands of police tape affixed to the entrance. Jimmy pulled out his wallet and fished out a credit card. "This is an old lock and an old trick that just might work."

Jimmy wiggled the card between the door and jamb, pressed the card up against the lock, and jiggled the knob. The lock clicked open.

"Impressive," Lisa said.

"From my days as a cat burglar," he whispered.

"Second-floor man?"

"Yes. And we're on the second floor."

The couple ducked under the tape, hurried inside, and relocked the door. Jimmy scanned the apartment

In the kitchen, glass still littered the floor. A pool of partly congealed blood covered the tile. "I feel lightheaded," Lisa said. "I'm getting out of here." She returned to the living room and called immediately in a low voice. "There's a desk here." Jimmy joined her and opened the antique drop-leaf secretary desk. A single drawer underneath the leaf contained only an old city telephone directory, a relic but still useful. Pigeonholes on the top portion held rent receipts and several letters from the West Coast. The envelopes were addressed to Bart in an elegant, antique style. The penmanship looked familiar. After a moment studying one letter, Lisa thought, *That's it!*

She told Jimmy the letter had the same script as the mysterious entry for lightbulbs on the After Dark bar shopping list. At the time Lisa didn't recognize the handwriting and no employees admitted requesting the fluorescent bulbs. It turned out the lightbulbs *were* for the basement ceiling. *It must be the female vampire's*, Lisa thought. There were four letters, all in the same florid handwriting, all signed at the bottom with an elaborately penned E. The letter envelopes all had the same return address.

"This must be where *she* is," Lisa said. "It doesn't appear she was too careful covering her tracks."

"Look at this," Jimmy said. "The last line of this letter. *Remember, Bart, destroy this and all correspondence I have sent. There must be no trace of our existence beyond After Dark.* He never listened. You still want to track her down?"

"You better believe I do. That vampire gave my father hope. He thought he would be cured of lung cancer, that he would live forever disease-free. Who knows what else they promised him? She's just as much responsible for his death as the stakes he was shot with."

"It would have been easier and infinitely faster to send Bart a text or pick up a telephone," Jimmy said. He made a puzzled face.

"I doubt if too many people who were alive in the Middle Ages know how to text," Lisa said, "even though they might have access or at least people who could do such things for them. They'd do what they knew best, what they were familiar with, and that was to write letters. It could be that the vampires didn't trust modern conveniences."

"I suppose. With technology today, even deleted messages can be retrieved. Maybe a letter through the post office was the most secure way to send a message. That might have been the last *modern convenience* she trusted. All Bart had to do was destroy the letter as he was told. If he had done that, we wouldn't have a clue. I wonder why he saved them. He definitely wasn't a hoarder."

"Maybe because the handwriting was so old. Everything else in here looks antique."

The couple split up and canvassed the rest of the apartment. Nothing seemed out of place. No ransacking. Bart appeared to have been compulsively neat. A jewelry box with an assortment of watches, gold necklaces, rings, and tie clasps, seemed to have been untouched. How could have the murderer not noticed it? Did he, she, or they panic and flee after a scuffle with Bart? Could one of them have been injured in a melee? It was doubtful Bart could hold his own in any fight, let alone injure an intruder. It was also odd that Bart had jewelry he didn't wear.

Lisa found the apartment too depressing and wanted to return to After Dark, which was hardly more comforting. The air in Bart's apartment, despite its central air conditioning, seemed oppressive and heavy. She wondered whether ghosts from After Dark had attached themselves to Bart and now gleefully huddled in a corner discussing the gruesome murder like the tenants still did outside.

When the couple returned to After Dark, police officers were waiting. The staff was aghast that Bart and Leon the bartender were murdered the night before in separate incidents almost three miles apart. Both had worked that same day. Then there were the overdose deaths of Jose and Miguel only days before. Although the police didn't seem to think the four deaths were connected, their proximity seemed to be too much of a coincidence, Lisa thought. Police had already questioned the employees, even the part-timers. Those not working were called into the bar and were interviewed in Bart's office. The constant traffic in and out made keeping the restaurant open a nightmare. The cops wanted to know about problems the victims had, among themselves or with others, disgruntled employees, past and present, arguments with customers, and any worries they might have shared. Detectives reviewed the cc TV videos of the bar and restaurant for several days leading up to the murders. It appeared, at least now, that there was no connection between the two crimes. The employees not working lingered in little groups, crying, and hugging as they shared stories among themselves and with workers on duty. After all, any one of them could have been killed the way Leon was. Although Leon had been relatively new on the job, no one knew his background. He was a popular employee, always eager to listen, but not share any personal information. No one realized that until he was gone. It was almost like he had no past.

Police asked Lisa to watch restaurant and bar footage recorded the night before. They were the last shots of the bartender alive. It seemed he had no altercations with any patrons. In fact, he smiled and appeared jovial in the recordings. Even Lisa was visible in one scene when she checked the alcohol inventory. *Oh, boy. I am really getting huge*, she thought, while watching the footage. As expected, there were people she recognized as regulars, some by name. However, among the people seated at the bar, alkies, lovers, and solitary drinkers, two large men caught everyone's attention.

Lisa did not know them. Neither did the waitresses, bartenders, and busboys who viewed the video. It appeared the men knew they were on camera because they kept their heads lowered, even when talking to the bartender. They were burly as if they might be construction workers, with longish, dark curly hair, possibly brothers they were so similarly built. Occasionally, one leaned toward the other to talk, even though it seemed no one was close enough to overhear them. Both cleaned their plates of food. They ate quickly. Drank soft drinks. Paid their bill with cash. They exited the restaurant as fast as they entered with heads down. Enlarging and enhancing video images revealed no facial details. They floated out of the restaurant and up the street to an unknown destination. Eventually, they walked out of the exterior surveillance camera's view, but they walked in the direction of the bus stop, where the bartender was later murdered according to the video's time stamp. The bar where they sat, the glasses they drank from, and the plates they ate off, were all by now cleaned. The money they handled was mixed with other cash. There was no trace of the men.

One cop said to Lisa, "What was the bartender like? Do you think there might have been a drug deal that went wrong?"

"I doubt it," Lisa said. "He didn't use and he didn't sell, as far as I know."

"Sex?"

"Leon had a girlfriend, so he said. Early on, he nicely repelled advances by a couple of the waitresses. He was about as straight-laced as they come."

"You're getting into the heart of junkie territory near the bus stop," the cop said, lifting an eyebrow.

"I don't know whether a junkie would have the strength to overpower Leon," Lisa said. "He appeared to be in shape. Worked out. Was always cautious. More cautious than even I am out on the street. I think it was a criminal. Somebody who wanted to rob him. He had a nice ring he wore on his pinky finger. It came down through his family, I think. I noticed it because my dad had a nice ring." Lisa paused for a moment. "Dad gave it to me not long before he died."

The police did not believe there were vampires and Whistlers in After Dark's basement. There were no such things and there was no evidence. Pools of mucous-like liquid and heaps of fine ashes did not a vampire colony make, even when one considered the wooden stakes that were scattered about and the shredded and bloody clothes. It appeared to Lisa the police were making cases for a robbery at the bus stop and something kinky in the basement that led to Bart's murder. She believed neither case would be solved. Both Bart's and Leon's families deserved closure.

CHAPTER SIX

THE BROTHERS WAITED ACROSS THE STREET FROM THE Grinder, a restaurant about two blocks east of After Dark, biding their time until the last police officer left, before going inside to order lunch. They no sooner sat down and the woman tending bar sidled up to Kazmer and started to share news of the grisly murders connected to After Dark while she pitched coasters in front of the men. The brothers wore newly purchased baseball team hats over their unruly hair and the same dark clothing they had on yesterday.

After the men gave the woman their orders, Lazlo said, "That's incredible." Lazlo slid one of the coasters to his right toward his brother. "What do the police know?" Both men looked amazed.

"Nothing they're talking about, but they asked nine million questions this morning. Here almost two blocks away from the crime scene. That tells me they don't know nothing."

"That's a lot of questions," Kazmer said. "Nine million? Who kept count?"

The bartender stopped and looked at Kazmer. "Maybe not nine million, but a lot. It took hours. I missed two breaks waiting for my turn to talk to two cops." The woman sounded frustrated. "You know how it is, good cop, bad cop, but both these guys seemed to be good cops. I bet they drank ninety-nine gallons of coffee each. Every time they finished a cup they pushed it toward me, across the table where they were set up, and I had to call the kitchen for more. Of course, it was gratis. They spilled sugar and creamer all over the place. Real slobs. I was ready to go through the roof because I knew they weren't cleaning it up. Looked like the type of guys who expected to be waited on. Felt like they had some privilege because they were cops.

"I used to work at After Dark," the bartender continued. "That's what it's called, not *The* After Dark, so it's more like a condition than a place if you know what I mean. But I never got along with Bart. He rubbed me the wrong way. So, I quit there and came here. Plus, it was so depressing at After Dark. The air even seemed heavy, especially with those creepy statues they hauled from old St. Vincent's Cemetery."

Kazmer grunted. "You can feel the dead inside."

"That's what I said. Bart was just as creepy. Licking his lips. Staring at your breasts. I couldn't wait to get out of there." The thin, young bartender inclined her head across the bar conspiratorially toward the brothers. "I heard Leon's head was almost severed by that garrote. That's what they called the thing he was killed with. The medical examiner figured it was a wire. That's what I heard. And the guy who did *it* was *very* strong. There must be nine million rumors floating around. Leon was always stingy with his tips, not too fast to share them with the busboys or dishwashers, let alone anyone else who was supposed to get a share. He should have handed the money over to whoever came after him. Was it worth it? Your tip money for your life?"

Kazmer grunted again, as if in agreement.

"I can see Leon fighting over a couple of bucks," the bartender said. "I think it cost him his life. I told the cops that too."

"You're probably right," Lazlo said. Kazmer nodded in agreement.

The lunch trade thinned. The bartender left to tap a draft for someone but soon returned as the brothers finished their lunches, and slurped down the last of their Coca-Colas.

"We ate at After Dark yesterday. We talked to a woman named..."

"Lisa," Kazmer finished the sentence for his brother.

"Do you know Lisa?" Lazlo said.

"Sure. We're BFFs."

What's that?" Kazmer wanted to know. His mouth hung open for a moment.

"You know. Best friends forever," the woman said.

"Of course," Lazlo said.

"Forever is a long time," Kazmer added.

The woman gave Kazmer a strange look.

"I noticed Lisa is pregnant," Lazlo continued. "Is she healthy?"

"Sure is, although her feet swell after a long day."

"Is that bad?" Kazmer said.

"It's not good. But common in pregnant women who stand a lot. Why would you care?"

"We have a large family," Lazlo said, smiling. "We've seen a lot of pregnancies over the years. Nieces and nephews. Lisa seemed nice. She should take it easy. That's what I told her."

"That's what I tell her, too, but she's a trooper. If we were busy and somebody needed a hand, she'd be mixing drinks, carrying food trays, taking orders, seating customers." The bartender smiled.

"This is good," Lazlo said. "And she can still work a full day?"

"Full shift plus, most days, so I hear. She's usually at AD until five or after."

Kazmer grunted, shot a look at his brother, and left the woman a nice tip from the money he took last night from Leon.

"Thank you, gentlemen," the bartender called, as the brothers walked away. "Come see us again."

Lazlo stopped and turned around. "We will. We're at the horror and comic book convention down the street."

"I hear they're a blast," the bartender said, smiling. "I always wanted to see one."

"We are having a great time," Kazmer said.

"Are you dressing up? You know, cosplay?"

"We always look like this," Kazmer said, "but our hats are new."

THE BROTHERS SPENT the rest of the afternoon in their van, observing Lisa's apartment, the second floor of a duplex accessible by a covered exterior stairway. No one came or went. The neighborhood was quiet. Despite the beautiful day, no one was outside. No children playing. No one walking. Some houses appeared vacant. On the way to Lisa's apartment, the brothers pulled over and changed the magnetic signs on the van's sides. The new sign read *Gill's Appliances: Quality For You Home*. The van's windows were open to let in the crisp fall air. Lazlo and Kazmer talked in hushed voices in the ancient dialect they used, as if someone outside might hear them.

Satisfied they understood the next move, Lazlo said, "My brudder, you always make the best plans." He patted Kazmer's arm.

The brothers exited the van and opened the rear doors. They pulled a washing machine box to the tail and eased it to the street. The box of thick cardboard was strapped to a hand truck and rolled to the exterior stairway. Although the box was empty, the brothers huffed and puffed, as if it contained a new washing machine. They pulled the box up the steps toward Lisa's apartment. Anyone seeing their progress would not be suspicious. They paused on a landing halfway up the stairwell.

While Lazlo climbed the remaining steps to pick the door lock, a woman stopped on the sidewalk and called up the stairway. "Hi. I'm Lisa's neighbor Susan. I live across the street." She pointed across the street. She too was visibly pregnant.

Kazmer nodded at the woman.

"Is Lisa getting a new washer? I thought she went to the laundromat."

"She bought a new washer," Kazmer said. "An expensive one. She has good job now."

"I didn't think she had room for a washer," the woman said, twisting her mouth as if trying to visualize Lisa's apartment.

Lazlo returned down the steps to join his brother. "She better have room," Lazlo said, smiling. "We deliver and install washers. That's our job. We don't want to take this machine back to the store."

"She's not home. Her car isn't here. How will you get in?"

"She leave key," Kazmer said. "You know. Under the mat."

"I'm surprised she would do something like that," the woman called to the men. She edged closer to the bottom step, clutching her open sweater to her throat. "I'm even shocked she would leave a key outside." She stared at the brothers.

"It is only one time. She trusts us," Lazlo said. "We're bonded. We do this all the time."

The woman paused, opened her mouth to say something, and closed it. After a moment, she said, "Well, okay then. I have to go. If you see Lisa, tell her to call me. I'm Susan, remember? From across the street." She held a thumb and pinky outstretched to resemble a telephone. "I want to show her my new ultrasound pictures of the baby."

"We remember," Kazmer said. "Susan, the lady across the street."

Susan walked away, craning her neck for one last look at the brothers.

"What about her?" Kazmer said.

"She has a baby. I don't like to kill an unborn. It might be bad luck for us."

"Me either," Kazmer said. "But she talks too much. She has seen us. Women like her have good memories. What do you call it?"

"Nosey."

Kazmer grunted.

"We have time to think about it, my brudder. We must decide if taking Lisa and killing this woman across the street will be too much, especially after the four lives we took, even though it's a big city and these murders would be miles apart."

Kazmer grunted. "Especially with two babies gone. We will have to talk about it after we are inside."

"Remember, my brudder, we must be very careful with Lisa. She cannot be harmed. The baby cannot be injured, or the mistress will kill us. She wants that baby. It is special to her for a great mass."

Kazmer grunted. "Maybe we will see this ritual with the baby when it is time."

"Maybe. It will be magnificent. It will be an honor."

The brothers hauled up the box the remaining steps. In a minute the men were inside with the box and hand truck, the lid removed from the box. A roll of duct tape for gagging Lisa and binding her hands and ankles lay on the kitchen table. The brothers sat at the table still wearing their work gloves, hoods raised over their heads. Kazmer's stiletto knife lay within easy reach. They waited silently for Lisa to arrive home. Occasionally one or the other brother sighed.

CHAPTER SEVEN

Bo shivered. It was damp in the vampires' underground lair, the destination they finally reached, a vast catacomb-like structure excavated in the hill above the old cemetery. Despite the wan illumination from torch light, he knew it was daytime because the caskets that lay scattered seemingly casually about were closed, their undead inhabitants asleep. Bo knew when it rained, too, by the way water dripped from the ceiling, along with occasional clods of earth that fell. Stone arches and, in some places, wooden timbers supported the high ceiling.

He wondered how long it had taken unknown workers to burrow into the ground, to produce this vast space with galleries and chambers leading in various directions, some of which he had not yet seen. Even in the central cathedral-like vault, there were holes gouged high in the walls, excavations only a vampire could reach. At places, there were steps and paths shoveled into the earth along the walls that led to the higher niches. Here and there were several great columns supporting the roof. Overhead, at the vault's highest point, there was always a flurry of bats, circling endlessly day and night. The creatures seemed to rest occasionally and clung to the high ceiling, gripping fine roots, dropping their guano intermittently to the floor below.

Of two large openings at opposite ends with heavy wood doors reinforced with iron, one led to the cemetery mausoleum exterior and the other uphill to another destination, a house boarded over so no light could enter or escape, where he and the vampiress bathed together before she went out to feed. Although the entire structure appeared ready to collapse, neither the vampires nor their black-clad human servants called Shadows seemed to fear a cave-in.

Today, Bo had managed to wiggle free from the vampiress's embrace and clamber outside. He sat next to the casket on a shelf cut into the wall. He was still naked and in ankle irons and wore the collar that identified him as Eva's property.

Vampire Shadows, who hoped someday to be turned, moved about on various errands. One carried a stack of freshly laundered clothes. Another dragged a long length of chain. A third covered a large blood spill on the floor with a mixture of sand and sawdust. The Shadows were mostly thin, had jet black hair—probably dyed, Bo thought— and pale skin. A few exhibited signs of puncture wounds and infections on their bare arms. Vampire bites. Not needle marks. Bo knew the difference by now.

The Shadows rarely acknowledged him, even when he called for their help. He begged for clothes, anything to get warm. They ignored him and continued to do their chores. Even those who talked did so briefly, furtively, without giving any information. Bo was neither a vampire to be obeyed nor a fellow Shadow to be respected. He was treated like someone who was already dead. He was merely a meal waiting for a vampire. He was somebody who would need burying at some point. He was work for the Shadows.

Bo had no idea how long he had been in this lair he was told was his new home. However, he knew the colony was on the United States' southwest corner, in a rundown section of a large city. No one would give him an exact location. His cell phone had been lost on the East Coast. His new Dodge Charger probably disappeared inside a chop shop. He had no idea how long it took to travel from After Dark to this new place. Much of the time he spent sealed inside the vampiress's casket. When he was allowed out at night, he was usually woozy from blood loss and exhausted from the vampire's sexual demands he could only imagine because he could not remember them. It was the price of being a virgin and a vampire pet. Pleasure he could not recall. Perhaps it was better that way.

In this new lair, Bo was often confined to the casket during the day, unable to move with the vampiress's cold corpse on top of him, the stained and crusty lining against his skin. Time seemed to have slowed, even stopped, because torch light in the caves seemed always the same. Several Shadows sat apart on the floor making more torches, wrapping handles with cloth dipped in a long-burning, potent-smelling flammable solution. New torches leaned against the wall in racks to dry. It was as if the outside world no longer existed. Bo heard no news. He didn't know what day or even month it was, although he expected it would be late fall because some Shadows now wore black hoodies or jackets on their comings and goings. They always wore black clothes.

It was dangerous to sit outside the casket when Eva was asleep. He could easily be prey to another vampire who was awake. They could move about during daylight hours but at diminished strength, although they were still as strong as several men and vastly stronger than Bo. He had developed a nagging cough during his confinement that defied cure, he imagined the result of breathing fetid air inside the casket, having his mouth pressed against the vampiress's dead lips. He also had rashes and patches of dry skin over his body, as well as various infected scratches, cuts, and puncture wounds. The fact that Bo was a virgin—sex with the vampire did not count because the fiend was dead—left his blood with an especially sweet taste, highly desirable, even intoxicating to a vampire, so his female keeper claimed. Most vampires would exsanguinate a virgin in a frenzy of blood draining and splatter, unable to control their cravings for the sweet elixir. Eva, however, was ancient, already old when Napoleon's armies swept across Europe. She had drained countless virgins. With Bo she had learned to curb her desire, draw out her consumption as if she were tasting expensive wines, sampling exquisite chocolates from a small box, or rationing an ever-shrinking food supply.

On the night they moved into the new colony, the entire undead population turned out, even delayed feeding, to meet this ancient vampire whose strength was greater than any ten of the fiends. The vampires, most of whom had been turned for only a single human lifetime or less, bowed en masse. Several were children. The vampiress was glutted with blood and appeared the same age as when she was turned at the age of nineteen human years.

She smiled and bowed back to the group. She and Bo stood naked before them. Bo was at her side one step behind, a move *she* made him practice in their nightly encampments for this auspicious event. The colony leader, who himself had been turned at age thirty with the dawn of the twentieth century, stepped forward. Although centuries younger, he still had old-world charms and called her Madam. The vampiress appreciated his manners, smiled and kissed his cheek, sniffed his neck. In turn, the male vampire kissed and sniffed her, then stepped toward Bo. Eva raised her arm to block his advance. The collected vampires grumbled at the affront. The male vampire smelled Bo's virgin blood in the air, and sensed his heart pounding. The vampire leader closed his eyes. His jaw grew slack as if imagining the pleasure Bo's blood would bring.

The vampiress snapped him back to consciousness. "I tell you this," she roared, looking from face to face among the thirty-odd vampires. The Shadows shrank from her shrill voice, hollow sounding, and moved behind caskets and columns. She delivered her words slowly, individually, in her European accent. "This is Bo. He is my pet, my little rabbit. When you smell his sweet virgin blood and hear his heart race you will ignore them. He is mine and only mine," she shouted. In a lower calmer tone, she continued, "You see he wears my identification."

Eva grabbed Bo's collar and hauled him to her side. "He is mine the same way any bobbles you paid for or stole that are around your wrists or necks, any rings you wear on your hands are yours. I have no right to wear *them*. You have *no* right to Bo. I refuse to share a single drop of his precious blood. He is, how do you say, *off limits*. I don't want to see anyone getting close enough to so much as sniff the air that surrounds him without my permission. It will be too much for you to handle."

She glared at the group. "Just so we all understand. I am stronger than *any* one of you, stronger than *any* several of you. Despite that strength and the power of my will that could crush you, I have decided not to become your leader. Fagan will remain in that role. He has provided stability to the colony. We all should be thankful for that. I am now a part of this colony."

Eva paused for a moment and looked from face to face again. Some of the vampires showed fear. Some compliance. Some contempt. She roared again, "Remember, leave Bo alone!"

Bo shrank behind the vampiress. He peed on the floor. His legs were weak and trembled. The vampires laughed suddenly. Eva looked back at Bo and laughed, clapping her hands. The Shadows, in their best goth outfits, complete with multiple piercings, emerged from hiding and laughed, too.

The ice had been broken.

The vampires separated, most leaving to feed.

"Well done, young man, Mr. Bo," Fagan said, swirling his tongue around his mouth to catch the faintest taste of his virginity in the air. "You saved the day."

The vampiress looked at Bo approvingly and smiled, cupped

her cold hand under his chin, and patted his cheek. Bo coughed and stepped out of the urine puddle he stood in.

Fagan turned and walked toward the vault's interior. The vampiress's casket had arrived earlier in the evening. The brothers carried it in and selected a spot on a shelf above the floor. It was away from the tracks left on the dirt floor. Bo should have minimal contact with other vampires and their Shadows. The brothers were already on their way back to the East Coast, this time using interstate highways, taking turns, driving continuously.

"Your casket is there," Fagan pointed toward the wall and its shelf some three feet off the floor. "Your Shadows placed it. If you want to move..."

"This will be fine. Lazlo and Kazmer have selected a good location. They think out everything for my comfort and safety."

"Have you fed, Madam?" Fagan asked, more out of politeness because it was obvious the female vampire was engorged with fresh blood.

"I have. What do they call them? An illegal immigrant? A hard worker with callouses on his hands. Absolutely delicious. It reminded me of a serf from Saxony."

"How did you dispose of the bodies? We can't leave exsanguinated corpses in the open to be found by humans, the police, or, even worse, the Brethren."

"I took every precaution. The human will never be found. My Shadows gave him a deep grave that will not be disturbed."

"The illegals and the homeless are easy prey, popular among our colony members," Fagan said. "These ones who are our food are rarely missed, even among their own kind. They come and go, move often, scatter to the wind. If the taken are missed, the people who miss them don't matter, have no voice, can't go to the police themselves."

"I do not like the junker blood," the vampiress said. "The taste is off."

"True, but we have grown accustomed to it," Fagan said. "You will, too. Sometimes there is no choice. We have too many of our feeders here to keep junkies until their blood clears as you did on the East Coast. Having humans inside the colony, other than our trusted Shadows, would cause unrest."

"Of course. You know, the Dark Ages are reviled in history, but for us, it was a glorious time. We were protected by superstition and fear. We could take whomever we liked. When we saw a villager and fancied an eye or hair color, we could pluck that person, man or woman, boy or girl, from his or her bed and feed as I feed on Bo, or we could drain every last drop of blood at once. Whatever pleased us. Deaths were blamed on plagues. The plague was sometimes blamed on us. They might search for us but more often preferred to hide and arm themselves with trinkets—holy relics, crucifixes, spells, garlic." The vampiress chortled. "Isn't that right, dear Bo? Humans are such fools. So easy to control."

Bo was silent and looked at the floor.

"My little rabbit. You still fear me. What would you do to escape from me at this very moment? Fagan, do you hear his heart hammering away in his chest? Isn't it wonderful? That tiny muscle moving volumes of sweet blood."

"I hear it, Madam. It is truly wonderful to imagine. It would be better to experience." Fagan's jaw grew slack again and he closed his eyes as if imagining Bo's sweet blood coursing down his thirst-ravaged throat to quench a voracious desire that could never be slacked.

"Let your ears enjoy what your mouth and throat cannot, Fagan. You will never taste his hot blood."

Fagan opened his eyes and stared a moment at the vampiress. His look was reptilian. It appeared he was not accustomed to such talk. Then he relaxed his face. "One more thing. As lovely as your body is, you must wear clothing when you hunt. Modern clothes that won't arouse suspicion. People might see you. Call the police."

"I believe Bo will shop for me. Buy me the clothes I will need. I told him I wanted to look like his sweetheart."

"Can he be trusted?"

"I control him completely," Eva said, pulling Bo to her side and placing an arm around him.

"To be safe I will have one of my Shadows accompany him. How much can he know about shopping for women's clothes? He is a virgin."

The two vampires laughed.

"All right. The Shadow must be a male. Bo would have no use to me without his virginity."

"I have a female Shadow I can send," Fagan said, "but Bo must have clothes too before he goes out. She will get him clothes."

"Do you require money for your Shadow?"

"No. The clothing is new and free. The Shadows call it boosting or shoplifting. They can steal the teeth out of someone's head. She will look at his body and know what to get. Bo will know his sizes."

"You know, Fagan, on the East Coast we never hunted. The cattle were brought to us. I look forward to returning to the hunt again, really, selecting victims, cornering them, and feeling their panic in the last moment of life. It's wonderful."

"I agree," Fagan said, "almost as pleasurable as the taste of blood itself. As a member of this colony, you will have to hunt for your own food. We must hunt together. Also, you must follow several imperatives."

Fagan stopped a moment as if to see how the vampiress would accept the new rules. "One, never reveal the colony's existence or entrance. That is utmost. Two, never allow a victim to escape or survive an attack, one who might lead authorities here. Our Shadows are helpful, but few are strong enough to ward off an attack. Your Shadows, the brothers Lazlo and Kazmer, are the exception, and now they are not here. Avoid the clean bloods, those who the authorities will attempt to trace if they disappear into the night, people with families, jobs—how do they say it now? —a footprint on the city. That includes anyone who will be missed, whose death or disappearance will be noticed. It's not like there aren't murders on any given day, but sometimes *our* work is difficult to mask. Shootings and stabbings go mostly unnoticed, I imagine, but someone drained of blood and covered with bite marks is fodder for the rabid press who will create a story when they can't find a legitimate one. Their headlines will blaze, *Ten shot,* but few will care. Should the headline say *Body found drained of blood,* there will be a panic."

"I understand," the vampiress said. "The colony's rules are agreeable to me."

"There's one more thing," Fagan continued. His eyes grew narrow. "There is a group, well organized, that hunt vampires across the globe."

"The Brethren," the vampiress hissed. "That's what they call themselves. They are almost as ancient as we are. They are smart, well-trained, and loyal. They carry crossbows. All are marksmen."

Fagan said, "They are actively searching for our colony now, in this city. We have lost five members over the last two years. What they lack in speed they have in stealth and knowledge. We will have no problems as long as our colony remains a secret. Tell me, did the Brethren decimate your colony?"

The vampiress laughed. "The group that entered our colony was a rag-tag bunch of junkers that killed my brother Gerrard, a new vampire we turned, and our malformed friends who hunted for us. No more than that." She lowered her voice. "They were not skilled, just lucky. But they knew our ways. Some of them had been our prisoners and escaped, also by luck, while we waited for their blood to clear. They banded together and attacked our colony. One among them is pregnant. I plan to bring her here and harvest her baby when it is time, in a few months. We will have *the* great mass."

"A newborn mass. How wonderful." Fagan raised a fist to his mouth in excitement. "I have never attended such a mass. None of our membership have. We've only heard of them. But can you conduct such a mass?"

"Of course. I have presided over such masses through the centuries. How do you think I have attained my strength?"

"Madam, it will be an honor."

"My Shadows are on their way now to capture her. We will slaughter the infant and mother the moment the child is born. Everyone will participate."

CHAPTER EIGHT

Lazlo and Kazmer sat in Lisa's kitchen. Every time the refrigerator compressor started its low hum Kazmer raised an eyebrow. Occasionally he toyed with his stiletto knife, which lay on the table in front of him. A Felix the Cat clock on the wall swished its tail and eyes back and forth with the passing time, adding a little more noise to the otherwise quiet kitchen. Finally, they heard the thump of slow steps up the exterior stairway. They looked at each other. "Remember, my brudder, be gentle to Lisa. We must protect the baby."

Kazmer grunted. "I don't forget. I understand the job we have." Kazmer stood and positioned himself behind the door. He stripped a length of duct tape to slip over Lisa's head and cover her mouth as soon as she stepped through the door. He handed the tape to his brother. Lazlo stripped off two pieces, one for Lisa's wrists, another for her ankles and hung the tape from the kitchen table edge.

The steps continued slowly, heavily, then stopped, seemingly for a rest on the landing halfway up. The apartment below was empty. The brothers had determined that earlier in the afternoon. There were no curtains, and the windows were dark. They weren't concerned about making a little noise during the abduction. If anyone appeared at the door, the brothers would say they were moving the new washing machine into place. Kazmer shot a glance at Lazlo. Kazmer thought perhaps Lisa suspected something was amiss. Had the hand truck gouged or scratched a step when the brothers hauled the empty washing machine box up the steps? Was Lisa going to retreat? Was their plan, Kazmer's idea, going to fail?

Finally, the steps continued. They grew louder. The brothers were relieved the steps continued up the stairs and shared another glance and tense, closed-lip smiles. Lisa was a prize trophy the vampiress insisted on having and sent her trusted Shadows to dispatch her to the West Coast. Lazlo nodded to Kazmer. Kazmer raised the strip of tape in front of him high enough to slip over Lisa's head. The steps stopped outside the door. The brothers expected to hear a key in the lock but instead heard a knock. They stood motionless. Shot each other another glance. The knock came again and after a pause a third time.

Lazlo motioned with his hand as if signifying Lisa might not have a key. Kazmer shrugged. Lazlo stepped toward the door, and was about to put his large hand on the doorknob when a voice called.

"Hey, It's Susan from across the street. I talked to you earlier." She knocked on the door again. This time louder. The door rattled in its frame. The brothers waited. They heard her heavy breathing. Lazlo's hand remained an inch from the doorknob. He pressed his back against the wall beside the door and remained unseen from the outside. The brothers watched each other. The doorknob turned back and forth. Susan pushed on the door without success. After a lengthy pause, Susan knocked again. "I know you're in there. I see your van in the street. What are you up to? Let me in."

The brothers traded more looks. Kazmer shrugged his shoulders.

"Maybe she'll go away," Kazmer whispered.

Lazlo raised a thick index finger to his lips.

"Are you all right in there? Let me in. It's Susan from across the street."

Lazlo turned the lock switch and opened the door a crack. Susan pushed the door open another few inches until it hit the toe of Lazlo's boot and stopped. Susan pushed a plump hand and wrist through the open space and waved it around as if looking for something that stopped the door from opening.

"What's going on in there?" Susan demanded. "I want to see what's going on. Lisa's my friend and I have a right to know."

Lazlo put his face to the opening. "We are still installing washer."

"In the dark. I want to see what you two are doing in there."

"Installing washer in other room," Lazlo said.

"What's taking so long? I could install a washer myself, you know." Susan's voice became strident. "All you have to do is connect the water hoses and the drain, then plug it in and test it."

"The washer connection was there but we had to do a little more plumbing," Lazlo said. "To prevent future leaks. My brudder and I are very thorough. It takes a while. We don't want a complaint about a leak."

Lazlo looked toward his brother. Kazmer nodded and put down his piece of duct tape. Then he returned his knife to its pocket inside the hoodie. Lazlo moved his foot and allowed the door to open. Susan stepped into the kitchen. She looked flustered. She wore a plaid wool poncho now over her sweater. Kazmer moved to his brother's side, which blocked a view of the tape hanging on the table's edge.

"The sign on your van has no phone number," Susan said, "so, I checked the internet and Gill's Appliances has no website, no reviews, no complaints..."

"We never have complaints," Kazmer interrupted. "Everyone loves us." He smiled, and raised a shoulder toward his ear.

"How would anyone know? You don't have a website! Who is Gill?"

"We are Gill. We are so busy we don't need website. How do you say it?" Lazlo thought a moment, head lowered, a large fist to his forehead. "Talk of mouth. We can hardly handle all the business. Have no time for website."

"We don't get a minute off," Kazmer chimed.

Susan investigated the washer's empty box. "You moved the washer?"

"It's already in place. Just a little more plumbing and then we will make the connection. Then the install will be finished and we will leave. Jimmy told us to lock the door before we leave. Put the extra key on the table." Lazlo smiled at Susan.

"I want to see where the washer is going," Susan said. She took a step toward the men, but the box and the brothers blocked her path. She waited with her hands on her hips.

"It is a surprise, the washer," Kazmer said. His hand tightened on the knife handle inside the hoodie as he smiled at Susan. "From her boyfriend, father of the baby she carries."

"Jimmy? Jimmy bought her the washer?"

The brothers nodded.

Susan clapped her hands. "What a man! I could eat him alive."

"Really?" Kazmer said.

Susan blushed. "Of course not, not literally. I'm married." Susan's voice was strident again. She waved her be-ringed left hand at the men.

Kazmer grunted.

"*Jimmy* say he wants Lisa to see the washing machine first," Lazlo said.

"She'll be…" Susan shook her head looking for the right words.

"Over the moon," Kazmer interjected.

"Exactly! Thrilled! I know she hated lugging laundry up and down these steps." Susan smiled. Looked around the kitchen. Then she twisted her mouth. Susan retreated a step. "But what about a dryer? The washer won't be much good without a dryer."

Kazmer's eyes glazed over He brought the knife forward. Repositioned his fingers on the handle.

"It come next week," Lazlo said, matter-of-factly. "On backorder. When the store gets it, then we deliver and install it."

"Isn't that the case with everything today? Lisa said, wagging her head. "It's probably coming from China."

Kazmer released his grip on the knife. "Who knows?" he added. "It comes from somewhere."

"But where will it go?"

Kazmer rolled his eyes toward his brother and retightened his grip on the knife handle.

Lazlo smiled. "Special order. It fits over washer. Takes up no room on floor."

"That will be fabulous," Susan said. "Lisa won't know what to do with herself. Listen, I don't want to hold up you gentlemen. Lisa might be home soon."

"We are almost finished," Lazlo said.

Smiling, Susan turned and exited the apartment, backing out, bending slightly at the knees. She called back over her shoulder. "Maybe I'll see you when you bring the dryer."

"Maybe," Kazmer said. After the door was closed, Kazmer turned to his brother. "She said *Listen*, listen for what? I don't understand Americans. They use too many words."

"I don't know, my brudder. Maybe Lisa's footsteps."

The brothers repositioned their tape strips and sat down again at the kitchen table.

After a day of police interviews, employees coming and going, call-offs from among those scheduled to work, and a large crowd of curious who milled around the restaurant—Lisa had to call in one of the bouncers—Lisa finally finished her work and left for home. She was tired. Her feet were swollen and throbbed inside her shoes. She couldn't wait to get back to her apartment and kick them off.

There is no shortcut when traffic is heavy, or so it seems, Lisa thought on the way home. Eventually, she pulled up behind a van with signs marked with Gill's Appliances. She stared at the sign for a moment and thought it was strange the lettering contained no phone number, no address, no website. She shrugged it off and approached her building. She turned back a second to ensure there was enough space behind the van and her car for workers to get in. Someone was lucky enough to get a new appliance or unfortunate to need one repaired.

Lisa grabbed the handrail on the steps and started the long climb to the second floor. Inside the apartment, the brothers stood at the first football on the steps. They took their positions. They looked at each other. It had only been minutes since Susan left the building.

Kazmer mouthed silently, "I hope she did not come back."

He checked his knife's position. The blade was back on the table. The steps were slow and heavy, as Susan's had been. Again, there was a pause on the steps, seemingly a rest on the landing. This time, however, the rest was briefer, and the steps continued. Finally, feet shuffled outside the door. The brothers heard keys jingle, A key slipped into the lock and turned. It had to be Lisa. Kazmer raised his duct tape strip high, ready to gag her as she walked inside.

The door pushed open. A hand reached inside and searched for the light switch. Lisa stepped inside. In one fast, smooth move-ment, Kazmer slammed the door with his raised elbow, slipped the tape over Lisa's head, and pressed it to her mouth. Then he grabbed her above the waist to pin her arms, avoiding the baby bump. Lisa launched herself backward, knocking Kazmer into the cabinets. He struck his head. She kicked wildly, but Lazlo pinned her legs between his arm and body and wrapped his tape around her ankles. It was difficult to breathe with her mouth taped shut. Lisa snorted air through her nose. She twisted her torso but could not move under Kazmer's strong grip. Lazlo dropped her bound feet to the floor. Lisa jumped, banging her head under Kazmer's chin. He staggered back a step. She swung her legs up backward, landing in Kazmer's crotch. He released Lisa and grabbed his groin with a groan. She dropped to the floor, then lunged for the table, grabbed the razor-sharp stiletto knife, and slashed madly through the air in quick short strokes. One caught Lazlo's arm. He hollered in surprise and backed away. Blood pumped from the wound. Lisa ripped the tape from her mouth. Panted for breath. She sliced the tape on her ankles and freed her legs. Then she turned the knife toward Kazmer.

Kazmer landed a punch to her jaw and Lisa slumped to the floor. The brothers bound the six-inch wound on Lazlo's arm with duct tape to prevent further bleeding. Then they examined Lisa for injuries. Satisfied, she seemed to be knocked cold, the brothers retaped Lisa, lifted her inside the empty washing machine box, and secured the box lid with more tape. Finally, they cleaned up Lazlo's blood with towels from the kitchen and bathroom, bagged the bloody items, and slowly, carefully, used the hand truck to convey the box to the front yard. It took only a few minutes to move the box downstairs and load it in the back of the van. The men worked casually, as if they were still on the clock, and tried to eke out a little more delivery pay.

The brothers pulled away and stopped around the corner briefly to remove the *Gill's Appliances* signs from the van exterior and replace them with *Kazmer Plumbing*, a little joke the men laughed at when they ordered the magnetic signs before starting their long trip. The mission on the East Coast was complete.

CHAPTER NINE

THE VAMPIRE HUNTERS LOWERED THEIR HEADS IN A MOMENT of silence for New Girl. They were scattered about Bad Nelson's garage at the end of his parents' yard. While waiting for everyone to arrive, Bad Nelson had collected the PVC potato guns he had converted to shoot wooden stakes, wiped them down and turned off the propane gas canisters used to propel the stakes. It was the morning after their assault on After Dark's vampire lair. After the moment of silence, Bad Nelson asked if anyone knew New Girl's real name. No one did.

They smiled and laughed at the descriptions of New Girl running down Fifth Street buck naked after she, Overboard George, and Mad Maggie escaped from the vampire lair. Later, she appeared on the street wrapped in a sheet, a toga, stolen from a backyard wash line, and garish running shoes too large for her small feet.

"She never talked much, but she was always thinking," Overboard George said, shaking his lowered head. He raised his eyes to look at the members of the group. "Man, could she run. She was a sprinter, even in that toga and weird shoes. It's a shame she didn't last long enough for a chance to get out of this city, this homeless-ness, and get away from the dope."

The others mumbled in agreement and mused silently for a moment, perhaps thinking of their own conditions, homeless, addicted, and virtually prisoners on the streets with little hope of escaping.

"She was so small you could keep her in your box, and she'd take up practically no room. Eat almost nothing. You wouldn't know she was there most of the time unless she said something, which wouldn't be often," Old Harriet said. "She probably could make a single fix last a couple of days."

"She could shoot a stake gun, too," Bad Nelson said. "Had an eye like an eagle. Wasn't afraid to face those vampires."

"Not after what she went through in that dungeon," Mad Maggie said.

"What we all went through," Overboard George added. "New Girl, me, you Maggie, and Bad Nelson, too. We all had a hard time."

"She was a screamer," Mad Maggie said, smiling at her memory of the young addict. "But when it came down to it, she was a warrior same as the rest of us."

"So, where do we go from here?" Bad Nelson said.

"We must be careful. We don't know what that vampire will do. She might be out for revenge," Overboard George said. "Who knows how many friendly people she has under her spell?"

"Bo for one," Mad Maggie said. "I think she had mind control over him. That's why he didn't help us with the attack. He just faded away—not that he could have done much against *her*. Especially in the weakened condition he was in."

"I'd be surprised if he was still alive," Overboard George said. He pointed a finger and moved it from person to person, "The other thing we don't know is how far the female vampire went. She could be still here in the city. Might be in the same block. Or, she might have moved to another state. Unless she shows herself, it'll be impossible to find her, even though I'd love to drive a stake through her dead heart and watch her incinerate. Remember we all have to be careful, especially at night when they can move around at will."

THE DAY AFTER LISA DISAPPEARED, the group assembled again in Bad Nelson's garage. Jimmy, the last to arrive, cried. "My Lisa is gone!" when he entered under the overhead door.

"How?" Overboard George said, taking a step toward Jimmy.

"Kidnapped. Last night. She didn't answer my calls."

"Maybe she skipped on you," Old Harriet interjected. Her thatch of hair was flat in the back from sleeping in her sweet box.

Tears rolled down Jimmy's cheeks. "No. She was taken. A woman who lives across the street said two men in a white van delivered a washing machine. They had a big box. The men told her I bought the washer for Lisa as a surprise. They were in Lisa's apartment a long time. Then the men left the apartment with the washer box after Lisa got home, but get this, there's no washer in her apartment and Lisa is gone. I never bought a washing machine. Her car is parked on the street. I think the men took Lisa away in the box."

"The vampire did it," Overboard George said. "I know it. Remember how protective she was of Lisa during the attack. Staying outside her cell. Wanting to escape, but not wanting to leave Lisa. The vampire chose her own safety only at the last moment."

"I remember how she roared. The look in her eyes," Old Harriet said.

Jimmy sobbed. "I know most of you don't like me because I doubted you about the existence of vampires, how I refused to carry one of the stake guns or a torch, but I'm asking for your help now. We must find Lisa." After a pause, he added, "I don't know where else to go."

"Police?" Mad Maggie said.

"I called the police. Had them talk to Susan, the neighbor," Jimmy said. "Susan thinks Lisa was kidnapped, too. Susan said the van had magnetic signs, Gill's Appliances, but there was no phone number on the signs. The store doesn't have a website. Not one internet comment on the store, good or bad. Susan checked it. The store doesn't exist."

"What about the police?" Overboard George asked again.

"I talked to two officers. They said there was no evidence of foul play, but I know Lisa's kitchen is different. She has OCD. There were little things out of place. The table was moved. Just a few inches, but Lisa wouldn't have moved it the way it is now. Things on the counter were different. The police think we had an argument, and she went to a friend's place. They even asked me if I hit her. We didn't, I didn't, I swear. When I told the cops that Lisa was pregnant, they said her hormones were off-kilter and that she needed a break from me. They thought Susan, who is also pregnant, had raging hormones and was cooky, too. I think the cops suspected me more than the idea Lisa could be kidnapped. The cops didn't like me either. I could tell."

Overboard George rubbed the stubble on his chin. "I don't know what to say."

"I know what to say," Mad Maggie said, pointing an index finger with its ragged nail into the air. "My research tells me vampires will sacrifice a baby, preferably at the moment of birth, and consume its blood and flesh in a ceremony, a black mass, very unholy, that will add strength to the fiend and any vampires who partake. It's so dark the devil himself might be invited. It's so dark *he* might show up."

"That sounds like Christmas dinner on steroids," Del Hatch said from his position in the corner. He wore his jumpsuit and a pistol in a holster around his waist. "Maggie's right. I'm more of a Bigfoot expert, but I've been doing research, too."

"Internet?" Bad Nelson asked.

"*Famous Monsters of Filmland.* I got an extensive collection of periodicals on the occult." Del winked at the group, snapped open a soda can, and took a long pull. "Those movies, the magazines, are designed to educate the public about everything unholy almost in a subliminal manner."

"Not again," Jimmy whined. He ran his fingers through his hair. "I have nowhere else to turn. Will you help me find Lisa and our baby?"

"I'll help, but where the hell would we even start to look?" Old Harriet said. She saw her reflection in the garage window and tried to right her flattened beehive hairdo.

Jimmy pulled a paper from his shirt pocket. "I think I know— it's a stretch—and it's going to require some travel."

The vampire hunters looked from one to another. Del Hatch smiled. "My go bag is always ready."

CHAPTER TEN

The vampire hunters crowded around Jimmy to see the letters he pulled from his pocket. Letters he and Lisa took from Bart's apartment the morning after he was killed. They marveled at the thick stationery and the elegant penmanship.

"That's definitely old handwriting," Old Harriet said. "I know it is. Had a teacher when I was little. A real bitch. Always sending notes home to my mother about how I acted in class. The writing looks similar. I'd say this was done with a fountain pen, too. Something elegant. Who uses a fountain pen today? Maybe the president to sign a bill that will take more money from our pockets and push us toward extinction."

Jimmy passed the letter around. They studied the penmanship, felt the stationary between their fingers, and examined the ink. No one said a word. Del Hatch held the letter at an angle.

"Look here," Del said. "This might be a fingerprint. A small one."

"The vampire had small features, although she herself is tall," Mad Maggie said. "At least that's what I remember when she was pulling my limbs out of their sockets."

Del looked at Maggie for a moment and returned to the letter. "I'd say it's a faint thumbprint. Just a smudge. Could be blood."

"What else would it be," Mad Maggie said. "She was probably draining some poor soul of her last drop of blood, licked her fingers, and turned to this letter. What a fiend!"

"I'll put a new edge on your machete, Mad Maggie. You think it's sharp now? Wait and see." Del winked at her.

Mad Maggie smiled. "You're a good man, Del. You're just like us now. Always thinking about the demise of the undead."

"How do we know this writing is the vampire's?" Overboard George wanted to know. He had been the least enthusiastic about the letter. "It could be anybody's."

"I'll tell you," Jimmy said. By this time the letters had circulated among the group and returned to him. He took a deep breath and started. "Lisa did all the ordering at After Dark. She had lists from the kitchen, the bar even, occasionally, the offices upstairs. The cooks, the bartenders, everybody added items to the lists. Lisa double-checked the items on the lists and called or emailed the orders to After Dark's various vendors. After a while, she got to know everybody's handwriting. Then this strange, very elegant, very old-fashioned handwriting shows up *once* on the list for fluorescent lightbulbs the restaurant, the bar, the kitchen, the offices upstairs didn't use. They were an odd size. Lisa thought someone ordered the bulbs to take home. She told Bart about the order, and he told her to put them through anyway. The next day he even asked if she had included the bulbs. As it turned out, the bulbs were used in the basement where the vampires were. Lisa was sure the handwriting belonged to one of the vampires. She was convinced it was the female vampire's because the handwriting was so elegant. Lisa thought it was feminine. And, of course, the male vampire died in the attack. He couldn't have written letters from the West Coast."

"Ain't nothin' feminine about that bitch," Mad Maggie said.

Overboard George looked at Jimmy. "You believe in vampires now?"

"I believe. I've seen them with my own eyes," Jimmy said.

"I believe, too," Del said, "and I haven't seen one yet. But if George says vampires exist, I believe they exist, too. Hell, I ain't seen a Bigfoot either, but I *know* they exist. There's enough evidence to make me believe in both."

Jimmy walked to the garage workbench and spread out the letters on the top. The group followed him. He added an envelope made of the same paper. Jimmy pointed with an index finger, "Up here is the vampire's return address. I believe that's where she was after she escaped from After Dark. She's probably still there."

"What if she isn't?" Old Harriet said.

Jimmy said, "It's a start. Lisa and I believed she was there. She wrote four letters to Bart from that address. If she isn't there now, maybe we can find out where she went. It's not so easy to drag a casket around the country, especially with her in it, a casket you can only move at night if you don't want to be seen."

"I'm with you," Old Harriet said. "I'll make the trip. Never been to the West Coast. There's a first time for everything. Even for me."

Jimmy stepped away from the workbench and turned toward the group. He looked nervous. "I've been thinking about this. I asked for your help, but I don't expect anyone to make this trip, to confront the vampire again. We won't know what the odds are until we get to the West Coast. She might not be alone. There might be more vampires. Frankly, I can't predict anything."

"You can't go without us, me and Mad Maggie," Overboard George said, placing a hand on Jimmy's shoulder. "Lisa was always kind to us. Saved us food from After Dark. We won't let her down. Besides, I figure *nobody* knows more about vampires than me and Maggie. We never stopped our research. We know more now than ever."

"Call me Mrs. Van Helsing," Mad Maggie said, smiling. "You

know, George, after we're all done with this and Lisa is returned to Jimmy, we can take our vows on the beach, in front of our friends here and the Pacific Ocean. I want you all to be our witnesses."

"Mags, that would be nice. I couldn't ask for anything more," Overboard George said. He wiped a tear from his eye.

"Del, I don't expect you to go. This isn't your fight."

"Fuck you, Jimmy!" Del said. He pointed a finger at Jimmy. Jimmy took a step back. "You whet my appetite about vampires and then pull the rug out from under me. I don't think so. I'm in. Besides, when we're done and that bitch is staked, I'll head up north. There're some fellas I met online from Washington State. We can do a little Squatch hunting. One is an expert howler. They'll be expecting me at some point."

"Thanks, Del," Jimmy said. He and Del hugged. The vampire hunters surrounded Jimmy to console him.

OVER THE NEXT THREE DAYS, the group gathered supplies, and finally, Bad Nelson hauled his potato guns to the game lands. The vampire hunters making the trip west shot and reloaded wooden stakes. They had learned a few lessons from the attack on After Dark. A vampire could outrun the relatively slow-moving stakes. It might be better to slow down a fiend with a few lead bullets before shooting the lethal stakes. They would try to fight from within direct sunlight. Individually, they were no match for a vampire. Although Overboard George and Mad Maggie maintained cruci-fixes, holy water, mirrors, and garlic were strong weapons against the undead, they had no direct experience, even though such devices had worked against Bela Lugosi, Christopher Lee, John Carradine, and other vampires portrayed in movies. Even *Famous Monsters of Filmland* magazine had touted the effectiveness of the items. So, they figured, there must be some legitimacy to the claims.

Del brought his stash of *Famous Monsters, Monster World,* and

Modern Monster magazines, as well as *Creepy* comic books, which Overboard George and Mad Maggie poured over while they sat on a blanket in the shade of a pine tree. The couple took copious notes on tablets. Del introduced a crossbow used for deer, which could shoot a bolt farther, faster, and more accurately than Bad Nelson's potato guns. Although none of the homeless had the cash to buy even the cheapest crossbow, they all took turns shooting bolts. Then Del pulled out revolvers and pistols. All took a turn shooting them. The guns were all small calibers. Del said it would be better to hit the vampire several times rather than miss her with a large magnum bullet whose recoil might make them miss.

After target practice, they sat in the forest on blankets and planned the trip to the West Coast. They would use Del's SUV and Jimmy's car. The passengers were Overboard George and Mad Maggie, Jimmy, Bad Nelson, Del, and Old Harriet. Megan would stay at home with her children. There was room for food, weapons, and of course, Lisa on the return trip. Del had already packed snacks, dried fruit, and trail mix, as well as individual meals that required water and activating a heating element provided in each pack. There was enough food to supply the vampire hunters and later feed Del on his trip north looking for Bigfoot. They would travel the interstates and make the trip as fast as possible, trading off drivers as often as necessary, although only George, Del, and Jimmy were capable of driving.

There was one rule all agreed to—there would be no drug or alcohol use allowed on the trip. Old Harriet agreed only reluctantly.

The group had been animated about the drive—the sights, the food, George and Maggie's impending marriage, even potty jokes about stopping to go. Then they were silent. A breeze made Old Harriet shiver. Then she sobbed.

"What's wrong, Old Harriet," Overboard George said. "You don't have to go. It's going to be a tough trip, maybe too much for you."

"It's not the drive," Old Harriet said, between sobs, with her head lowered. "Or the fight. I'm not afraid of vampires. It's our poor Bo. I believe he's alive and he's in trouble. I think that vampire has Lisa and him."

"Bo's either dead or on the lam. He might have gone back to his home, wherever that was," Bad Nelson said.

Old Harriet raised her head and cleared her throat. "No. I feel Bo is alive, the vampire has him, and he is in trouble. The vampire has Lisa, but Lisa is not with the vampire—yet. She is on her way to the vampire. Kidnapped. It's a vision I had in my mind when the wind blew. It was like I saw photographs all at once, so fast I could hardly tell them apart. Now they're gone." Old Harriet looked from face to face. "Over the years I've had such visions, a glimpse into the future. They've always proved right. I get the visions when I get goose bumps like just now when the wind blew. But I don't get visions every time the wind blows, or I get goosebumps. My grandmother, my mother's mother, saw things, too. I predicted my grandmother's death. I knew my mother was pregnant with my sister when I was a little girl, even before my mom knew." Old Harriet raised her hands and let them fall in her lap. "Sometimes the visions were years apart. I haven't had one in a long time, especially with the dope I been on for so long. I think the dope clouded my visions."

"Did you see where Lisa is, where the vampire is?" Jimmy said. The group leaned toward Old Harriet and waited for an answer.

"I couldn't see that," Old Harriet said, finally, slowly, barely above a whisper. "I know something, though. Lisa will be safe until the baby is born, *even* with the vampire. Without help, I doubt whether Bo will survive this day."

CHAPTER ELEVEN

Lisa woke with a pounding headache. Her jaw was sore. She was jostled back and forth, side to side in the dark, and was in an uncomfortable position with her knees tucked up against her chin, an especially difficult position for a pregnant woman. However, she couldn't move much. There was no room to stretch her legs or arms. Her wrists and ankles were bound and, therefore, she had to settle for transferring her weight from one hip to the other after one position became painful. Her other senses came back slowly. There was a taste of blood at the corner of her mouth. That probably was the reason her head and jaw hurt. She smelled cardboard. New cardboard. She pressed her back into the stiff wall behind her. It gave a little. It felt like cardboard. She was in a cardboard box. A big one.

She pushed her palms against the roof. Definitely was cardboard. She was in a vehicle. And could hear the engine accelerating now. She was bound in a box in a moving vehicle, probably a van that had just entered a highway from a ramp. The engine no longer revved but ran smoothly. At times she heard the tailpipe below rattle. She heard cars and trucks passing and vehicles going the opposite way in the distance. It was still daylight because there were holes in the box and pinholes of light slit through the sides like swords in a magician's act.

Lisa raised her hands to one of these light streams, no larger than a pencil, and saw her hands were bound with duct tape. Immediately she gnawed on the layers of tape, stopping every few seconds to see if a tear in her constraints could be ripped wider. The tape was tight and cut off circulation to her hands. Her fingers felt numb. She clenched and unclenched them to keep blood flowing.

What had happened? She remembered arriving home from a long day at After Dark, the news of Leon and Bart's murders, climbing the long stairway to her second-floor apartment, pausing on the landing midway for a breather. She fumbled with her keys outside the kitchen door. It took a few seconds to find the correct key. Then she paused. She remembered seeing some gouges on two steps near the bottom, but the landlord had said he planned to paint the entire stairway before winter. No big deal. She would stay with Jimmy while the work was done and the paint dried. His first-floor apartment would be a godsend. Just three steps in and out. She might move there when the baby's birth was closer. While she looked for the kitchen door key, she noticed the carpet outside the door was askew. She kicked it back in place because that's how she was. Everything had a place, and everything had to be in its proper spot. Still, no alarms went off. Maybe Susan had come over or a gust of wind moved the mat. Lisa shrugged off another peculiarity in a day filled with murders, police interviews, and trying to keep the restaurant and bar open. She remembered thinking as she opened the door, *all I want to do is sit down and put my feet up.*

Now she remembered the fight. There was a washing machine box in her tiny kitchen. Someone had grabbed her. Tried to put tape over her mouth. There were two of them. Very strong. She fought with all her might. Kicked and slapped, using methods she learned in a self-defense class she had taken. She had picked up a knife that did not belong to her. It was a knife that looked like a weapon, almost surgical, not meant for, say, slicing cheese. She slashed the knife through the air repeatedly, fighting off grabbing hands, and hit something. There was a gasp of surprise and pain. Just as the hands on her seemed to retreat there was a shock and a flash of pain. Then there was oblivion until her senses returned slowly and she discovered herself bound in a box. Ahh, Lisa thought. She was in the box that sat in her kitchen. The box was in the van that had been parked at the curb. Where was Susan, her nosey friend, when she needed her? Lisa had been kidnapped. But by whom?

At last, Lisa chewed through the duct tape on her wrists. She spit out threads in her mouth, adhesive plastered to her lips while working on the tape at her ankles. Meanwhile, the van appeared to settle into a steady speed. They were on a highway. Lisa found the end of the tape, peeled it loose with difficulty, and carefully unwrapped its many layers from around her ankles, trying to make as little noise as possible. At last, her ankles were free, and she flexed her feet to get back the feeling. If only she had her purse. *She did have her purse.* She found it when she moved to ease the pain in her butt and hamstrings. It was the small leather purse with a long strap she wore across her shoulder. Her abductors must have taken it from around her neck and thrown it in the box when they lowered her inside. Now she rooted slowly, quietly, through the purse, feeling items—hairbrush, compact, wallet, a wad of tissues— and found her mini flashlight. Lisa clicked on the flashlight to illuminate the purse's interior. Her fingers moved through the contents a second time. Her cell phone was gone. Of course. She held it in her hand when she was attacked. It dropped to the floor. Probably kicked away during the melee. Finally, at the very bottom of her purse, Lisa's fingers scraped the item she wanted, prayed was still there, had been transferred among the things from her larger purse a few days before. Pepper spray. A can Jimmy had bought her.

Thank God, Lisa mouthed silently. When the van lurched after hitting a pothole, Lisa changed her position to sit comfortably cross-legged. The van roared on. Light from the box pinholes dimmed as time went on, but Lisa had her flashlight and pepper spray. All she needed was the chance to see her attackers. Should she move around in the box and force them to pull over, or wait for them to select a spot? Either way, she would not have a decision on the terrain and a path to escape. At least if her abductors decided where to pull over, they would not suspect trouble from her. The element of surprise gave her an advantage. She decided to wait. Lisa had been a medium-distance runner in high school who had remained in shape and now, remembering how the men had gasped for air during her abduction, thought she could outrun them, even pregnant. Meanwhile, she mapped out several scenarios. She could spray her abductors when they opened the box and run like hell, or at least as fast as a pregnant woman can run. Or, if possible, run first and spray them when they followed.

Eventually, the van exited up a ramp, slowed down, made a series of turns, and pulled to a stop. Lisa could smell meat frying. They probably stopped to eat. She heard mumbling from the front. It didn't sound like English. The abductors sat silently for a while. Then a van door opened and closed. She heard a sigh and then what she imagined was a sudden curse. Again, it was not English. After being raised in a broken home and working in a bar, there were not many curses she had not heard. It appeared one of the abductors had remained in the van. After a while, one returned, and the second left. The aroma of fried food filled the van. Lisa's stomach groaned. It was a welcome relief from the stale smell of a strange tobacco that had been present. Eventually, the second one came back.

"I got something for her," a gruff voice said after the second one returned. It was English, but in a strange accent. European sounding.

The other appeared to grunt.

That grunt confirmed to Lisa there were two men up front.

Immediately the aroma of the food became stronger. Sitting in her dark cardboard enclosure, Lisa imagined the men ate in silence with some occasional lip-smacking. Finally, she heard air sucked through straws followed by two prolonged burps and chuckles. Then they took turns leaving the van again, possibly to use the bathroom. This would be a good time to run with one man gone. However, she was still a prisoner. If she got out of the box, there was no telling whether she could open the back of the van from the inside. Lisa slipped her flashlight inside her jeans pocket. She turned the pepper spray can over and over in her hands. Suddenly, she heard both van doors open and close. There was a key in another door lock.

"I want to make sure she is still breathing. Let some air in that box," one man said in his strange accent. "Unless you want to do it?"

"You do it, my brudder. She already slit my arm. She is a hell cat. Drop the food in. Tell her to stay quiet, or we will take her baby away and cut it out of her. Kill the baby and her."

"I hope she is still breathing. I am afraid I hit her too hard."

"Anyone that strong will be all right. Don't worry. Maybe we should drive somewhere else to check her."

"There are not many cars here. I am worried. She has not moved since we are on the road."

"All right, my brudder. Check her breathing. Satisfy your curiosity. Here is the roll of tape when you need it to seal the box."

Lisa heard tape pulled from the box lid, strip after long strip. The box lid lifted a few inches and struck the van's roof. Light and fresh air, heavy with the aroma of frying meat, flooded the box. They stopped at a fast food joint, Lisa thought. Lisa knew she could not spring from the box. There was not enough room. A man tried to put his head into the crack. A baseball hat bill loomed over the box lid. An amount of unruly, black hair. The head strained from side to side.

The men seemed to curse. Again, it was not in English.

"What's wrong, my brudder?"

"I cannot see. I am worried. She has not moved. Not made a noise."

"Maybe she is playing the porcupine. Tip the box and look in."

Meanwhile, Lisa flexed her calf and thigh muscles, and rubbed her hamstrings, preparing to launch herself from the box. Meaty fingers slipped over the box's upper edge. The man pulled the box toward him, but it snagged on the van roof. He bumped it several times, and caught his fingers on the lid. Cursed more in the strange dialect.

"Close the lid, my brudder. Then it will tip."

The man let the box go and it righted itself. The lid slid shut.

The man pulled the box forward. Stopped a moment. "I still don't hear anything."

"Tip it over, my brudder while no one is watching, and we will see for ourselves. The eyes know more than the ears."

Lisa had the pepper spray ready. She held it away from her, nozzle pointing out. The box eased down on its side. Lisa slipped from the box bottom to the side. Just as the fingers appeared inside the lid again, Lisa delivered a kick with both feet that sent the man sprawling. The fingers disappeared with an unintelligible oath. One man was on the ground, and the second was shocked for an instant. Lisa released the pepper spray at the standing man. He turned away, grimacing, rubbing his eyes, choking, stamping his feet. Lisa slipped from the van. The man on the ground caught Lisa's leg. She reached down and sprayed him in the face. It was Kazmer, and he rolled away choking, gasping for breath, but he managed to knock the pepper spray can out of her hand. It rolled under the van.

Lisa ran. Her cramped legs did not fly as she thought they would. She almost crumpled to the ground but managed to catch herself. Her baby bounced. She cradled her belly with one arm. The other swung as she ran. She surveyed the fast-food chain parking lot. There were only a few cars scattered around. A half-dozen vehicles waited in line at the drive-through. A worker paused, mouth open, as she cleaned the glass on the front door. Lisa screamed for help. She zigzagged through parked cars. Crushed a paper soda cup. Lost her footing for a moment on the spilled ice. A few people stood watching but no one came to her aid. She waved at the diners inside, but everyone looked away and continued eating. She surveyed her surroundings while she ran, trying in an instant to decide an escape avenue. She ran behind the restaurant and entered the truck parking lot en route to a busy intersection, where she hoped she would find safety from the men who, she imagined, now clumsily pursued her, fighting off the effects of the pepper spray. Already her legs ached, her lungs burned. She hoped she would make it to the intersection.

Then she heard him. "Over here! Over here!" It was an odd, high-pitched voice, more like a warble, that belonged to a trucker who had just pulled his semi in and slipped from the cab.

Lisa ran to him. "Help me! Help me!"

"What is it darling?" the man said in a calm voice, looking around the parking lot over Lisa's shoulder.

"Two men are after me. They kidnapped me," Lisa cried, between gulps of breath, "but I escaped. Just now. Hit them with pepper spray. Please. Call the police."

"You're safe with me," the trucker said. "I'm Don. Do you still have the spray?"

"No. One of them knocked it out of my hand. The can rolled away."

"Good. Don't want you hitting me with it by accident." Don was already opening the sleeping compartment to his cab. He smiled with discolored teeth. "Now, you climb in the back here. You'll be safe. If they come back here, I'll tell them you ran around the other way.

Lisa looked at the man. She was still breathless. She couldn't run anymore. Don nodded eagerly. His jeans were stuffed into his scuffed cowboy boots. He had spindly, bowed legs, a little beer belly that almost made *him* look pregnant, scrawny arms hanging from a faded T-shirt, and a long graying ponytail of unruly hair. Lisa looked back. The brothers hadn't appeared around the restaurant yet. She climbed inside the truck. Before Don moved toward the restaurant, he returned to the cab's passenger side to open the door. Lisa pushed her head through the curtain that separated the sleeping compartment.

"It's only me," Don said. "Just want to get my phone, and just in case there's any trouble, my pistol. Hang tight. I'll be back in a few. What's your name, anyway?"

"Lisa. Lisa Van der Meer."

That's a nice name. Sounds royal. I always liked those 'vans' and 'vons,'" Don said with a smile as he rummaged through a compartment, grabbed some things Lisa couldn't see, closed the door, and walked away.

While Don sauntered around the side of the restaurant, Lazlo and Kazmer approached him. "You see girl running through here, maybe?" Lazlo managed to say. The brothers still rubbed their eyes and coughed.

"It looks like you boys got hit with pepper spray," Don said, smiling.

"The girl do it," Kazmer choked out.

"Her name Lisa?"

The brothers stooped with hands on their knees and nodded.

"I got her up in my rig. She's safe. Not going anywhere. Scared shitless, but not of *me*."

"She is ours," Lazlo said, standing straight, towering over Don. "We take her now."

"I don't doubt she's yours." Don grinned at the brothers. "All I want is a little time with her before I give her back. If you know what I mean?" Don pulled the pistol grip from his side jean pocket to show the men.

The brothers looked at each other for a moment. "How much time?"

"Just a little. You can even watch. I ain't modest. When I'm done you can have her. Do whatever you want, because I never met you two."

"Where?" Lazlo said.

"I got a spot. Up the highway about five miles, there's a closed-down mall. Highway sign says RAMP CLOSED. Go up that ramp to the top of the hill and hang a left. Go around the mall. Nobody's ever up there. I park my rig up there all the time. I sleep up there. Nice and quiet.

Lazlo and Kazmer shared a long glance.

"I'll tell you what, to show you I'm a decent guy, I'll give you this," Don said, reaching in his back pocket. He pulled out a small brown bottle and a white rag about four inches square. "It's chloroform. Ever use it?"

Kazmer took the bottle and rag and sniffed the cloth. "We know chloroform."

"Good. You can even knock her out with it, and I can have my fun while she's unconscious. No problem. I already got her, and she trusts me. I'll drive her to the old mall. You guys get cleaned up. Wash that pepper spray shit out of your eyes. Get your breathing back to normal. Then you join us. If we're already done, you get her back right away. But you boys take your time."

The brothers looked at each other again. Glanced toward Don's pistol. Finally, Lazlo said, "You must not hurt Lisa. You must not hurt the baby. That is very important. She does not belong to us. She belongs to someone who has great importance."

"I've been in more positions in the back of my rig than there are in the Karma Sutra. The baby'll have a good time, too. Nobody gets harmed. You got it, gents? I'll see you up the road in a little."

"Don't let her get away. She run like a deer," Kazmer said. "She like a hell cat."

Don winked. "They never get away on me."

CHAPTER TWELVE

Lisa woke, again with a headache. She swayed gently back and forth, as if she were on water, a lake, but realized in an instant she was trussed up and back in the washing machine box. In addition, she wore a gown and was barefoot. She struggled to free herself but couldn't. Her hands were tied behind her back now. It appeared her abductors had used more tape this time. They were taking no chances. She'd never get free. Lisa was in the van again. She smelled the box's cardboard and the men's strong tobacco. The aroma of hamburgers was gone. She had not eaten and was famished.

Lisa sobbed, but after a moment shook her head and stopped. Tears ran down her cheeks and she couldn't wipe them away. She had escaped once. Another opportunity would present itself. All she had to do was wait for her chance. She knew now she could outrun the men, not for a long distance, but far enough to find help. As her sight returned slowly, Lisa noticed the men had cut a hole in the washing machine box on the side that faced the back of the vehicle, presumably to check on her without tipping the box. They had learned from their mistakes. Now she must do the same. There was blood on the gown. She didn't think it was her blood.

Lisa never should have got in the truck with what was his name —Don—to escape the men. Don, with his bowed legs, bad teeth, and glasses full of fly specks. She should have used Don to slow down the men, used him as a buffer, while she increased the distance between her and the abductors. And what had become of Don? Did he simply hand Lisa over to the men with the promise he would not be harmed? Did the men pay Don for the location of Lisa's hiding place, the rank-smelling rig's sleeping compartment? What had happened? How did she end up with the foreign men again?

It all seemed so distant as if a fog covered the present from the immediate past. Lisa immediately started on the tape, rotating her wrists, and spreading her ankles. Despite the pain, she worked on. She was now accustomed to pain. It was painful to sit, painful to fight the tape, painful to open her mouth. She didn't care how much noise she made. If the men pulled over, that opportunity for escape might present itself. What could they do, hit her again?

At least the hole provided some light inside the box, let in some different air, even if it had the aroma of the men and their tobacco. Lisa gritted her teeth. The longer she worked her wrists the easier it became to move inside the tape. However, her wrists were sore now. Probably bruised, she thought. Something trickled down her palm. It must be blood, she thought. *I don't care. I'll do whatever it takes to save myself and my baby. Our baby.*

For the first time, Lisa thought of Jimmy. What must he wonder? Does he think she left him without saying a word? Will she ever see him again? But the most haunting question was: *Is Jimmy still alive?* because now Lisa believed the men who abducted her were the men in the After Dark CCTV video. They had probably killed Leon and Bart.

Tears rolled down Lisa's cheeks again. She sniffed back her runny nose. Still, she worked on the tape. It still held her firmly, wrists and ankles, but it was definitely looser. Her wrists were sore. Her legs ached. The highway miles ticked on. Large trucks—trucks like Don's—rumbled by, shaking the van in their wake. Smaller-sounding cars whizzed by. Meanwhile, the van seemed to cruise at the posted speed, taking no chances with the law, biding its time as it moved toward—who knew where? Slowly, Lisa's recollection of the scene in the restaurant parking lot came back.

DON POPPED BACK inside the cab. "Well, that was a close one. I got them going six ways to Sunday." Lisa poked her head out of the curtain separating the cab from the rank-smelling sleeping compartment. "Let me pull out of here and get on the road. Once we're clear of those bad boys you can move up front here with me or stay in the back. Wherever you're comfortable."

Don drove to the end of the parking lot, stopped for traffic, and pulled out slowly. He spun the steering wheel, huffing, to make the turn and ran through several gears.

"You can drop me anywhere," Lisa said. "I should be safe now, with them all confused. I saw a sign for a hospital, but I don't know which way it is from here. If it's not too much trouble. You've already done so much." She had crawled through the curtain opening, sat in the passenger side, and buckled her seatbelt.

Don took his eyes off the road a moment and grinned at Lisa with yellow, broken teeth. His mouth reminded her of the vampiress's, and Lisa shivered. "Hell! I'll do better than that. Hospital? No way. What's a doctor going to do for you? Other than check your papoose. Hang with me a few miles on the interstate," Don said, pointing a crooked, nicotine-stained finger up the road, "and I'll drop you at the state police barracks."

"That would be great," Lisa said. "What a relief. I can't thank you enough."

"No need for that," Don said. "I'm happy to do my part. Have a daughter myself about your age. I wouldn't want to see her in any trouble like this."

Don turned his attention in earnest to the road again and deftly navigated a series of tight turns, watching the rig's tail follow in his side view mirror. He entered a ramp, gunned the engine, shifted again, and sailed up the ramp to the interstate.

After they were on the interstate and he had run through more gears, and was up to cruising speed, pointing to a radio, Don said, "You can play some music if you like. I usually do on long trips."

"That's okay," Lisa said. "I'm fine. How far is the barracks, anyway?"

Don pursed his lips. "Ooohh," he said slowly, rubbing his stubbled chin. "I don't know exactly. I know we ain't passed it yet because there were no signs. It's up the road. I can't give you an exact mileage, though."

"If I had my phone—" Lisa said

"We'll reach it directly," Don interrupted.

Lisa looked out the cab's side window and spun back to Don. "According to that sign, we're going west. I want to go east—to where the men caught me."

Don flushed. "Well, the exit for the state police barracks is on the westbound side. I had to go this way. It might be out of the way a little, especially for me, but that's okay. I should have explained my plan. The important thing is making sure you're safe. This is a big barracks that covers a lot of the interstate, miles and miles. Those coppers will throw a dragnet out that those boys won't escape. You wait and see. Next thing you know, those boys will be in custody, in a lineup and you'll be identifying them."

Lisa shook her head and flushed. "Sorry, Don. It's just that I've been through a lot over the last few days and—"

"I understand," Don interrupted with a soft chuckle. "I wouldn't trust me either, being a stranger and everything. Sometimes I get up and look in the mirror. I say, 'Who's that ornery old cuss?'"

Lisa smiled.

"Up that ramp there," Don said, pointing his crooked finger again, was a mall. It's closed now. That's why the ramp has a closed sign. Used to be a nice mall, too. A bunch of big box stores, nice chain restaurants, and a giant parking lot. Me and many of my trucker compadres would pull in to get a good, quiet night's sleep, away from all this traffic. Did it for years. Now it's all empty."

"You don't park there anymore?"

"Naw. There's safety in numbers. If I'd get up there now and be all alone, I'd have to sleep with one eye open. You never know what kind of a twisted son-of-a-bitch might be lurking around, or what their intentions might be. Plus, in the old days, I could get a bite to eat, use the bathroom, you know, shoot the shit with a few of the other drivers. We always liked to talk about what we hauled, the price of diesel, things like that."

"What are you hauling?" Lisa asked as she watched the countryside pass by.

Don turned his head to her and said, matter-of-factly, "Caskets. Got a whole trailer full of them."

Lisa turned her head toward Don. "That's creepy."

"Well, they ain't used, like you buy somebody else's car. These come right out of the casket factory. Brand new. That's where I pick 'em up. Almost every week. It's a sweet gig. It's a full load and a light load at that. Some caskets are custom jobs—fancy paint, fancy inscriptions. Personalized, I believe they call it. There's quite a demand for them. People are always dying."

Vampires, too, Lisa thought. "It's just that I thought, you know..."

"I know. It is creepy in a way. But they're all new. Never been slept in, unless some lazy, hungover factory worker crawled in one to take a snooze. They say the caskets are comfortable, but I never tried one out." They laughed. "I'm not ready for that."

"I hope not, Don." Lisa returned her gaze out the side window.

They drove on through the late afternoon. Lisa watched mile

markers whiz by. Traffic had thinned. Finally, she felt uncomfortable. "How far is the barracks, anyway?" Lisa tensed.

"If I'm not mistaken it's the next exit."

A few minutes later a ramp loomed ahead.

"There's no sign for the barracks," Lisa said, as Don maneuvered the rig off the interstate and up the ramp. He geared down as they approached a stop sign.

Don turned and winked. "This is a shortcut I know. We'll be there in a jiffy."

Lisa looked out the side window again at rolling farm meadows. She took a deep breath and relaxed again. Don halted the rig at the stop sign with a jolt.

"That's not good," Don said, rubbing his face.

"What isn't?"

"Sounds like the load shifted. We'll have to check it out. We dent one of these custom numbers and I'll be in a world of hurt. The dead don't like waiting to be buried while another casket is fabricated. That's what they call it in the casket industry. *Fabrication.* If I damage one, the next thing you know I'll be hauling loads of live chickens. I can tell you from experience that ain't no fun. Talk about stink and all those feathers. I'm sorry, Lisa." Don looked contrite. "It'll only take a minute to check. I think there's a road up here we can turn down. It ends in a place I can swing around and get out. Don't want to tie up traffic."

"Whatever," Lisa said. She was tired of Don and couldn't wait to leave his rank-smelling rig.

"Good. As the crow flies, that barracks is just over the rise." Don pointed in the opposite direction. Hardly more than two miles away."

Don swung the truck down a grassy lane. Limbs and saplings scraped at the sides. The road ended in a large clearing, where Don swung the rig around to exit where he drove in. Don stopped the truck, set the brake, and slipped from the cab, promising to be back in a minute. He walked around the cab, waved at Lisa, and walked down the side of the trailer, stopping momentarily to inspect the tires. Lisa watched his progress in the sideview mirror and giggled at his funny bow-legged gait until he disappeared behind the trailer. There was a racket in the back. Then Lisa heard the trailer doors swing open. There was more noise from the rear. Don was soon back at an exterior compartment on the driver's side. Lisa had seen his approach in the outside mirror. He appeared agitated when he poked his head in the cab.

"Just as I suspected. We got a loose cannon. I need a tool to strap her down again. Won't take a minute and we'll be on our way." Don winked.

"Do you need help?'

"You wait here. If I need a hand, I'll call."

Don closed the door. Lisa watched his reflection waddle off against the trailer's side.

A few minutes passed. There was more noise from the back of the trailer. Don now trudged toward the cab on Lisa's side. He opened the door and said, "I hate to ask you, but can you hold this strap in place for me? It won't take any effort. Every time I start to cinch it down the darn thing slips."

"Of course," Lisa said.

Lisa climbed from the cab, taking Don's hand. Don let her precede him along the trailer. She turned the corner at the trailer's rear, and saw an empty trailer, an open and empty casket on the ground. Just as she noticed a mint green gown hanging on the trailer door, Don pressed a cloth to her face. There was a foul smell. She coughed and darkness followed. However, the chloroform had not put her completely under. She retained enough of her senses to feel Don strip off her clothes and dress her in the green gown, chortling all the time, talking an incomprehensible babble. With difficulty, he zipped up the dress, which was barely large enough to accommodate her growing baby. He tried to jam high heels on her feet, but they were too small and left her barefoot. At one point Lisa saw Don's face looming over her, red and sweaty, eyes bulging from exertion, fly-specked glasses askew, drool hanging from the corner of his mouth. He lifted her into the casket. Then his face disappeared. Meanwhile, she was powerless to move. She heard him return and felt him apply eyeliner, powder, and lipstick to her face. With his amateurish makeup skills completed, she could smell the powder, and taste the lipstick.

Lisa's vision and her other senses were still numb. She felt she would pass out again. Lisa lay in the casket. Don was above her. He grinned and was giddy. He unbuttoned his shirt and peeled it off, pulled down his pants. He lifted the front of the gown and patted her bare thighs. Lisa was powerless to stop him. Through her drowsiness, from the corner of her eye, Lisa saw one of the men who first abducted her approach. He raised a finger to his lips. She tried to scream, but in that instant couldn't make a sound. In the day's dying sunlight, she saw a blade flash and heard the impact of Kazmer's knife slicing into Don. Surprised, Don pursed his lips. His eyes bulged again, and he coughed up a mouth full of blood, which spewed over Lisa's gown and splashed on her makeup. Don's body collapsed beside the casket. Lisa closed her eyes, not wanting to see more.

"What a mess this is, my brudder," one man said.

The other grunted. "This man is...freak."

"He tried to trick us. That never work. We are too smart."

The other man grunted, as if in agreement.

"Take Lisa and her clothes. Leave him as he is. We must get back on the road before she wakes up. Remember, my brudder, she is a hell cat."

The other man grunted and carefully lifted Lisa from the casket as if she weighed no more than a child. He cocked his head. "Nice dress. Nice casket, too. Our parents would be proud to have such caskets. Do you want to return to the back roads?"

"No, my brudder. We will stay on the interstate. We'll get to the colony as soon as we can. This one," he nodded toward Lisa, "is a lot to handle. Too much trouble, even for us. I wonder how her man handles her."

The man holding Lisa grunted.

CHAPTER THIRTEEN

Bo vomited. He hung upside down, spinning on a chain suspended from a wooden beam. He was already exhausted and could no longer scream. He was hardly strong enough to cry. Two vampires, barely fifty years since they were turned when they were children, spun him wildly in a high doorway that led to an underground passage off the main vampire vault. They raked his naked torso with their claws, licked the blood from their fingers. They shrieked in their high-pitched children's voices, danced around Bo's spinning body. Every time one of the vampires took a swipe at Bo, he whimpered. The children were careful to not to injure Bo severely. At least not yet. They wanted to torture him for hours, sample his terror-infused virgin blood. At the point of death, they would exsanguinate the vampiress's pet.

Had these two not been turned at early ages, they might have tortured small animals and developed into serial killers as adults. While they played, several other fiends stood in silence, watching, sniffing the scent of Bo's sweet blood on the air, rolling their pointed tongues around their mouths to enhance their pleasure. The vampiress's threats to the group hadn't affected the young vampires. It was daylight and most vampires were in their caskets, including the vampiress. Bo had been nauseous inside the casket from the vampiress's reeking odor and climbed out. He had barely climbed out when the children pounced on him. Despite their small size, they had amazing strength. Meanwhile, the older fiends stood at bay, wanting to throw themselves at the swaying Bo and tear him apart, but they feared the ancient vampiress, her threats, and her ancient strength from the black masses, which could only be imagined.

Occasionally, dirt fell from where the beam was secured in the dug-out doorway. It cascaded over Bo in handfuls, and stung his eyes and wounds. Bo choked on the gravel, which delighted the children. The vampires caught Bo to stop his spinning. They paused to lick the blood and dirt from his wounds. They were intoxicated, at the point of swooning, and copulated on the floor. The other vampires tittered. Several more joined the orgy. Finally done, the children swung Bo back and forth, as one would push a swing, ever higher, giggling again, until the male vampire gave the human pendulum a nudge and Bo collided with the tunnel's rock wall, showering more debris to the floor. The impact knocked what little wind was left in Bo's lungs into the cool, damp air.

Then Lazlo and Kazmer came into the vault, just arrived from their East Coast trip. Lisa remained in their locked van outside the cemetery, trussed up. The brothers saw the commotion and approached across the vault. They had been careful not to mingle with other vampires and their Shadows during their brief time in the new colony. They exclaimed an oath in their ancient tongue when they saw Bo, naked and suspended upside down, his entire body bloodied. They intervened, stepping between the vampires and Bo.

"You must stop. This is our mistress's pet," Lazlo said, looking squarely at the vampires. A direct gaze from Shadows was forbidden, especially with a vampire to whom they were not sworn, but the brothers were loyal to their mistress, ready to fight to the death.

"You are out of place, humans, the female vampire snapped in her child's voice, thin but loud on the vault's still air. The sound affected the swirling bats above and they dipped out of formation a moment before returning to their endless loops. The male snarled, twisting his little mouth, showing his small, pointed teeth. Still the hollow noise he emitted was also loud. The assembled vampires, who now numbered almost ten, stepped back. The children's Shadows moved closer to the brothers, with torch handles ready. The little male raised his hand and the Shadows retreated.

"Step away, you ugly cretins," the male vampire told the brothers. The Shadows giggled.

"No!" Kazmer shouted. He withdrew his stiletto blade and gripped the smooth handle tightly in his meaty hand.

"We will not move. We are sworn to defend our mistress's property. You have no right to touch Bo," Lazlo said. "*She* said so. She will sense what you did. She will awake and kill you."

The children looked at each other and laughed.

"Your mistress hunted all night and came back just before dawn without feeding, starving like a human," the little female said. "We were here. We fed well at the border until we could hold no more blood. She could not even catch one of the homeless that infect the streets like lice."

"All humans are like lice, even the ones who think they are secure in their gated communities, with their private security forces, armed to the teeth," the male said.

"Your mistress went to her casket this morning exhausted, aged," the little female said. "We watched her. She is weak. She will sleep through our playtime."

"She will know you injured Bo," Lazlo said. "He doesn't heal like a vampire."

Kazmer grunted an affirmative. The brothers stood determined. They rocked side to side, lifting their feet, stepping in place. Their eyes darted back and forth in the event of any attack from the side.

The female giggled. "We did not expect to injure your precious

Bo. We are not sorry he is bloody and bruised. Scared so much he can't make a sound. After we are done playing, we plan to drain every drop of his virgin blood and share it with our friends." The vampire waved her small, pale arm toward the gathered vampires. The waiting vampires twirled their tongues around their lips, clasped their clawed hands, and whined with expectation. The group took a step forward.

"You see? There will be no trace of your Bo when she awakes. We and *you* will tell your mistress Bo has escaped into the daylight. That he is gone. Picked up by the police. That the police think he is raving mad."

"We will never betray our mistress," Kazmer snarled.

"Then you will be drained, too," the girl vampire said. She grinned at the brothers and cocked her small head. "You stupid brothers chased Bo and were gunned down by the police. Beating and molesting a naked boy in broad daylight. Tsk-tsk. That will be our story. I have witnesses."

The vampire waved toward the other vampires again. The group smiled in unison and edged closer. Expectant. Some had returned unsuccessful in their own quests for blood. They formed a tight group like a choir, heads tilted back, tongues swirling.

"Your Shadows will not, cannot, lie to our mistress," Lazlo said. "She will know the truth. She will smell who drank Bo's blood, and they will be destroyed."

"What Shadows?" the boy vampire asked and spread his arms.

The brothers looked around. The Shadows had slipped silently from the vault. None were visible now.

"Our mistress can command Bo from far away. He does her bidding. She controls his mind." Lazlo pointed a finger at the girl vampire. The other vampires gasped at Lazlo's impudence. "Bo could never escape. She would sense him and bring him back. He would not get beyond the outer door. If you kill him that connection will be cut. She will know he is dead."

"Bullshit!" the little male vampire called in his tiny hollow voice.

The adult vampires chattered nervously among themselves, then swirled their tongues more, agitated.

"We should ask Fagan," one of the vampires said. "We could wake him. He won't be happy, but he might know. He knows much for a young vampire."

"Fagan might stop the children," another vampire said.

"He wouldn't. Not if we are all behind *them*," a third said.

The brothers and the gruesome children eyed the nervous adult vampires.

"Move out of the way," the little female vampire demanded of the brothers.

"Bo has reached the end of his rope, or should I say, chain," the boy vampire quipped.

Several of the expectant vampires tittered.

The brothers set their jaws and showed their resolve to protect Bo. Kazmer flashed his stiletto knife. The adult vampires waited eagerly to feast on Bo. Sniffed the brothers' fear in the air. The little female vampire, in a blur of movement, caught Kazmer's knife arm and tossed him to the left. She batted Lazlo to the right. He crumpled against the wall. Kazmer charged again. The vampire caught him, lifted him over her head, and threw him twenty feet into the vampiress's casket.

The little vampires extended their claws, bared their fangs, and approached Bo, who sobbed, had stopped swinging and saw them close on him, seeing everything upside down. The brothers were stunned. The adult vampires followed the children toward Bo, moving cautiously. The children's tongues swirled. The adults were expectant, giddy. Adult virgin blood was rare, especially when it was mixed with terror, hot and pumping from a racing heart. It was an elixir rare among vampires. It was so rare they would fight for the blood spilled in the dirt.

Bo was about to lose consciousness when there was an explosion. The vampiress's casket lid flew into the air and banged off the wall. She stood and roared. The deafening hollow noise echoed through the vault, and caused dirt to crumble from the ceiling and walls, waking other vampires in their caskets. The bats circling high above went into a frenzy. A few collided and fell to the floor, momentarily stunned. The vampiress saw Bo and roared again. The adult vampires withdrew to their caskets, bowing as they went, stepping quickly in unison until they scattered. Other caskets sprang open, their occupants alerted to the roar, fearing an attack on the colony. The brothers stirred. Found it difficult to stand. Bo twitched like a dying fish on a hook.

The children glanced at each other as the vampiress stepped slowly from her casket. Her claws extended, sharp, and dagger-like. The fangs lengthened, black eyes rolled back for an instant, returned to the front, and focused on the children.

The vampiress stooped in rage and then straightened. "How dare you! I warned you not to touch my pet. His sweet blood is mine. Anyone who tasted a drop of his virginity will be destroyed."

"You are weak, old woman," the male child called, smirking. "Look how her flesh hangs like an old hag's."

"We know you didn't feed last night," the female screamed. "You are no match for *us*, who gorged ourselves on fresh blood. We will pull the flesh from your ancient bones, snap them like twigs, and suck your ancient marrow. Then we will share your strength. Then, we will consume your pet for dessert."

"Stop!" Fagan screamed, but his voice was not as loud as the vampiress's rage. It didn't free dirt from the ceiling. He stepped closer to the vampires. "This is forbidden. There must be no infighting among colony members."

"You rule by *our* pleasure," the young female said. "Your ordinances don't apply to us. We don't accept them. We only adhere to keeping this colony safe and a secret."

The vampiress snarled.

"I won't allow it," Fagan shouted.

The children attacked, their own diminutive claws and fangs grew. They shrieked. The vampiress howled. To any human, the three vampires disappeared in a blur of unholy screams and teeth gnashing. Only the bravest vampires dared look from the safety of their caskets and saw the melee as it unfolded. The children catapulted themselves at the vampiress, their small arms and legs flailing, but the vampiress was faster. Their swipes, their kicks, missed. They attacked from two sides, but the vampiress launched herself out of their reach. She laughed devilishly.

The vampires in the vault shrank back. Lazlo and Kazmer were the only Shadows present. They saw only the blurs and heard the Doppler Effect of the strident howls the vampires made as they raced around and above the vault floor. At times there were three separate blurs racing at breakneck speed around the vault. Then there were two blurs of equal size. Eventually, there was one large blur, ever-changing colors, as the three vampires locked in combat. The motion whipped up a little cyclone of dust that trailed after the blur. The brothers, who still sat on the floor, choked on the airborne grit. They shielded their eyes. The blurs disappeared down passages. The wind that followed them sounded like a hurricane. The brawling vampires exploded from the tunnels like cannon shots, only to disappear down another passage.

The blurs returned to the main vault and circled around the edge of the great room, forming and separating, pulsating like a living thing. Caskets were lifted and thrown at great speed, bursting into pieces when they struck the walls. The howling continued. Finally, a single blur, now shrinking, turned red, and slabs of flesh flew to the floor and rolled through the dirt like breaded meat. Then a small arm corkscrewed over the floor and stopped under Bo. Bo barfed bile, convulsed, twitched with dry heaves. The arm was followed by a little girl's bloody leg. A great gash exposed inches of femur. The roars and shrieks continued. In a split second, the male's head rolled from the ever-shrinking blur, coming to a stop, his dead eyes staring as if in disbelief, mouth open in a silent scream. The little male's torso eventually rained down, missing an arm and a leg, its buttocks chewed, bone denuded.

Finally, the vampiress came to a stop. She was naked and drenched with blood. She sucked mightily again and again on the girl vampire's neck. What remained of the body was exsanguinated in a few gulps, and desiccated within seconds. The vampiress dropped the corpse with disgust, looked around, and belched. She coughed up a mouthful of blood and gouts of flesh, letting them fall to the dirt. She cleaned her lips with the swirling tongue. The children's remains burst into flames and were soon reduced to a fine ash.

Then she roared. "Who in this colony will have the...audacity to defy *my* mandates and touch *my* pet or *my* Shadows?"

The vampires cowered before her. They answered, "Not I," or "Not me, mistress."

"Now I have another pet. One that no one must dare look at, or that vampire or Shadow will be destroyed. I will take one of the high empty chambers for my pets, my Shadows, and myself. None will be allowed inside my new crypt! None will raise their eyes to its location!" Then she roared "EVER!" Dirt fell again from the walls and ceiling. Another bat fell to the ground, stunned.

The vampiress moved to Bo, lifted him tenderly from the iron hook that held his leg shackles, and rested him on the dirt bench beside her overturned casket. Bo stirred.

"How are you, my little rabbit?" the vampiress asked.

"I don't know," Bo answered. "I need to rest."

"Of course, little rabbit."

The vampiress brushed dirt from him, cupped his chin in her palm, and examined his closed, swollen left eye. "If you were one of us, you already would be healed," she said.

Bo managed a smile. "Thank you," he said. "I'm just glad it's finally over. I'd never want to be a vampire." Bo moved his limbs and stretched his back. No bones seemed broken. The brothers, shaking their heads, joined Bo and the vampiress.

"You did well, my Shadows. You saved Bo. I am thankful. Your rewards will be considerable and deposited into your accounts."

Lazlo and Kazmer bowed. Bo thanked the brothers. "I saw what you did. Risked your lives for me."

The brothers smiled. "It was our duty," Lazlo said.

Kazmer winced in pain. Held his arm. "It might be broken," he said. Kazmer removed his hoodie and rolled up his sleeve. He pursed his lips to inspect a bruise on his upper arm.

Bo staggered from the bench and picked up a T-shirt from one of the children who landed nearby in the fight. Kazmer watched him with interest. With difficulty, Bo tore the shirt into one long strip to make a sling for Kazmer's arm.

"How does that feel?" Bo said, after applying the sling and tying the two ends behind Kazmer's neck. "I learned this in Boy Scouts."

Kazmer let the sling take his arm's weight. "Much better, my friend," he told Bo. He smiled at Bo and reached out to take his hand. A tear trickled down Kazmer's begrimed cheek. "I will not forget this kindness. Neither will Lazlo."

CHAPTER FOURTEEN

Kazmer still nursed his injured arm, although he no longer wore Bo's sling, which he had kept nestled inside his hoodie. He sat with Bo in the main vault. The vampiress had ordered extra food for Bo to speed his recovery and bought him jeans, T-shirts, underwear, socks, shoes and his own hoodie. All were black. She also removed the leg irons. The collar, a sign of his indenture, remained, however. At last Bo was warm. Bo thought he looked like a Shadow, but he was a mere toy. While Shadows performed arduous work for their vampires, in the hope they someday would be turned, all Bo did was perform for the vampiress. The real Shadows, most just as gaunt as Bo, seemed to dislike the vampire pet even more now that he dressed like they did.

The Shadows huddled together making torches or folding clothes, sniggered when Bo passed, making sure he would hear them. That was the point. Although they scattered when the vampiress appeared, they had little regard for Bo. They envied his closeness to the vampiress. Still, they thought it ridiculous he was worn out from sex but could not remember the wild, marathon sessions the vampire demanded. The funniest thing to the Shadows was that Bo was still a virgin. Although she still tapped Bo's veins regularly, the vampiress demanded less sex. The fiend now copulated regularly with Fagan but usually returned to her casket by dawn. A mere human could never outperform a vampire, and Bo's apparent inadequacies inside the casket was another point for mirth.

Her casket had been moved to a large chamber high on the main vault, vacated by a vampire the Brethren had staked six months earlier. The chamber was reached by a long, narrow path dug in the wall that switched back to the opening. To prevent Bo from wandering, the vampiress had the brothers destroy part of the path at a high point. Planks were used to re-connect the gap. Although this opening would stop Bo, any vampire could scale the vault wall or jump the gap with ease. So far, none had dared. None probably would after Eva tore the two children vampires to pieces and drank their blood. The children were small in stature, but had the strength of adult vampires, were vicious hunters, and cruel to their prey. Still, most colony members doted on the boy and girl, who had been playmates in their human lives. Their disappearances decades ago were still police cold cases. The children liked the attention the adult undead showered on them. Although vampires rarely made attachments of affection among other vampires, and especially with humans, some in the colony held grudges against this new female who had passed centuries like mortals pass years, who had strength and mental powers of many of their kind. What these colony members did not know was that the vampiress knew who among them hated her. She had a cold smile, usually accompanied by a stare that was frigid. Even the strongest vampires avoided her.

Now the vampiress's chamber had two new members—Lisa and a female Shadow. Despite his injured arm, Kazmer helped Lazlo cut the gap in the path to the crypt and dug out a chamber for Lisa and her new Shadow off the vampiress's chamber. They smiled and worked long hours under the vampiress's approving nods. They added curtains at the doorways and torch holders on the walls in the two rooms. After they were finished, the brothers hauled a single bed and mattress up the path to Lisa's chamber. The female Shadow, Patty, was a gift from Fagan. At first, she resisted her new job under the vampiress and the two brutish-looking brothers but soon settled in. Patty was not so emaciated as other Shadows and still lived at home intermittently with her parents. Her job was to cater to Lisa's every whim. A refrigerator in the house above the vault was dedicated to Lisa—no hungry Shadow dared remove anything—and had a variety of foods to cater to a pregnant woman's cravings—ice cream, pickles, hot dogs, fruit, yogurt. If Lisa wanted something not in the refrigerator or kitchen cupboards, Patty made the trek, regardless of the time or weather, through the mausoleum and cemetery, to a rundown, twenty-four-hour convenience store a block away. The vampiress herself had little contact with Lisa, other than to watch the progress of her growing belly. She often stood in the doorway while Lisa slept, parting the curtain to check on her welfare. She quizzed Patty almost daily on Lisa's moods, her diet, and her general well-being. Patty stood slightly taller than the vampiress, with her head lowered to avoid eye contact, answering every question truthfully. The vampiress, meanwhile, seemingly scrutinized each answer, as if it were delivered in code and had to be unscrambled before she posed the next question.

<hr>

THEY WALKED down the gently sloping tunnel from the main vampire colony vault to the mausoleum pressed into the cemetery hillside. Lazlo walked ahead and was out of sight. After he reached the mausoleum's backside, he slid the heavy marble door open enough to walk through. Opening the door, which glided on casters and a lubricated track, was difficult, even for a human with Lazlo's strength. A vampire, however, could open the door with a finger.

Lazlo crossed the marble floor with its ornate engravings, the names of its long-dead inhabitants, and waited at the heavy, reinforced exterior door. There were vases inside the mausoleum on the floor in corners, filled with the remnants of shriveled flowers, their glorious blooms decayed to brown husks. The vampiress and Fagan soon arrived in the mausoleum. Lazlo opened the exterior door and stepped into the night. He paused at a wrought iron gate at the edge of the mausoleum's portico, the colony's first line of defense against humans in the cemetery. The air outside stirred gently, swept into the crypt, rattled the dead flowers in their vases, raised dust off the floor, and turned a page in the guest book on a lectern. The pen was missing. The last entries on the yellow pages were decades old. The three listened for a minute to the night noises in the cemetery. Insects were still active and hummed all around. The vampires' hearing was more acute than Lazlo's, therefore he stood tense, ready to slam the interior door if there was trouble, and waited for a nod from Fagan to unlock and swing open the gate. The heavy gate was noiseless on often-lubricated hinges. Lazlo took a deep breath and stepped into the cool night air. After another minute, the vampires followed. That was the drill. At least one Shadow always preceded a vampire into the night, into the unknown, to take the brunt of any attack. Fagan and the vampiress sniffed the air and swirled their tongues around their mouths to pick up any trace of human activity. Leaves had begun to turn color, dry, and fall. Fagan motioned for the vampiress to descend the mausoleum's three broad steps to the ground below. The vampires both wore jeans and boots. Fagan wore a long-sleeved white shirt and black leather vest. The ensemble was completed by a string tie with a turquoise clasp. The vampiress wore a similar shirt, only red. Suddenly there was the sound of someone running down the passageway from the central vault. All three turned to find a breathless Shadow appear at the gate.

Fagan hissed, "Fool! Do you want to wake the dead?"

"I'm sorry I'm late, master."

"Noise travels far on still, night air," Fagan said. "Our enemies could be anywhere. Their listening devices can detect your movement. You could give away our location."

Fagan gave the young man his reptilian look and the Shadow cowered. "Please, sir."

"Do not disappoint me again," Fagan said in a low voice, "or you will regret it. I want you to keep the doors locked and oil the hinges again. Hide until our return. We have other members out feeding tonight, if there are other Shadows nearby, don't mingle with them. Be prepared to defend this doorway with your life."

"Yes, sir. You have my promise."

"Madam, do you want me to remain outside, too?" Lazlo said.

"Return to your brother. Keep watch over my pets," the vampiress said. She patted his cheek with her dead hand. "You and your brother have worked hard over the last few days. Take turns resting. There are enough Shadows here to protect until our return."

Lazlo bowed and backed away.

The vampires watched Lazlo return to the mausoleum, mount the steps, swing the silent gate shut, lock it, and then close and lock the exterior door. The Shadow melted into nearby bushes.

The vampiress surveyed the surrounding marble gravestones. Acid rain had obliterated some names and melted the features on cherubs and other statuary. Farther in the darkness were a fallen tree, high grass, and thick underbrush. She raised her head and sniffed the air.

"Do you sense something?" Fagan said.

"Only the Shadows. They are out there."

"You can smell them?" There was surprise in Fagan's voice.

"Of course. My powers are greater and will be—how do they say it?—enhanced more after the black mass. Our colony's strength will be boundless." She patted Fagan's arm, touched his cold face. "There is Johnson, the one with the great hooked nose, behind that tree," she pointed. "We interrupted him from completing the act of pleasuring himself. Betty, with her bad complexion, is beside the next mausoleum, the vegan lad—is it Barry?—is in the bushes over there. He smells like a vegan. What will he eat if he is ever turned? They are all frightened." She tittered softly.

"Of us?"

"They are afraid of the night. Merely a human condition. How foolish. This is a wonderful cemetery," she said. "So much decay. The night, the darkness, is beautiful."

"Truly. Generations of dead lie here. Most of their descendants have either died off, too, or moved away. And, of course, this new generation of humans tends to forget the dead, no longer honors them, as in the past. Now these are forgotten." Fagan spread out his arms. "Even time is now erasing their names on the marble. As memorials go, granite is harder but more difficult to chisel. Eventually, nothing will be left. Even their bones will dissolve to dust."

"And we go on," the vampiress said with a smile. "Who knows how long?"

"Forever," Fagan said.

"I wonder," she said. "What is forever? What is nothing? Even we don't know such answers. I like being among so many dead," the vampiress said. "It is comforting. I like imagining their wretched lives, filled with sickness, fear, and always loss." She swept a finger across the grounds. "Did any of these dead give their lives for you?"

"No, Eva. Not these," Fagan answered. "Most were interred before I was born as a human."

"I hope they are at peace," Eva said. "Some night after I am gorged with blood, I would like to find a quiet spot in the oldest part of the cemetery and sit with my memories until just before dawn. Among the peaceful, quiet, old dead."

"They are mostly at peace," Fagan said, "although some specters are active at night. We might see one if we follow this path."

"What do these ghosts do?" Eva said. "Where do they go at night when they crawl from their rotting coffins?"

"Who knows? It doesn't have to be night. Some walk in daylight. They never communicate. They don't seem to see *us*. Even care about us. Perhaps they believe we are ghosts, too."

"What a pity, especially if we can see them."

"That's the mystery," Fagan said. "They just might see us but don't care to communicate. That's a pity because there is so much they could share, even with you who have lived so long."

The vampire's vision is better than that of any night predator. Fagan led the way down a barely discernible path through high grass, among old gravestones, some cracked, toppled, or leaning, covered with moss and lichens. They stepped down a small embankment and onto a cobblestone road, barely wide enough for a modern hearse to navigate, and followed it uphill past free-standing mausoleums and family plots defined by small walls or metal rails. There were many crosses, large and small, whose presence had no effect on the vampires, and here and there tall obelisks. A breeze scattered dry leaves on the lawn.

"The cobblestones. Do they take you back to another time?"

The vampiress stopped a moment and smiled. "There's a cat up here on the left. It has caught a mouse. The mouse is still alive in the cat's mouth, but just barely." She cocked her head and raised her index finger. "There. The mouse's heart has stopped. The cat is afraid of us, but it has stopped to lick the mouse blood. How exciting. The find. The chase. The capture. The food. After we've moved on, the cat will eat its little trophy and return home happy. Oh, to be a cat!"

"To have nine lives?"

"One life would be enough when death does not haunt you," Eva said. "To be untroubled by it, like a cat that will fight to live but doesn't realize it will someday die." As they walked on, a large tabby streaked across the cobblestones in front of them and disappeared in the high grass. It still clutched the mouse between its teeth.

"I could not sense that cat, the mouse dying," Fagan said, glumly.

"The cat is pregnant. There are tiny heartbeats waiting to breathe on their own, catch their own little mice, even among all these dead."

"Amazing," Fagan said.

Eva smiled at him. "You will sense such things, eventually. Perhaps after we consume Lisa's baby."

"How do you keep all the sensations separated, say, a cat embryo's heartbeat from the mouse's. Can you sense a Brethren lurking in the bushes ready to unleash a crossbow bolt?"

"Of course. You will learn that, too," Eva said. "You will—how do they say it?—prioritize. The important thought will jump to the front—like the cat's heartbeat. The embryo kitten heartbeats you will sense and find amusing, perhaps, but still less important."

"It's this way," Fagan said, walking off the cobblestones and into high grass again. The vampiress followed across a flat lawn. More old tombstones leaned this way and that. A few were on the ground. Clouds parted and light from a half-moon shone, brightening the grave markers. It also made deepening Shadows. The insects stirred. Their chorus increased.

Eva stopped and touched a small stone obscured by the grass. "A child. How sad. She never had a chance to live. Experienced next to nothing."

"Look at this old fellow, Eva." Fagan stood next to an ancient oak, patting its trunk and heavy bark with branches that resembled long-fingered, clawed hands.

Eva smiled and raised her head to look into the canopy. "Its root system must be incredible. I wonder how many bodies it crawled through, licked, with its tendrils, sucked nutrients from eyes and organs high into the limbs, the foliage." She stooped to pick up a leaf. "This may contain the final thoughts of one of these humans. Isn't that amazing?"

"You have a morbid way of thinking," Fagan said.

"I always did. You know, before I was turned I was accused of being a witch. I wasn't, of course. The town elders wanted to burn me at the stake. Imagine that. Me! A royal! My brother Gerrard freed me. We escaped to a real witch and vampire. After a time in servitude to the witch, she turned us. After that, Gerrard and I were inseparable for centuries until the junkers, friends of *Lisa*, killed him. We had a perfect arrangement at After Dark. Soon Lisa will know the horror of watching her baby sacrificed. And after she sees us consume the child, she will join it."

The level ground gave way to a gentle slope with more leaning stones, then flat ground again with large trees. "This area of the cemetery is closed to new burials," Fagan said, matter-of-factly, as if he were a guide on a haunted tour. "Too many tree roots everywhere. And the stones are too close and brittle to dig proper graves with the modern machines they use. Still, there are vacant graves." Fagan stopped for a moment. "Oh, look!" he said pointing into the shadows. "Watch. Here she comes."

A white mist emerged from the darkness. At its core was a female figure, more corporeal than the mist. The woman was thin and wore a long dress, flowing white around her. She had long hair that reached the middle of her back and she seemed to float over the landscape, moving away from the vampires. The surrounding mist, which appeared somehow attached to her, moved also. The apparition's legs were not visible within the long dress and mist.

"How wonderful!" the vampiress said, clapping her hands once. The report carried on the night air. The specter stopped, turned her head, as if to look at the vampires. Its face showed no emotion.

"Hello, I am Eva," the vampiress said, expectantly in her shrill, hollow-sounding voice. Then the mist and the ghost evaporated, disappeared before their eyes.

"That's what she does. Disappears if you attempt contact. In a while, she'll reappear at her grave, over there," Fagan said, pointing. "She makes a circuit almost every night. She stops at a particular grave, Herbert Filmore, over there." Fagan pointed again. "The mist spreads over the grave."

"He could have been her lover," Eva said. "How exciting to imagine."

"He died before she did. Her name was Minnie Barnes. She is buried with a husband, Frederick Barnes. So, who knows? After pausing at Herbert's grave, as if to pray, she moves on, takes a winding circuitous path back to her own grave. Then she does the whole thing again. A never-ending loop."

"Interesting."

"If you like ruminating over humans," Fagan said, as if dismissing the matter. "I thirst. Let's feed."

He led her away from the ghost. They skirted a large, twisted tree limb, fallen, that looked like a giant arm rising from the ground. They walked toward a barely discernible stone wall in the distance, that defined the cemetery boundary. There was a wrought-iron gate askew, off its top hinge. The gate bottom dug into the ground. Fagan paused at the threshold in the wall, listening, testing the air. Eva waited behind him. Then he proceeded, taking a single step outside the cemetery, and paused again, as if he had entered an uncharted no-man's land filled with danger.

"It's safe," Fagan said. "Or perhaps you, who can detect kitten fetuses, should tell me."

The vampiress smiled. "It is safe."

"I will show you a place where illegal immigrants come into the United States. It's on the bank of a large river. We will wait on its bank, completely hidden, and surprise the stragglers. There are always weak ones who fall behind, and exhaust themselves crossing the river. They are easy prey. After they're drained, we slit open the abdomens to let out gas that will form, and launch them back into the river, like little boats, where they will sink or float to the ocean."

"What if the government stops this...migration of illegal immigrants?"

"There are plenty already here to consume, enough for a hundred years. Many don't speak English, so, if a family member or a friend disappears, they have no one to tell. Who will believe a hysterical immigrant who should not be here in the first place?"

"A wonderful plan," the vampiress said.

"We will walk through this city like lovers, hand in hand," Fagan said. "It's not a long walk, but we will be seen by other humans. If gang members try to rob us, we will kill them. Take their guns for our Shadows and *our* defense. There is a point where we can blur. We won't stop until we reach the river. Then we will wait."

<hr>

THE VAMPIRES SAT at the river's edge. "What if no one comes across tonight?" Eva whispered. They sat motionless hidden among brush. Water lapped at the river bank a few feet away.

"It happens. They may cross in another location. We can go downtown," Fagan said, matter-of-factly. "There are places respectable humans don't go, especially at night. It is easy to be accosted, be dragged into an alley, a dark building. We might even be separated. They will try to steal money or sell you drugs. That is what they will think you want in *their* part of the city. And if one stabs you or shoots you, wait till you see the surprise on that face, that their weapons have no effect. It's quite amusing."

"I don't like the taste of junker blood," Eva said.

"Sellers are not necessarily users," Fagan countered. "You can pass on a human user if you like because you detect drugs in his blood. Just kill him. Here." Fagan made a motion at his throat. "There is not a day that goes by in this city that there are no murders, especially among the gangs and drug sellers. Competing gangs are always at war. The news will report the numbers, the mayor will appear on camera and denounce the shootings or stabbings for whatever is politically convenient, and they will be forgotten because the murdered were already forgotten, abandoned, and lost. Tomorrow will bring a fresh number of killings. There will always be a new batch of undesirables the politicians won't care about."

"It is a strange world where humans cannot work together to help themselves. Imagine what they could accomplish. How advanced they would be. That would be real enlightenment." She watched the moon, which had slipped from behind clouds again. "The moon is like humans. It never changes. It looks like it did in the Middle Ages. When the moon was full, I told Gerrard it winked at me."

"And what did he say?"

"He said he winked at me because his complexion was so bad he couldn't find a lover with a face like that." She looked at Fagan. "How we laughed! How I miss Gerrard. My brother was a wonderful lover."

The vampiress stopped and held up a finger. "People are coming. They are still far away.

"I hope it's not border patrol officers, or worse, Fox News. If it is, we will have to move and make no contact. They make such a fuss over these immigrants."

"They have stopped to rest." The vampiress swirled her tongue around her mouth. "They are tired. I can smell their sweat. Their fear. They might be *illegal*." The vampiress raised an eyebrow and smiled at Fagan in expectation.

"They have stopped to rest before crossing the river. That is the most difficult part. The current can be strong in places. It swirls against their legs. The bottom is slippery. There are many rocks to stumble over. The water saps their strength quickly."

The vampires waited. Their tongues swirled around their lips. Water lapped nearby. At the river's middle, the current was fast and muddy and roiled. Clouds covered the moon again as if the pock-marked face did not want to see what was about to happen. The people stood to continue their trek and marched toward the water. The vampiress sensed there were elderly among the group. They moaned at the stiffness in their joints. There were young too, tired, begging to be carried. Eva cared nothing for their plight, their desire for a new life, jobs, or an existence in luxury paid by the government and rich Americans, or the chance to expand their criminal activities in a land where illegal immigrants were held higher than real citizens.

"One carries a rifle," the vampiress said. "I hear it rub against his body. It is a noise I remember among the armies that fought Napoleon."

"The one with the rifle must be from a drug cartel. He is their guide They paid the cartel for safe passage to America."

"Does he stay here then?" The vampire looked quizzical, an expression Fagan could see in the low light.

"He returns for more illegals."

"Tonight?"

"Probably not tonight, but tomorrow perhaps. It is a never-ending process. Many want to make the journey."

The vampires heard splashes from the river's opposite bank and saw the first illegals enter the water. Their splashes were noisy. They recoiled at the feel of cold water, cried, and shouted as the current tried to upend them, rocks tripped them. The man with the rifle stood on the opposite bank, barked what seemed to be orders in Spanish, and hurried them into the river. He wore a bandana over his face. The vampiress watched with interest, calculating their progress and the point where she imagined they would emerge from the water. It was like an old problem from high school physics. A boat crossed a river at a certain speed. The water current ran perpendicular to the boat at another velocity. If the teacher were a little sadistic, she might add measurable wind, either aiding or hindering the boat. Given all the speeds in miles per hour, how long would it take the boat to reach the opposite bank, a finite distance? Of course, neither vampire had ever had high school physics, but they started to move, cat-like along the riverbank, noiselessly, remaining in the brush. They stopped at a gap in the bushes, where a well-worn path led from the water up the muddy bank. It seemed to be a predictable crossing. Would the illegals have the strength to reach the well-traveled bank, or would the current force them farther down the river?

The vampiress sensed there was panic among the illegals. They were in the river's middle now. The current pulled them downstream. They tripped on unseen boulders on the riverbed. They fought the current to reach the path. Children cried. The elderly panted. Men grabbed for the elderly, women, and children. Arms flailed. The man with the gun cursed and jumped into the river to help the weak. It appeared he had made the trip across the churning water many times, the vampiress thought. Even he stumbled, holding his rifle above his head with one arm, herding the illegals with the other, grabbing the hands of people ready to go under, cursing their slow progress. The illegals spread out across the river, often going single file.

A floating log struck a white-haired man in the back. He screamed, collapsed into the water grabbed the log, wrapped his arms around it, and sailed into the distance. Others in the train called after him in Spanish. Eventually, his bobbing white head disappeared under the murky water. An old woman who had held his hand stood in the current and screamed. Then her feet flew up and she floated downstream. It appeared none knew how to swim. Finally, the first survivors reached the bank. They had fought the current to reach the path up the bank. Others were pulled farther downriver. They clutched for grass, branches that extended over the water. Anything to escape the current. Exhausted, the man and woman below the vampires kneeled at the water's edge coughing, trying to catch their breaths. Others still struggled to cross. Some had only made it to the middle. The man with the gun exhorted them to move faster.

Eva and Fagan slipped down the bank, patted the illegals on their backs, and reached for their arms. The immigrants shivered and thanked these strong people for their help. The vampires lifted the couple with ease and guided them up the bank. They pulled the people out of eyesight from the river and bit into their necks. The exhausted illegals did little more than whimper. There was no fight left in them. The vampires greedily gulped down the hot blood. The couple were exsanguinated within a minute. Eva returned to the river and rescued a girl of about twelve. The girl seemed to be alone on the trek. Eva hoped the child would prove to be a virgin, but she was not. Eva drained the girl in another minute, taking huge swigs, and tearing out her neck. Meanwhile, Fagan returned to the river's edge and hauled up another man. He exsanguinated the illegal in short order. The vampires waited for the remaining immigrants to scramble up the bank and disappear into the night. Fagan and Eva returned to the water with the corpses, opened the dead body cavities with their claws, and threw the corpses back into the water.

"Let's go," Fagan said. "We have had enough." He grabbed the vampiress's arm, but she pulled it away.

"Not yet."

Eva returned to the water's edge as the man with the gun waded ashore. Her cowboy boots sank in the mud. He tried to push people out of the water toward Eva, but she grabbed the rifle, slit his throat with a fingernail, took a healthy gulp, opened him from sternum to groin with her thumbnail, and released him into the swirling water.

Eva belched a fountain of blood into the river.

The illegals were aghast. They screamed and cried, "Diablo! Diablo!" and raised their arms to heaven. Some let the water close to the shore carry them away to a safer location. Others tried to recross to Mexico, and now exhausted, were swept away in the current. Those who had mounted the riverbank tore into the flat land and brush, screaming all the way.

Eva was delighted. She clapped her bloody hands. Threw back her head and roared a hollow-sounding devilish noise. She regurgitated more blood down her chin and mopped it quickly with her swirling tongue. "How I love killing humans!"

"There are cars coming," Fagan said. He sounded annoyed. "I don't like the illegals to see us. You shouldn't have killed the cartel runner. It could be dangerous."

Eva pressed a bloody palm against her hair as if to fix it. "Perhaps I will give a—what do you call it?—an interview to Fox News." She laughed again. Both vampires were bloated with blood. Their skin was tight and youthful looking. Fagan's eyes bulged. Still, the raging thirst for more blood remained.

"It is either a border police patrol or this landowner. We should go."

"Blur?"

"Yes. Back to the cemetery gate," Fagan said.

They took turns leading the way, jumping over cars and fences, streaking down alleyways, nipping at each other in blurs that were at times separate and sometimes appeared as one. They raced around groups of junkies on sidewalks, paralyzing them with fear, before flying away. No human would have known what the blurs were—fog, localized weather anomalies, something the wind blew —or perhaps footage to send to a paranormal television show. The vampires were bold this night. It would be sunrise soon. Neither was sweated nor breathless. They arrived at the cemetery gate they had exited through. The sky was starting to lighten, changing from black to a plum color. They pulled off each other's clothes and copulated on an ornate vault, a so-called altar grave, near Minnie Barnes's grave. She was still making her tireless rounds of the grounds between her and Herbert Filmore's final resting places.

The vampires' sex was also a blur. A human, even a paranormal investigator at work in the cemetery, accustomed to oddities at night, might have been delighted or perhaps frozen in terror by what they might think was an apparition.

What the vampires didn't know was the Brethren had installed trail cameras in the cemetery at various locations, in an attempt to see Shadow activity. They would not be disappointed.

CHAPTER FIFTEEN

The vampire hunters met early in the morning at a convenience store to gas up their vehicles and hit the road west before rush hour. It was still cool, overcast with some fog in the distance. Del Hatch had predicted a scorcher by afternoon, despite the season, after the clouds evaporated. Del was that kind of guy—always predicting things. Del's SUV was parked next to the first gasoline pump. It had a bumper sticker that read SASQUATCH ON BOARD. Jimmy Young's sedan was behind it. Del had paid for the fill-ups as well as two large sacks of snacks he carried from the store with a broad smile. After Old Harriet rooted through the bags and gave her approval, Del stowed the food in the SUV's rear compartment, closed the hatch, and checked Old Harriet's chair on wheels, which was lashed to his roof in the luggage holder. Old Harriet knew her sweet box would be gone by the time she returned, occupied by another homeless person, or even removed by city workers. Homes on the street were temporary, but she was not going to lose her chair on wheels.

Del was dressed in his jumpsuit with pantlegs bloused inside his polished boots and wore a jacket of highly reflective silvery material with the large image of an ambling Sasquatch in profile on the back. Aviator sunglasses and a baseball cap also emblazoned with a Sasquatch completed his attire. The other vampire hunters were dressed less conspicuously. His outfit was always good for starting a conversation with strangers, possibly finding someone who had a Sasquatch encounter.

Armed with the vampiress's suspected new address and the place where Lisa was most likely held prisoner, the group lined up with Del driving Overboard George and Mad Maggie, and Jimmy hauling Old Harriet and Bad Nelson. The group's weapons, including Bad Nelson's stake guns, Del's BAR, assorted carbines and pistols, and a cache of explosives, lay safely hidden in the SUV's rear. There was ample ammunition for the firearms and enough stakes and propane canisters for a small skirmish with the undead. In addition, Del had supplied walkie-talkies to allow communication between the vehicles. George, Jimmy, Nelson, and Del would trade off driving to keep the vehicles on the road as much as possible.

Old Harriet and Mad Maggie hadn't ridden in a car in years. Although there's not always a lot to see from interstate highways, both were enthralled with the passing landscapes. Old Harriet wanted a window open; and the air rushing in buffeted her beehive, making it shimmy as if it had a life of its own. Del and Jimmy, the first drivers, traveled a few miles above the speed limit to keep up with most traffic but not fast enough to set off police radar. If caught speeding, a group of people with no identification hauling a cache of weapons would complicate their mission.

As they drove, Overboard George poured over Del's *Famous Monsters of Filmland* magazines, taking copious notes. "Every article I read has some new details about vampires I didn't know," George called from the back seat, seemingly amazed.

"Hey, George, I hope someday we can have a TV and watch some of the horror movies that are in the magazines," Mad Maggie responded dreamily as if imagining she and Overboard George next to each other on a sofa, sharing a big bowl of popcorn. "I think whoever wrote the articles was warning everybody, in a clever way, that monsters are real."

"They real all right," George said, reaching over the back seat to stroke Mad Maggie's hair. "Don't we know it!"

Miles ticked by amazingly fast. Eventually, they needed gasoline, bathrooms, lunch, and to stretch their legs so they pulled off at an interstate rest area. Old Harriet remained outside with Del's SUV and the chair on wheels, walking figure eights around the SUV and Jimmy's car, pumping her arms all the time. She waited for her pizza and Pepsi. Old Harriet stopped her laps around the vehicles when a boy started to follow her.

"Hey lady," the boy called.

Old Harriet was surprised. She couldn't remember when someone called her a lady.

"Is that an antique?" the boy asked. He appeared to be about ten and still wore pajamas. He pointed at Old Harriet's chair on wheels strapped to Del's luggage rack.

Old Harriet eyed the boy suspiciously. "You better believe it's antique. That's why I take it with me. So nobody steals it."

"Did you just buy it?"

"It's been in my family for years," Old Harriet said. "Generations. My great-great-great... Why do you ask so many questions?" She squinted at the boy.

The boy stepped back into a tall man.

"She's squinting at me, Dad," the boy said looking up.

"What's wrong?"

"This your boy? He had designs on my antique chair on wheels."

The man pointed at Old Harriet's chair. "That piece of junk?"

"I tell you it's antique."

"I know an antique from junk, and that is junk. Not museum-grade. It's yard sale junk," the man said, resting his hands on the boy's shoulders.

The boy looked up at his father. "I know junk, too, Dad."

The pair grinned. "Let's get out of here, Paul, before this old witch puts a hex on us."

They turned to leave.

"What's a hex, Dad?"

"I'll tell you in the car. How would you like to have a head of hair like that?"

"It's creepy. She belongs in the nut hatch like Nanna Carlson."

The father laughed and the pair meandered away, zigzagging among the parked cars.

Old Harriet snapped her fingers at the pair, although they did not see her.

Soon, the vampire fighters returned with food and moved to a picnic table nearby. Old Harriet positioned herself to ensure she could watch Del's SUV and her chair on wheels.

"I wish we had a tarp to cover my chair on wheels," Harriet said.

"Don't worry," Del said. "I checked the weather along our route and there shouldn't be a drop of rain."

"It's not so much the rain," Old Harriet said tearing off a piece of pizza crust. "The chair could use a good washing. It's the bugs. I'll be scraping off bug guts for weeks."

"We'll help you clean up that chair when we're done, Old Harriet. Maybe even let you ride on top like Granny Clampett." Overboard George was the last to settle on the picnic bench seat with a sigh next to Mad Maggie. She handed him a napkin and plastic utensils. "Isn't it strange? We just spent all morning driving and the first thing I want to do after we stop is sit down again. Don't make sense."

Jimmy smiled. "This is a different kind of sitting. It's more relaxed. Even if you're not actually driving, being in the car, on the highway, makes you tense. At least that's the case with me."

With his mouth full of food, George nodded his head in agreement. After swallowing, he said, "This is good grub for the interstate."

"Huh! How would you know, George? When you been on the interstate lately to stop and take a meal?" Old Harriet sat with her hands on her hips.

"Well, maybe not lately, but I spent my fair share of time on the interstate."

"You're right," George," Del Hatch said. "This isn't bad food for the interstate. I did some Squatch hunting about a hundred miles north of here with a local Bigfoot society a few years back. I got interviewed on that show *Bigfoot Uncovered*. I think we stopped in this very plaza, but it was at night."

"See anything?" Mad Maggie asked.

"Everything but a Bigfoot, although we did find tracks and some hair. The society made some nice casts. They're in contact with a professor, an anthropologist, in Idaho. That's great Bigfoot country out there. We had trail cameras positioned and we picked up some bear, fox, deer—the usual suspects you'd expect to find."

"I wouldn't mind seeing a Big Foot someday," Overboard George said, "when we're done with this vampire mess."

"I'm with you," Mad Maggie said, smiling, taking ahold of George's arm.

"I'm in, too," Old Harriet said. "I'll have my potato gun primed."

"We only want to photograph them. Something that will prove to everybody that they exist," Del Hatch said. "That's our mission."

"Do you have room for a mother and baby?" Jimmy said.

"You bet we do," Del said. "What a headline! First baby to encounter Sasquatch."

The group laughed and continued eating. And so went the trip west, although as they neared the coast tension in the cars rose. The vampiress's letters with their elegant penmanship were passed around and circulated from car to car until they were smudged with fingerprints. Every word was scrutinized, every loop in the script examined. Eventually, everyone knew the return address as if it were their own.

Using Del Hatch's GPS, the vampire hunters reached the city just before dusk, drove to the very outskirts of the neighborhood, and stopped a block away. It was a cool, cloudless evening. They had all the car windows open. The group huddled on the sidewalk between the two vehicles. Del Hatch ate peanuts from a bag. He had already passed around the last of the potato chips.

"I say we knock off for the night. Find a motel where we can get showered and start in the morning," Overboard George said. "That way we'll all be fresh, and the vampires will be at their weakest point."

"Not me," Jimmy said. "I want to drive past the house, make sure it exists, and is still there, so we know what we're up against. See how many doors and windows there are. How we can get in without being seen. We can use tonight to make a plan."

"Myself, I'm spent," Old Harriet said. "I vote for the morning."

"I'll go with you, Jimmy," Del said. "I agree. It's better to see the place tonight and make a plan for tomorrow. We don't want to go off half-cocked in the morning. It won't hurt to do a drive-by, even make a couple laps around the block. That shouldn't raise any suspicions. After all, it's still light, and if you look up the street, there aren't too many houses around."

"Okay. I'm in," Old Harriet said, reluctantly. "But don't expect any hand-to-hand combat from me now."

"You leave that up to the men," Overboard George said.

"If you want my opinion," Old Harriet added, "my chair on wheels on Del's roof makes us look very...nonchalant...like we just come from some expensive antique sale." Old Harriet smiled broadly.

Del shrugged his shoulders and looked from member to

member. Each shrugged his or her shoulders in return. They climbed into the two vehicles.

Mad Maggie pulled her machete from its sheath. "Just in case," she said and smiled at the group.

Del led the way in his SUV. The block ahead had few homes left. It appeared most had been razed in recent years. The vacant lots were overgrown with saplings and untrimmed hedges. At the top of the hill, two homes remained, one on the left and one on the right. Both looked abandoned. The home on the left had a caved-in roof, ready to collapse. The home on the right was rather large and sat back off the street. It must have been the jewel of the neighborhood years ago. The property was surrounded by a six-foot chain-link fence, rusted and torn in places. The house itself was covered in dark clapboard, probably originally from the early 20th century. The windows and doors were covered with plywood sheeting. Rust stains from screws ran down the wood. No one was around the house with the address they knew or the more derelict one across the street. Del drove on, descended the hill, and stopped halfway down. He could either continue downhill or make a left turn to go around the block. The terrain on the right sloped down and dropped off into an old cemetery. Del climbed out of the SUV, told the others to wait for him, walked to the curb, and plowed through tall grass.

"Watch for snakes," Old Harriet called from the car's open window. "I don't want to see you bit."

Del raised his hand, as if signaling he got the message, and stopped where the bank became too steep to descend farther. He peered down at the overgrown cemetery with its toppled and leaning gravestones, litter, dropped tree limbs, and a row of old mausoleums built into the hill. Some crypts had concrete roofs. Others had coverings of earth, sparse grass, moss, and weeds. Del scanned the silent grounds. A large tabby hunted through the high grass. Then something caught his attention. The cat crossed a barely discernible path in front of the mausoleums.

Familiar with tracking Sasquatch and its suspected prey. *Where there was prey there was Sasquatch*, Del Hatch said to himself, "I'll be damned. Looks like a game trail. Maybe not animals, though. Could be humans not careful enough to make sure they don't leave tracks."

Del pulled a pair of binoculars from his Sasquatch jacket, sat down in the grass to hide his location, jammed a stick of chewing gum in his mouth, and panned the area below. In some instances, he could almost read the inscriptions on the tombstones, but most were unrecognizable as if melted from the marble by wind and acid rain. Del checked the sky for the sun's location.

"This is most interesting," Del Hatch said, continuing to talk to himself while he chewed the gum. "The trail goes west, curves around that outcrop in the bank, and heads toward...I don't know... too many trees to tell for sure...but it appears to be a stone wall. Perhaps there's an exit, a breach in the wall, even a gate. Must be the edge of the cemetery. But the most interesting thing is the trail stops at one particular mausoleum. It doesn't go farther to the right. It's as if there were an invisible wall right there to stop the *game* that made the trail in the first place. Most curious indeed. We'll have to investigate that trail, that cemetery, that wall, and, of course, that mausoleum."

Del stood and moved to his right, walking cautiously along the bank's edge until he reached the chain-link fence that surrounded the dilapidated house. Del held out his arm straight, as if measuring a distance between two points. "What's even more strange is that *that* mausoleum, where the trail ends and this old house up here on the hill are in a direct line, straight as an arrow."

Del trained his binoculars on the back of the house. He studied the roof with missing shingles, the boarded-over windows, a back door covered with plywood, the siding, basement windows filled in with bricks and mortar, and overgrown grounds around the house that appeared not to have been walked over in years.

Then Del spit out his chewing gum. A long, low whistle exited his pursed lips. He smiled. "Now that's the strangest thing of all. Here we have an old rundown home sitting high on a hill, no other occupants around, right above an old cemetery with a mausoleum. You might think the mausoleum is abandoned, but yet it appears, even from up here, to me, an old Sasquatch hunter, that it's visited quite often." Here Del Hatch paused a moment for his surveillance to sink in. Then he continued, excited now. "And to beat it all, there's an active electric meter hanging on the back of the house, where almost nobody can see it unless you crawl halfway down this bank. An electric service with a fairly new-looking wire going inside. There's electricity to that old, abandoned house—200 amps, judging from the wire size. Who would have imagined that? That's a lot of electricity for who—rats, cockroaches, spiders? Maybe. Maybe not. Possibly for vampires!"

Del Hatch shot up from his seat. With his binoculars, he took one final look at the trail in the cemetery. Confirmed it ended at the mausoleum. Turned the glasses back to the house. The electric service was definitely connected. He spun and hurried uphill back to the street, putting his binoculars back in his inside jacket pocket. He couldn't wait to tell the vampire hunters about his find. He was sure he had found Lisa's location. She was either held captive in the house—probably—or in the mausoleum—less likely. Surely there was a passage between the mausoleum and the house. There was no evidence anyone moved above ground between the mausoleum and the house. That meant they must move underground, just the way a vampire would like it. The tunnel of the undead. The vampire hunters would have to determine how large the vampire colony was and the best way to attack it. The long shot of long shots had paid off. Del Hatch had had little hope of finding Lisa—let alone alive—when the group started their trip. Now they were closer than ever to freeing her. *The odds might be swinging in our favor.*

Del slipped on the tall grass and had to scramble on all fours as he neared the top of the bank. He imagined assaulting the old home with his BAR, with its 30.06-caliber armor-piercing bullets slamming into the wooden siding, disintegrating the plywood and front door, leaving gaping holes in the facade. The ear-shattering sound ripped through the abandoned neighborhood. Spent shells streamed from the gun. The Shadows inside shrieked and fled. Vampires awake during daylight were ripped to pieces by the firepower. Del slapped magazine after magazine into the weapon to keep up a constant fire. Blood sprayed everywhere. Del Hatch was covered with gore. He wiped his goggles with a gloved hand. The carnage left the floors slippery.

Meanwhile, his friends followed, staking the fiends with their converted potato guns while the vampires lay helpless, waiting to recover from bullet wounds, hoping their severed limbs, and mangled torsos would grow together before the lethal stakes struck. Mad Maggie brought up the rear, machete flying, decapitating the vampires before they disappeared in fireballs. Lisa was rescued and ushered to safety from the house. The flaming vampire corpses set the house's dry, old wood on fire. The structure was consumed in minutes. The fried electric service exploded in a great fireball.

The vampire hunters escaped in their two vehicles and peeled out just ahead of firefighters arriving on the scene. The firefighters wet down the grounds around the house to prevent a brush fire from spreading. There was little they could do to save the home. They watched it burn. After all, there was nothing inside to save. Any evidence would be lost in the blaze. The collapsed ruins would smolder for days, giving the vampire hunters ample time to escape east. Del, meanwhile, would head north to his Sasquatch hunt. His camera was ready.

Del Hatch mounted the final hillock, and stood breathless, hands on hips, grinning toward the street and his fellow vampire hunters. The memory of his imagined assault on the old house was fresh. Both vehicles and their occupants were gone.

CHAPTER SIXTEEN

Lisa turned in the small bed the vampiress had provided for her. Another sleepless night. Or was it daylight? She still had difficulty telling. The large vault, the vampiress's crypt, even the boarded-up house above the cemetery had neither clocks nor calendars. Shadows didn't wear watches or carry cell phones visible to her. The Shadows either ignored her requests for a date and time or said they didn't know. A few said they couldn't provide that information. Most avoided her as if she had the plague, suddenly changed directions when they saw her coming with Lazlo and Kazmer. Did they fear her or the brothers, she wondered. She knew they were terrified of the vampiress.

Even Bo was no help, because he didn't know the date or time, even though he recently was let outside. No one carried newspapers or magazines. Bo had asked Lazlo for comic books, but the man only eyed him suspiciously.

"Comics are for children," Lazlo said. "You should want to be a man. Maybe a vampire one day. One of the undead, like my brudder and me will be."

"I would never want to be a vampire," Bo said. "I'd rather be dead."

However, Kazmer brought Bo three Superman comic books within a few days. All were old and couldn't establish a date. One appeared to have blood stains on it. Bo didn't ask where Kazmer got them. He just thanked his new friend, feigned interest in their pages.

"Show no one," Kazmer had said, "or I will be in trouble with *her*."

Bo stashed them under the padding in the vampiress's casket, the last place anyone, including the fiend, would look. After all, the casket never got cleaned.

Lisa now knew the brutish men who had kidnapped her were brothers, and they provided no information. If she asked Lazlo a question, he replied, "I will ask my brudder. He might know," and walk away, as if he were on a mission to deliver her question.

Likewise, Kazmer said he would pass questions to his brother because, "He likes to think he's the boss when it comes to questions."

Both men eyed Lisa suspiciously and usually left the crypt when she stirred. The brothers exited to sit at the crypt's opening beyond the privacy curtain on a bench they had dug into the side of the vault. There they smoked their vile cigarettes, sighed between puffs, and watched the bats circle overhead. Sometimes Bo sat between them. However, if Lisa craved certain things—yogurt, a club sandwich, bananas, grapes, saltine crackers for a jittery stomach, kiwis, spaghetti and meatballs—the food arrived soon, sometimes within the hour. The brothers never complained. They had enlarged Lisa's room to accommodate a bistro table and two chairs they hauled up for her and Bo to sit. Kazmer's arm now appeared healed.

The Shadow named Patty, who usually ran for the food and was responsible for Lisa's direct care, was also little help. She mostly sat in Lisa's room on a rug on the dirt floor listening to music on earbuds and biting her nails, which looked mutilated from her constant gnawing. She seemed to feel little loyalty to the vampiress or the brothers and next to none to Lisa. After all, she had been Fagan's Shadow. Patty's disdain for Lisa was evident. She ignored Lisa's questions and refused to enter conversations. There was no girl talk between them.

On one such occasion, Patty snapped, "I didn't ask for this gig to be a nursemaid to you. I had prestige when I was attached to Fagan. Shadow for the colony leader. Back then some Shadows bowed to me. Me! Now I'm stuck up here in this hole in the wall, catering to your every whim, the sacrificial lamb. I clean the bathroom in the house before you get washed. Make sure there are enough towels. Empty your...chamber pots. Clean up after you eat. I even have to take orders from Tweedledee and Tweedledum."

"You can always leave and go back to the real world," Lisa said. "Go back to school. Get a job. This is no life. I'll help you go. I'll go with you." She looked at the scrawny girl who did little to care for her appearance and might be attractive after a salon visit.

"Like I would fit in anywhere but here." Patty spun and left the room.

Time passed. The baby grew. Lisa sat on the bed, rubbed her stomach gently, and talked to the child. "What are you?" she cooed. "Boy or girl. Your father and I never got a chance to discuss names, even decide what sex we'd prefer you be. Who knows now? I wish we could get to a doctor. The only thing that keeps me going is *you* and the fact I know Jimmy is looking for us. Even now. This very minute. Whether it's day or night, I know he is."

Lisa tried to talk cheerily to the baby, but she thought, *Where would Jimmy begin to look for me? I hope he saved one of those letters from Bart's apartment. That return address would be something. But it was so far away. Three thousand miles at least. And what of the others—Overboard George, Mad Maggie, Bad Nelson. They were all held captive by the vampires. They escaped. Would they help find me, or go back to the streets and their addictions? Lisa* smiled. *And what could have become of Old Harriet and her chair on wheels? How she loved that ugly thing. It was on the street because somebody threw it out. Where could Old Harriet be right now? I wonder. Sometimes I feel there is almost a connection between us.*

When there was no concept of time, it was difficult to note the passing. When they were tired, Lisa and Bo slept—although not always at the same time. When they were hungry, food usually arrived soon. Either the brothers or Patty delivered meals, set them on the bistro table, and retreated to the larger room where the vampiress's casket lay. Rarely were they asked what they wanted to eat or given a menu to select from. Food arrived. What wasn't eaten at one sitting was removed, so the captives learned to eat what they were served, sometimes hiding morsels for later. Usually, they sat across the bistro table and shared or traded food.

"Take some fries."

"You want my pepperoni?"

"I hate lima beans. Why does it always have to be lima beans?"

"Why does it always have to be bleu cheese dressing? Who orders this stuff?"

"What I wouldn't give for a cup of coffee."

"Me, too."

Rarely were they alone. Patty or one or both brothers hovered nearby—it seemed more to eavesdrop than serve them—although occasionally Kazmer dropped off coffee.

"How did you know?" Bo would ask.

"I hear you tell Lisa you want coffee," Kazmer would say, with a hint of a smile. "I like coffee, too. But maybe it is not good for the baby. I don't know. I am not a doctor."

On the few times they were alone, Bo told Lisa how to determine the time of the day, even the weather, by what the Shadows wore on their comings and goings—jackets, sweaters, rain gear. There was always activity in the vault, even among the vampires during the daylight. The Shadows arrived and parted at all times of the day and night, depending on their apparent assignments. Bo used his time wisely on the bench with the brothers. There never seemed to be a pattern in their movements. At night, however, most vampires were gone, hunting, including the vampiress. It appeared they hunted either alone or in twos, never in a crowd that might raise suspicion. At times they returned quickly. On other occasions, they filtered in just before dawn, because they went directly to their caskets. They were always practically noiseless. If they arrived in a blur at their hyper-speed, Bo might miss them completely if he blinked.

Over one meal—they figured dinner—Lisa said, "You need a haircut, Bo. Your hair was always shorter when you came to After Dark with your friends."

Bo gave Lisa a nod, which to her indicated they were alone for the moment.

"You should ask Kazmer to take you for a haircut," Lisa added in a whisper, leaning as close to the table and Bo as her stomach permitted. "He seems to like you. I see the coffee and the bags of pretzels he brings.

"I think you look better than you did when they first brought me here, Bo." Lisa smiled. "You look healthier. Somebody might see you on the outside. I think Jimmy is looking for me. Maybe the others, too. It could be that your friends look for you."

"My friends, Ridge and TJ, were killed at After Dark," Bo said glumly. "I saw their clothes in the pile in the basement. Covered in blood. Slashed to pieces. We had an argument the night they were taken. Went our separate ways. The Whistlers got them. Other-wise, they might have gotten me, too. The worst thought I have is that without the argument maybe none of us would have been taken."

"I'm sorry, Bo."

"Nobody's looking for me," he said. There was a tear in his eye.

"To be honest, the team all thought you were dead. You disap-peared when we attacked After Dark." Lisa became resolute, but she lowered her voice to a whisper. "I have hope. Jimmy and I found a letter from the vampire to Bart. I think the return address was the place on the outside, the house above the cemetery. At least it was a place to start. You should make a break for it when you get outside. You can outrun the brothers. I did. Or should I say *we* did."

"But *she* controls me. If I ran she might be able to will me to return," Bo said. His voice rose too. "She willed me to leave After Dark and join her for the trip here."

"*Might?* I'd risk it," Lisa said. "If you get far enough away, who knows. You might escape her pull."

"You can't imagine what she'd do to me. I saw her torture people on the way here across the country. It was horrible. She loves being cruel. I don't want to go like Ridge and TJ."

"Still, I'd take my chance. I'd take off if I got anywhere near a door out of here. You should see the vamps line up when I walk up the tunnel to go to the bathroom in the house. They stand shoulder-to-shoulder, large and small, twirling those hideous tongues around their mouths. You'd think their lips would wear away. And when I come back after a bath, they're lined up again. I'm always with Patty and Eva. If not Eva, then the brothers. Patty with her goofy walk. Eva has a smirk on her face as if she is challenging the rest of them to make a move on me."

Lisa leaned over the table toward Bo. "I don't know much about motherhood, but I know this baby moves a lot. Most firstborns arrive late. Having a due date doesn't do any good when you don't know what today is. Let's face it. I'm really big. I'm afraid the baby will come early. Who knows? She or he might be born tonight. I'm running for our lives the first chance I get."

"What if you're caught?"

"They won't hurt me or the baby until it's time to give birth. I don't think the vampire would hurt you, either. Not really. She likes your—"

"Virgin blood. Go ahead and say it. I know everybody thinks it.

Hey, news flash. I'm a fucking virgin. Even Patty sniggers when the vampire calls me to her casket."

"I wasn't going to make an issue."

Bo still had feelings for Lisa. He recalled entering After Dark, scanning the bar for her. Now she was pregnant by a man she loved. She was in dire trouble, and Jimmy was powerless to help.

"Now that she hunts with Fagan, she leaves me alone mostly. She drinks her fill of blood and doesn't have room for mine. Plus, I'm sure she has better sex with Fagan." Bo thought a moment. "That's probably why I look healthier, feel better."

"That's why I'd ask the boys for a haircut and make a run for it when you get some people around you. What the hell. Once you get in the barber shop you can tell them you need to use the bathroom and maybe slip out a back entrance or crawl out a window."

"I worry she might be losing interest in me, now that she has Fagan," Bo said. "My days might be numbered, too. I'll give an escape plan some thought."

"I'm sure you're terrific in the sack or casket. No pun intended."

Bo grinned and drained the last of his Coke. "The upside about being a virgin and having sex with a vampire is that she is dead, technically doesn't exist anymore."

"So?"

"So, even though I remain a virgin..."

"Technically."

"Technically, the sex with a vampire doesn't count and I don't remember it. It's supposed to be a curse but it's more of a godsend."

"Thank God." Lisa shuddered.

After their meal, Lisa returned to bed and slept fitfully. Despite the dampness underground, she was too warm. She threw off the blanket only to grow cold after a while and pulled it back up under her chin. At some point, she felt chilly again and reached for the blanket, but it was gone. There was a dim light from the foul-smelling torch in the wall across the room. The torch was just about consumed—Patty should have replaced it by now—and gave off an oily black smoke that crawled across the ceiling and began to push lower. The blanket was not at the bottom of the bed. Neither was it on the floor. The smoke intensified. Through the murkiness Lisa saw a group of people crowded together. Their heads were raised, their long, pointed tongues swirled in unison around their mouths. Vampires! They had breached the vampiress's tomb. Where was *she*? Where were the brothers? Where was Bo? And where was Patty, the keeper of the torches?

Lisa sat up on the edge of the bed. Smoke filled her throat, although she didn't cough, and she couldn't scream for help. Couldn't even talk. She stood, ready to flee past the group, but the smoke was thicker, stronger nearer the ceiling. She dropped back on the bed. Her vision was blurry. The vampires moved as if a single entity like the Whistlers had. The vampires stepped toward her. They stopped before her and surrounded the bed. The night-gown she had worn was now missing, too. She was naked. She tried to call Jimmy's name but couldn't. Pale arms reached toward her. Their fingers had thick, claw-like ridged nails. Cold dead hands clamped on her head, her shoulders, her arms, her legs.

Lisa was raised off the bed like she weighed no more than a feather and was carried from her room, through the vampiress's crypt, passed her open and empty casket, through the curtain to the main vault. The vampires carried her in a procession down the ramp the brothers had built. She was powerless to move. The baby inside her kicked furiously, as if it, too, tried to escape. The pain was excruciating. They crossed the planks that covered the gap in the ramp and continued downward. On the vast floor below stood a host of vampires, many more than the colony held. They stood with heads raised, tongues swirling, to capture every molecule of Lisa's and the baby's scents. As they reached the floor, the vampires in the procession remained solemn. The other fiends assembled were expectant. They moaned in anticipation. The bats high above had landed, hung quietly upside down on the ceiling, and squeaked as if also waiting a turn.

The great door from the cemetery opened silently. Fagan and the vampiress entered slowly. Both were naked and proceeded toward the gigantic vault's center. A naked retinue of colony vampires followed. The last was Patty, still in her black-clad Shadow uniform, carrying an ancient-looking, long, curved knife. The vault's perimeter was lined with local and visiting envious Shadows. Patty grinned, enjoyed the honor she held, and kept her eyes lowered on the shining blade.

The tongue swirling was audible from around the crypt. Then it halted. The vampire heads lowered. The assemblage parted as the vampiress, Fagan, and their retinue continued their slow, measured march, then fanned out to form a crescent near an ornate altar the Shadows had assembled at the dome's center. The procession carrying Lisa approached slowly from the opposite side. Her abdomen had grown, nearly doubled, and appeared hard like a drum. The baby moved inside against Lisa's belly. Its handprints, even its face, were visible momentarily as it pressed on the womb as if it fought to get out. Lisa screamed.

The vampires laid Lisa on the altar and tied her wrists and ankles with rope. It was impossible for her to move. Lisa was wet with sweat. She glistened in the torchlight. Patty laid the knife above Lisa's head, picked up an ornate jar and long-handled brush, as if for painting, and handed them to Fagan. He, in turn, gave them to the vampiress.

The vampiress lifted the jar, sniffed its contents, and smiled. She sampled a taste, closed her eyes, and shivered slightly. The assembled vampires moaned with anticipation. The vampiress raised the jar over her head. "The blood of a virgin, for your pleasure, my friends…"

The vampire tongues swirled again.

"...the blood of an adult male virgin, most rare."

The vampires whimpered with expectation and rocked from side to side.

"He was my pet. How I will miss my dear Bo."

Lisa cried.

The vampiress inserted the brush in the jar, brought it out trailing a thick red liquid—Bo's blood—and dabbed Lisa's swollen abdomen with ancient-looking runes. Satisfied with her artwork, the vampiress nodded. Lazlo and Kazmer brought a large crock forward, tilted it, and spilled blood over the length of Lisa's body. The altar's raised lip caught and held the blood that surrounded and covered Lisa's body.

Lisa still could not move. She gagged at the blood's hot, metallic smell.

"It's still warm, friends," the vampiress said with a smile. "My Bo, my little rabbit, was drained in the last few minutes. Lisa's warmth will help keep his blood warm until you drink."

The vampire assemblage moaned louder. Some cried out in delight. Yapped like canines. The bats, hanging in place, beat their wings.

Eva stepped to the altar next to Lisa and looked down at her face. Lisa cried. She cringed in pain as the baby increased its efforts to escape.

"At last, it is time Lisa," the vampiress said in a whisper, leaning over Lisa so only she could hear. "You who have caused me so much distress. I want you to know that while these fiends tear you apart and become intoxicated on Bo's blood, I will slice you open to take your baby. I will flee with my servants. The others will never notice. Lazlo and Kazmer will pronounce the black mass in a safe place while I feast on your baby's flesh. My strength will grow tenfold. You will slip from this life to oblivion, never knowing your child, never seeing it. What a horrible mother you are."

Lisa could only manage to shake her head.

The vampires waited expectantly with clasped hands, fangs

and claws extended. The vault was quiet except for the vampires murmuring and the bats above beating their wings.

Then something caught the vampiress's attention from afar. She turned toward the door with a quizzical look. Cocked her head. The large door from the cemetery blew apart in a deafening explosion and concussion. Wood splinters of all sizes were propelled toward the vampires, striking them all over. Some were lethal, causing the fiends to burst into flames immediately. Impaled vampires shrieked in surprise and pain, and scattered, pulling out the shrapnel. A man in a powder blue jumpsuit stepped from the smoke and rubble and fired a rifle from his hip. It made the unmistakable sound of the Browning Automatic Rifle (BAR) set for automatic fire. The gun had spelled safety for GIs and doom for the Wehrmacht during World War II. The name tag above the jumpsuit breast pocket read HATCH. The man howled. The gun roared. He fired long burst after burst. Flames leaped from the rifle barrel. He slapped clip after clip into the rifle's action. Vampires were decapitated. Limbs were blown off. Blood sprayed everywhere.

The spell over Lisa ended. She rolled out of the blood and off the altar to the floor, seeking cover. Dirt covered her like breadcrumbs. The gun roared. Bullets whizzed by and shattered the altar. Spent shells spewed from the rifle, and clattered on the floor. While the injured vampires began to heal, and pulled themselves back together, sinews dragging bloody slabs of meat through the dirt to the riddled torsos, more fighters arrived, shooting crossbows and long PVC pipe guns. Their wooden projectiles were accurate and fatal to the vampires. They shot and reloaded quickly. Fires and ash piles spread across the vault's dirt floor. Hatch paused a moment, turned the BAR on the Shadows fleeing in terror and mowed them down.

Lisa's face was buried in the dirt. Then she felt someone at her side. It was Bo. "You're alive," she gasped. "But the blood!"

"It was a ruse. She killed a Shadow. Used his blood." Bo panted and cringed from the withering BAR fire, the screams of panic, and the orderly shouts from the other marksmen. "She planned to steal your baby for herself while the vampires drank the blood on the altar. She thought nobody would notice her leave. The brothers have a van outside. That's why she insisted the black mass be held during daylight. Nobody could follow. But she never planned for this."

"Bo, you look like Moe Howard." Lisa was incredulous.

"It was Kazmer's idea. We got the same haircuts."

"No." Lisa shook her head.

Bo made a face. "Yes."

Lisa woke with a start. Her heart pounded. The baby kicked.

Bo shook her shoulder. Patty stood behind him nonplussed.

"I heard you scream," Bo said. He patted her arm now.

"Oh, I had a terrible dream," she said.

A dream?"

"A nightmare. I dreamt..." Lisa looked up at Bo's face. "You got a haircut. You do look like Moe Howard!"

"It..."

"I know," Lisa said. "It was Kazmer's idea."

"Yes, it was. He's a fan. He got one, too. He thinks the Stooges are modern. Still alive."

"What about Lazlo?"

"He didn't get a haircut. He might know the difference."

CHAPTER SEVENTEEN

Bo sat on a plastic chair with rusted metal tubing legs listening to clothing tumble in a laundromat dryer. It was only the second time he was allowed outside the colony, even though a Shadow accompanied him. He washed the vampiress's and his clothes, taking extra care to scrub blood stains from Eva's apparel before throwing them in the washer. The fiend was such a slob, drinking too much, burping up mouthfuls of gore that often covered her shirts and pants. He hated cleaning blood from the seams in her leather boots before polishing them. The sound of the dryer was monotonous. The other machines running were just as annoying.

Bo stared out the window. He wondered whether he could escape the vampiress's mind control, as Lisa had suggested, but he feared what she would do to him if caught. She could break his bones, savage his body with a single swipe of her arm, although he hadn't been bruised in her rough sex in a while. It seemed most of her energy was spent on Fagan. There were times Fagan shared her casket during the day and Bo was left to roam the vampiress's crypt high on the wall in the colony's main vault.

He was afraid to venture into other parts of the colony. He was left to talk with Lisa or the brothers, who were not communicative. Kazmer at least had brought him a blanket to ward off the grave's chill.

Whenever Bo asked Kazmer what the date was, the man would pause, stare at Bo as if he had asked a trick question, and answer, "Not really sure." That's how Kazmer was.

Bo would sigh from the vampiress's crypt ledge, return his gaze to the bats overhead, smelling the damp odor of death from below. "Well, what month is it. I don't know even that. You must give me something."

"Fall. Winter will come soon. The mistress doesn't want us to give you too much information. She says it could be dangerous." Kazmer pored loose tobacco on a cigarette paper and began to role a smoke.

"Even a date? You know she controls me. She can make me do things with her mind. Things I don't want to do."

"Maybe not so much?"

"Are you saying her control wears off with time?"

"I say nothing. It's not allowed."

"Does she control you and your brother, too?"

"Nobody controls us. We serve the mistress at *our* will."

"You know, I don't hear her in my mind as much as I did. She was always probing my thoughts."

"Maybe your mind is not interesting."

Bo thought a moment. "Still, she must have some control. Do you think I'd choose to sleep with a corpse?"

"When you become a vampire, you will want to sleep with vampire corpses. Even the men, maybe. Who knows what makes vampires...what is the word...tick?"

"I'd rather be dead."

"Don't say that. It is our job to protect you, the virgin boy, and to preserve your blood for her. Your blood is the only thing that keeps you alive. Remember, you get laid, she or the others will tear you apart. Your...value will be gone. Your days as a pet will be over."

"Another reason to save myself for the wedding night."

"I don't understand."

"You wouldn't."

Bo turned his attention back to the dryer. There were still a few minutes left to tumble. The Shadow guarding him had stepped outside the laundromat for a smoke. He was not visible at the moment. Bo thought, even in this weakened condition, he could outrun the Shadow. After all, he had outrun the Whistlers in the park on the East Coast, narrowly escaping their claws and snapping teeth. Bo had been doing exercises to strengthen his legs and increase his lung capacity when no one was around. He watched a large lint ball roll down the aisle, pass him like a tiny tumbleweed in a Western movie, powered by the air from a vent overhead on the water-marked ceiling. It continued toward the front door, as if it had a mind of its own, but stopped suddenly when the door opened, and retreated up the aisle toward him. Eventually, it rolled by him again, crossed the aisle, and lodged under a dryer. Bo saw in an instant the Shadow who guarded him was at the large front window, cigarette dangling from his lips, checking on Bo and the young woman with long jet-black hair who had just entered the laundromat, a wash basket of clothing on her hip, weighted down by detergent and softener bottles, a bag of more laundry clutched in her free hand. A large black leather purse hung over her shoulder. Amid the laundromat's humid air scented with a myriad of sweet-smelling detergents, Bo could smell the woman's more delicate perfume as she passed him.

The Shadow had finished checking out the young woman's tight jeans. Satisfied Bo hadn't strayed, he tapped out another cigarette from a pack and moved away from the window out of sight again.

"Are you using these machines?" the young woman asked, with a smile.

"I'm almost finished. Just drying." Bo saw she was attractive. Was in shape.

The woman opened the doors on two washers, tossed in her laundry—it was already separated into whites and darks—spilled in detergent and softener, swiped a credit card to pay for the loads, and started the machines.

The woman checked the laundromat's front window and settled into the plastic chair beside Bo. She gave him a hard look and dropped her eyes toward Bo's arms. "I'm Persimmon."

"My name's Bo."

She smiled at Bo. "What's your addiction? I might be able to help if you want help."

Bo smiled at her. "You can't help me."

"Try me. Trust me. You might be surprised."

Bo looked at the front window. The Shadow had not returned. "All right. I'll tell you, but you're the one who'll be surprised."

"Really?"

"Yeah. To begin, these aren't needle marks." Bo raised his arms to give Persimmon a better look at the infected wounds.

"I know. They're bite marks," she said matter-of-factly.

Bo looked incredulous.

"I said *you* would be surprised," Persimmon said.

"I was...kidnapped on the East Coast. By a vampire!"

A Latino woman at the other end of the laundromat, who stood folding clothes, swiveled her head toward them a moment, then returned to her folding.

"Shush," Persimmon hissed, raising an index finger to her lisps.

"She keeps me in a casket most of the time, in a crypt with other vampires." Bo stopped. He looked at Persimmon.

She stared back. "I believe you."

"She forces me to have sex with her in the casket. At least I think she does. I can't remember. She controls my mind. She drinks my blood little by little. It keeps me weak. The wounds are infected, and sore as hell. I have no strength."

Persimmon took one of Bo's arms and held it tenderly, examining the wounds. "They do look nasty." She looked into Bo's eyes. "I could give you antibiotics, but she would taste them in your blood. That would give *me* away. How long have you been under her spell?"

"I don't know. I don't even know what day it is. They won't tell me anything. I wanted to buy a newspaper today, but..."

"The Shadow outside wouldn't let you," Persimmon said.

"You saw him? Recognized him?"

"Of course. They're easy to spot. You must have a strong will. Otherwise, they'd let you come here alone." Persimmon told Bo the date.

"I don't even know who won the World Series," Bo moaned.

"Sorry. I'm not a baseball fan."

"That's okay. I have bigger problems right now."

Persimmon checked the window again.

"I don't want to put you in danger," Bo said, checking the window himself.

"That Shadow?" Persimmon laughed. She pulled her purse open to show Bo the contents. She reached in and palmed a pistol. "It's for Shadows, a 9mm." Then she dug to the bottom of the bag and pulled up three wooden stakes and a hammer. "These are for vamps." She smiled. "I have a crossbow, too, in my car. It's more effective but I can't bring it in here."

Bo's dryer rolled to a stop. He rose to pull out the clothes and threw them on a table to fold.

"Need help?" Persimmon said.

"We better play it cool in case he comes back."

"We can still talk."

The Latino woman finished her folding, placed everything in a basket, and left the laundromat. Bo and Persephone were alone. Bo separated his clothes from the vampiress's.

"Is that her stuff?"

"It is. Looks like I missed a blood spot. She probably won't notice."

"Most fiends tend to wear the same styles that were popular before they were turned," Persimmon said.

"Not this one. She's ancient. Hundreds of years old. She looks it, too, when she hasn't fed."

"That's who controls you?"

"Unfortunately, yes."

"That could be a problem. She will be incredibly strong." Persimmon frowned. "She's not your run-of-the-mill vampire. Obviously, you haven't drunk her blood."

"No, but she drinks mine like it's a rare aperitif. A sip here and there. Claims my blood is sweet. She enjoys the hell out of it, and it takes a lot of self-control not to drain me. I can tell."

"Then you're a virgin?"

Bo blushed and lowered his head. "Thanks for reminding me."

"It's nothing to be ashamed of. It's lucky you are. Otherwise, you would have been killed long ago. There's still hope, Bo, even with such a strong vampire in control. She might not be too wise in the ways of the modern world—computers, video, that kind of thing. That could work in our favor."

Persimmon moved to a chair closer to Bo, where he stood folding laundry. She unfolded her tale of the Brethren, a secret society hundreds of years old sworn to fight evil. Most Brethren were legacies, whose parents and grandparents going back generations fought evil, first in Europe and then in the Americas. Some were brought into the fold as orphans whose families were killed by vampires. In the Dark Ages the Brethren was exclusively a male society. The members wore armor and traveled on horseback. Later they wore robes. Eventually, women were admitted. All endured rigorous training in hand-to-hand combat and were experts in the use of weapons. The Brethren knew how to track, locate, and kill vampires. They eliminated undead colonies either piecemeal or by full-scale assaults. Brethren casualties could be high. There were always openings for new recruits. The training was long and arduous, not for the feint of heart. When she was finished, Persimmon moved back to her original chair.

Bo said, "If I can get out of this, I want to fight beside you. I lost two friends to the vampires back east. I want to join for them. I want to kill that bitch myself."

"Killing an ancient one is difficult. It usually takes many of us. We'll see how you feel when this colony is cleaned out. After you see the carnage. After you've recovered your health. Then I'll get you an application."

"You have applications?"

Persimmon cocked her head. "Really, Bo?"

The Shadow was at the front window. He peered in with his hands cupped over his eyebrows. His great hooked nose pressed against the glass.

Persimmon's washers chugged to a stop, first one, then the second. She stood to attend to her laundry. As she passed Bo, Persimmon said, "You're cute, Bo. I'd like you better if you got a haircut."

"I just got one."

"Really, Bo?"

"It wasn't my choice. I can't wait for it to grow back. Now tell me, how do we stay in touch?"

"First, get me the exact number of vamps in the colony. I don't care how you do it. I'll see you here again. Take care of yourself, Bo, and grow that hair. Next time, I'll cut it. Moe Howard is so uncool."

The Shadow came through the door and walked toward Bo.

Persimmon loaded wet laundry from the washers into dryers and started those machines. She moved away from Bo, returned to her original seat, picked up her cell phone, and started to text.

"Done?" the Shadow asked Bo.

"Done, Johnson."

The Shadow shot a glance at Persimmon. "Let's go."

Bo carried the folded laundry in a basket and led the way up the aisle toward the door. The Shadow followed. When they were outside, Johnson spun Bo around and almost made him drop the laundry basket. "What the fuck you doing, calling me by name? You know it's forbidden."

"What isn't forbidden around here?" Bo fired back. "I'm sick of your shit."

"Watch your mouth, Bo."

"Or what? I'm not afraid of you."

What will you do? Tell your mistress. I'm not afraid of *her*." Johnson stared at Bo.

"I'll tell *her* Shadows, Johnson. The one who is my friend, who brings me things, has a knife. I've seen it. Razor sharp. I've touched the blade. Watched him slice *things*. It passes through hard cheeses and meats like slicing a hard-boiled egg. What I like about that knife is that he can kill you with it in a second, or he can insert it in a slightly different spot a centimeter over and you will die slowly. The blade will nick a vein in your lung. He knows just where that vein is. He knows anatomy better than a doctor. Even if you wore a coat, he could find that vein. That's how many people he's killed. That little vein he nicks, it will leak blood slowly." Bo pressed his face toward Johnson and the Shadow retreated a step. "And you will drown in your own blood. Every heartbeat will pump a thimbleful at a time, maybe less, until blood fills one lung and spills over into the other. It will get more difficult to breathe. Eventually, when there's no room for air, you will experience a slow, agonizing death. All very painful."

Johnson swallowed.

"All I have to do is ask him for a favor. And guess what? I'm not afraid of your vampire, because my vampire could kill him in a second."

Bo looked through the window and saw the hint of a smile on Persimmon's face. For the first time in a long while he felt elated.

Johnson pointed a finger at Bo. "You made eye contact with that girl. It's forbidden."

"You're crazy. I tried to avoid her. I moved away when she sat near me."

"No. You looked through the window and she smiled back. Just so you know, I've seen her here before. This is how it works at the colony. She doesn't know it yet, but I have a claim on her, and no one can touch her except me."

"Be careful what you ask for, Johnson. She might be more than you can handle." Bo moved along the sidewalk toward the cemetery.

CHAPTER EIGHTEEN

D EL LIFTED HIS S ASQUATCH BASEBALL CAP AND SCRATCHED his head. Both cars were gone. His friends had left without him. He was stranded in a city he didn't know. It was getting dark in a neighborhood suspected of having vampires. More puzzling was where did his friends go? Surely, they would not return to the motel without him or go out to eat, because usually he picked up the tab. They had to have noticed he didn't return to either car when they pulled out. He was driving one of them. Did the passengers in each car believe he was in the other? Had something scared them away? The sun on the horizon was covered by clouds.

What Del didn't know was that while he was transfixed by the fact that the old house had an electric service, a black SUV screeched to a halt next to the vampire hunters. He was down the bank and didn't hear what happened next. Through the open passenger-side window, Persimmon slapped the door exterior with her palm. She stuck out her head. "Hey, what are you doing here. Follow me! There're vampires in that house and it will be dark soon."

"So says you," Old Harriet said, climbing from Jimmy Young's car. "This is a public street. Mind your own beeswax. We know how to handle vampires. We've done it before."

Persimmon exited the SUV. "Let's go. You all are in danger. Follow us to a safe place. We can talk. We know what you're doing. Please!"

"Come on, Old Harriet. Listen to her. Get back in the car," Jimmy Young called.

"Well, doesn't she think she's somebody," Old Harriet said. "All hoity-toity." Old Harriet snapped her fingers at Persimmon, returned reluctantly to Jimmy's car.

Overboard George had already climbed behind the wheel of Del's SUV and gunned the engine in neutral.

Old Harriet threw up her arms. "It always has to be drama with these people. Afraid of their own shadows." She climbed in Jimmy Young's car.

"We got a man over the bank reconnoitering," Overboard George yelled to Persimmon. "We can't leave him."

"I'll come back. I had him in my binoculars. He looks like a survivalist."

"He's a Sasquatch hunter," Old Harriet interrupted.

"A what?"

"Bigfoot. He hunts Bigfoot in the wilderness," Mad Maggie added. "He has a hell of a big rifle."

Persimmon's mouth dropped open for a moment. Then she recovered. "We'll get people inside the cemetery. He'll be okay for now. But *we* must get someplace safe." She jerked her head back toward the house for a second. "We're pulling out. Follow me."

The SUV drove away while Persimmon jumped in, still had one foot on the ground. She shut the door and raised her window. Overboard George and Jimmy Young followed. The cars drove downhill, made a left at the corner, and flew out of the neighborhood. By the time they drove two miles away from the house darkness settled. The sun, a red ball, had dropped behind the horizon.

The moon was visible. The sky turned darker by the minute. All three vehicles had headlights on. The lead SUV turned down a quiet street, mostly dark, and into a parking lot at Cove Home for Funerals. The SUV whipped behind the building with Overboard George and Jimmy Young following. The three vehicles pulled in side-by-side. Persimmon was the first to emerge. She held a crossbow and carried a leather satchel over her shoulder. A ground-level door at the building's rear opened, shining a swatch of light on the asphalt. Two men emerged from the building, both carrying crossbows. Persimmon stood by the door, waving everyone inside, her weapon on her hip.

The vampire hunters entered the building cautiously, followed by Persimmon's driver and the door guards. Persimmon was the last to go through. She pulled the door closed and locked it. Three large bolts. They stood in a hall, bright with white paint, that inclined upward slightly. Persimmon took a deep breath and exhaled. She introduced herself and the three men with crossbows. She pointed at the vampire hunters and—one-by-one—each introduced him or herself. Persimmon smiled and waved an arm for everyone to follow. She walked up the hall and tapped on a door. A woman opened the door and admitted them to a room with a stainless-steel table equipped with a drain that emptied through the floor, a desk, various mismatched chairs, some machinery, and shelves with books and bottles. The ceiling was stained around the HVAC vents. The vampire hunters scanned the equipment and the walls, looked from one to another, and found seats.

Persimmon cleared her throat to get the vampire hunters' attention. "You don't have to be an architect to guess this building was originally a church. After it closed, the building was converted to a funeral home. The way people die you'd think business would be steady, especially with Covid, drug overdoses, murders, all the homeless, disease, and old age." Persimmon raised a finger in the air. "But it's rumored there were...improprieties and the state closed the place. Now we own it. You probably guessed that the hall we came up was how bodies were delivered. And, yes, this is where they were embalmed, dressed, and had their final makeup applied. I'll show you the rest later."

"There's more?" Old Harriet said. "This is some place."

"Why were you so...insistent we come here?" Overboard George said. The vampire hunters all nodded.

Persimmon looked from one to another. "You all were in danger near that home just before nightfall. There are vampires inside. The sun was covered by clouds while it was still over the horizon. Vampires would be protected from its direct rays. They could have attacked, even before true sunset, while you sat inside your cars. Vampires could tear off car doors, even when they're locked, and drain your body of blood before you knew what happened. That's why I was so *insistent*. You put us in danger, too."

Old Harriet stood. "What about our friend Del. He's the one been taking care of my chair on wheels."

"Hatch," Persimmon continued. "We know who he is. We know all of you."

The vampire hunters mumbled. The men with crossbows chuckled.

"We are the Brethren," Persimmon said slowly. "A worldwide organization devoted to destroying the undead. Just as there are vampires everywhere, we are everywhere. That's why we know who you are and what you did at After Dark. With no training, no vampire knowledge, you brought down the mighty Gerrard and the malformed vampires that hunted for that colony."

Mad Maggie smiled. "Overboard George and me did have help from *Famous Monsters of Filmland*." She touched Overboard George's arm, and he smiled at her.

Jimmy rolled his eyes and shook his head.

"Well done, vampire hunters. You used what tools were available. Gerrard and his evil sister Eva have been on our radar for years. We finally got an implant in After Dark, a bartender named Leon, but, unfortunately for our cause, he was murdered."

"That wasn't that long ago," Mad Maggie said, barely above a whisper, "and yet it seems so long ago."

"What's most remarkable is that some of you escaped from the vampires. That's incredible, unheard of. In the history of fighting vampires, that almost never happens. You are to be commended."

Overboard George, Mad Maggie, Jimmy Young, and Bad Nelson raised their hands. Persephone and the men with crossbows applauded.

"I kept the hearth warm," Old Harriet said. "But I ain't afraid of no vampires."

———

DEL HATCH SAT on the bank, scratched his head some more, and thought aloud. "To be honest, which I always am, especially with myself, I'd rather be down in that cemetery than up here in the open if those vampires decide to take a stroll."

Del searched the pockets in his pant legs, pulled out two small aerosol cans. One was insect repellant; the other was labeled *Sasquatch sex hormone—Male and Female.* He sprayed himself liberally with both and set off for the cemetery, half walking, half sliding down the long, steep incline. *That ought to confuse the sons of bitches,* Del thought. *It'll either scare them away or make them horny.* It was dark when Del reached the mausoleum next to the one where he suspected vampire activity. He stepped onto the roof where it met the bank. He had no sooner flattened himself on the surface than he heard voices and footsteps coming. From what he had learned from his friends, he suspected they were Shadows arriving for work details. He knew a vampire would be silent and might arrive in a blur. Sasquatch was silent, too, unless it wanted to be heard.

Two black-clad women walked up the barely discernible trail, talking about music. Both had long, stringy hair and were amazingly thin, anorexic looking. "You know, they're coming to town for a concert in December. I'd love to get tickets. Just to say I saw them live before they disbanded or killed themselves. You know how it is with music and bands. They all overdose at some point."

"While we're still alive?" The woman chuckled. "I'd like to see them, too," the second Shadow said, "but what if we pull guard duty or some other shit work?"

"That's it. Try explaining a concert to a vampire. 'We have concert tickets.' They wouldn't understand."

"Do you think, after we're dead, I mean when we're turned, we'll still like music?"

"I hope so, but from what I've seen, it looks like all the vampires care about is blood and sex."

"So what's the problem with that?"

The women squealed and hugged. They arrived at the mausoleum, sat on the marble steps, and waited. "I hope that asshole Johnson isn't going to let us in. He keeps asking me for a date, but I know all he wants is sex. I couldn't stand that big nose snorting at me while we did *it*."

The other girl sniggered. Then she said suddenly, "It's so quiet tonight."

"More than usual. Even the insects are quiet. I hope the vamps aren't on the prowl already."

Del rolled over on his hip slowly, silently, felt for his bear spray, and pulled the can from the elastic band on his belt. The can was new, never used. *Shots in the face would take care of the two Shadows and any more who came outside. Vampires? That remains to be seen.* Del regretted letting his gym membership lapse. He might need some cardio before the night was over. He wished he had brought a few of Bad Nelson's wooden stakes, even his Bowie knife, but he hadn't expected to be abandoned at the vampire house. All he wanted was a fighting chance.

Del inched himself forward to the mausoleum roof edge. The Shadows sat on the portico steps of the next mausoleum. He imagined they could not see him. Then Del heard a key turn in a lock.

After a few seconds, another key turned. Del imagined two doors opened silently. The Shadows stirred on the steps of the next mausoleum.

"Johnson?" one of the women said. "Where have you been? Pleasuring yourself?"

"You're early," Johnson said. "I have vampires to let out."

"I'm all bit up by mosquitos."

"Me too."

"Lucky mosquitos," Johnson cooed. "When will you two let me taste your blood?"

"Never!" the women answered in unison.

Johnson mumbled.

"Fuck you, Johnson!" one Shadow said. The other women laughed. "You're not so mucking futch!"

Del smiled and rolled away from the roof edge. The Shadows moved into the grass away from the steps. Bowed toward the mausoleum. Two vampires emerged. Stopped. They rolled their heads back. Sniffed the air. Del heard their tongues twirling around their mouths.

"Why so much noise out here?" the taller male vampire said.

"Master, we apologize. We won't displease you again."

"Do you smell that?" the second vampire asked.

"I do, but don't recognize it."

They sniffed the air again. There was a growl. The mortals seemed to retreat a few steps. Possibly genuflected before the vampires.

"Have you Shadows perfumed your bodies?"

"No, masters," one of the women said, whimpering. "Perfumes are forbidden for the Shadows. We would never—"

"Silence!" the taller vampire hissed. "Come here. One at a time. If I detect perfume on you, I will flail you alive."

The Shadows approached the tall vampire, one at a time, sobbing. He sniffed each carefully. "Your breath, too. Who knows what you people eat? Perfumes agitate us. They confuse our sense of smell."

"Yes, master," the three Shadows answered in unison.

"What work do you have tonight?" the taller vampire asked.

"I am to clean in the house."

"I am to sit with Lisa. Patty is doing wash."

"Lisa, Lisa. The colony revolves around Lisa," the shorter vampire said with disgust.

"You'll sing another tune when you taste her infant's blood."

"Perhaps."

"And you, Johnson?"

"I work for your pleasure," Johnson said.

"Good. Do you have keys to get in?"

"Yes, master. I am one of the few who are trusted with keys," Johnson said, pronouncing the words slowly as if they were important.

"Wait out here for our return. Stay hidden."

"Will you be gone long, master?"

"That's none of your business. You serve at *our* pleasure. If you must know, we are attending a gay party."

"Oh?" Johnson said.

"It's all blood," the shorter vampire quipped.

"Then we will feed. Tomorrow you will read there was a hate crime. Don't you love the insipid media?"

"I do. How like cattle they are," the shorter vampire said. "Worse than Shadows but just as obedient."

The male vampires laughed. There was a sound of a breeze, but Del noticed none of the branches nearby moved. The vampires were gone. Del twisted his mouth. *That must have been a blur. There's a first time for everything. Even if I saw it, I might have missed it.*

The female Shadows mounted the last steps. "You locking up, Johnson?" one said.

"Not until I get some bug spray. It's in my pack up in the house.

I didn't expect to spend all night outside. It's worse than doing laundry with Bo."

"You better hope *they* don't find out you went back in. Your job is out here."

"Who would tell them? I know you girls won't say anything. Get yourselves in trouble with the masters. You know the drill. Slight one vampire and you slight them all. If one Shadow is wrong, we all are wrong and share the beatings."

Del heard footsteps enter the mausoleum. Now was his chance to get away. He stood, walked to the back of the roof, stepped on the bank, and descended the space between the mausoleums to the cemetery grass. He pressed his back, now wet with sweat, against the tomb where the Shadows had entered, and moved along its length toward the front. Del turned the corner and slid along the portico to the gate. He pulled off his hat and peeked inside. Not only was the gate open, but the exterior door and the sliding door at the back of the crypt were open. Del looked up the dug-out passage. Intermittent burning torches cast a wan light. He pulled out his phone and snapped several photos, inside the crypt and up the passage. Then he stepped back and photographed the mausoleum exterior with the name Hammer above the portico. He heard movement inside the tunnel and saw a dark shadow trail along the dirt floor. Del ran to the next mausoleum and hid behind the side facing away. In a moment, a thin young man exited and looked around the cemetery. It had to be Johnson returning. Did he suspect something? Had he heard Del scurry away?

"Oh fuck!" Johnson said from the last marble step, loud enough for Del to hear. "Skunks!"

That Sasquatch sex spray must work, Del thought. He smiled. *It stinks enough for even a human to notice. By God, it was worth every penny.*

Johnson returned up the steps. Del heard the interior door slide shut, Johnson grunting with exertion. The exterior door closed, and a key turned in the lock. Dell had seen and heard enough. He would make his way in the direction he had seen the Shadows come. Follow the trail in the grass, which he could see even in the dark. He doubted he had anything to fear from vampires inside the cemetery. They would either be on their way out to hunt or return too full of blood to bother with him. Besides, the interred dead had little to offer the fiends in the form of food. Otherwise, the grounds would be vacant.

Del walked carefully and slowly, making as little noise as possible. He avoided branches on the ground but occasionally snapped a twig in the high grass. Other Shadows might be on guard, even this far away from the mausoleum. Or they might use this very path. Ever vigilant, Del noticed three game cameras tied to trees. Someone was watching the trail. There might have been some closer to the mausoleum that he missed. Who would be interested in Shadows? Certainly not vampires. They already had the Shadows under their thumbs. He would have much to tell his friends when they were reunited. Del moved off the path when he thought he heard a noise. Something moved stealthily through the grass ahead. He stumbled over downed branches and crawled over a fallen tree. Eventually, he found the trail and followed it again. Clouds parted overhead and the moon brightened the landscape. He turned his head to see the fallen limb he tripped over. After a moment, he resumed a slow pace in his original direction. In the distance, he saw the stone wall he glimpsed from the top of the bank near the abandoned house. He continued toward it.

To Del's right, a patch of fog seemed to hover. He left the trail to investigate. The fog was stationary, concentrated at the center with misty tendrils at the edges that curled in spirals near the ground. What would cause such an anomaly? This would be another item for his journals on hunting Sasquatch and—now— vampires. *The world's almost as strange as its people*, Del thought. The closer he got to the mist he noticed the temperature dropped. A low-hanging branch obscured the fog's center, and he changed direction to get a better view. Del passed the branch and saw a specter, the form of a woman in a long dress, standing at a grave, hands folded, head bowed. She faced him as he approached but took no notice. Her apparition at the dense core was well-defined. He made out crepe, and small buttons on the dress. Her hair was long, piled high on her head, cascaded down her back. *She was a looker in her day*, Del thought. Still, her face was drawn, careworn in middle age, certainly not old enough to die.

Del stopped. Studied the phantom. Was she real? Was it a trick played by cool night air and moonlight? Did her features remind him of someone from his past? Was it merely his brain, his eyes, disconnected for a few moments, playing tricks? Did his brain want to assemble a rational view of these strange occurrences? Or was it that darn Sasquatch sex hormone addling his mind? Eventually, the apparition looked up. Their eyes met, Del imagined, and she, showing no emotion or signal of recognition, evaporated slowly until the mist disappeared. The warm air returned to the spot.

Del walked to the place where she had stood. *Herbert Filmore. Not even her own grave*, Del thought. *I wonder where she's planted? Maybe you're Mrs. Filmore. Maybe old Filmore was your honey. Then again, maybe you're looking for a date. We'll probably never know. One thing is for sure, though. I know there are vampires. Now I know there are ghosts. Sasquatch must exist.*

Just as the specter disappeared, Del heard movement on the trail. He dove behind Filmore's gravestone. Whoever was coming walked at a slow pace, Del soon realized, stopping intermittently, then starting again. There were several people, too slow for Shadows on their way to work or vampires, unless they detected him. They were silent, looking for something. Del stooped behind Filmore's large stone. He was silent. His heart pounded. He got his bear spray ready. Somebody would get a puss full of the nasty stuff if they came close.

"Pssst," someone said. It was a man's voice. "Hey, Sasquatch man. Where'd you go? We had you on FLIR."

Forward-Looking Infra-Red, Del thought. *That can't be a*

vampire or Shadow. These people are the real deal. They know how to hunt at night. They're hunting me. I hope to hell they're friendly.

"Don't make us look for you," the same voice said. "We're here to help get you away from this place. Take you back to your friends."

Footsteps approached Filmore's grave. Dell made sure his bear spray was pointed in the right direction. "Okay, I'm coming out. Don't shoot," Del whispered.

Del heard several people chuckle. "We won't shoot, Del."

They know my name, Del thought, with a smile. *It's not the first time my reputation has preceded me.*

Del poked his head over the top of Filmore's gravestone. Waved his arm.

"There he is," a female voice said. "I got him back on FLIR. Over there."

Footsteps jogged toward Del. He saw four people. All carried crossbows. The woman with the FLIR goggles carried her weapon in a sling around her shoulder.

The man with the now-familiar voice said. "Let's go. We'll worry about the introductions later."

"I'm Persimmon, by the way," one woman said.

"I have some stories to tell you that you won't believe."

"I don't doubt it," the young woman with the camera said, patting Del on the shoulder.

As they walked in the moonlight, Del saw the stone wall ahead and the wrought iron gate askew. Suddenly, there were four distinct popping sounds in the distance. Everyone stopped. The noises were followed by twenty more hurried pops.

"Extended magazine," Del said, loud enough for the others to hear.

"Vampires aren't the only creatures that hunt at night," Persimmon said. "You can bet at least one is dead. Probably gang bangers."

"Where are we going?" Del wanted to know. They began walking again and Del fell in line.

"The mortuary," Persephone said.

"Mortuary?"

"That's right. It's our base."

Del grinned. "After what I saw tonight, that doesn't surprise me one bit."

CHAPTER NINETEEN

Persimmon led Del up the mortuary ramp and tapped on the interior door. He heard people stir behind the door and locks turn.

"Hey, it smells like..."

"Death?"

"Pizza."

"I hope you're not lactose intolerant, because that's your dinner," Persimmon said.

"When it comes to food, I'm all Italian."

After the door opened, Del saw his fellow vampire hunters seated on the various chairs, chowing down on slices. He entered the room to a chorus of hellos from his friends, although all seemed to have their mouths full. Old Harriet was perched on her chair on wheels, her feet dangling over the floor. Bad Nelson stood at the desk, rummaging through a stack of pizza boxes.

"You're just in time, Del. Pepperoni?" Bad Nelson asked.

"It's my middle name," Del said, moving to the desk, and helping himself to a slice. Persimmon grabbed the next piece and handed Del a paper plate. Del and Persimmon found seats and the group ate in silence and passed around soft drinks and bottled iced tea. They traded smiles and nods and eventually returned to the desk for seconds.

Finally, one of the men tossed his plate in the garbage and wiped his mouth with a napkin. "For you East Coasters, I'm Radish, a member of the Brethren. You've already met Persimmon. She's our leader. Right now, her mouth is full."

The group laughed.

Radish continued: "We kill vampires. For the Brethren, this is Mr. Hatch, Del Hatch."

The half dozen Brethren murmured.

"I saw you interviewed on that Bigfoot TV show," one man said.

"Which one? Del said, with a self-depreciating chuckle. "I've been on a few—*Bigfoot Encounters, Bigfoot is Real,* and there was *Modern Fossils,* a documentary. Also, I had a small part in the movie *Bigfoot Cave.* I was the first to get killed, that's why I say it was a small part. Really, I was more of a technical advisor on the movie, but then one actor didn't show, found a better gig, and they gave me the job in a pinch. It turned out I was the worst actor among the bunch, so it was a blessing to kill me off early. But my name's on IMDB. You can look me up."

Radish cleared his throat. "Mr. Hatch..."

"Call me Del, please."

Radish continued. "Del had a distinguished military career after his years as a radioman in the Navy. Saw real combat. Knows what it means to be under fire."

Del blushed.

"He's also an expert tracker," Radish said. "He could enter the wilderness armed with only a toothpick and come out alive a month later. He's an expert survivalist. In a tight squeeze, there is nobody I'd rather be with. Not to mention he's a demolition expert."

Radish paused a moment, while the group ate. "The Brethren

already know the East Coasters took down the vampire Gerrard this past summer at After Dark."

"How many people did you lose in the fight?" one of the Brethren asked.

Mad Maggie piped up. "We lost two. New Girl and…"

"New Girl? Persimmon said, cocking her head.

"That's what we called her. New Girl. She was a captive of the vampires and me and Overboard George sprung her when we escaped. Then she started to hang around with us and helped us attack After Dark. We never knew her real name. She's probably just a number affixed to the name Jane Doe. She didn't say much, but she was a pistol, fast as a freight train, liked to wear togas she made from bed sheets, and could hit the bull's eye with one of Bad Nelson's stake guns."

"Who else did you lose?" Persephone said.

"A young man named Bo Bentwood. He was helping us, but we think was under the female vampire's power. He's surely dead by now."

"Bo is alive. He's still human, a slave to Eva the vampiress," Persimmon said. "I've seen him. Talked to him. He's weak. Eva drains his blood. Still controls him with her mind."

"What about Lisa Van der Meer?" Jimmy Young asked.

"The pregnant woman? She's a captive, too."

Jimmy cried. Bad Nelson rubbed his shoulder.

"You're the baby's father?" Radish said.

Jimmy nodded his head.

"By all accounts, Lisa is safe and healthy," Persimmon said. "She and the baby are extremely important to the vampire colony. I don't know how to say this a better way, but Eva plans to sacrifice the baby during a black mass the moment the child is born. That will give her incredible strength. She will be virtually invincible. If she shares the child with the other vampires, the colony and its members will be unstoppable."

"Do you know when she is due?"

"We believe it's around Easter," Jimmy said. "If my math is correct. It comes early this year."

Persimmon slumped in her seat. "That indeed is a bad omen."

"How come?" Old Harriet said.

"Due dates are seldom accurate, but a vampire black mass conducted on a Christian religious holiday like Easter will make Eva even stronger. We would have no chance against her. The vampire could wipe out an army of Brethren. You can't begin to imagine her strength."

"What do we do?" Jimmy said. "What can we do? Has it ever happened?"

"It has," Persimmon said. "Our oldest texts warn about such ceremonies, but they are rare. The vampires believe in them. Therefore, it must be true. There's only one thing to do. Break the cycle. Eliminate the possibility of such a black mass."

The Brethren mumbled in agreement.

"That must include freeing Lisa and saving our baby," Jimmy said.

"Don't forget about Bo," Overboard George said. "Control or no control, we have to get him away from that vampire, too."

"Our plan is to destroy the colony—every vamp," Persimmon said. "Bo is part of the plan. For you East Coasters, we know where the vampires are. We know how they come and go. When they come and go. We know the Shadows' schedules. We've been observing them for weeks."

"Well, what the hell are you waiting for?" Old Harriet said. She jumped off her chair on wheels and stamped her foot. "We need action. Not observation."

Radish moved to Old Harriet. Placed his hands on her shoulders. "I agree, Old Harriet, but we don't know how many vampires are in the colony. To attack it, the way you did After Dark, might be suicide. Even though there are always more Brethren to fight, to be called from other locations, the vampires would know they'd been made. Just so you understand, we have killed several of the colony's vampires over the past few years, mostly by accident when they discovered us spying on them. There is always some vampire attrition." Radish paused a moment and looked over the group. "If the vampires realized what we know, they could move their colony en masse or break it into smaller parts. It has taken years to find this group as it exists. Now we have the colony and Eva."

"I believe I speak for our group when I say you can count us in," Overboard George said. The East Coast vampire hunters agreed. "We'll do anything we can to help."

"I was hoping you would say that, Overboard George," Persimmon said. "You and Mad Maggie, especially, have gained quite a bit of insight into the vampire colony. That will be valuable. After all, you were held captive. You saw them operate."

Overboard George and Mad Maggie smiled at each other. Maggie winked at George.

Taking turns, the Brethren members explained what they had done during weeks of observation. The most complex act was watching the cemetery and the Shadows moving in and out. They were photographed from hiding places and by trail cameras.

Over centuries, the Brethren had amassed thousands of pages on vampires and their movements, tracked them through Europe and the New World. Despite the vampires' immense strength, ability to move faster than the human eye can detect, heightened senses, unnatural life spans, and the ability to control mortals with their minds, daylight and certain blessed religious artifacts evened the playing field. Vampires were also dependent on human Shadows to help and protect them during the day. Each vampire normally had a Shadow, possibly two, although some detested humans and preferred to have none. There was no direct way of knowing how many vampires were in the colony, but by counting and identifying Shadows, the Brethren could determine roughly how many vampires there were. The Brethren deemed most

Shadows little or no threat, useless in a fight, and more likely to flee in terror in a showdown.

In summation, Persimmon said, "So, that's why we study the Shadows. There are a few big brutes. We think they're attached to Eva. We know a Shadow cares for Lisa around the clock. We're at the point where we haven't seen any new Shadows coming and going. We have a photographic record, similar to what the FBI might collect in a case, of this colony's Shadows. We've even given them names. Most are sad sacks that probably wouldn't make very impressive vampires, but the vampires use them as willing slaves. Most are never turned but discarded after they're no longer useful, either drained of blood or just murdered. Meanwhile, there's a waiting list of losers hoping to join the ranks of the undead."

Several in the group chuckled.

Persimmon cleared her throat and continued. "We want to do more observing. For instance, it appears no one enters or leaves the house on the hill. Our trail cameras have picked up no activity, except Del sliding down the hill on his...butt."

The group laughed again. It seemed the group needed a light moment, even if it was at the expense of Bigfoot hunter Del Hatch.

Persimmon said, "We must determine whether to do a frontal attack on the mausoleum or two-pronged from the house and mausoleum. It would be nice to blow up the house on the hill, dynamite the crypt door, and charge in, but that would bring down police, firemen, etc. How would you explain we're after vampires?"

"We could torch the house, just like the villagers did in the original Frankenstein movie," Mad Maggie said.

"I vote we torch the house and blow up the crypt," Old Harriet said. "With fires, and gunshots all over the city every day, who's gonna notice?"

The Brethren erupted in laughter.

"We like to operate more on the Q.T.," Radish said. "We don't like to expose ourselves to the public, especially the police."

"One more thing," Persimmon said when order was restored. "I met Bo by accident at the laundromat near the cemetery while on reconnaissance. I'll see him again. Meanwhile, he'll get us an exact number of vampires. That will make our preparations easier."

CHAPTER TWENTY

Overboard George, Mad Maggie, and Persimmon leaned against the chain-link fence near the corner of a soccer field, their elbows on the top rail. Overboard George's chin was planted on his large, tattooed forearms. It was Saturday morning and games had started among what appeared to be five and six-year-olds wearing youth league team jerseys. The Hornets and Ravens battled now. Other kids in different-colored jerseys, early arrivals, gathered on the sidelines waiting for their turn to play.

Their vantage point gave the trio an air of ardent youth soccer fans, but they watched the adjoining cemetery for vampire friendlies moving to and from the undead lair where Lisa surely was a prisoner. Among the Brethren it was known vampires preferred to make their lairs in the quiet of old cemeteries. Similar watches were underway across the city in other cemeteries, where other, smaller colonies or even individual vamps might rest. This cemetery in particular always showed promise because it was old, overgrown, and seldom visited.

The adjoining Cecilia Powers Brown Park with soccer and baseball fields, walking trails, and pavilions were active mostly on weekends. Even when the park hummed with life—Friday evening food trucks, Saturday night family outdoor movies, concerts at "The Shell," fundraiser walks, and various games, few people paid attention to the dead and their overgrown graves. The committee that oversaw the cemetery, now in the hands of a church, recognized a chance to profit from a large swath of yet unused cemetery land and sold it to the city for part of the park.

Shadows would be visible even among the high grass, overgrown bushes, and tall tombstones as they slunk in their drab clothing to and from the vampire lair concealed within the cemetery. Watching the Shadows' movements and numbers would help estimate the number of vampires inside, should Bo fail to get a count on the number of vampires. It seemed only Persimmon believed Bo would come through. The team's reconnaissance had already moved inside the cemetery, always new teams strolling during daylight, different Brethren, pretending to do genealogy research, vlogging with their cell phones on gimbles, even taking etchings off old gravestones. With the aid of trail cameras surreptitiously placed, the Brethren had pinpointed the lair's entrance. It was confirmed by Del Hatch and the photographs he took. After the vampires' numbers were determined, the assault would be planned. Everything had to be organized quickly, because as Persimmon said, "Vamps are squirrely. They can move their entire operation if one stinker sniffs something wrong. Their entire operation will disappear in a single night. Then we're back to square one."

Parents and grandparents soon set up folding chairs inside the fence in front of the vampire hunters. The smell of coffee perfumed the air. Overboard George sidled away from the group along the fence.

"Watch it, George," Persimmon said. "Poison ivy coming your way on the right, climbing all over this fence."

George moved behind his friends and avoided the parents and the vines. "Good to know. Had poison in the Navy. Don't know how I got it—was on leave somewhere—but ended up in the infirmary. My eyes swelled shut and my throat closed. I was almost a goner. Thank God I had a good Navy doc."

The game moved toward them. The little players in their shin guards and cleats kicked at the soccer ball furiously, with few connecting in the slow-moving scrum. Fans shouted encouragement. Coaches yelled instructions that were mostly ignored. Some kids stayed away from the action, jumping, skipping, and kicking crazily even though the ball wasn't near. The vampire hunters were amused but still kept an eye on the cemetery.

"Come on, guys," Mad Maggie cheered, enjoying the play. "Kick somebody in the stones."

A family matriarch turned in her folding chair and said to Mad Maggie, "I beg your pardon."

"Mind your own business, Grandma," Mad Maggie fired back. "Park those fancy sunglasses on the field and let us alone."

A few other soccer fans craned their necks toward the trio briefly and returned their attention to the field.

Overboard George nudged Mad Maggie and chuckled. He whispered, "Just because they own a home doesn't mean they know how to treat people when they go outside it."

"Got that right," Persimmon said, with a nod.

Aside from the seated fans stood two string-bean dads in their identical soccer attire, black long-sleeved shirts and leggings, despite the early-morning heat.

"Jason, go for it!" one called.

"Harry, attack the ball. Like I showed you! Attack!" the other screamed.

"I think Thomas and Bryson would make better coaches than the guy we have," a heavy-set blonde said of the string bean fathers. "Our coach lets the kids do anything they want."

"But they're so gay," her plump friend giggled as she smoothed a crease in her yoga pants that were as tight as sausage casings. "Besides, how can you impose your will on a five-year-old without starting a meltdown? Especially someone else's kid. I know my John would look for another team if Thomas and Bryson wanted to be coaches."

"Why don't you coach? You played soccer," the plump woman in yoga pants said.

"That was ages ago," the grandmother with the fancy sunglasses, interrupted. "You probably couldn't run across the field anymore."

"Mom!" the blonde retorted.

The grandmother shrugged. "I call 'em like I see 'em."

The plump friend with yoga pants giggled.

"Like I have time to coach soccer. A practice and a game every week. I can hardly keep my house in shape."

"You have that little chili pepper cleaning your home. Her illegal *brother* does your pool. Anyway, half the games are canceled. Rain, too hot. Coach can't make it," the grandmother said. "Do you know how many times I showed up here at an empty field? Plenty! A courtesy call would help."

"Mom, I wouldn't have the time to coach," the blonde said. "We have a T-ball game after this mess. God, I hope it rains! I need my own space, too."

The plump woman in yoga pants giggled some more but changed the conversation. "Thomas and Bryson can't be that bad. They adopted those twins. It's a shame nobody else wanted the kids. They'll probably end up gay, too."

"If they had to adopt, you'd think they'd pick normal kids," the grandmother said. "Both those boys look *slow*."

"Mom, it's not like going to the pound for a puppy," the blonde said.

"First of all, who would go to the pound for a puppy?" the grandmother said. "We always had pure breeds. Raised a few litters myself, if you remember. That was real work."

The play returned to the sideline and the smallest girl planted a kick that sailed over the fence and through Overboard George's outstretched arms.

"Who said all the blacks, if that's what you call them nowadays, play basketball," the grandmother grumbled.

"Mother!"

The chunky woman in yoga pants giggled again. "You two are too much."

Persimmon retrieved the soccer ball and served it volleyball-style across the fence to the eager children. They jumped and cheered. The string bean dads smiled and waved.

Nearby a girl cried. The woman she was with said, "Don't you want to go in the game and play, have fun with your friends?"

"They're not my friends. I hate soccer. That boy with the red hair kicks me in the shins."

"You have shin guards, Shauna," the mother said. "They're *supposed* to work. Getting kicked is part of the game."

"It still hurts when I get kicked."

"Well, I've never seen bruises on your legs."

"The bruises go away."

"So, what's the problem, Shauna? Stay away from the boy. Do you have any idea what it cost to register you for soccer, how much I pay for this silly equipment? And that doesn't include the soccer camp you're going to next month. Besides, your father wants you to play. That settles it. What would you rather do on a Saturday morning?"

"Watch TV," Shauna said.

Overboard George and Mad Maggie watched the grownups across the fence with bemused interest, occasionally giggling themselves or trading sidelong glances.

"Glad we don't have kids," Mad Maggie said.

"Not yet, anyway," Overboard George said. "At least I think we'd do a better job of parenting, even on the street."

"Even on the street," Mad Maggie answered. She looked at

George. "At least they wouldn't have TV to rot their brains. But really, I hope we never have to go back...to the street."

"I know. You can't sink much lower than living on the street with an addiction. I never want to go back. Live in a box or a tent. Have nothing of your own. No place to go when it rains or it's cold. Begging for money just to get by." Overboard George paused a moment. "But what would we do? Who would hire us? We're both on the police radar. We wouldn't stand a chance."

Persimmon had moved out of earshot and away from a new group of fans who set up their chairs for the next game.

"I've been thinking about that OG," Mad Maggie said. She touched his arm. "We could have a future with the Brethren. They seem to like us. Even Persimmon said we have a lot of knowledge about vampires. And we already fought them. Were prisoners. That's more than a lot of them can say."

"I don't know how that works, Mag. Do they invite us to join, or do we ask to sign up and request an application? Like a job. What if there would be only one opening?"

"It probably isn't like that, like a normal job," Mad Maggie said. "It's real secretive. Look at the name—the Brethren. And the names. You don't see any Bobs or Bills or Bettys. Nobody uses a real name. They're all vegetables or fruits, things like that— Persimmon, Radish, Turnip, Butterscotch, Raspberry, Gooseberry."

"Okay, what name would you take, Mags?"

"Beetlejuice. Like in the movie."

"That's what I was going to say," Overboard George said. "We could trade."

"No way. You snooze, you lose. You'll have to pick another and hope nobody else has it." Mad Maggie gave a resolute nod of her head.

Overboard George thought for a moment. "Zorro. That's it. My name will be Zorro. I liked reruns of that show when I was a kid. Even had my own little mask."

"Sounds good," Mad Maggie said with a smile. "Zorro has a certain ring to it."

"It wouldn't hurt to ask," George said, after another pause. "The Brethren don't seem to go hungry and always have a good roof over they head. Heat and AC in the proper seasons. They have nice vehicles and money to spend. They probably get allowances. I was thinking about the money coming in. Nobody seems to work—other than fighting the undead. Maybe the Brethren wouldn't look so hard at our backgrounds. The way I see it, there's going to be more than a few openings after this job. We don't know how many vamps there are or how strong they are. We know the bitch vampire has plenty of strength. We've seen that. Fast, too. The vamps are sure to get some of us. That's a given. Look at New Girl. Who knows? She was killed in an instant. Maybe we'll be in the number of goners."

"You talked like that before we stormed After Dark," Mad Maggie said, laying her head against Overboard George's shoulder. "We'll be okay, OG. Don't forget. We have superior knowledge of vampires. Know their strengths and weaknesses. If we play it smart, we'll be just fine."

Overboard George smiled. "Whatever we do in this next—in this new life after we free Lisa and Bo—the important thing is we'll be together."

The game ended abruptly with a whistle tweet, and the kids huddled around the coach for a pep talk and instructions for the next practice. The huddle dispersed after a series of high-fives with the coaches and other players. Fans folded their chairs, gathered their children and water bottles, and walked toward the parking lot. Two new teams took the field and started warm-up exercises. The string bean dads crossed on the other side of the fence in front of the trio.

"I noticed Jason and Harry's plays have improved," the one man said.

"So did I. Our practice sessions really help."

"I agree."

"Don't forget your coaching."

"You helped, too."

Two slim kids, obviously twins, ran up to the men.

"Boys, who wants ice cream?"

Persimmon moved closer and gave Overboard George a jab in the ribs. He turned to share a smile, but she leaned into his ear. "Shadows at three o'clock."

"Oh. I see them now," Overboard George said. "Look worse than the homeless."

"That's the truth," Mad Maggie said. "Not dead yet and not really alive. I thought the Shadows didn't use dope."

"The dead don't like junkies," Persimmon said, "especially among the people they depend on to keep their secrets, keep them safe during daylight."

Two male Shadows walked carefree through the cemetery, making no effort to hide their identities or their missions. They entered the trail their kind had blazed through the cemetery grass and continued toward the row of mausoleums. At first, they walked single file but then talked and moved side-by-side. One was animated and made circles with his hands, patting the other's back occasionally. They even laughed. Made it easy for the vampire hunters to follow them at a distance, using trees, bushes, and large tombstones to duck behind as they moved. Overboard George stepped on a stick in the grass and there was a large crack. Everyone froze, including the Shadows. The vampire hunters ducked for cover. The Shadows spun around.

"You hear that?" one Shadow said. The vampire hunters were close enough to hear the Shadows' voices.

"I heard it," the other said. "Take a look."

"What if we're being followed?"

"It's better to know."

"Then what do we do?"

"Run like hell. We'll split up. Run right by the mausoleum. Make a wide circle back to the gate in the wall. I'll meet you there."

"I don't like it."

"We can't give the entrance away. Fagan will kill us."

Overboard George peeked through a dense bush and saw the worried looks on the Shadows' faces. Persimmon was ahead of him. Mad Maggie was behind. Persimmon drew a knife from her waistband. George doubted she wanted to use it. Even though he thought Persimmon could take the two Shadows, even without a knife, he readied himself to charge forward to help her. He hoped Mad Maggie was well hidden.

Overboard George imagined Mad Maggie was behind him somewhere flattened in the high grass, hiding behind a tombstone. He loved Mad Maggie. They had been rivals less than a year ago, racing daily to the McDonald's drive-thru window to beg for change. The first one there got the spot. The loser looked for another place. Now they were lovers. He wondered what kind of future would be possible for them. Neither had much of an education, although recently they had become experts in vampirism through horror movies and old copies of *Famous Monsters of Filmland*. George was AWOL from the Navy. Maggie had murdered her abusive stepfather, stabbed him, emasculated him, and flushed his privates down the toilet. Then she escaped from a mental hospital and years later was still on the run. She might not be public enemy number one, but George knew she, like him, was still somewhere on the police radar. He didn't believe Mad Maggie was nearly as crazy as she liked everyone to believe.

The Shadows stood a moment, quiet and alert. One elbowed the other and motioned with his head to move forward. Investigate the noise. No one moved at first. There was gunfire in the distance, multiple pops, followed by sirens. The Shadows listened, as if waiting for a signal to move. The air was crisp and quiet. One Shadow took a step forward. Then another. The second Shadow moved forward, joined the other. They traded glances. The first took another step. A tabby cat burst from cover, darted across their path, paused, streaked again toward George, and suddenly zigzagged away from him among the tombstones.

The Shadows laughed. Breathed sighs of relief. Gave each other little punches in the arms.

"A fucking feral cat," one Shadow said. "I've seen that one before. Let's go or we'll be late."

The Shadows continued toward the mausoleums.

Stupid shits, Overboard George thought. *No cat could snap a stick and make that much noise. The cat made a good excuse to retreat.*

The vampire hunters followed the Shadows, moving like soldiers, hunched over from cover to cover. The Shadows arrived at the mausoleum. One man dug keys from a pocket. He mounted the marble steps and opened the gate, then opened the exterior door. The vampire hunters watched from their hiding places. After the door and gate closed and they heard keys turn in the locks, the vampire hunters gathered on the roof of the neighboring mausoleum, where Del Hatch had found cover the night the East Coasters arrived in the city.

They sat cross-legged in a circle on the mausoleum concrete roof. Persimmon said, "It seems like some Shadows, probably the most trusted, have keys to the place. We'll have to move our trail cams closer to the mausoleum to identify them. It's risky. Someone might see the cameras, especially the vampires, even though the cameras are camouflaged."

"How soon do we go against them?" Overboard George asked.

"We'll see what the latest trail cams caught. We haven't been getting any new Shadows. When we have a finite number of Shadows, more or less, we can estimate the number of vampires. Then, we'll ensure we have enough Brethren and attack. Of course, you East Coasters are invited. You are more than ready. And who knows? Bo might give us an exact number. That's what I hope for."

"We wouldn't miss it," Mad Maggie said. "How did you get

involved? It hardly seems the kind of work for such a pretty young woman."

"I've always been in *it*," Persimmon said. "My parents were Brethren. Both were killed by vampires when I was still young. In fact, Gerrard, who you guys staked, killed my mother. The Brethren raised me. Taught me how to fight. Like it does everybody. I have lived all over the world. I've never known any other life. I wouldn't want to be anything other than a vampire killer, not, say, a corporate lawyer or real estate agent or surgeon or even stay-at-home mom."

"What about later?" Overboard George said.

"You want to have another pizza party after we stake them?" Persimmon said. "That can be arranged."

"I meant the future," George said. "After the pizza party."

"You know about us now. Soon you'll know how we operate. If you have a taste for the fight, this life, the invitation is open."

"We'll take two applications then," Overboard George said.

"We are secretive. There are no applications. We will keep files on you, though. We always will know where you are. And you will always need to be ready to fight. No drugs. Minimal alcohol."

"I think George and I are beyond that," Mad Maggie said. "Neither of us wants to go back to the streets. We feel we have bigger things to do in life."

CHAPTER TWENTY-ONE

Bo sat on the vampiress's closed casket, slumped against the dirt wall. Lisa held a compress to the new wound Eva opened in his shoulder. Bo was naked but didn't care. He was that weak. Kazmer hunched over Bo, hands on his knees, watching his friend's shallow respiration.

"She's going to kill you, Bo," Lisa said.

"I think that's the idea," Bo said in a weak voice, barely audible.

Lisa removed the compress and dabbed it over Bo's wounds a few times to clean up the blood on his skin.

"There. The bleeding has stopped. Finally. That's a deep wound she inflicted. I hope there's no nerve damage. It already looks infected. What possessed her to..."

"She was thirsty. Couldn't contain herself, the way she usually does," Bo said. He moved the arm under the wound and grimaced.

Lisa turned to Kazmer. "Do we have any bandages?"

Kazmer handed a bandage he had ready. "I keep them just in case," he added. "You never know when one is needed. And here is the sling Bo made me. You can put his arm in it. I hope it helps."

Lisa winced. Took a step back. Straightened suddenly, wobbled. Kazmer caught Lisa's hand. Let her get steady again.

"How do you feel?" Kazmer said.

"Not as bad as when you connected with that right cross in my apartment," Lisa said. "I just had a cramp. The baby kicked really hard. I saw stars."

Kazmer grunted. He looked at the ceiling. "I think the baby will come soon."

"If I knew the date, the month, I could be some help," Lisa said. "I believe my due date is near Easter Sunday, but it's just a guess."

"I am not permitted to tell you the date, not even the time of day," Kazmer said. "It is what *she* wants. If I tell you she might know."

"Please don't tell her about the cramp," Lisa said. "She'll know soon enough."

Kazmer grunted.

The vampiress arrived in a blur, appearing suddenly amid them, coming into focus in a split second. Only Kazmer was not surprised.

"My children all together. What is it you conspire?"

"Union meeting," Lisa said.

The vampiress, dressed like a cowgirl, including a hat she had pushed her hair under, said, "I don't understand." She looked at Kazmer, who shrugged his shoulders. He looked confused, too.

"I will tell you when I think something is...funny," the vampiress said.

"You almost killed Bo, drained too much blood," Lisa said.

The vampiress smiled.

"I don't think that's funny," Lisa said.

"Be careful how you address me, little one. I can make...things painful when the time comes. As far as Bo, he is not your concern. He is my pet. I treat him the way I want. Drink his blood when I crave it. Have sex with him when I desire it."

"He is weak, Madam," Kazmer offered.

"Silence!" she shouted at the trio. Her hollow voice rang off the walls. Lisa and Kazmer shrank back a step. Bo remained motionless, too weak to move.

The vampiress approached Bo and placed two fingers on his neck. "Poor little rabbit heart. So weak. It is true. I enjoyed you too much. We will let you rest until you regain your strength. Then we will see."

"Bo needs antibiotics," Lisa said. "He has infections in the wounds you gave him." Lisa moved closer to the vampiress. "The new bites and the old ones. He might not be able to fight it off. There's no telling what germs are in your mouth. He could die if he gets sepsis. He might already have it."

"Be careful, little one. I can take your baby now if I like. You are becoming quite bothersome."

"I doubt you'll do anything to me," Lisa said. "It will show the other vampires you are weak, that you let a human get to you."

The vampiress stared at Lisa. Her clenched fists, with claws extended, dug into her palms and dripped blood.

"I was going to recommend antibiotics too," Kazmer said, his eyes lowered to the ground. "For the infection."

The vampire stepped toward Kazmer. "It's so nice to see your concern, Kazmer." Her face twisted when she pronounced his name. She thought a moment. "Is it concern for me or for Bo? I wonder. Very well. Get the antibiotics. Go through the usual channels for medicine. We will let Bo heal and the medicine to clear from his system before I sample again."

She ran her fingers through Bo's hair, streaking the side of his head with her blood. "I want to see him gain some weight. Have his hair cut, too. He looks like a serf."

"I will have my own fun tonight. I am going with Fagan. He is teaching me to line dance. It's western, you know. Then we will feed until we can hold no more. The nights are longer now. We will have more time. Long nights are my favorite time of the year. Afterward, we will pleasure each other until dawn." She clapped her hands together and laughed. Then disappeared in a blur.

The vampires arrived in the Wagon Wheel Country Saloon parking lot, appearing from their blurs, first Fagan, who led the way, and Eva a step behind. They checked the surroundings to ensure humans hadn't seen them appear as if from thin air. Satisfied, they looked at each other, smiled, and reset the cowboy hats they had removed at the cemetery gate. Fagan helped push Eva's hair under her hat in the back. The parking lot was filled with vehicles, mostly pick-ups and jeeps, and couples ahead of them flocked toward the saloon. Country western music spilled from the place for a few seconds every time the doors opened and snapped shut. The vampires walked hand-in-hand to the entrance, where Fagan paid the cover charges. He held out his hand for the bouncer to stamp. As Eva followed, the man re-inked the small, round stamper on an ink pad that sat on a stool. He took her hand in his when she offered it for stamping, but he never touched Fagan. The bouncer dropped Lisa's hand immediately, and recoiled from the corpse's hard, cold touch.

"You just step off a plane from the North Pole?" the bouncer said. "You feel frozen."

Eva threw back her head and laughed. "No. I just got off a train from hell."

"I believe it." He looked at her warily.

Eva offered her hand again in a fist and the man stamped it quickly, then looked away. The vampires held hands again and stepped inside the saloon. Fagan stopped and surveyed the room. "We'll have to stand at the bar until some seats open. It's the custom. The place is packed. That's the problem when you have to wait for sundown."

"Where would you like to sit?"

"A table near the dance floor would be nice," Fagan said. He pointed. "Over there, away from the spotlights."

Eva walked toward the dance floor, stopped at a table where a western-clad couple sat in conversation, and turned to Fagan. He nodded his approval. Eva lowered her head to the couple. Talked to them briefly. They looked at each other, stood, and exited the saloon as if in a trance. Eva pulled out a chair for Fagan, cocked her head, and took a seat on the table's other side. Fagan joined her.

"What did you tell them?" Fagan said.

"I told them they should go to the parking lot, find their machine, climb in, and make the most of this night."

The vampires ordered drinks they didn't touch, bounced into humans on the dance floor as they navigated line dance steps awkwardly and laughed with other revelers. When there was a break in the music they sat at their table again.

"I didn't like this place when I came in," Eva said. "It reminded me of a stable."

"That's the idea. Humans call it atmosphere. Ambiance."

"How quaint. It doesn't smell like a stable."

"Do you sense any virgins we can tap?" Fagan said.

"Not yet. There are too many odors. Individuals. And the perfumed bodies. It's disgusting. We'll have to circulate. I'll need to get close to a virgin to sense one, a virgin like Bo. That damned perfume is confusing."

"What will you do with Bo?" Fagan said.

"I don't know. He is weak. Has infections." She held her drink in one hand. Pretended to sip from it, and raised a straw to her lips. She set down the glass and stirred the contents. The ice had melted. The waitress came over and asked whether something was wrong with their drinks.

"They're dead," Fagan said and smiled at the woman who clutched a tray to her body.

Eva smiled at the selection of his words. He ordered two more.

The waitress scooped up the old drinks and carried them back to the bar.

Eva continued. "I told Kazmer to get Bo medicine. I'm sure he will. Bo will recover." She paused a moment as if thinking through a problem. "I don't trust Bo, Lisa, even Kazmer at times. They spend too much time together. I realize Bo and Lisa knew each other back at After Dark, but I don't know how well. They seem to be protective. And Kazmer has become especially attached to Bo. That worries me the most."

The waitress returned with their new drinks. "I hope you like these better. Let me know if there's a problem. We have a new bartender."

Fagan smiled at the woman. Nodded his head. Touched two fingers to his hat brim as he had seen Gary Cooper do in an old Western film. The waitress hurried away to another table. "The solution is simple. Have Kazmer kill Bo. It should mean nothing to your Shadow. He serves at your will. How many humans has he already killed? I doubt if even Kazmer could tell you."

"I would hate to lose that sweet blood. I've become attached to Bo myself. I know it's very unlike a vampire to form attachments, especially to humans."

"How long have you had him?"

Eva pressed a finger to her mouth and rubbed it against her lips. "Longer than any pet I ever owned. Even the rabbit I had as a girl. When I was a human girl."

"I'm not telling you what to do, but I would sacrifice Lisa and Bo at the black mass."

"That is, how do they say it?, an idea," Eva said. "It would give you and me more baby blood. The colony could share Bo. After the mass, you and I would make a team more formidable than Gerrard and I were. It is a thought. I like the idea and will think more about it. After all, we must think of *our* survival above all else."

"The absence of Lisa *and* Bo would do much to bring harmony back to our colony. It is *our* colony now that you are a member."

It was after midnight and the scent of humans made the vampires hungry, so much so that they had difficulty keeping their claws and fangs retracted. They decided to leave the saloon and hunt. They walked to the back of the parking lot, as if they were looking for a car, then blurred away. Midway through their flight, Eva smelled a virgin, the slightest hint of sweet blood in the air. She stopped suddenly. Fagan came back to her side.

"What is it?" he wanted to know. "Danger?"

"Virgin blood. Female." They smiled at each other.

"We have to be careful," Fagan said. "We can't take someone who will be missed. We can't endure a sensation, especially with the Brethren so close. They will suspect us."

"I understand. Still, we can—as they say--check it out. If we can't take her, we can always go for the homeless. There's a tent camp nearby. I can smell the stench."

The vampiress followed the faint smell as it lingered almost imperceptively on the calm night air. She was able to follow just a few molecules of air the virgin breathed. They came to a cross-roads. Eva stopped, sniffed the air, and swirled her tongue. She pointed and made a left.

They continued down that road. She turned to Fagan. "It's getting stronger. I think we have her." She pointed at a convenience store ahead. Eva blurred a short distance and stopped at a car parked at the gasoline pumps. She sniffed the car's interior through the open driver's side window. She turned to Fagan, closed her eyes a moment, and nodded. "This is the virgin's machine." There were no other cars in the parking lot. They moved toward the entrance. Inside, a young woman paid for gasoline, snacks, and a carton of ice cream.

Eva feigned interest in automobile air fresheners, Fagan in beef jerky. He grabbed a handful of meat snacks. Eva gave him a quizzical look. "For the boys back *home*—Bo and your Shadows. I'm sure they will eat it."

The male clerk, still a teenager, spilled coins into the girl's palm, counted out three singles, and gave them to her.

The doors slammed open. Three men wearing hoodies and masks charged in, brandishing guns. A car pulled up, waiting outside the store. Two emptied merchandise into garbage bags, raking their arms along shelves. The third pointed his pistol at the clerk and demanded money. The kid behind the counter froze. The robber waved his gun in the kid's face and screamed for him to empty the cash register. The customer shrank away, dumped her ice cream and change on the floor, and dropped to her knees, sobbing. The two thugs had filled their bags, produced two more empty ones, and continued to pillage. The third man jumped over the counter, pushed the kid away, and hammered on the cash register. It didn't open. He grabbed the kid and pulled him to the register.

"Open the fucking drawer," the man screamed.

The kid's hands shook. He fumbled over the keys. Finally, he hit the right button, and the cash drawer flew open. The thief hit the kid on the head with the butt of his pistol. The kid bled. Crumbled to the floor. The thief scooped cash from the drawer into his own small bag.

"Hurry up, man! We gotta go," one man called.

"I got it. Fucking drawer wouldn't open. Almost done." He looked up. "Hey, grab some of them Slim Jims."

The scent of the cashier's blood in the air was intoxicating to the famished vampires. They moved to the counter, blocking the thief's exit.

"Out of the way," the man holding the cash said.

The vampires smiled back.

All three robbers stopped to look at the vampires. They laughed.

"Look at this, will ya? Mr. and Mrs. Country Fried. Man, where'd you leave your rig?" the thief sneered, waving his pistol.

The vampires were silent. Continued to smile. Sniffed the scent of blood in the air.

The robber with the cash pumped three bullets into Fagan's chest. One clipped the end of his string tie. Black blood seeped from the wounds but stopped almost immediately. Three flattened rounds pushed through the holes in Fagan's western shirt and bounced on the counter as if they were dropped coins. The stunned thief backed into a wall of cigarette cartons. Packs rained over his head. The girl on the floor whimpered and lay prone in a growing puddle of swirling Neapolitan ice cream. The clerk moaned and regained consciousness. The chunky getaway driver honked the car horn furiously, and gunned the engine, spewing the exterior air with fumes. The two thieves behind the vampires held their pistols sideways. The vampires turned to them and snarled. The gunmen emptied the magazines in a blaze of fire. Bullets sprayed everywhere. Windows broke, cans exploded, potato chip bags burst, and streams of corn oil and detergents mixed as they glugged to the floor. The robber with the cash was hit three times, twice in the head, and died before he hit the floor. Both vampires were hit multiple times. Healing started immediately. Eva took a round above the eye, blew out the back of her head, and scattered brain and skull fragments across a recently emptied shelf.

Despite their wounds, the vampires blurred in an instant, caught the thieves, tore open their necks, and drained their blood taking huge sucking draughts. Fagan dropped his exsanguinated man on the floor, and wiped his mouth with his shirt sleeve. Eva threw the other body through the store's broken door window. It landed on the getaway car hood. The corpse's head remained attached to the body by only a few threads of flesh. The driver peeled out and fled the parking lot. The head flew off and bounced away, but the body remained on the hood until he turned onto the street. It slid off the car leaving a bloody smear on the hood and then the asphalt. Meanwhile, the young female customer and the teenage clerk had found each other, now hugged, hidden behind a display of shot-up and bloodied confections —cookies and cupcakes infused with brain matter and bone, like jelly-filled sweets, until the vampiress's scattered gore ignited. The couple was covered in gore. Eva walked to the teenagers, looked down, and smiled. The pair grimaced in terror and held each other tighter. Eva's right eye was still missing, just beginning to grow back. Nerve threads grew, whipping around her face wildly until they finally attached to the head. The wound on the back of her skull closed.

Eva rejoined Fagan and exited the store. "So much for our virgin," he said.

"There'll be others." Her voice had an unusual sound, which exited partly through the hole in the back of her head as if it were a ventriloquist's trick.

"We can always come back. You might be able to follow her scent."

"Did you see them embracing? After tonight, I don't think she'll be a virgin."

CHAPTER TWENTY-TWO

Approximately fifteen Brethren and the East Coast vampire fighters assembled in the mortuary's viewing room. The mood was lighthearted. Brethren had been called in from their various reconnaissance missions at city cemeteries, and neighborhoods with abandoned buildings. It was impossible to blanket the entire city at any one time, and the Brethren shifted surveillance often. The Brethren showed their mosquito bites, told stories of encounters with raccoons, rats as large as house cats, even coyotes, and, of course, junkies and homeless who roamed the streets like zombies, always looking for so-called bandos, abandoned properties where they could crash. Some were harmless. Others had mean streaks. They all wanted money. This was nothing new to the East Coasters. They had lived the life of homeless people. They had begged themselves and spent time in abandoned buildings until they were chased out.

Coffee percolated in a large urn. Breakfast sandwiches, doughnuts, and fruit lay on a long table. Everyone chowed down. Overboard George and Mad Maggie sat on folding chairs away from the others, plates balanced on their knees, taking in the sights. Some of the Brethren were new to them. They came in a variety of shapes and ages. Most packed sidearms and had machetes on their hips. Were always ready for a fight with the undead.

Overboard George leaned toward Mad Maggie. "I got to give these Brethren credit," he said. "They know how to eat. Good food and plenty of it."

Mad Maggie nodded her head, her mouth full of a bagel covered with a thick layer of cream cheese. After swallowing, she said, "They say breakfast is the most important meal of the day."

Del Hatch made his rounds among the Brethren, holding coffee and a doughnut, a paper napkin tucked in the neck of his olive green jumpsuit. He put down his food to explain a Sasquatch patch on his sleeve. Old Harriet was perched on her ornate chair on wheels, which Jimmy had hauled into the mortuary for her, eating a banana, swinging her legs, taking in everything. Jimmy and Bad Nelson sat together, also away from others. Voices in the room got louder as three more Brethren entered, and went directly for the food. Occasionally, laughter erupted from the small groups scattered around. In pantomime, one Brethren acted out his encounter with a feral dog.

One of the new arrivals bellied up to the food table, tilted the coffee urn, and called, "Persimmon, we need more coffee."

She, standing at the end of the food table with another woman called "Pear," pointed at the urn. A man in the corner hurried to the small kitchen off the viewing room and started another batch. After everyone had emptied their plates, even taken seconds, especially the East Coasters who still never knew when their next meals would arrive, settled into the folding chairs, and waited expectantly. The viewing room's floor lamps, potted plastic plants, and even a church truck for wheeling around caskets, were pushed into a corner. A lectern and screen were arranged near the center at the front of the room. Brethren swung the food table around, cleared the plates at one end, and set up a computer and projector. A hush fell over the room when everything was organized. Persimmon stepped to the funeral home's lectern and put on black-rimmed glasses, which gave her a studious, softer look. Closed, mauve curtains hung on the windows behind her.

Persimmon looked across her audience. Smiled. "Any vampire encounters we don't already know about?"

Those assembled scanned the room, looking among the faces.

"I heard something interesting on the radio this morning, not directly a vamp encounter, but..." The man who had been worried about the coffee level raised a hand. "There was a convenience store robbery last night. Two teenagers survived. The robbers—three gangbangers—were killed. Two had their throats slashed. One was decapitated.

"Blood loss?" Persimmon said.

"The radio news didn't mention any. I heard it in the car as I pulled in."

"It was vampires, alright," a woman said, just entering the room from the mortuary.

"Tomato. You're late, as usual," Persimmon said.

"I just left my cop friend," Tomato said. She was tall, thin, and dressed in black. Looked like a Shadow. She spoke while she loaded a plate with food. She stopped. Looked at Persimmon. "No lox?"

"You snooze, you lose, Tomato," Persimmon fired back. "You know the drill."

Tomato smeared cream cheese on a bagel. Tore a huge chunk out of it, chewed, and swallowed. She threw back her head. Relished the taste. Poured the last of the coffee. Slurped a mouthful. Burped.

"Ready now?" Persimmon said.

"Ready," Tomato said and sighed. "My cop friend said, as best as he can figure—oh, there's cc video too—these three gangbangers enter the convenience store, demand money. There's a girl inside buying ice cream. She hits the deck. The clerk, who was eighteen, froze. One of the gangbangers jumps behind the counter, pistol whips the kid. He's dazed for a moment." She stopped to take another bite. Gulped more coffee. She pointed the remainder of her bagel at Persimmon. "There's also a man and woman in the store. Our vamps. You can't see them at first because they're not in the camera's frame. They're dressed like cowboys—hats, boots, belt buckles, and string ties. The only thing missing is the buckboard parked outside."

Instead of laughing, the Brethren sat in rapt attention. Overboard George stifled his smile.

"The cowboys approach the checkout counter. That's when they come into view. Meanwhile, one thief empties the cash drawer. The cowboys block his escape. Just stand there at the counter. The thief shoots the cowboy three times in the chest. It has no effect. The video shows blood oozing from the wounds. The vamps turn to the other two gangbangers. They empty their guns. Bullets spray all around. They're not exactly marksmen, although the female vamp takes one in the head. Blows the back of her head out—brains and all—all over a shelf behind her. Again, the bullets have no effect. A couple of slugs clip the third gangbanger and kill them on the spot. The couple disappears out of the camera's view. We don't see the exsanguination, but there are two bodies left. One is decapitated and in the parking lot. The female comes back in frame and looks at the kids huddled in a puddle of ice cream on the floor. She takes off her hat. Puts her finger through a bullet hole. Looks pissed. The head wound is already healing. You can watch her scalp come together. Then she disappears in a blur. Is gone."

There are murmurs from the group. "What does your cop friend say?" Persimmon asked.

"He's spooked. Doesn't know what to say. The kids are, too. They're both in the hospital, in shock."

"Mental ward, no doubt," Mad Maggie said, with a knowing wag of her head. "That's where they send people with that kind of...*visual* trauma. Poor kids."

"The official version?" Persimmon leaned over the lectern.

"There was something wrong with the camera. Rival gangbangers killed the thieves. The thieves bled out, even though there was next to no blood on the floor."

"Clean-up in aisle five. I'd like to see that video," Persimmon said.

Tomato held up a flash drive between her index finger and thumb. "You want to watch it now or later?" She smiled and finished off her coffee.

"How?" Persimmon said, shaking her head in disbelief.

"I have my ways. Leave it at that."

Persimmon suggested a break. They'd return in ten, watch the video, discuss it, and continue the meeting. There was a full agenda that would continue through lunch and the evening.

Overboard George winked at Mad Maggie, and whispered, "What I tell you? These people make all they decisions on a full stomach. That's the best decision you can make."

AFTER THE BREAK, the smokers returned inside, Pear made another urn of coffee. Persimmon returned to the lectern. Tomato played the soundless video, and showed it on the screen. Reran it three times for the group. The Brethren watched in silence, then discussed it at great length, often asking for the video to be rewound to certain spots. They debated every detail in the video.

"One more thing," Tomato said before the meeting returned to its original agenda. "The first three bullets the male vamp took—his body pushed them out. They fell on the counter. Three flattened nine-mill slugs, and a piece of his string tie that got shot off. My friend the cop found them. He was one of the investigating officers. He thinks I'm crazy, believing in vampires..." The group sniggered. "When we first met, it was outside a cemetery. I told him I did genealogy for fat cats who wanted a family tree but didn't have the time to do the work themselves. He bought it."

It was now evening and dark. Persimmon cleared her throat

and returned to the agenda. "We've reached a point in our reconnaissance where we're not seeing any new Shadows. We think we have them all identified unless there are Shadows who remain inside the colony full time. We don't think that's the case. They come and go, always returning to the colony."

Persimmon showed a series of photos on the screen, taken mostly in the cemetery. Some were shot outside a run-down laundromat blocks away from the vampire house on the hill. She talked while the slideshow continued on the screen.

"You will see some Shadows were photographed multiple times. They seemed to be more active than others, perhaps more trusted, and given more important assignments. If you study the photographs closely, you will see some Shadows are armed. You can see a bulge in a jacket pocket or a pistol grip in their pants. We believe, from experience, the vampires give the guns to their Shadows after they kill gangbangers or other criminals. We don't feel the colony has an arsenal, even extra ammunition for the guns. There is no reason to think the typical Shadow can hit the broad side of a barn, let alone use a gun with any skill. We believe the only bullets they have are the ones loaded in the guns. Some guns might have only a few rounds."

Persimmon looked into the audience. Paused. Photographs continued to hit the screen every few seconds. "We've identified thirty-eight Shadows. Therefore, those who pack should carry their weapons and extra ammo. From experience, we don't think the Shadows will offer much resistance. Still, we don't want to get into a firefight and face multiple guns. We want to stake vamps, not be slowed down by losers.

"Therefore, with the idea that a vampire will have one or two Shadows—some are loners and won't have any—we suspect there are between twenty and twenty-five vamps in the colony. That number might change. I'll tell you why in a minute. First, we're calling in extra Brethren, a few from Florida, three from PA, and some from Europe. All are on their way now. We'll have to hit the house and cemetery at the same time. Leave the vamps no way to escape. The house is boarded up. As far as we know, there are no ways in or out. Any ideas?"

Del Hatch stepped forward. He removed the paper napkin from his jumpsuit neck. "If you don't mind a little noise, my BAR, with armor-piercing bullets, can knock down any door. It's lethal, but you have the noise factor." Del grinned sheepishly. The crowd chuckled.

"Thanks for the offer, Del. We might have to use it at some point, but we want to go quiet on this raid, even though the neighborhood is mostly deserted."

"I see your point," Del said, as he returned his napkin to his chin and headed to the food table for another doughnut.

From her chair on wheels, Old Harriet said, "Why not torch the house? Burn them alive. We *East Coasters* know all about making torches."

"Again, we have the noise factor," Persimmon said. "We don't want fire trucks arriving while we're still staking flaming vamps. We don't want to be exposed or see civilians injured."

"Bad for your image?" Bad Nelson said. His head was lowered.

"That's the point," Persimmon said. "We don't have an image, a persona." The Brethren mumbled in agreement. "The outside world doesn't know we exist. The only ones who know about us are the vamps and now you East Coasters. We want to keep it that way."

The photos on the screen continued to flash by. I want you to study the Shadows. Get to know their faces. Remember who's packing. As you see, most of the pictures we got are good quality. There are some photos of animals, especially a tabby, probably feral. There's some other critters and some mist, which we can't explain. Might be some anomaly."

Del stepped forward again and pulled the napkin from the neck of his jumpsuit again. He swallowed a mouthful of doughnuts. "You won't believe me, but that mist is a ghost, an apparition I saw the night you found me in the cemetery. She has a long dress and I saw her move around the cemetery." Dell spread his arms as if he expected laughter. There was none. "I saw her walk. If you can call it a walk. It's more like a float. I couldn't see her legs. There was that long dress and that carpet-like mist that moved with her. Then she vanished. Her and the fog."

Del looked around. The Brethren had leaned forward in their seats to hear him. Now they mumbled among themselves, as if in agreement. Del continued. "My view was if there are vampires and ghosts, Sasquatch ought to be out there, too."

Old Harriet screamed and pointed. "It's our Bo. I just saw him. He's alive!"

Persimmon stopped the slide show, and reversed it until Bo's photo showed. She froze the image.

"That's Bo," Jimmy called. "He's one of us. We thought he was dead."

"I talked to him at the laundromat a few blocks from the vamp house. They let him out to do laundry. He's under their control. I'm not sure to what extent, at least not enough to give us up to the vamps, I hope."

"We figured that," Overboard George said. "The day we stormed After Dark Bo was supposed to work the door outside. Pass us ammo, whatever we needed, but he disappeared. He was gone when we came out after the fight."

"I almost didn't recognize him," Mad Maggie said. "Look at all the hair on him. It's safe to say the vamps don't have a barber."

Persimmon looked across the group. "Bo is working for me now. I gave him an assignment. To find the exact number of vampires in the colony. From now on, I'll be at the laundromat every day, waiting for him to come back, to get his intel. So, I'm going to need everybody's dirty clothes."

CHAPTER TWENTY-THREE

BO SAT ON THE EDGE OF THE CRYPT WITH KAZMER ON THE bench the brothers carved into the wall. They talked little, mostly watched the bats fluttering overhead. Bo had his blanket draped over his shoulders like a shawl. He thought it was early evening, perhaps not yet sunset. The vampire exodus to the outside world had not yet begun, but a few vampires had left their caskets, milled around on the main vault floor, talking to one another, as if preparing to leave, waiting for sundown. Bo had given up asking Kazmer the time of day and date. Although Kazmer wore a watch, he said it didn't work. He claimed he did not own a cell phone.

"I see the vampires are stirring," Bo said.

"Stirring what?"

"They're leaving their caskets for the night."

Maybe." Kazmer looked at Bo, as if he suddenly didn't trust him.

"You get around, Kaz. How many vampires are there in the colony?"

"Who wants to know?" Kazmer's eyes narrowed. Cigarette smoke drifted over his face. He squinted an eye.

"I did. I wondered if there were plans for expanding. Digging more vaults. It seems..."

"That is not my concern," Kazmer said abruptly. "My job is to protect you and Lisa. To do what the mistress tells me. She tells me to protect you and Lisa. I won't dig places for other vampires unless she tells me."

"It seems, some vampires I see often, maybe every day. Others not so often—like they're here for a visit."

"I don't notice such things. It's not my business. I think you sit outside too much. Sitting outside the rooms might get you in trouble."

Above, bats scurried, circled lower, flew toward the exit. The large wooden and iron door to the cemetery passage glided open. The bats flew out. A Shadow stumbled in, all arms and legs, spider-like. "Farber's been staked," he screamed. "I saw him blow up at St. John's, outside the mausoleum he used."

The Shadow collapsed to the floor, rolled over, and was covered in dust. Fagan blurred to his side, lifted the Shadow as if he were a doll, held him off the floor at arm's length. "What happened?" His hollow-sounding voice echoed off the vault walls. One amazing thing the workers who excavated the vault did, probably without intention as they dug, was to create incredible acoustics. Bat wings fluttering, conversations on the floor, could be heard from the vampiress's crypt.

"You should go inside," Kazmer told Bo.

"Why, I'll still hear it."

"Better not to be seen." Kazmer grabbed Bo's wrist, but Bo shook off Kazmer's hand.

"I'm staying here."

The Shadow coughed and cried. Fagan shook him. "Tell me!" the vampire demanded.

"I took Farber the clothing he wanted," the Shadow said between sobs. He was covered with dirt from the floor. "It was before dawn. I did everything as instructed. I was on the cemetery road to his mausoleum. I didn't know Farber was there. He returned in a blur. Appeared on the mausoleum steps, ready to go inside. I heard his key in the door. Then there was a whiz. A couple whizzes. Arrows struck him—from crossbows—one in the head, two in the heart." The Shadow looked around at the vampires who had assembled, then back to Fagan, who lowered him to the floor, but still held his shoulders, and brushed dirt off his jacket. "I know it was the Brethren. I didn't see them, but they shot crossbows. They were hunting us."

"When did it happen?" a late-arriving vampire said.

"This morning, before dawn."

"Why did you wait so long to report?" Fagan demanded. He squeezed the Shadow's shoulders and the young man winced in pain.

"I had to make sure I wasn't followed. I was careful. Took two buses, then an Uber."

Fagan stared at the kid. Released him. "You did well."

"Johnson!" Fagan called. Johnson scurried over and bowed to Fagan. "Get this lad food and drink. See that he is comfortable upstairs in the house."

Fagan looked at the vampires, scanning the assembly as if doing a head count. "Now that we are all here, let this episode be a lesson. You see what happens to those who decide to live alone. There is safety inside the colony. We still have three, no, four loners. I want them back inside until we clean out these Brethren. I want Shadow protection inside the entire cemetery, all day and all night. I want everybody armed. If there are not enough guns, trade them off when watches change."

Johnson had led the dirty Shadow toward the passage to the house. He stopped and turned. Johnson said, "If we need more guns, I know a guy who can get them. No questions asked. It will be expensive, but..."

"Do an inventory of the weapons," Fagan said, pointing a finger at Johnson. "Decide how many more we need. Then buy them. I will give you the cash."

Johnson nodded and led the other Shadow toward the passage to the house.

"What about recruiting more Shadows?" one vampire said. "I would take another one."

"Not yet," Fagan said. "With the Brethren, they might try to get a spy inside. We will wait. We know the Shadows we have are trustworthy. There are more than enough. If anyone sees a Brethren, follow that person to their lair. Do not engage. Then *we* will attack."

The vampires voiced agreement.

"Hunt in twos until this crisis is over. Now..." Fagan smiled at the group. "Feed well."

The heavy door to the exterior swung open and the vampires left. The last bats circling the door fled, too.

Bo took a deep breath. *So much for old Farber. Gone and forgotten almost immediately*, Bo thought. Kazmer looked at Bo, eyes narrowed to two slits. "Did you get your count?"

"Count?"

"How many vampires are in the colony? You heard they were all together below."

"I forgot. They move too fast to count. What use would that be? I was just curious."

Kazmer grunted.

After a long silence, Bo said, "What was it like growing up?"

Kazmer looked at Bo and exhaled cigarette smoke. "Not good. We were not happy. Children should be happy. We were poor. That is it. I don't like to think about it."

"Are you happy now?"

"Lazlo and me..."

"I"

"Thank you, Bo, for helping me with English."

"Lazlo and I are working toward something greater. We have

been...oppressed all our lives. When we become vampires, we will be the masters. We will have our own Shadows and sex with other vampires. Sometimes humans. That is our plan." Kazmer smiled and took a drag on his hand-rolled cigarette. "Lots of sex."

"I hope you remember it."

"We remember. We will get fancy caskets—like the mistress has. The other thing Lazlo and m...I decided is that we will be nice to our Shadows. Maybe you will be my Shadow someday."

"I don't think I'll live to see your...*graduation* to vampires."

"You never know. Graduation. Yes. That's what it will be. I will graduate. I never graduated from anything." Kazmer patted Bo's arm. "Don't worry. I have been thinking. Even Lazlo doesn't know. I will buy you from the mistress. Give her virgins and slaves for Shadows. Such things are possible. You will be expensive, but I will do it. Someday, I will turn you, if that's what you want. If not, you can remain my Shadow and retire when you are old."

"What would I live on? I won't even get Social Security."

"We pay you for being a Shadow. It will be a good life, you will see. Save your money. Retire a wealthy man. Play golf. Women throw themselves at you when you are rich. Women go to the golf park to look for rich men. Even rich old men. Lazlo and I are already wealthy. We have investments. We have a nice apartment in a secret place. We collect things we like to look at. We have many fine clothes and jewelry. Some does not fit us, but we can look at the nice things in our closets and that make us feel rich."

Kazmer stubbed out his infinitely small cigarette. Crushed the butt between his fingers and sprinkled the remaining tobacco flakes to the ground. He immediately started to roll another one.

"Smoking isn't good for you, Kazmer. And that tobacco stinks. Smells awful."

"I know smoking is not good. This tobacco is strong, but I like the flavor. I quit when I become vampire. Maybe. Maybe not. After I become vampire, my health doesn't matter."

"I hope you make it."

"Me, too. I want to live the dream as they say. To be vampire."

The men traded smiles. Kazmer lit his new smoke, which flared at the end when he first applied the flame. They sat in silence for a few minutes.

Bo doubled over and grabbed his stomach. Then he placed his hands over his ears.

"What is it?" Kazmer's face showed concern.

"She's calling me. Wants me inside the crypt. I'm trying to resist."

"Don't. She might kill you if she thinks her control is gone, even getting weaker."

"What if she drains me?"

"She won't. Go to her. You must obey."

Bo's hands dropped to his lap. His mouth grew slack. "I must go."

Bo stood, dropped the blanket off his shoulders to the bench, and shuffled off inside the crypt. Kazmer picked up the blanket, folded it neatly, and placed it at his side. Eva waited beside her casket. Bo saw the curtain to Lisa's dugout move. He knew Lisa listened inside with the Shadow Patty.

"I am happy when you are obedient to my summons. My little rabbit. Give me your arm."

Bo offered his arm. "Are you going to take blood?"

"Not tonight. I want to see your wounds." She took Bo's arms in her cold hands and raised them to her nose, sniffed. "The medicine works. You look much better."

"I feel better. Thank you for the antibiotics."

The vampiress ran her fingers through Bo's hair. "I do not like this haircut. What was Kazmer thinking."

"He got one just like it," Bo said.

"Let Kazmer do what he wants. But you? I want a better haircut for my rabbit. Let me hold you."

The vampiress pulled Bo to her. He felt the cold body, the same temperature as the damp air inside the tomb. He shivered.

"Your warmth is pleasant." She sniffed his hair, then his neck. She parted her lips, licked the skin, and rubbed her fangs gently over Bo's carotid. She had never taken blood from his neck.

"How your little rabbit heart thunders, Bo."

"Are you going to kill me now? I'd like to know before you do it."

"My little rabbit." She held Bo at arm's length. "Why the tears? I enjoy your blood—even your company—too much to kill you. I have plans for you. They are still developing. In the meantime. I want you to go to the laundromat tomorrow. I have clothes that need washing." The vampiress returned to her casket and pulled out bloodied clothes, boots, and a hat. "See what you can do with the hat. It has a bullet hole. See?" She pushed a finger through the bloodied hole. "Some...asshole shot me. Fagan said it was a gang-banger. Do you understand?"

"I do," Bo said. "You should be more careful."

The vampiress smiled. "I'm fond of this hat. I'll get another, if necessary. You can shop for it. Now I must feed. Fagan is waiting. I plan to keep my promise. Some night we will go to see a movie. Just the two of us. You will pick the show. Just for—how do they say it? —fun."

CHAPTER TWENTY-FOUR

Bo gagged. The back of his hand, protected in a neoprene purple glove, flew to his mouth in a reflex action, then dropped just as fast. Gagged again. He was back at the laundromat, pulling bone fragments from the vampiress's cowboy hat. Fragments that didn't incinerate. He peeled back the interior hat band and dislodged the last fragment, a rather large piece. Bo mopped sweat from his forehead with a forearm, took a deep breath, dropped the fragment in the waste can between his legs. Johnson was outside the laundromat smoking, laughing at Bo through the plate glass window. Bo was alone in the laundromat. His washing machines chugged. He had picked up a manicure brush in the bathroom of the vampire house on the hill and gently scrubbed the dried brain material on the hat's interior, He gagged again, vomited the chocolate cake Kazmer brought him earlier in the morning. The cake was hurled into the waste can, mixed with the skull shards, lint, and a broken, zipper. Johnson loved it. He walked out of sight. Bo tapped the top of the hat. The gray material, now a powder, sprinkled over his chocolate cake like powdered sugar. Bo groaned.

The vampiress's head had healed within hours of the shooting, apparently complete with her memories from centuries ago and all her meanness intact. He wondered why the material did not incinerate and ignite the cowboy hat.

It was unusually warm for a fall day. Leaves dropped in the cemetery when he walked through it with Johnson on their way to the laundromat. Other Shadows were already on guard duty, not very conspicuously hidden. Inside the laundromat, the air-conditioning ceiling vent down the aisle dripped. Nearby ceiling tiles were stained and looked soggy. A wet-floor placard covered the drip and blocked part of the aisle.

Bo looked up to see whether Johnson had returned. He was still gone. Persimmon pushed open the door, carried in a basket of wash. She scanned the laundromat and winked at Bo.

"Did you see Johnson outside?"

"No. Maybe he's around the side of the building. Probably playing with himself."

"We'll have to talk fast. He's outside a while. Might be back any second. He saw you last time we talked. Already has the hots for you." They talked in hushed voices. Bo's washers rolled to a stop. He scooped out the clean clothes and threw them in dryers.

"We staked a vamp at St. John's Cemetery, downtown. He was a loner," Persimmon said, as she threw clothing into washers down the aisle, away from Bo.

"I know. News reached the colony through a Shadow. The vampires were like a hive of angry hornets. Be careful. They have Shadows hidden—some of them not too well—all over the cemetery, around the clock. The plan is to arm them all with guns. They hope to spot the Brethren, follow them back to your hideout, and wipe you out."

"We're always careful. It won't be the first time a colony tried to track us." Persimmon smiled. We have two places. The main one and a backup.

"The vampires had a meeting. Their leader, Fagan, said they

were all there. I counted twenty-nine vampires. And there's four more of what you call loners out in the city. They're supposed to come back to the colony."

"Good. We'll get them all at once. Now that we know the number of vamps we can finish our plans." Persimmon grabbed Bo's hair and shook his head playfully. "I can't wait until your Moe Howard haircut grows out. I'm going to style it then—just the way I like it."

Bo couldn't help smiling, but he said, "Be careful." He looked around furtively and checked the front window. "Johnson's packing, too."

"So am I. I have more good news. Your friends have joined us. We call them the East Coasters. Let me see, there are Overboard George, Mad Maggie, Old Harriet, Bad Nelson, and a guy you might not know—Del Hatch."

"What's a Del Hatch?"

"He's OG's friend from the Navy. A Sasquatch hunter. On his way to Washington state. Believe it or not, he fits right in."

"Why wouldn't he? A Sasquatch hunter?"

"He brought a lot of firepower with him. Doesn't seem afraid to use it. Oh yes, there's one more, Jimmy Young."

"He's Lisa's boyfriend. Her baby's father." Bo smiled. "She'll be thrilled."

"So will Jimmy. He seems kind of depressed. Do you see Lisa much?"

"Every day. They keep us in the same crypt with the vampiress, a Shadow named Patty, and the brothers Lazlo and Kazmer. The brothers are Eva's Shadows."

"Is Lisa well?"

"Yes, although they won't let her see a doctor. I suppose vampires don't need doctors, dentists, chiropractors, witch doctors. You know, Lisa's due in early April, so she thinks. They don't let us know the time of day or the day of the week."

"I know. Jimmy told us. We'll destroy this vampire colony long before that. We don't need Eva getting any stronger."

Bo's eyes filled with tears. *At last, I see a way out.*

Persimmon moved down the aisle to a chair in front of her washers. She pulled out an old magazine, *Famous Monsters of Filmland*, and pretended to read.

"Overboard George?" Bo whispered from up the aisle.

Lisa smiled. Nodded her head. "OG wanted me to *bone up*. You know, the East Coasters were right about a lot of things, especially vampires."

Johnson appeared at the window. He cupped his hands around his eyes to peer inside. He headed directly for the door when he saw Persimmon. Entered the laundromat and sat between Bo and Persimmon.

"How's the wash going there, champ?" Johnson said to Bo. "You remember my dryer sheets?"

"Almost done...chief. You want dryer sheets, add them yourself."

Johnson scowled at Bo. He turned his attention to Persimmon. "Nice day. Too nice to do laundry."

"Well, the clothes are dirty, and I have the time."

"Yeah. I know what that's like. Where do you work?"

"County government."

"Good job?"

"Coroner's office." Lisa smiled. "How about you?"

Johnson thought a moment. "Cemetery. Head groundskeeper. Bo, here, is one of my assistants. He does my laundry. I cut him some slack. He's an alright guy but doesn't have much drive."

"Interesting."

"I've seen you around. Want to go out for coffee later?"

"No, thanks."

"Just coffee. Maybe some pie. A little chat. I bet we have lots in common."

"I'm engaged."

Bo and Johnson's heads snapped toward Persimmon.

"I don't see no ring," Johnson said.

Persimmon smiled at the Shadow. "I don't wear it downtown. It's a real rock. I'm afraid some creep might try to steal it."

"I wouldn't let that happen," Johnson said. Then he sulked. Stared at the floor. He waited for the dryers to stop and Bo to fold the clothes. As Bo packed the last of the clothes into his basket, Johnson stood and exited the laundromat. He stopped outside and peered through the window.

When Bo walked by Persimmon, she whispered and smiled. "Bo, I'm not really engaged."

Bo smiled back. This time, when his heart jumped, he enjoyed the feeling.

— — —

PERSIMMON RETURNED to the mortuary and dumped the clean clothes on the embalming table. "Come and get it," She hollered. Brethren sauntered into the room to retrieve their wash. "I hope you guys didn't forget how to use a washing machine. This laundry service won't last forever. We have the information from Bo we need." The Brethren were in high spirits. They dug into the pile of unfolded clothes.

Persimmon said to one man, "Really, Mercy? Sponge Bob underwear? I would have thought you could do better than that." She stood near the table with her hands on her hips.

Mercy, who got his name for showing no mercy when it came to vampires and their Shadows, had burn scars from close contact with dying vamps and shrugged his shoulders. "I like Sponge Bob. They were a gift. I got a whole pack of them."

"Somebody doesn't like you."

Everyone laughed and teased Mercy, a large man with a shaved head and tattoos on his arms. Persimmon said she would call a meeting after the evening meal when everyone was present. In the meantime, she decided to go to the convenience store where the vamps had caused havoc. Persimmon drove to the store, filled up the black SUV with gasoline, and pulled in front of the store. The shot-up door glass and front window had been replaced. A few diamond-sized safety glass shards lay on the pavement outside. Inside the store, curious people wandered up and down the aisles, more intent on the scene than spending money, pointing at bullet holes in the ceiling and shelves not yet restocked.

"Were you here three nights ago when the shooting happened?" Persimmons said when she got the kid alone after shoppers massed in the back of the store to watch a repairman replace a door on the ice cream case.

"Sure was. Right where I'm standing now," the teenage boy said. He was gangly and bucktoothed. "I told the TV news reporter that I was just ready to throw those guys out when the man and woman stepped up."

"You were going to throw the robbers out?"

"Looked like they were up to no good. I don't take any shit from people. Know what I mean?"

"Sure." Persimmon smiled at the kid.

"I figure the man and woman were Texas Rangers. With the cowboy hats and all. Out of their jurisdiction because they weren't packing. That's why they didn't hang around. Probably up here after some cartel members. Anyway, that's my theory. That's what I told the authorities. It's not that farfetched. The cops wrote down everything I said. Even took my name."

"Did you see the security video?" Persimmon pointed at the camera.

"The cops took it. Wouldn't let me see it. After all, I was here. I don't need to see it."

"I'm sure you were a little unnerved. That's understandable."

"Unnerved. Not me. I was more scared for the girl who was in the store. Her name's Lydia. She's my girlfriend."

"Lydia?"

The kid rubbed a palm across his face. "Well, she wasn't my girlfriend three nights ago, but she is now." The boy smiled.

Persimmon thought for a moment. "I can't understand what brought the *Texas Rangers* inside the store. Is Lydia a virgin?"

"I don't know her that well—not yet anyway." The kid blushed.

Persimmon cleared her throat. "Are you a virgin?"

"Hell, no," the boy shot back. "I'm what my grandfather used to call *a man of the world*."

"I'm sure. Sorry. I had to ask."

"Why would someone being a virgin bring in the Texas Rangers? It's not like they could smell it. I mean, Lydia smells good and all."

"Did you see the Texas Rangers kill the gangbangers? See it happen?"

"I didn't see the killings. At that point, the one robber had hit me over the head with his gun. I fell on the floor, and crawled from behind the counter." He paused a moment as if gathering his thoughts. "I was going after the other two but stopped to comfort Lydia. She was really shook up."

Persimmon stared at the boy who looked uncomfortable now. "Do me a favor…"

"Jake," the boy said.

"Jacob? A Biblical name."

"That's right. My folks are religious. Been that way since their own childhoods. Not born again or nothing like that, but you could qualify them as real Bible Thumpers."

"That's good, Jacob. Now, make me a promise. You and Lydia— don't go off by yourselves. It's dangerous. There are gangs, illegal immigrants, and all kinds of people who carry weapons and can hurt you. I'd hate to see that happen. Go to the movies. Stay around other people. You'll both be safer."

"I understand. My folks say that man and woman weren't no Texas Rangers, but demons walking the Earth disguised as people. Imagine that."

"Your parents might be right, Jacob. Listen to them."

"I wouldn't expect that from someone like you—young and snatch. Pretty, too."

"Really?"

"Well, my parents are older. Plus, they don't know what I know, and they weren't here at the time of the shooting, and I was."

CHAPTER TWENTY-FIVE

The baby woke Lisa with a powerful kick. She groaned and rolled on her side. The baby quieted. Surely the child was destined to play soccer. Lisa rubbed her swollen stomach with fingertips. Another fitful night—or was it a day—of sleep. She never knew. Each collection of waking hours brought the birth and her and the baby's execution date closer. At least she now had hope. Jimmy, her fellow vampire hunters from the East Coast, and now new brothers and sisters in arms, the Brethren, trained to kill vampires, were planning a raid to rescue her and the baby and exterminate the colony.

All those pale faces leering at her comings and goings to the house on the hill would soon be gone. Piles of ashes. She lay facing the dirt wall. She could tell the single torch near the door to the vampiress's chamber was nearly burned out by the low yellow light it cast, the sound of its flickering flame. Lisa rolled herself over with difficulty to watch the torch that occasionally emitted little colored sparks, released a thin, curling stream of black smoke, near the end of its life. Patty, who dozed in the corner, might wake before the torch burned out, but she was lazy and sometimes slept through

Lisa rising and dressing. Once, the vampiress beat Patty severely, bruised her face and body, when she caught the Shadow napping. Eva made Patty strip and pummeled her with iron-hard fists, scratched her with claws. Later, Patty blamed Lisa for not waking her in time to avoid the mistress's wrath.

Lisa thought of Jimmy. She missed him terribly and was concerned for his safety. What could he be doing at this very minute? If it were night, he might be sleeping. If it were day, he might be planning the raid, possibly at this moment sneaking up on the place, his stake gun primed and ready to fire. The great fight between good and evil might start at any moment. She must be ready no matter what happens. Tears welled in Lisa's eyes. She remembered her quiet times with Jimmy, lying in bed, staring into each other's eyes, cuddling, suddenly giggling, tickling contests, showering together, and sharing breakfast in her little kitchen. That all seemed so long ago. She wondered whether those good times could be retrieved from the nightmare they had lived recently.

It must be morning, Lisa thought. Although it was quiet, other than the brothers 'snoring in the outer room and the torch flame flapping, she smelled regurgitated blood. The vampiress had fed well, too well, and again drank more blood than she could hold during her frenzy of gluttony. Lisa shuddered. She hoped the fiend puked on the floor and not over Bo, which happened at times when he was ordered into her casket.

Lisa stood and reached for the maternity clothes she now wore, stolen by Patty at a thrift store. Lisa coughed on the pungent torch smoke. Patty stirred and dropped back to sleep. Lazlo was at the curtain. "Are you all right, Lisa?" he whispered. "I heard you cough."

"I'm fine, Lazlo, thank you," Lisa said.

Patty was awake. She sighed and frowned. "Need a bath?"

"Please. Thank you, Patty."

"No problem, but I'm going to grab a smoke first. Just a quick one. To wake up. We have no coffee."

"Sure," Lisa said.

"You decent?" Patty said. "I'm going to open the curtain."

"Go ahead."

Patty pulled open the curtain. Kazmer stood in the door opening. "Smoke later. Attend to Lisa *now*, or I will tell *her*."

"Okay, already." Patty shook with anger and knotted her fists. "Give me a sec to make sure the bathroom is clear."

"No smoke," Kazmer said. "We all go now." His eyes narrowed to two slits. Lazlo stepped into view behind Kazmer and appeared equally stern.

"What about Mr. Bo?" Patty wagged her head.

"Bo is always ready," Kazmer said. "He is a man."

Patty made a disgruntled sound and blew between her teeth. "Come on, then. Let's go."

Patty grabbed her boots and sat on Lisa's bed to put them on.

"Not on Lisa's bed. Only Lisa sits on Lisa's bed," Kazmer said. He stepped into the room.

"Okay," Patty said, showing frustration. She returned across the room and sat on a straight-backed chair, pulled on her boots, and laced them up. Sighed again.

As occurred almost every day, Lisa, Bo, Patty, and the brothers made their way from the vampiress's crypt to the old house on the hill and its working bathroom. Lisa and Bo carried clean towels, clothes, and bags with their toiletries.

Bo whispered on more than one occasion, "I wish we had some deodorant."

"I know." Lisa would whisper back and smile. "Someday we're going to escape. It wouldn't hurt to be ready. At least smell decent. Damn vampires. It's not perfume."

Most trips to the old house were uneventful. Patty always led the way, followed by Lisa and Bo. Lazlo and Kazmer were close behind. The brothers stepped ahead at the gap in the trail from the crypt to the vault floor and dropped the planking to continue their journey. Ever watchful, the brothers scanned their surroundings.

Even if a vampire attacked the group during the day, when the fiends were weaker, the brothers were not strong enough to fight one off. Still, the vampires feared the ancient vampiress and her incredible strength, especially after the children vampires were decimated. The boldest might stand and stare, twirl their tongues around their mouths, but did not approach the group. Patty had learned to walk slowly on the trek, especially when they began the climb between the vault floor and the house basement, where the air smelled of death, But Lisa needed to rest. At some points the passage was so steep Shadows had installed stone steps. Here the group slowed more. Usually, Lisa would ask them to stop for a moment. It was a ruse to make her keepers think she was weaker than she was. After all, she had been a track star in high school and might need to run again.

If the group encountered someone in the passage, a Shadow would press himself or herself against the wall, and lower a head. Vampires would turn suddenly, either retreat in a blur or find a niche in the walls to enter until they passed. The last seven steps to the house's basement were especially steep and guarded by two Shadows. After Farber the loner vampire was staked by the Brethren, the Shadows were armed. It seemed almost everyone carried a gun. The guards knocked on a heavy wooden door. Two guards inside opened the door to admit them. The basement was filled with old, broken furniture, festooned with cobwebs. Everything was dusty. The air smelled of mold and dust. A path led through the clutter to the basement steps. An ancient rusting boiler sat along the way. Old steam pipes ran along the ceiling, making it necessary to duck in places, and knob-and-tube wiring was strung through the massive wooden joists.

Patty coughed on the dust. Bo's nose ran. Allergies, he claimed. They climbed the steps to the first floor, which was hardly cleaner than the basement, with its sagging furniture, crumbling plaster, and graffiti-covered walls. Lounging Shadows waited for assignments. It was the perfect hangout for losers.

Electric lights provided the same wan light as in the vault, only the lightbulbs didn't spew foul-smelling smoke. There was a working kitchen at the rear of the first floor. A Shadow emerged from it slurping from a steaming plate of SpaghettiOs, and changed directions to avoid the group.

"That smells good," Lisa said. "Haven't had them since I was a kid."

"You," Kazmer directed at the Shadow. "Make another plate."

"Get your own, dickhead."

Kazmer pulled the stiletto knife from his hoodie in an instant and waved it in front of the Shadow. Pressed it against his neck "The plate is for Lisa."

The Shadow bowed. "Coming right up. I'm sorry. I didn't know it was for Lisa." He put down his plate and spoon on a cluttered table and returned to the kitchen.

Kazmer stirred the SpaghettiOs with his knife tip, licked the sauce, and raised an eyebrow. "Make plate for Bo, too," Kazmer called after the retreating Shadow.

"Of course."

They climbed the stairs to the second floor. The stench of death was heavy. Some vampires preferred to keep their caskets in the house. The group walked down a hall over faded, threadbare carpet to the bathroom, which had been enlarged, and remodeled. There were two walk-in showers and two bathtubs. Two small changing rooms. One bathtub was reserved for Lisa. Still, Patty cleaned it and turned on the water to fill it. She asked Lisa to check the temperature. The Shadow returned with two steaming plates from the microwave. He handed them to Lisa and Bo. Before he retreated, Kazmer caught him by the throat. His powerful hand squeezed. The young man coughed. Struggled to breathe.

"If I see your spit in the food, I will cut out your tongue." Kazmer lifted him off the floor.

"I would never do that. Please," the Shadow choked, gasped for breath, and peed his pants.

Kazmer released the kid, who fled downstairs.

Kazmer turned to Lisa and Bo. "Enjoy." He smiled. Kazmer added as suavely as he could manage. "Bon appetite, as they say. I think it will taste well."

"Good," Bo corrected.

"Good, too," Kazmer said. After they ate, Lisa bathed and Bo showered. The group returned to the vampiress's crypt. Like other days, Kazmer went out to buy coffee for Bo and milk for Lisa. The seemingly unending days of boredom continued.

CHAPTER TWENTY-SIX

Persimmon talked to the group, but to Jimmy Young it sounded like she was in another room, her words further diluted as if by sound proofing. About every third word registered. All the Brethren and the East Coasters were assembled in the mortuary's viewing room for the latest update on the vampire colony. It was evening and everyone anticipated a vampire attack at any time. They relaxed only after dawn. After the lone vamp Farber was staked, the vampires knew the Brethren were close. The undead were as skillful as the Brethren. They had enough time to find their headquarters, no matter how careful the Brethren were.

Del Hatch sat in the back. His BAR lay across his lap. His jumpsuit pockets were filled with extra clips. More newly loaded clips balanced on his knee. The Brethren handled their loaded crossbows, the East Coasters had their primed stake guns. Mad Maggie inspected the edge of her machete. Old Harriet perched on her chair on wheels, took notes on looseleaf. Bad Nelson drew a prototype on a tablet for an advanced stake gun. Their folding chairs were arranged to cover every entrance. The mortuary's doors and windows had been reinforced. No assault would go unheard.

They would have the time to swing their weapons at any opening, fill the space with bullets, lethal bolts, and stakes, hit even blurring vampires. They could divide and cover multiple entrances at the same time.

Their tactics had been developed in Europe centuries ago, proved to be effective on the undead as far back as the Crusades. The entire group was divided into platoons. Each platoon had three tiers. After the first tier fired, the second shot. Meanwhile, the first reloaded. The third fired after the second shot and reloaded. The first shot again while the third reloaded. The Brethren, armed with enough bolts, could keep up a steady, uninterrupted fire, inflicting heavy casualties on vampires. All Brethren assembled were seasoned warriors. All had staked vampires. They knew how vampires burst into flames when they took a lethal stake to the heart. They knew how to shield their eyes from the resulting fire. They were familiar with the odor of burning vampire flesh, the stench that surrounded vampires. Each Brethren was assigned to a platoon and only shot when the platoon shot. Firing individually might mean gaps in their barrages. A split second without covering fire would allow a vamp inside their ranks, where it could decimate several Brethren with a few swipes.

As the East Coasters were taught the tactics, Del Hatch said, "It's just like the continental army fighting the British."

"Or the British fighting in that movie *Zulu*," Bad Nelson said, looking up from his drawing. "Very effective."

"And I'm the new wrinkle," Mad Maggie said, brandishing her machete. "Any fanger hits the floor, I'll mop them up, sever their heads with this baby before they can get those choppers working. Overboard George put an edge on it that's sharp as a razor. Maybe sharper." She raised a large pair of pliers with her free hand. "This is for fanger dental work. George said he'd make me a necklace. I hope I have the time to pull teeth before they burn."

The group laughed.

Jimmy Young sat alone at the edge of the group. He was

unarmed, although one of Bad Nelson's stake guns lay on the floor nearby. It was not ready to fire. The sudden laughter brought Jimmy from his reverie.

"Jimmy, you feel alright?" Persimmon asked from her spot in front of the group. Her crossbow leaned against a nearby chair. She wore a Bowie knife on one hip, a 9mm holstered on the other.

Jimmy had thought about his road to the West Coast. It began as a troubled alcoholic, passed out in the gutter in the rain, filth washing over him, gagging him. Then he met Pastor Bob Shenkel. He went to his Lutheran church. Alone in the nave he found God, covered in dazzling sunlight suddenly lighting his way through stained glass windows. Pastor Bob got him a job at a local trucking company. Jimmy worked his way up from clerk to head dispatcher. He devoted his extra time to the homeless, junkies, distributing water, food, and invitations to attend church. Then he met Lisa. Their world seemed perfect. His life had turned around, until After Dark and vampires entered it.

Jimmy thought of Lisa and their times together—date night, getting caught in the rain, sharing their beds. Then Lisa went missing. The quest to find her was hopeless until the vampiress's letter to Bart turned up, a return address on the West Coast. With his new friends in tow, they drove west. Now the Brethren had taken them in. Trained them how to really fight vampires. Their success at After Dark had been a fluke. Now they had to go up against a larger colony and the ancient vampiress.

Where would it all end?

Jimmy looked at Persimmon. "I'm fine. All this mayhem is not my bag. What would happen if I shot a real person?"

The Brethren called Topsoil called across the room. "If you're talking about Shadows, it's like stepping on a bug. One of those Shadows, trying to be a man, killed my sister. Just for fun. To impress his vampire. That's how I got involved."

"They are still God's creatures. Even the Shadows," Jimmy said. "They're misguided and must be shown the right path.

There's no reason to kill them. The vampire is different. It is unholy. Already dead. There's no question about that."

"They're both unholy," Topsoil said. He stood to allow Jimmy to see him. "It's just a matter of degree. True, the vampire is closer to Satan, but the Shadow is on the vampire's shoulder. Right behind him. Waiting for the chance for his own audience with the devil."

"Still, a Shadow is a human life," Jimmy said.

"What would you do if a Shadow pointed a gun at you or put a knife to Lisa's throat or pressed the point against the baby inside her? Your baby. What would you do?"

Jimmy lowered his head. Paused a moment. "I'd have to defend myself, protect Lisa and our baby."

"You see then," Topsoil said.

"What if the vampires have innocent people in their colony— not Shadows who chose to be there, who accept that lifestyle, but those held against their will? The way it was at After Dark. I was held against my will. So was Lisa. We might have been killed if the Brethren burst into that basement."

"None of us choose to be murderers," Persimmon said. "I don't enjoy killing, although there is satisfaction in staking a vampire who would go on killing through the years, through many lifetimes, if not stopped. The ancient vampire Eva has killed thousands, possibly tens of thousands of people over the centuries. Most of them will be unknown, forever forgotten. Most of them disappeared without a trace. Their families, people who depended on them, never knew what happened."

Persimmon walked to Jimmy and placed a hand on his shoulder. "You have seen such a small amount of the evil that vampires spread. You were a victim. I was a victim. My parents were killed by vampires. My brother was killed by vampires. The Brethren took me in and trained me how to fight. I wanted to be a nurse when I was a girl. Dreamed of working in a hospital, helping people get better. That wasn't meant to be. Today I am a warrior. I lead a band of warriors. If I could snap my fingers, make this all go away, wake up tomorrow, and drive to work at a hospital, maybe a children's hospital, carry a stethoscope instead of strapping on a 9mm, I wouldn't change a thing. I know first-hand what evil the vampires represent.

"We don't always target the Shadows. They aren't much good in a fight. Those who can retreat run. Those who can't usually surrender. Even the ones with guns. They want all the glory and power they imagine a vampire has, but they don't want to take that step and risk their mortality to gain it. As far as vampire prisoners—they are usually easy to spot. Don't appear to be menacing. They cheer us on. Sometimes they tell us where a vamp is hiding." Persimmon looked around at the Brethren. "We've all been in multiple engagements with vamps. Has anyone ever misidentified someone and killed an innocent civilian? Even in the dark?"

The group was silent.

Topsoil, who had sat down, stood again. He stroked a long beard. "There's no mistaking civies for vamps. It's impossible. Civies don't move like vamps. Vamps don't beg for mercy, like Shadows, blubber about the end of their miserable lives, kneel and plead for another chance. Even when you got a vamp just where you want him and he knows he's going to get staked, all he'll do is stare at you and hiss. And if it's an old vamp who might be able to screw with your mind long enough to turn the tables, you stake the son of a bitch as fast as you can."

The group mumbled in agreement.

"What about Lisa and Bo?" Jimmy said.

"Their photos have been circulated among us," Persimmon said. "With the stories you East Coasters have told we feel we know them already. None of us will accidentally kill either."

"What if they use them as human shields?" Old Harriet said. "Or kill them out of spite?"

"That's an unknown," Persimmon said matter-of-factly.

"Unfortunately, it goes with the territory. That's why we must hit them hard and fast before they can think of such plans."

"I don't know if I can rush in there, shoot stakes all over the place," Jimmy said. "I know there will be a lot of confusion. There was at After Dark. And I was in a cage. What if I shot Lisa?"

Persimmon stared at Jimmy. "Then we'll find another job for you," she said.

CHAPTER TWENTY-SEVEN

PERSIMMON HAD GONE OVER THE ATTACK PLANS THREE TIMES. Everyone had a job, and everyone knew what to do, what was expected. The Brethren had all been through this before. Some had played the same parts before. The East Coasters were new to such complicated plans. That's the reason she repeated the entire attack three times, stressed the East Coasters roles. The Brethren were antsy to end the meeting, return to whatever they had to do that evening—laundry, call loved ones, catch up on sleep.

Persimmon looked at her notes and checked the large whiteboard at her side, where she outlined the attack. The Brethren sensed the meeting was over, were fidgety, pushed back on their folding chairs, prepared to stand. "That's about it. Any questions?" Persimmon said. She looked around the room. No one raised a hand. She checked her notes one last time. "Wait. I see we have one last item."

The group let out a collective groan.

Persimmon smiled. "Although most of you don't know it, today is special, especially to one among our ranks."

The mumbling rose again. Shoulders shrugged. Members

looked around the room, from face to face. Tomato and Topsoil had slipped from their chairs and retreated to the kitchen mostly unnoticed. The kitchen door flew open, and they emerged with a large sheet cake decorated with candles. The icing on top read *Happy Birthday Old Harriet.*

Old Harriet, perched on her chair on wheels, clapped her hands. Her lips quivered. "I don't remember when I ever got a happy birthday cake with candles. Maybe never." Tears rolled down her cheeks.

Persimmon turned the wheeled whiteboard around. Red and blue erasable marker read in large letters HAPPY BIRTHDAY OLD HARRIET!!! Old Harriet was delighted. The crowd approached Old Harriet, kissed her, and hugged her. Some even presented small gifts wrapped in bright paper.

"Is this what they think of me?" Old Harriet burst into tears again.

Tomato and Topsoil placed the cake on the table they used for food. The crowd led Old Harriet to the table. Persimmon gave her a knife to cut the cake.

"Make a wish," Persimmon said, "and blow out your candles."

Old Harriet leaned over the cake, took a huge breath, and blew. It took two such breaths to extinguish all the candles. Everyone cheered. Old Harriet smiled.

"We would have got more candles, but that's all the store had," Tomato said, hugging Old Harriet.

Persimmon led the group in singing *Happy Birthday.* Just as they reached the loudest part, *Happy Birthday, dear Harriet,* the front window glass broke. Guns fired through the mauve drapes. Bullets sprayed around the room. The whiteboard, lectern, and chairs were hit. Bullets flew into the ceiling. Cheers erupted outside. More bullets followed. One creased Tomato's shoulder. Another caught Topsoil in the groin.

Del Hatch stood, released the safety on his BAR, and fired

through the windows. The mauve drapes danced as his bullets shredded them. The outsiders screamed.

"Kill the lights," Bad Nelson screamed. Someone hit the switches.

"We can't see them," Mad Maggie called.

While Del slammed another clip into his rifle, Persimmon launched herself toward the window, took a running jump, grabbed the mauve drapes, and pulled them to the floor. She rolled away from the exterior wall. Shadows, who had regrouped after Del's volley, shot again. Del returned fire. Shadows fell. There were screams and moans. Vampires in the background encouraged their Shadows to charge. The humans scattered. The Shadow Johnson wrapped a heavy chain through the window bars and dropped out of sight. A pick-up on the lawn gunned its engine, and sped away, tires spinning, throwing up dirt. The chain snapped tight. The window bars shook. The truck fishtailed wildly across the lawn. The engine roared. The bars flew from the wall and were dragged away by the truck.

Persimmon stood. "In your ranks! Get ready to fire!"

The Brethren separated into rows. They reacted calmly and with precision, aimed their crossbows at the windows. Some pointed at the front door, which still was locked. The Brethren Tulip slipped through the viewing room's back door. "We have six Shadows coming up the ramp. Some vamps, too. They smashed the camera." About half the Brethren spun kneeled, and re-aimed their crossbows to protect the back door.

The shouting, Del Hatch's BAR, and the Shadow gunfire all stopped. The room and exterior were eerily still as if someone had asked for a moment of silence. Gun smoke hung in the air, making the room hazy. Persimmon looked at the ceiling and noted the errant bullet holes, barely visible in the emergency lighting that had kicked on. A bullet had hit one of the speakers that pumped recorded organ music into the room for funerals. Persimmon had activated the switch accidentally when she hit the lights. Organ music, "Onward Christian Soldiers," crackled lowly through the damaged speaker. A grandfather clock ticked in the hall, seemed too loud. Then it chimed the quarter hour.

Everyone remained focused on the three entrances—the front window, now missing the bars the Brethren had installed, the front door, and the rear door. Del Hatch checked the action on his BAR and loaded a new clip as silently as possible. All eyes shifted to him for a second and returned to their targets. Del grinned, as if he apologized for the noise, sweated profusely, and shifted the rifle's weight while he dried his palms on his powder blue jumpsuit. Breathing in the room was deep and measured. They waited in the near darkness, in the calm, for the attack's next phase.

That's when the whimpering started. It came from within the room, grew louder in increments, and turned to a wail. During the attack, the BAR's roar, the gunfire from outside, the Shadows' screams, the mauve drapes grabbing, the blackout, Old Harriet tried to save her cake that still held yellow candles poked in the icing. She tripped on a wrinkle in the carpet and fell on the table. The cake slid to the floor and broke apart. Old Harriet tumbled on top. She stood now sobbing. Cake covered her face, her clothes, and her hair. It was in her eyes and ears. The sweet icing was smeared all over. She shoveled chunks into her mouth between sobs.

"It's so damn good," Old Harriet bawled.

Overboard George and Bad Nelson, moved her to cover. Turned over the chair on wheels and put her behind it. Brushed clumps of cake from her.

"We might be able to save some of it for you," Overboard George said. "If not, we'll get another just as good."

While Old Harriet screamed, no one noticed the Shadows, with help from the vampires and their strength, breached the mortuary door and were about to explode into the viewing room from the back. Meanwhile, Shadows had assembled outside the front window, prepared to vault inside the viewing room from the front, their weapons reloaded. Vampires would follow.

From her crouching position behind Old Harriet's overturned cake table, Persimmon wished they had another way to escape, undetected by the vamps. *Live to fight another day*, she mused. They didn't have another exit. Their second hideout a mile away would. However, it might be better to face the vamps head-on. Kill as many as possible tonight. Keep Brethren casualties at a minimum and fight a reduced force later, before the vamps regrouped, while they were still reeling from this defeat.

With Old Harriet quiet, the stillness returned. The organ music stopped. The speaker had finally failed. Tomato, with a superficial shoulder wound, waited to turn on the lights, a surprise the vamps wouldn't expect. Topsoil was treated by Brethren medics in a triage set up in a corner. The bullet he took passed through him. Blood loss had stopped. He received plasma through a needle in his arm. Although he couldn't handle a crossbow, he was propped up, holding a .45 caliber 1918 CAP in his free hand. Extra clips lay at his side. He planned to take out as many gun-wielding Shadows as possible. After all, he might kill the one who shot him.

The silence continued. Occasionally, someone inside coughed or cleared a throat. There was no reason to stifle it now. Their positions were known. The grandfather clock sounded the quarter hour again, a few modulating dongs. Overboard George let out a loud sigh everyone heard.

Outside a walkie-talkie crackled. Someone said, "Now!"

Shadows spilled over the front windowsill, shouted, and fired their guns. The rear door burst open, and more Shadows entered and opened fire. Tomato hit the lights. Shadows screamed in confusion. The Brethren returned fire in both directions, cut down Shadows, and wounded others, who dropped their guns and limped toward the exits. The larger group fired on the front lawn and hit vampires. Some shrieked in shock. Two took lethal bolts, burst into flames, and set the dry grass outside aflame. The Brethren fired volley after volley with deft precision and caught two more vampires blurring through the front windows. They erupted in flames, and sailed through the air in fireballs, scattering glowing embers that ignited the mauve drapes on the floor. The dry-rotted material flamed up and caught the carpet on fire. A conflagration started. The room filled with smoke quickly. Del Hatch shot from the hip. His BAR roared. The 30.06-caliber, armor-piercing bullets destroyed what was left of the security bars, and ripped through the exterior wall. Shredded vehicles are parked on the street. Topsoil killed Shadows inside and outside the room.

The smaller attack at the rear door was over quickly. Two Shadows dead. Two vampires were reduced to ash piles. The rest fled in terror.

Sirens wailed in the distance and grew louder. It seemed they were on a fast track to the old funeral home. The attack ended abruptly. Vampires blurred away into the night, leaving their Shadows to fend for themselves. Before dispersing, Shadows slashed tires in the funeral home parking lot, stranding the Brethren, they thought. Some vehicles were already disabled. The Brethren's best cars were parked away from the funeral home.

The front room was soon an inferno. Black smoke roiled across the ceiling. The intense heat spread the fire. The Brethren escaped through the back, and took what weapons and ammunition they could carry. Some conducted a body count. The total dead: six vampires—finally, really dead, as Old Harriet exclaimed—nine Shadows, names unknown, two Brethren, Topsoil, who took a round in the head from one of the last fleeing Shadows to leave the room, and Spinach, who was shot several times. Shadows killed outside were thrown back into the raging fire inside. The Brethren dead were pulled outside, and picked up by other members. Everyone escaped ahead of police, paramedics, and firetrucks, headed for their second safe house a mile away.

CHAPTER TWENTY-EIGHT

Survivors of the funeral home attack crammed into available vehicles and fled to the Brethren safe house. They attended to the injured and dead and carried weapons and supplies salvaged from the funeral home. The cars were scattered around the neighborhood to prevent Shadows from targeting them. There were Brethren, recent arrivals, guarding the new safe house. Those who had survived vampire captivity—Overboard George, Mad Maggie, Bad Nelson—were already legends and the new Brethren were eager to introduce themselves and hear the East Coasters' stories in person.

"We'd sing happy birthday again for you Old Harriet, but seeing what happened an hour ago we better save it," Peach said. She was among the new Brethren at the safe house. She was tall, blonde, blue-eyed. She looked like a surfer. However, she carried an AR instead of a surfboard.

"I don't mind," Old Harriet said. "A birthday's just one day out of the year. It was the thought that was touching, everybody was thinking of me. That poor cake. It was a dandy."

A Brethren member announced the fire was on the ten o'clock

news. Everyone gathered in front of the flat-screen television in the ranch home's living room.

The flaming former funeral home was visible on screen, a jumpy cell phone video supplied by Bargain Videos. The news anchor said authorities suspected arson. Numerous pops had been reported, either gunshots or possibly propane tanks. The place was an inferno. Firefighters could do little other than watch the building burn. They spent their energy protecting neighboring properties. The investigation would continue. Nothing was said about people outside or bodies found in the rubble.

"That was some fire," Old Harriet said. She smoothed down her frizzy hair and cleaned cake from her face with a towel. It was then she remembered her chair on wheels had remained at the funeral home and now probably was reduced to ashes. She burst into tears again. "Didn't anybody remember to bring my chair on wheels? It was the only thing I could call my own. Jimmy always took care of my chair on wheels." Old Harriet twisted her face. "Anybody see Jimmy Young?"

Everyone looked around the room. Overboard George called his name. Persimmon flew down the steps to the basement, where there were beds for the wounded, and cots in makeshift barracks for the fighters. She returned in a moment, shaking her head, a scared look on her face. The fighters from the funeral home were separated from the group and asked what cars they were in and with whom they drove. No one had seen Jimmy, alive or dead.

Everyone assembled and crowded into the living room. There was a long silence. This hideout was different from the sprawling funeral home. The rancher had smaller windows, already barred, reinforced doors, and a basement as large as the house was upstairs. Only one-and-one-half bathrooms for so many people. The kitchen was small. In the morning, the Brethren would inventory supplies and weapons, make orders, and begin the search for another backup safe house.

Bad Nelson raised a hand. He had been working on repairing a damaged stake gun. "I remember Jimmy leaving the meeting. He went through the back door before the birthday cake came out. I figured he went for a...leak. Maybe wanted some privacy after the meeting and everything. All that food."

"I can't believe we left Jimmy there," Persimmon said. "We don't do that kind of thing." The crowd grumbled. She pounded a fist in her open palm. She thought a moment. "I'm going back. I'll drive around and walk around a bit. Pretend I'm a vlogger doing my thing."

"I'll go with you," Bad Nelson said. "I feel responsible."

"It's not your fault," Persimmon said. "I'm going alone. There wasn't time for a head count. The police would have been hot on our trail."

"What if there are vamps or Shadows still in the neighborhood?" Overboard George said.

"I know how to blend in," Persimmon said. "Other than fighting, that's what I do best. I'll be seen but not noticed. If Jimmy's in hiding, he can reappear and we'll book it out of there. I need a gimble, so I look like a legit vlogger, and keys for Del's SUV. Jimmy might recognize it."

Persimmon drove back to the funeral home, parked as close to the police line as possible, and surveyed the scene from inside the SUV. A late-arriving TV station reporter was setting up an interview with the sweat-soaked fire chief for a live feed. Her cameraman panned over the still flaming building—now mostly collapsed—and returned to her face. She, meanwhile, fixed her hair and looked at her makeup in a small mirror. An all-news radio station reporter interviewed a cop down the block. There was good illumination from flood, street, and headlights in the area. Vamps were not good at hiding themselves. They had a tendency to stand awkwardly in plain view. Shadows were a little better and seldom stayed in the shadows.

Persimmon attached the gimble to her cell phone, turned on the device, and exited the car. "Hey all," she crooned into the phone as if vlogging while she walked. "It's Little Livey Live here for another fire. How many have there been this week? I'm at the point where I think I'll take some stock footage and just show that every night, instead of crawling down here to the scene. Just kidding. I know you want to see the real thing, and that's what I'm here for, the details no one else sees. But I suppose a fire is better than a shooting. How many of them have we had?"

Persimmon walked by a policeman. She pointed toward the fire as if asking for a closer vantage point, but he shook his head no. She walked on. "I love a man in uniform. I'd love him more if he acquiesced. For those of you who don't know what that means and are too cheap to own a dictionary, it means I'd give him my phone number if he let me duck under the tape for a few minutes. You know what happens when a man in uniform gets *my* number.

"Laugh on, Mr. Policeman. You had your chance. Let's try over this way for a better view of this great conflagration. Another good dictionary word. Stick with me, dear viewers, and I will make you a smarter person."

Persimmon swiveled the phone off her face to the surroundings. She thought the video might pick up someone in the dark her eyes didn't catch. She meandered through the crowd of onlookers, some in pajamas or holding cans of beer, toward a tree line near the funeral home parking lot. She kept the loud banter going.

"Friends, viewers, countrymen, we have lots to catch up on after I get back to my *studio* for our weekly live gabfest. You won't want to miss it. I want to tell you about my new boyfriend. His name begins with the letter B, but his name isn't Bob. It's shorter than Bob. But he isn't if you know what I mean. He has a mole on his...well, you'll want to know where it is. I have a photo I might share if I have a big turnout. It's a cute mole, really, not a hideous one that turns into skin cancer. It doesn't sprout hair or anything like a witch's mole."

Persimmon walked and talked until she was out of earshot. Most seemed to pay no attention to her. She approached the trees, and started again, this time louder, singing. "I have another boyfriend named Jimmy. That's J-I-M-M-Y. Don't know what happened to him. Don't know where he is. He done disappeared on me during the middle of a fight. We weren't the ones fighting, of course, he and I. We were fighting with other people. Wish I had Jimmy back right now. I have a new place he'd want to see that's safe." She continued to shoot video into the darkness and talk. No one stirred.

Finally, she returned to the SUV, and drove up and down one block after another, hoping to see Jimmy, who did not know where the safe house was. He was a stranger in a foreign city that had gangs, murderers, rapists, illegal aliens, Shadows, and vampires. He was alone, on foot, weaponless, and did not have even a street map. And, Persimmon thought, he couldn't fight his way out of a wet paper bag. Persimmon started over, and drove through the same neighborhoods again. Would he recognize Del's SUV? Did he have money and his cell phone? Could he find a corner with street signs and call an Uber? Then where would he go?

At 4 A.M., Persimmon returned to the safe house. The night guard poured her coffee. Her head pounded. She wanted to cry but wouldn't allow it. The disappearance of Jimmy Young was now a bigger mystery than the whereabouts of Lisa Van der Meer.

CHAPTER TWENTY-NINE

Johnson had taken a bolt through one butt cheek and out the other during the raid on the Brethren. It was said among the Shadows, and the vampires laughed, too, Johnson was lucky he had such a big ass, or the dart might have hit him in the hip, so Kazmer told Bo. Johnson was relieved of his Shadow duties temporarily and healed in the vampire house on the hill. About the only thing he could do comfortably was lie on his side on the rundown sofa, complete with springs that poked through misshapen cushions here and there. Getting to that position and standing was excruciating. Other wounded Shadows recuperated in rooms throughout the old house.

Bo had wash to do and was accompanied to the laundromat by Patty, who drug along Lisa's and her clothes. The normally sullen Patty was happy to get out of the vault, away from the brothers, but complained about doing laundry.

"It's bad enough I have to serve Lisa hand-and-foot, twenty-four-seven, now I have to do her wash. The next thing you know I'll be giving her baths."

"It could always be worse," Bo said as they left the mausoleum and walked up the path through the cemetery toward the wall and its broken gate. "You could be sleeping with a corpse every day."

"I wish."

"You could have been involved in the raid. If that was the case, you might not be here to do laundry. As far as I see, Lisa doesn't make many demands on you." They each pulled a wire basket on little wheels behind them with dirty clothes.

Patty pulled a snub-nosed .38-caliber revolver from her hoodie pocket, waved it around, aimed at various tombstones, and said, "Pow. Pow. Pow. I should have been there. I would have taken some of the Brethren down. They're not so special. No different than we are. That's what Fagan said."

"Is that thing loaded?"

"Of course. Why wouldn't it be? Eva gave it to me this morning. Said she took it off a Mexican she drained last night."

"Don't point it at me and take your finger off the fucking trigger unless you're going to shoot. If you shoot me accidentally—"

"If I shoot you, it won't be an accident, Bo. It'll get you right here." She touched the gun hammer to her forehead. She put the revolver back in her pocket.

"You have extra ammo to go with it?"

"Not yet, but I'm getting some. You'll see. I'll be in the thick of things on the next raid. Soon as we figure out where the Brethren moved. That won't be hard. We have parties looking now, going block by block. Meanwhile, Fagan turned three Shadows, the most loyal, the longest serving. Their cocoons are hanging in a little chamber in the vault. They should emerge in a few days."

"This is the most I ever heard you talk, Patty."

"I'm pumped. Every time a Shadow gets turned, I move up the seniority list."

Patty's laundry basket cartwheels squeaked. Bo and Patty fell silent. They rounded a curve in the asphalt road. Several used needles littered the road. Her cart's little wheels jumped over the needles, and the cart itself rocked from side to side. Ahead to their left the cemetery was flat, treeless, and newer looking with all ground-level headstones. A crying woman knelt at a new grave covered with fresh flowers. Nearby was a mound of leftover dirt. Bo stopped. He could hear the woman's sobs. Patty made a face and grabbed Bo's arm to hurry him along. Bo shook his arm free, left the laundry cart standing on the road, and walked toward the woman.

"Get back here," Patty hissed. She crouched as if to project her voice more.

Bo looked back a moment and continued. Patty abandoned her cart, ran after Bo, grabbed his arm again, this time harder, and spun him around.

"Leave her alone, Bo. You can't bring back the dead."

"I want to talk to her. Tell her it's not safe here."

"You going to tell her this is vampire territory?"

"Something like that, but not exactly."

"I want to leave." Patty stared at Bo.

"Go ahead. I'll catch up. I'm not taking off on you."

Patty reached into her hoodie pocket. "That's what this is for. To make sure you don't run. *She* told me to use it, if necessary. There's a lot going on in the colony. You would be expendable when it comes to our secrets."

"Did you ever lose anybody close?"

"No. I never been close to anybody."

"Well, I was. My younger brother. We called him Boo. Died of a drug overdose. He was still in high school. He died under the football stadium bleachers with a needle in his arm. I want to show her a little compassion." Bo stared back. "You can wait here or go. Either way, I'll catch up."

Bo pulled his arm free and walked toward the woman. Patty maneuvered their carts off the road and waited. She kept a hand inside her hoodie pocket on the gun. She would kill them both if necessary. Bo approached the woman and startled her when his shadow crossed the grave. She stood suddenly and faced Bo. Her eyes darted toward Patty and the carts. Then back to Bo. She relaxed.

"Sorry. I didn't want to scare you."

"I don't have any money. I didn't expect anyone would be around."

"That's not it. I only wanted to say I'm sorry for your loss."

"My father. I was out of town on business when he died. It was a long assignment—so long he was buried before I got back. I always checked in on him regularly. He was healthy. He was just at the doctor's, and got a clean bill of health. I don't understand how things like this happen."

The woman wore a white blouse, floppy straw hat, and tan slacks with knees muddy and grass-stained. "Thank you for stopping. I appreciate the kind words."

"I know something about tragedy. My younger brother got mixed up with drugs, nobody knew, and I was away at college. He overdosed."

"I'm sorry," the woman said. She reached over and touched Bo's arm. "The cemetery was supposed to haul that dirt away, but—as you can see—nobody did. I wanted to clean up the grave a little. I suppose I'll just sit here for a while."

"That's the other thing," Bo said. He looked back at Patty and lowered his voice. "This isn't a safe place. You shouldn't be here alone, not even during the day."

"I haven't seen anyone until you walked up."

"It's a big cemetery. Junkies shoot up here. Gangs roam day and night. Then there are the lone criminals. I'd advise you to leave soon. I'd stay with you, but I have things to do."

"I see your girlfriend is getting antsy."

"She's not my girlfriend. I know her and we happened to be on the way to the laundromat. Started walking together. I have her detergent in my basket. It's a big bottle and it's heavy."

The woman smiled. "I'll take your advice and leave in a few minutes."

"That makes me feel better," Bo said.

"It was nice meeting you, Bo." She winked.

"Now wait." Bo looked confused. "I didn't tell you my name."

"It doesn't matter. You better go. Your Shadow is waiting."

Bo and Patty arrived at the laundromat. Patty got a soda from the vending machine and took a big slug. "You made us late, asshole. You can start my laundry and your precious Lisa's. I'm going outside for a smoke."

"Can't wait to sniff your undies."

"Pervert. Smell them all you want." Patty snarled and walked outside.

Bo loaded his and the vampiress's clothes into separate washers. Touching her corpse in repose was bad enough. He didn't want his clothes washed with hers. Then he separated Lisa's and Patty's wash and started them. Patty sat on the sidewalk outside the front window. Bo could see her head and its parted red hair through the glass, watching the plastic Mountain Dew bottle lift when she took a swig. A trail of thin cigarette smoke rose, encircled her head like a crown, and eventually climbed upward until it disappeared. Patty looked relaxed. Her cigarette pack and lighter rested beside her head on the windowsill. Persimmon passed Patty, and darted into the laundromat. Persimmon pretended to check clothing in an empty dryer. Patty followed Persimmon through the window a moment and returned her gaze to the street.

Persimmon smiled at Bo. "I got a call. I understand you met Gold."

"Gold?"

"It's short for Goldenrod. She's one of us." Persimmon walked away from Bo and took a seat across from the imaginary clothes she dried.

After Patty swiveled her head to check on Bo again, Bo said, "So she wasn't mourning her father."

Persimmon shook her head no. "Vamps killed her dad years ago. The fresh grave was convenient."

"I told her the cemetery wasn't safe."

"She knows. She's packing. She has three black belts. Could kill anything—excluding maybe a vamp at night—that comes her way. She thought you were cute, but I told her I have the first crack at you."

Bo smiled nervously. Patty's head was missing outside the window. "I don't see her."

Persimmon stood, walked to the window, and pretended to check the weather. "She's at the apartment building next door talking to some dude. She took her smokes and lighter."

"I have more news," Bo said. "Can she hear us?"

"No way. It's safe."

"From what I picked up since the raid, the vampires think they scored a victory, despite their losses. They think most of the Brethren were shot by the Shadows, died in the fire, or were arrested by police. They think the Shadows slashed all your tires, eliminated any way to escape."

"Police aren't saying much," Persimmon said matter-of-factly. "Probably don't know what's going on. Can't explain it."

"The vampires think the threat is mostly over but remain on alert. Fagan turned three of his senior Shadows. They're in cocoons now, in the vault. The vamps have reduced the goon watch outside. They don't have the numbers anyway. All their efforts are directed to finding the new Brethren stronghold."

"Good to know, Bo. We'll be extra careful with our comings and goings. That's all I'll tell you. The less you know the better." Persimmon paused and looked around the laundromat. "It's strange. It seems there's never anybody here when I come in."

"I don't think the people in this neighborhood roll out of bed until noon. It gets busy late afternoon and at night. That's why we try to get here early." Persimmon stepped closer, looked into his eyes, and touched his arm. "I better go before she comes back. Thanks again for the intel."

Bo pressed several pages into Persimmon's hands. "Here's some maps I drew. They're not to scale but pretty close. Any idea when you're going to make your move?"

"Sooner than later."

"Lisa is big. The vampires go crazy when she passes. Sniffing the air. Twirling their tongues. The Shadows are building something in the vault. It looks like some of them know carpentry. They bring in wood almost every day."

"An altar for the ceremony, the vampire black mass."

CHAPTER THIRTY

Bad Nelson sat on a basement cot in the Brethren's new stronghold the morning after vampire raid on the mortuary. He waited for glue to dry on one of his PVC stake guns that was damaged in the fight. It was dropped, kicked, and stepped on. Bad Nelson blew on the glue that reattached the gun's trigger guard. Only three of his original eight guns survived. Five were left behind at the funeral home in the raid's confusion and fire. The Brethren gathered up their crossbows and bolts, some food, before everyone fled. They didn't bother about Bad Nelson's guns, which they deemed inferior to the technologically advanced crossbows the Brethren carried. The stakes fired were slow moving, but the East Coasters knew the converted potato guns were effective and had rid the world of the ancient vampire Gerrard, and one of the fiends in the attack last night. Still, the Brethren said their crossbows didn't require priming combustion chambers, hoping there was enough propane in the canisters for another shot, finding another canister to change when one emptied. The crossbows were just load, cock, aim, and fire. The bolts were faster and more accurate.

Still, the East Coasters preferred Bad Nelson's models, despite their clunkiness. That is what they were accustomed to.

Bad Nelson thought of Megan, his high school girlfriend, safe back on the East Coast. They would have been married years ago. Her children would have been *their* kids if alcohol and homelessness hadn't intervened, been the cause of their separation. Now he, like Jimmy Young, was sober. Bad Nelson and Megan were an item again. She had remained on the East Coast while Bad Nelson decided to help his friends rescue Lisa, a woman he barely knew. He understood what Lisa went through. Bad Nelson had been a captive of the vampiress and Gerrard at After Dark. On the day he was to be strung upside down and his blood drained he played dead. The vampires' Shadow, Charles Van der Meer, had kicked him and beat him with a baseball bat until he was almost senseless, but Bad Nelson never made a sound, not the slightest movement. Charles dumped a naked Bad Nelson on the street, thinking he had died in captivity. He would look like another casualty of homelessness, the victim of a fight among city tent dwellers who even stole the clothes off his corpse. As soon as he was able, Bad Nelson stood and shakily walked away from After Dark. He returned to his parents' home, and immediately began work modifying PVC guns to shoot stakes instead of potatoes. Bad Nelson no longer wanted to work for Winchester making guns, he wanted to slay vampires.

No matter how busy their schedules were, Bad Nelson and Jimmy Young, the East Coasters' resident alcoholics, had managed to find a quiet place together to talk about their feelings. Both missed the women they loved. At times both had an unquenchable thirst for alcohol. They helped each other through these feelings and even managed to attend a few AA meetings inside the city.

Jimmy felt the worst of it. Whereas Bad Nelson could reach Megan almost anytime, accounting for her work schedule at After Dark and their time differences, Jimmy was left to worry about Lisa. He knew her life inside the vampire colony was always in peril. The Brethren had compiled profiles on the vampiress, Eva, and Fagan, similar to ones the FBI might build during an investigation. The other vampires were lesser known, newer to the disease. The profiles predicted how they might act in various situations—cornered on gluttonous rampages or starved for blood.

Now Jimmy Young was gone, too. Was he a vampire captive again, or killed in the raid, unaccounted for, perhaps wounded and suffering somewhere near the old mortuary?

The Brethren didn't know about the East Coasters' addictions. The topic had never come up. They had been too busy planning against the vampires. The Brethren had a strict policy about using drugs and alcohol in the field. The East Coasters decided—Overboard George and Bad Nelson—to set things straight. Finally, as a group meeting was ready to adjourn, Overboard George asked for the floor.

"We've all been together for a little while now," Overboard George said in a halting voice. He cleared his throat several times, and walked to the center of the living room in the rancher they now called home. "We've learned how some of you got involved with the Brethren. It's all very interesting. But I suppose you don't know much about us—other than the fact that most of us were held captive by the vampires on the East Coast."

"It's not important, OG," one of the Brethren said.

"I beg your indulgence a minute," Overboard George continued. "I know we all have things to do. I hope we don't need another safe house, but if we do I pray it has more than one-and-a-half bathrooms." The crowd agreed.

Old Harriet said, "Especially the way you make one bathroom off-limits for a while after you use it. We could use a bathroom with a bigger exhaust fan."

George looked perplexed until the laughter died. "We—the East Coasters—decided you should know most of us have addictions, with the exception of Del Hatch.

"And I'm an alcoholic," Bad Nelson said. He stood and raised his hand. "If he were here, Jimmy Young would want you to know he's an alcoholic, too."

"I'm a junkie, heroin user," Overboard George said.

"Me, too," Old Harriet said. "I'm not proud of it, but it's true. To tell the truth, I'd pull out my hair for a fix right now. If I had the stuff I'd shoot up right in front of you all."

Maggie stepped forward. She fingered the edge of her machete blade. "I'm not a user but I am crazy—have mental issues. I suppose I always have. That's why they call me *mad*. So, now you know."

"Mad Maggie and me are hunted by the law for past crimes," Overboard George said. "The others ain't. We're not public enemy number one, but Maggie and I would probably go to jail if the cops got their hands on us. That's why we like to lay low. Keep our real names under wraps."

The Brethren were silent and looked at one another.

"One thing I can tell you," Overboard George said, glancing around the room, pounding a fist into his palm, "none of us has had a fix or one drop of alcohol since we started this quest to free Lisa— and now we know they have Bo, too, maybe Jimmy Young—and none of us will use until they're free. I hope to God we stay on the right path all the days of our lives, with God's help. If you don't want us, don't trust us in a fight with the vampires and those Shadows, just say the word and we'll move out and go back to fighting the undead ourselves. This ain't over yet."

The group remained silent, motionless. Persimmon approached Overboard George and patted his arm. "I'm glad you came forward. We all are. Some members asked about your backgrounds since you joined us, suspected some were addicts. They knew what to watch for. As long as you follow our rules you are all welcome."

"I have Megan back home, along with her two boys to raise," Bad Nelson said. "I'll never raise another drink. And Jimmy and Lisa have a baby on the way. I know how he feels. He's been sober longer than I have."

"This is the longest I ever been clean," Overboard George said.

"I like the feel of it. I hope one day Mad Maggie and I can be a part of the Brethren. Seems like we've been fighting vampires all our lives, one way or another."

Everyone looked at Old Harriet. "I sure miss my chair on wheels. Ain't too many chairs that get to travel across the nation, have such a nice, padded seat, real leather too, and fancy scrolling. Made me feel all hoity-toity when I sat on it."

There was a long silence. "If there's no other business, the meeting is adjourned," Persimmon said.

Before anyone could move, Old Harriet said, "This is usually the point where the vampires break in."

The home's back door did fly open. The group gasped. Goldenrod walked in. She was begrimed with soot. Dropped a bag on the floor. Someone offered her a bottle of water. She took a big chug. Persimmon waited patiently. Smiled.

"Just came from the mortuary. Helped the cops look for victims."

"How?" Persimmon said, shaking her head.

"Told the cops I was looking for my mom's ashes in an urn. That the funeral home still had them."

The group laughed.

Gold took another swig from the water bottle. "They were done with the evidence gathering, so they let me poke around. They found nine bodies inside and outside the mortuary—Shadows. Some were blown apart, hardly recognizable. Others were burned bad."

"That would be the BAR's work," Dell Hatch said.

Gold smiled at Del and continued. "I counted six ash piles—vamps—that they wouldn't recognize, along with some assorted jewelry. Rings Pendants. Pretty nasty stuff."

"Do they have a cause in mind?" Overboard George said.

"Gangbangers. Drugs. Money. That's what they're saying," Gold said.

"What are they thinking?" Persimmon said.

"Gangbangers. Drugs. Money. Maybe they were starting a meth lab, were stupid, and blew up the place. I asked the guy in charge if he thought a staked vampire caused the fire."

"Gold!" Persimmon said.

"Just to get a reaction. There was none. It'll go down as gang-related."

"That's good for us," Persimmon said.

"One more thing," Gold said. She retrieved the bag she had dropped and removed two ornate chair legs. "Old Harriet, I thought these would make a couple of dandy stakes. All you need are some sharp points."

"I'll get on the points," Overboard George said.

Old Harriet took the chair legs, one in each hand. There was a tear in her eye. "My chair on wheels lives."

CHAPTER THIRTY-ONE

Jimmy Young sat in one of two men's room stalls in the mortuary, an employee bathroom off the hall between the back door and the embalming room. A ceiling fan hummed, starting immediately after he turned on the overhead lights when he walked in. A lower-pitched fan started somewhere and pumped in cool air from the A/C. Chalk up another one for the Brethren. They ate well and maintained clean bathrooms. While he sat, his jeans around his ankles, Jimmy's mind returned to this raid on the vampire colony that was planned.

He thought there were too many undead to confront. Too many unknowns. The place was too large. Vampire Shadows were armed, even if they weren't marksmen. They could do damage. Make some lucky shots. Jimmy thought the Brethren were too cavalier, despite their experience with the undead. Now that contact was made with Bo at the laundromat, Jimmy thought a better plan would be for Bo and Lisa to slip away during daylight hours when the vampires were in their caskets and the unsuspecting Shadows lounged around lazily. They could have a car waiting inside the cemetery, the doors open, ready to speed away. Lisa and Jimmy would flee back east in his car. Get her to a doctor. The Brethren could attack the colony when their plans were formed. The so-called East Coasters could join him and Lisa or the Brethren. A frontal assault on the vampires would end in a blood bath that could get Lisa killed. If they were to move on the colony soon, Jimmy would not participate, carry a gun, or shoot at Shadows. After all, they were people.

He was not a murderer.

He wondered what job would be left for him—driver, triage nurse. He could decide to sit out the vampire campaign. Someone had to remain behind to guard the mortuary. Lisa's chances might be better without him inside the raid. He would worry about her, and she would worry about him. The slightest slip-up could mean his, her, or both of their deaths. What was even worse was the prospect that one or both of them would be recaptured by the vampires.

Jimmy Young was resolute. He made his decision as he flushed. He would not take another human life. He was undecided about killing a vampire. Only if he, Lisa, or another were threatened. Would he be able to kill one of the undead? Would he be fast enough? Would he have the courage?

Jimmy pulled up his pants, flushed again, and washed his hands. The remnants of the funeral home's liquid soap had a wonderful scent he could not place. The ceiling exhaust fan suddenly squawked higher in pitch. Must have a bad bearing, Jimmy thought. The AC still hummed. The filling toilet was loud. The pipes were noisy. Water splashed in the sink as he soaped his hands again, pumped the dispenser a few times, to relish the soap's aroma one more time, and raised his palms to his nose.

Jimmy cocked his head. Sounded like several pops. He turned off the sink water to hear better. The toilet finally filled and was silent. The AC shut down. Despite the howling exhaust fan, which had now grown louder in an apparent death throe, Jimmy heard more pops.

"Now what?" he mouthed silently. "I hope to God it's not champagne. I thought these guys didn't drink on duty."

More pops erupted. Then there were shouts. "That's gunfire," Jimmy said, this time aloud.

Jimmy turned toward the door. It burst open. Two lanky Shadows leveled pistols at him. Jimmy raised his arms. One Shadow pointed his weapon at Jimmy's head. Jimmy's knees shook.

"Don't shoot, man. He's the one we're after. The one *she* wants captured alive."

"Lisa's old man?"

"He's the one."

"You know what this means?"

"B-O-N-U-S."

The taller Shadow sucker-punched Jimmy in the gut. Jimmy crumpled to the floor. The Shadows grabbed him under the arms and dragged him from the bathroom. Jimmy regained his legs halfway down the corridor to the back door, but he was still doubled over. Floral-scented soap dripped from his hands.

"Got a real prize here," the taller Shadow shouted as they emerged into the night. "Got Lisa's old man."

The Shadows roared in approval. A vampire blurred to Jimmy's side, opened his mouth, and extended his fangs.

"*She* wanted this one alive," a Shadow whispered.

The vampire stepped back suddenly and closed his mouth. "Very well. We will give *her* this prize."

Meanwhile, gunfire continued. There was the pop-pop-pop of handguns and the roar of an automatic rifle, stopping only a second to reload. Panting Shadows arrived at the rear door. They were exhausted. Vampires blurred to a stop. They seemed to assess the situation. Count their decimated numbers. One by one they blurred away, leaving the Shadows. There were shouts from inside.

"We got to get out of here," said the tall Shadow holding Jimmy's arm. "Anybody got ammo left?"

No one spoke immediately. Then a woman said, "I got bullets

in my pocket, but nobody showed me how to load. I don't even know if they're the tight ones."

"All right. Back to the colony. Spread out the cars near the cemetery. Before the Brethren attack."

"Bring the wounded," a woman hollered. "Get them in the cars."

"Bag this one," the tall Shadow said. "I heard he already escaped once."

Someone produced a white plastic store bag and stuffed Jimmy's head in it. Jimmy gasped for air.

"Don't choke the man," the tall Shadow said. "We can't take her a dead body."

A woman stepped up and raised the bag above Jimmy's nose. He gulped air immediately. The female Shadow fixed the bag to cover the top of his head and eyes and tied it off tightly so it wouldn't slip.

Jimmy couldn't see. He heard car engines start. He was shoved forward, pushed roughly, and fell on another body. The person screamed in pain. "Watch it, asshole," the tall Shadow said, whose voice was now familiar.

"I can't see!" Jimmy screamed.

Someone clubbed him over the head. He was pushed toward the car's middle. A person was sitting next to him. The backseat passengers moaned. Another was placed up front. He heard the seat belt snap into place. Jimmy thought they must be injured Shadows. He couldn't understand what had happened. Cars pulled out one at a time. Then the car he was in pulled out. The driver swerved, then straightened the vehicle, as she phoned ahead. The wounded cried in pain.

"We have multiple injuries inbound. We'll need stretchers and the doc. See you at the cemetery drop off in a few."

The car accelerated. The driving became less erratic. There seemed to be little traffic at this hour—whatever time it was. The driver never braked, not for a stop sign or traffic light, but sped on. If only a cop would see and chase them.

Jimmy thought they traveled through residential neighborhoods. Every time they swung around a corner the Shadows moaned in pain. The one to his left was quiet now. Possibly dead, he thought. This was someone's child, someone's sister. He ran down all the possible relations she might have, concluding with someone's mother. It smelled as if someone's bowels let loose. They turned often. The Shadows moaned. Jimmy's head throbbed where he was clubbed. Both his shoulders were wet, probably blood from the Shadows as the bodies rocked back and forth against him. His nostrils filled with the metallic smell of blood. Finally, the car made a ninety-degree turn, slowed, possibly to navigate a tricky entrance. Slowed more, crept across a hump in the road. Must be a speed bump, Jimmy thought. They continued to drive, much slower now, rounding curves. They pulled to a stop. People outside the vehicle tugged open the doors. The bodies were pulled out.

"This one's gone!" someone said, of the woman who had rode next to Jimmy.

"I need a tourniquet STAT!" a man called from another vehicle.

"Get a stretcher over here!"

"Is the doc here yet? Is that his car?"

"I haven't seen him."

"Quiet everyone."

Jimmy was pulled roughly from the car.

"Looks like this one has a head wound,"

"That's a prisoner," the familiar Shadow voice said.

Jimmy was cuffed again. Left to stand by himself. He leaned against a fender. His wet shirt was sticky and seemed glued to his skin. He hoped the blood wasn't his. He felt cold in the light breeze. Suddenly, he could smell the soap from the mortuary bathroom. *Lilacs. That's what it is.* Jimmy sobbed, wondering whether he would see Lisa, even for an instant, before he died. He prayed that they would kill him and not turn him into one of the undead to fight his friends and kill others through the ages. And if he were turned, he hoped one of his East Coasters would shoot a wooden stake through his heart. Use one of Bad Nelson's guns.

"We have a prisoner."

The murmur of a prisoner circulated among the Shadows in hushed tones.

"We need more help. People to carry stretchers."

The tall Shadow returned to Jimmy. Shoved him. "I can carry a stretcher," Jimmy said. "Please, take off this blindfold."

"Why would you help us?"

"We're all God's children. I don't expect to see the outside again. I can help. Please take off the blindfold. I don't want to stand here helpless when people are wounded."

"We need a stretcher carrier," a woman called. Her voice was loud, strained.

The tall Shadow leaned in. Jimmy smelled his fetid breath. "This won't help your cause."

"I understand."

The Shadow placed his hand over Jimmy's head and roughly yanked off the plastic bag. Jimmy was not ready for the carnage. Shadows lay about with temporary bloody bandages. Some moaned. Others cried. The uninjured moved among the wounded. Emptied vehicles pulled out, turned around, and drove away. The smell of car exhaust hung in the air. Some Shadows were useless. Stood dazed or squatted to vomit.

"Over there." The tall Shadow pushed Jimmy toward a stretcher waiting to be moved.

The cemetery was pitch black. There was no moon. A few Shadows with flashlights waved the beams back and forth, causing shadows that seemed to jump. Jimmy approached the stretcher. The Shadow on it was unconscious. Jimmy nodded to the other stretcher bearer. He ignored Jimmy. They lifted together and started the trek along a barely noticeable path in the tall grass. The lead bearer was silent. Jimmy thought about dropping his end and running. In a moment all the reasons not to run became apparent. He didn't know the cemetery. He could trip in the dark. The Shadow at the other end of the stretcher was packing and might shoot him. In a lawless city, gunfire was common and would go unnoticed and unreported. Foremost in his mind was the chance to see Lisa. The Brethren might move up their timetable to attack. Suddenly, the assault looked different as a captive from the inside.

"You still there?" the Shadow stretcher bearer said. "You strike me as a talker."

"I didn't know you wanted to chat."

"I don't, but when a person isn't talking he's usually thinking, making plans, up to no good. You drop your end and take off and I'll shoot you in the back. I don't care what a prize you are. We're going to drop this one off and go back for another."

Jimmy had already nixed the escape-at-night plan. They rounded a curve and approached a row of mausoleums. A faint light shined from one where the door was open. Two Shadows stood on the steps and guided the stretcher through the crypt and up a passage to a large, beehive-like vault. Other wounded were already on tables, attended to by Shadows. The Shadows seemed nervous, and worked frantically on their friends, unaccustomed to seeing so many casualties among their own. Several vampires stood in a cluster, their heads raised toward the ceiling, their tongues swirling around their mouths. Two had received what would have been mortal wounds for a human. One bullet hole was in the vampire's head. Jimmy watched the vampire heal. Hair and skin grew over the large entry wound. An ear was just about reconstructed. An already reconstructed eyeball slid across the man's face and into its socket.

Jimmy and the Shadow placed the wounded man on a table. The man convulsed. The Shadow pushed the stretcher at Jimmy, and jerked his head, indicating they would return to the cemetery for another victim. They moved toward the vault's exterior door.

The stretcher was heavy. Jimmy looked at the high ceiling and noted bats flying in circles above. The air inside the vault, despite its size, was fetid. Jimmy wondered whether it always smelled like this or did the stink come from the wounded. The Shadow told Jimmy to hurry. Jimmy complained the stretcher was heavy. The Shadow grabbed an end. As they walked toward the entrance, Jimmy glanced around the walls. He saw the interior door. That must lead to the old house on the hill he had heard about. Other smaller vaults were carved into the walls. His eyes caught a trail dug into the wall. He followed it to the top, where there was a larger door covered with a curtain. Two figures stood on a stoop outside the curtained door. They were Lisa and Bo.

CHAPTER THIRTY-TWO

THE LAST OF THE WOUNDED SHADOWS WERE BROUGHT INTO the vampire vault, gently set on makeshift tables where the torch light was strongest. Some moaned. Some cried. Some shrieked in pain. Those with a modicum of medical knowledge ministered to the injured. There were broken bones, bullet, bolt, and stake holes, burns, even a twisted ankle. There was little the nurses could do other than apply bandages to stop bleeding and console the injured. A growing number of Shadows and vampires collected around the triage. The Shadows hugged one another, cried about their friends' wounds, tried to account for those who were missing. The vampires' heads lolled. They sniffed the air. Their tongues swirled. They were intoxicated with the smell of so much blood in the air.

Johnson lay on his stomach grimacing. Someone had pulled down his pants to reveal his bare ass, entry and exit wounds across both cheeks. Although he was bandaged and the blood loss stemmed, Johnson was weak and in pain. His forehead rested on his arms. Occasionally he turned his head to look at his neighbors, assess their wounds. There were severe wounds that required medical attention beyond what the Shadows could provide. Bones had to be set. Medicine administered, especially pain meds. The humans spoke in hushed voices, as if they were visiting a hospital room and didn't want the wounded to learn their prognoses. The vampires swirled their tongues. The wounded moaned. One man shrieked in pain every time his wound was touched, but pressure was necessary to stop the blood flow and he writhed on the table.

Fagan and Eva arrived, back early from a night's hunt. They were surprised to see the carnage. They did not go on the raid, left it to others to conduct it. Fagan thought the attack would surprise the Brethren. They would be caught without weapons and their group destroyed. It would be a glorious night for the vampires and Shadows who participated, especially on the eve of the colony's impending black mass. Their colony would be famous. As leader, Fagan would become a legend even in Europe, even among vampires who were older than Eva. He quickly learned the Brethren were formidable. They cut down six of his vampires, killed nine Shadows, wounded more. Now the mortuary was crawling with police and firemen. The Brethren had lost two members and scattered into the night, were probably massing at a new location. Perhaps they would attack the colony, would learn about its location if they didn't already know.

Fagan looked at Eva.

"Your colony is too large," she said. "This was bound to happen." She flicked a piece of flesh off her shirt.

"There are larger colonies across the world," Fagan said.

"Yes. Among third-world populations, where *nobody* is missed. Where the peasants are not believed. *Vampires!* Don't you know that is superstition? The people are ignorant, fools." Eva folded her arms and looked over the wounded.

"Our colony has a good location, especially now among thousands of the homeless and immigrants," Fagan said. "They are superstitious. No one misses them. They would die from drug overdoses and disease anyway. We do humanity a favor. We cull the imperfect, the weak."

"They are countless and like cattle," Eva quipped. She paused and then became thoughtful. "Why should anyone care? Most humans avoid the homeless, the junkers, and despise immigrants. Still, how did the Brethren get involved? Why would they come here to hunt us? It's not like they have an advertisement in what you call the Yellow Pages."

Fagan stared at her. "You pose a good question. Why are the Brethren here? Because that's what they do. They hunt vampires. But why are they *here*? Suddenly among us. It might be related to Lisa. Perhaps they imagine they can rescue her."

"Nonsense. How would they know she exists? I think they have been watching, and planning for a long time. Since...before I brought Lisa here. They know our numbers. They watch our Shadows. They probably know where we are by now."

Fagan smirked. "Then there is Bo."

"My little rabbit?"

Fagan's eyes were two slits. "Your little rabbit has been out in the daylight. He walks around. Perhaps he made contact accidentally. Perhaps his friends have traveled west from After Dark.

Eva clapped her hands, threw back her head, and laughed. "His friends were a group of misfits, homeless themselves. How would they travel so far in such a short time? I doubt any of them have a machine to travel in."

"They might have help now," Fagan said.

The vampires sensed the tension in their leader and stopped their tongues swirling, staring uneasily at Fagan and Eva. So did the Shadows. Then one Shadow called, "Where's the doc? We need him."

Other Shadows agreed. The wounded cried for the doctor.

"Turn me, please turn me," one of the wounded called.

"Silence!" Fagan shouted.

The Shadows clustered together and stepped back.

Eva continued. "Help? Who would help such a group of... misfits? Who would believe vampires took their friend?" Eva stopped. Turned her head toward the passage to the old house. Patty emerged crying. "Help! Help! They're going to kill him! They won't stop!"

Eva blurred up the passage and stopped before two Shadows pummeling Jimmy Young, who was rolled in a ball, covered with dirt.

Fagan was at Eva's side in an instant. "What have we here?" he said.

Patty caught up and bowed before the two vampires. The two male Shadows kneeled. Jimmy Young looked up. His scalp was cut. Blood covered his bruised face.

"This is Lisa's man," Patty said. "He was with the Brethren. He was captured at their fortress."

The vampiress cupped her hand under Patty's chin and lifted her to her feet. "Were you injured during the fight?"

"No, mistress. I was here. Not one of the lucky ones who went."

"Indeed."

Patty's eyes filled with tears. Her lower lip quivered.

The vampiress pulled Patty to her, sniffed her, and patted her red hair. "Don't be afraid, Patty. You have done well."

The vampiress nodded her head, licked a tear from Patty's cheek, and tasted its saltiness with pleasure. "Before dawn, you must come to my chamber. We will have a chat, as they say. You must tell me about the attack. Do you have an account?"

"Yes, mistress. If you need money..."

The vampiress smiled. "How considerate. You are a good girl. Tomorrow, Fagan will deposit in your account a handsome sum."

"Thank you, mistress. You are too generous." Patty bowed. She shifted her eyes toward Fagan. He smiled back.

"Finish your work. Then come to me." Eva stroked her hair again and released Patty from the embrace. Patty retreated up the passage toward the house.

"Jimmy," the vampiress cooed. "It is Jimmy? Again we meet."

Jimmy looked up at the vampires, wiped blood from his eyes, and blinked in disbelief.

"How good of you to return. Lisa will be so happy to see you. Her belly is swollen with your child. You won't believe it."

The male Shadows responsible for the beating kneeled below a dying torch. They pressed their faces into the dirt floor and remained quiet and motionless. Little clouds of dust blew from their rapid breath. The noisy flame licked the air. The vampiress approached. "I smell neither gunpowder nor blood on you men."

"We were drivers," one Shadow said. "We didn't see the fight."

"Let's see one now," the vampiress said.

Eva picked up Jimmy Young with one hand and marched him down the passage and into the main vault. She deposited him roughly on the ground. Then she returned up the tunnel, returned with the Shadows. Threw them on the vault floor.

"For those of you who didn't see a fight tonight, we will have one now. A fight for life."

The vampiress's eyes were black. Her claws and fangs were extended. "Commence until one of you is dead."

The Shadows gasped. The vampires turned their attention to the two Shadows.

"We can't afford to lose more Shadows," Fagan said. "Not even one."

"Please, mistress," one Shadow implored. "We are friends."

"Fight!" the vampiress screamed and her voice echoed off the vault. Dirt fell from the ceiling. Bats above dropped from their endless loops as if her voice's sound waves stunned them momentarily.

"We can't fight," the second Shadow said. "Not after tonight. Some of our friends died."

"They're right," Fagan told her.

Jimmy Young was horrified. He looked toward the curtained doorway high on the vault wall where he had first seen Lisa and Bo.

They stood there, now joined by Lazlo and Kazmer. All four watched him.

Eva stepped toward the Shadows. They stood side-by-side and bowed their heads. She paused before them.

"You will not fight?"

"No, mistress," the Shadows answered in unison.

"Very well."

There was a brief silence. The Shadows seemed to relax.

"Then wear the mark of cowards."

Eva raked her claws across the Shadows' faces, leaving deep, wide incisions. The men screamed, collapsed to the ground, and cried in pain. They grabbed their faces. Blood flowed between their fingers. They rolled in the dirt in agony. The collected vampires moved forward a few steps.

Eva smiled.

The vampires showed renewed interest and swirled their tongues.

The Shadows walked backward a few steps when the vampiress looked at them. She turned her gaze to the vampires, and they retreated a step, stopping the tongue swirling. Even Fagan stepped away from Eva. She raised her hands. Her claws dripped blood and shreds of flesh.

"*Now!* Now you see what happens when you fuck with my stuff! We will have a vampire black mass soon and it will be a joyous event. We will all be happy. The Shadows will have substantial deposits made in their accounts. They will eat well. We vampires will be drunk on the blood of innocents. You will remember the night through the centuries. You will be famous because you were here. Act like you are *real* vampires."

Individual Shadows called again. "We need help."

"Where's the doc."

"This one has a compound fracture."

"They need medicine to survive."

"Turn them."

Fagan inspected the injured and walked slowly among the tables set up in the vault. Here and there he touched an arm, patted a cheek, offered encouragement. Some of the most seriously wounded asked to be turned. Fagan smiled gently at them and nodded his head. For a few, he stopped and thanked them for their devotion to the colony.

A female Shadow approached Fagan, bowed, and whispered his name.

"Yes, my beautiful. What is it?"

"Where is Doctor Finney? Did someone call him?"

Fagan looked sad. He said to the girl, "Oh, yes. Doctor Finney. He is on vacation. Far away. He is not available until next week. We don't have a backup. Unfortunately, we are on our own."

The Shadow burst into tears and returned to her group.

Standing alone, Fagan said to himself, "We will have to recruit some medical people, nurses perhaps. They should make intelligent Shadows. What nurse wouldn't want to live forever, vivisect anyone he or she pleased? See how the living body works." He smiled at the thought.

The Shadows renewed their interest in treating the injured. Someone brought scissors from the house and cut the clothes from the wounded. Most were soon naked, lying on their blood-soaked tables.

Fagan walked again among the wounded. The first in line was Joan, a thin woman with large breasts.

"It's just your shoulder, Joan."

"It hurts so much. I need something for pain."

"You will recover." Fagan smiled. "Do we have anything for Joan, for her pain?" He looked among the Shadows' faces.

"No, master. We gave out everything we had, which wasn't much," a Shadow answered. She was the one who inquired about Dr. Finney.

"Give Joan some whiskey, then," Fagan said.

"There is none allowed in the colony," the female Shadow said.

"None?"

"None, sir."

"Whose idea was that?"

Your edict, master."

"Mine?"

The Shadow nodded her head in the affirmative.

"Well, I didn't want a bunch of drunken Shadows stumbling around. Medicinal use is another story. Have someone go for some. Where's Johnson?"

"Here, sir," Johnson answered from among the wounded. He managed to raise an arm and drop it again.

"It's the middle of the night. The stores are closed," the Shadow said.

Fagan grabbed Joan's toes. Shook them until she winced. "Let's get everyone some whiskey in the morning, as soon as the stores open."

"Yes, master. Just for the wounded?"

"Of course, for the wounded." He paused and raised a finger to his lip. "In fact, get everyone who's not wounded a pint. No more. Take the edge off everyone. Just this once."

"Yes, master."

The next wounded Shadow was a male, barely twenty years old. He lay on his back. had an exit wound through the stomach. The youth was unconscious, but the blood flow had been stopped. Fagan felt a pulse on his neck and watched the chest rise and fall.

"What happened here?" Fagan said.

"Friendly fire. He stepped in front of one of ours just as he pulled the trigger."

Fagan made a face. "Our shooter?"

"Dead."

"This wound looks serious."

"Yes, master." The woman hesitated. Cleared her throat. Spoke meekly. "One of our members suggested taking the wounded to the hospital. Dropping them off. Just to get them help."

Fagan thought a moment. Twisted his face. "No. There'd be too many questions."

"But people get shot every day. I don't think the hospital would notice. Would care. The doctors would treat them."

Fagan turned away. He wiggled one of his gnarled index fingers toward the Shadows. "Move this young man to the center of the room," Fagan said.

"Do you want me to call for the cars? To take them to the hospital?" the female Shadow asked.

"Not yet," Fagan said.

"He might not have much time."

Fagan looked at the Shadow. "He doesn't have much time." The vampire snarled with his reptilian look.

The Shadow shrank away.

The vampire leader continued down the row of injured, assessing the injuries like an avuncular old family doctor, occasionally stroking his chin. The man with a shattered leg and the woman with a wheezing chest wound were moved to the vault's center. When he came to Johnson, Fagan patted his bare ass. "I thought you would go for our whiskey. You always seem to do a good job taking care of errands. This errand you will miss, but there will be others."

"Now? Can I send for the cars?" the female Shadow called from her group.

"Not yet, child." Fagan turned to the vampires. "These Shadows have served us well," he said pointing to the three moved to the vault's center. "They shed their blood for our defense. What blood is left in them they now offer freely."

The vampires swept over the tables, sinking their teeth into any flesh they could find. One table collapsed under the weight.

Another was tipped over. Muffled cries among the three stopped as fast as they were voiced. Within minutes three exsanguinated corpses lay in the vault's center. The bats circled overhead. The Shadows cried. The vampires walked away, blood-covered and smiling.

CHAPTER THIRTY-THREE

After the three wounded Shadows were drained of blood, their bodies lay at grotesque angles on the floor. The vampires had fought viciously for places at the tables, breaking bones, dislocating joints, and tearing flesh, to suck on the bodies. Some vampires attacked their own loyal Shadows. Now that the three were exsanguinated, the vampires dispersed leisurely, although a few blurred to the exterior to hunt more, this meal failing to slake the vampire disease thirst for blood. As the final vampires strolled back to their caskets, a murmur rose among the Shadows, who huddled and moved toward the tables.

Individual voices rose among the group. "You could have saved them."

"They were our friends."

"We could have dropped them at the hospital."

"They served you."

"They were loyal."

"Why didn't you turn them?"

The vampires who had fed on the Shadows ignored the group and continued their slow walks. They licked their lips and fingers of blood, and savored the final tastes, dispersing to their various crypts and the daylight rest of the undead. Vampires made no friends and cared not about one another's well-being. The vampires would beat their Shadows when they woke before they hunted again. Some Shadows would be beaten severely for insubordination and join the ranks of the wounded, needing a period for recovery themselves. Others would be punished less harshly. Not all vampires had been Shadows, lived through a term of servitude, and yearned to be a vampire. There were those who came to vampirism reluctantly, even against their wills, but after the transformation period inside the chrysalis, they emerged with an all-consuming thirst for blood and self-preservation. Males and females might be turned by vampires because they were handsome or comely. Sometimes they might be turned by a family member or friend who didn't want to see their beloveds grow old and die. These reluctant vampires might tend to be lenient with their Shadows, perhaps have no Shadows, even live alone outside a colony and fend for themselves. Whoever they were in life, as undead they were still reduced to animalistic instincts and a lust for blood.

The Shadow hoots continued and became bolder. They faced the last two vampires in the vast crypt, Fagan and Eva. Jimmy lay crumpled in the dirt, still bleeding. Patty lay in supplication to the pair. Finally, Fagan could take no more.

"*Silence!*" he roared. His voice echoed around the chamber. Some bats flew up the chamber path to the house. A few handfuls of dirt spilled from the ceiling. Eva looked toward the dome's top and smiled.

The Shadows shrank away and drew into a closer group. The bats returned to their circles at the dome's top. Several landed and clung to the ceiling.

"Enough," he said in a lower voice. "A trip to the hospital would raise suspicion. Our doctor is out of town. We had no alternative. A new vampire must be trained the way you needed to be trained as Shadows. We have three hanging now. Three more would be too many. I regret your friends' passing. Would you prefer to let them writhe in agony until they expired? You will forget about your friends at the black mass."

Fagan blurred away.

The vampiress looked down and stroked Patty's hair. "Get up, child, out of the dirt."

Patty stood and trembled. Tears ran down her cheeks. She averted her eyes from the vampiress.

"Look at me, Patty."

Patty obeyed.

"Have you ever been pleasured by a vampire?"

"No, mistress."

"Clean yourself. Change your clothes. Do you have a grave shroud?"

"Yes, mistress."

"Put it on, then come to me. I will pleasure you as part of your reward for helping to keep Jimmy alive."

"Yes, mistress." Patty bowed, walked backward a few steps, turned, and ran toward the house passage.

INSIDE THE HOUSE'S BATHROOM, there was confusion. Shadows cried, argued, screamed at one another, drew hot water into buckets and pans in the bathtubs, washed bandages in sinks, wrung them out. The floor was slippery and wet with blood and water. Shadows carried fresh water from the bathroom. Others returned with pails with blood-soaked rags and towels. Their shoes slipped and squeaked across the tile. Patty grabbed the last clean bath towel and slid herself toward the shower. She pulled open the plastic, curtain, and found a Shadow sitting inside on the floor holding his head in his hands.

"You can't take a shower now. We need the hot water, even that towel."

He looked up at Patty, and reached for the towel. She held it behind her back.

"*She* told me to take a shower, change my clothes, go to her crypt."

"Oh." The young man stood, looked at Patty for a moment, left the shower, and closed the curtain for Patty. Patty undressed and turned on the water.

THE VAMPIRESS PICKED up Jimmy by the collar, held him off the ground, and looked into his face. Jimmy returned the gaze. His one eye was swollen shut from the beating. Blood seeped across his forehead from a cut on his scalp. The vampiress swiped an index finger across the blood flow, examined it, sniffed it, and licked it off. She smiled.

"Have you ever been pleasured by a vampire?" She giggled. "There's a first time for everything."

Jimmy looked at the curtained entrance high on the vault wall. Lisa, Bo, and the brothers were gone. The vampiress lowered Jimmy until his feet touched the ground. Then she half-dragged him to the path on the wall that climbed to her crypt. He tried to walk but could take only one step to her two. Jimmy struggled to free himself. She laughed. Ahead, Lazlo had lain the planks to connect the gap in the path. The vampiress marched over the planks, continued up the ramp, and drug Jimmy past Lazlo. Lazlo scanned the surroundings, removed the planks to reestablish the void in the path, and followed the mistress inside the crypt.

LISA, Bo, and Kazmer were in Lisa's chamber in the vampiress's crypt. Lisa heard a commotion outside on the ramp. She knew the vampiress approached. Her footsteps stomped. It sounded like she dragged something with her. Lisa's heart sank. Could it be Jimmy? Was he all right? She last saw him prone on the vault floor. The vampiress's sudden entrance into the outer crypt moved the curtains and made the torches flutter in their wall brackets. Lisa held her breath. Jimmy staggered through the curtain and fell on the floor. Kazmer moved to his aid but stopped when the vampiress appeared inside the curtain, holding it back with one arm. Lisa rushed to Jimmy and knelt at his side as fast as she could lower herself to the ground. She turned Jimmy's swollen face to her and burst into tears.

"You fiend," Lisa cried out. "You didn't have to hurt him."

"I didn't do it. It was the Shadows," the vampiress said. "He'd be dead and drained now like the other wounded if it were not for our pretty little Patty. She alerted us to the beating. You saw I punished the boys who did it."

Lazlo arrived in the doorway behind the vampire.

"Do you want me to thank you?"

The vampiress returned a cold gaze. "No, but I like to, how do they say it, set the record straight."

Jimmy looked up at Lisa and smiled with his swollen lips. "I never thought I would see you again."

"Oh, Jimmy. I'm so sorry they got you again. I thought one of us would survive—you at least."

"Never mind," Jimmy said. "We're together."

"The three of us."

Bo jumped off the bed, where he had been sitting. "I'm feeling a little horny myself," he told the vampiress. "You want to knock one off? You can have the top, as usual."

"Come to me, Bo."

Bo obeyed. Stood in front of the vampiress.

"You are so...clear. Is that the word, when I know what you're plotting?" She took a handful of his shaggy hair.

"Transparent," Kazmer offered, smiling. "Bo is helping me with my English."

"How wonderful," the vampiress said, smiling broadly, exposing her stained teeth. "Don't teach Kazmer too much, Bo. He might become reckless like the Shadows below."

"I would never disobey you, mistress," Kazmer said. He bowed. "I wanted to serve you better by learning more English language."

"Good," she answered. "Excellent. Don't become too fond of Bo, either. You know he has a purpose, and when that purpose is gone..."

"Yes, mistress," Kazmer answered. "I understand."

"As for my sweet Bo, he wants to give Lisa and Jimmy some time together. Let them trade stories. We will allow that."

She pulled Bo closer, turned her attention back to him, and stared into his eyes. "Look at me, Bo. I've neglected you recently," the vampiress cooed. "You smell wonderful." She took Bo's arm, and rolled up the sleeve. "Your wounds are almost healed. The medicine is out of your blood. Soon I will make new wounds, but not tonight. I have other plans. After I drink your blood again, your mind will be open to me. Completely open. Now it is dark. You resist but you will not keep me out long." Bo staggered back a few steps and sat on the bed.

There was a cry for help from outside. The vampiress smiled. "It is Patty. Make the bridge for her, Lazlo. Remove it after she crosses."

Lazlo retreated. They heard him drop the planks across the path gap. He hauled them away immediately. Patty entered Lisa's room dressed in a white burial shroud.

"The vampiress smiled. "Come to me, Patty.

Patty crossed the room hesitantly as if she were trying to resist. The vampiress put her arm around Patty's back and stared into her eyes for almost a minute. She adjusted the thin shroud straps that covered Patty's shoulders. Checked the cleavage. Looked down the gown's length that ended at her ankles, and exposed her bare feet.

"Kazmer. Watch our three love birds while I reward Patty for her service. Come, Patty."

Kazmer bowed.

Patty turned to leave the room. As she reached the curtain, the vampiress slipped the shroud from Patty's thin, pale shoulders and it fell to the ground. Patty stepped over it and continued naked toward the vampiress's casket, unable to protest.

CHAPTER THIRTY-FOUR

The vampiress's casket rocked. Patty's muffled cries were audible inside Lisa's chamber. Lazlo and Kazmer walked outside, paused at the casket and smiled at each other for a moment, then continued outside to smoke on the ledge above the main vault, their shoulders slouched as if they took a break after a long day's work. On the floor below them, the dead Shadows had been removed. It was unknown how their remains were handled. Were they buried in the cemetery or dumped on the street? It might never be known. Meanwhile, the wounded were transferred one at a time on stretchers up the long passage to the house, where there were electric lights, running water, and presumably better care. Occasionally, one cried out in pain during the process.

Looking toward the vault ceiling, Kazmer said, "I don't like the way dirt falls sometimes. It is only a little but who knows? It can make me sneeze."

"If you sneeze, my brudder, the whole place will cave in."

The men laughed.

"It is natural, my brudder," Lazlo continued. "You remember what it was like in the mines. Dirt, rocks, timbers, something always falling. It was dangerous work. That's why we had hard hats. If this place falls, we will dig ourselves out. That's why I keep our tools close." Lazlo pointed to picks and shovels arranged next to their bench. "We have already done that, dug ourselves from cave-ins when it was thought we were lost."

"A few times," Kazmer added. He smiled. "We are smart. We know about mining."

Kazmer rolled cigarettes for himself and his brother, passed one to Lazlo, and struck a match to light them. The men inhaled deeply, held the smoke in their lungs a long time, as if it were a contest, and released it together with sighs. Kazmer cleared his throat and spit over the edge. Both men watched the spittle drop and disappear.

Kazmer tapped off some ash. "What do you think she will do with Bo?"

"Who knows, my brudder. It is not our concern. He is only a pet."

"I am afraid the mistress will like Patty more than Bo."

"Patty is not a virgin."

"How do you know?"

"I know certain things, my brudder. I am older. Trust me."

"I like Bo. He was kind to me. Made me sling for my arm when it was hurt. I still have the sling." Kazmer pulled out the ratty sling from inside his hoodie to show Lazlo and stuffed it back.

"How is your arm, my brudder?"

"Stronger than ever." Kazmer made a fist and flexed his bicep.

"Good. We will need your strength in the fight with the Brethren."

"I thought they were dead. That is what some of the Shadows said. They were killed or arrested."

"You know how the Brethren were in Europe. They were not like vampires. We could kill them, but there were always more. They looked for us night and day. They know how to fight us. I believe most of the Brethren got away and are planning to attack."

Kazmer grunted. "I hope you are wrong."

"What did you read in the newspaper you get every day," Lazlo said. "I know you buy them. Let Bo read them."

"Bo likes to read. He is helping me with my English. I want to be able to talk good—like you. So what if he knows what today's date is?"

"It does not matter what day it is, but the mistress does not want him to know. If he knows what day it is, Lisa knows, too. Time can be our enemy." Lazlo put a hand on his brother's knee. "Lisa will know when the baby will be born. Be careful, my brudder. You do not want to cross the mistress."

"I always am." Kazmer inhaled the cigarette and released the smoke after a long moment. Wiped loose tobacco particles from his lips.

"What does the newspaper say, my brudder? About the fight with the Brethren?"

"Nothing about the gunfire. Just a story about the building burning down. A complete loss. Things about insurance I didn't understand. There was another story about the robbery at the convenience store. Nothing about us. Always the investigations are continuing. The police must have many investigations. Maybe they are too busy to solve anything."

"That is good." Lazlo smiled at his brother. "When the police are busy, they don't have time to notice us. Who would believe it anyway?"

"Bo said not to believe everything I read in the newspaper."

"Bo is smart," Lazlo said. "But don't believe everything Bo tells you."

Kazmer grunted.

Inside, Lisa, Jimmy, and Bo sat on the bed. They finished hugging and crying. They wiped their eyes, blew their noses, and cleared their throats. They grinned at one another. Jimmy's injuries had been cleaned and bandaged. Then they were silent.

Finally, Lisa said, in a whisper, "Who's gonna tell me the latest? When the hell are you going to get me out of here?"

"Don't forget me," Bo said. "I want a ticket out, too. I've served my time."

"You heard about the raid?" Jimmy said. They moved closer on the bed and bowed their heads together, keeping an eye on the doorway to Eva's crypt.

"Patty said it was a great victory. Most of the Brethren were killed."

"I'm sure that's a lie," Jimmy said. He lowered his head. "I was in the bathroom when it all went down and was captured by the Shadows. It was embarrassing, but I know the vampires and the Shadows booked it out of there, me with them. I wouldn't call that a win. It looked like the bad guys were in full retreat."

Bo said, "The vamps killed three more Shadows that had serious wounds. Drained their blood instead of taking them for help. The Shadows are pissed, thought they should have been dropped off at a hospital for better care. Another nine or ten need to recover. Will be out of action for a while. We watched it from the ledge."

"Right," Jimmy said. He paused and shook his head. Looked at Lisa. "I get the feeling a rescue isn't the Brethren's top priority."

"Why?" Bo said.

Jimmy paused again. "The Brethren want to kill vampires. That's what they do. That's what they train for. The fact that you— now we—are inside the colony complicates things. Bo has been a tremendous help in giving Persimmon actual numbers of the undead and maps of the place. A plan is underway. More Brethren have been called in. But they had to refit a new stronghold. That moved the attack back. Nobody knows when it's coming. There's going to be two attacks, one from the house, one from the cemetery. It will be during the day, when the vampires are either asleep or at least weaker. It will be shock-and-awe. The idea is to catch everybody inside unaware. Persimmon used Bo's drawings to find a choke point in the passage to the house where everyone will be pushed. I hope you're a good artist, Bo. That choke point is crucial. Then the massacre begins. No prisoners. Vampires and Shadows. They'll all be cut down."

"The vampires move so fast," Lisa interrupted. "How will it be possible?"

"The Brethren are slick. They have a system for fighting vampires. The other thing is this is going to be quiet. We don't want a call to the police, even though there are multiple shootings in the city every day. Crossbows and Bad Nelson's stake guns. We have a new guy named Del Hatch, ex-Navy, a survivalist, and a friend of Overboard George's. He has some mean firepower, but he's only going to shoot it underground, where nobody'll hear it outside. It's a BAR from World War II. I hope it works. But from what they say, it'll rip the place apart."

Lisa looked at the dirt ceiling. "I think I've seen him in a dream. He shot the crypt up. It's hard to remember. I hope he doesn't bring the whole place down on our heads. Dirt falls on my bed now—almost every night. I asked the boys," Lisa jerked her head toward the exterior, "to move the bed, but they said the vampire wants it where it is, where she can watch me from the door."

"I thought that might be the plan," Jimmy said. "To blow the place up."

"Entomb the vampires?"

"Exactly. Del Hatch has grenades. Plastic explosives. He wanted to give me a few but I said no. I heard the Brethren talk about C4. I know they have it. I thought we could rescue you and Bo, blow the place, cut our losses. But the Brethren say the vampires have to be staked. Killed outright. If we bury them in an avalanche, they'll just dig themselves out. It might take a while, but they'll come to the surface and go back to killing."

"Apparently the Brethren take no chances," Lisa said.

"None from what I've seen," Jimmy said. "You know, they actually scare me."

"If we knew the exact time of the attack, if we could contact Persimmon, we could hide, let her know where to find us," Bo said. "I know places to hide. They could get us out of here."

Jimmy looked at the dirt floor. "I asked about getting you two out. Several times. She always said she was working on it."

"But now you're here, too," Bo said.

"I don't think that matters," Jimmy said. "If it comes down to killing all the vampires or killing *most* of the vampires and getting us out, they will kill all the vampires. That will be their priority. I think we'll be on our own."

After a long silence, Bo said, "Then we have to make our own plan. It has to be very fluid, ready to change at a moment's notice, depending on how the attack goes, where it comes from. We'll have to be ready to move fast."

"The vampires will be faster," Jimmy said.

"I'm pregnant, remember?" Lisa said. "I'm not that fast anymore."

Bo responded immediately. "I think the Shadows will be the bigger problem. They might shoot us. The vampires fear the mistress. She has told them we are off-limits. Most of the undead avoid us. When the attack comes, I think the vampires and the Shadows will be too busy to worry about us. We might be able to waltz out of here. That's what I'm thinking."

"Waltz?" Lisa and Jimmy answered in unison.

"You know what I mean. There will be so much confusion they won't notice us."

The casket had become quiet. They heard the cover open. Someone got out. Groaned. The vampiress giggled with her hollow voice. Patty parted the curtains to Lisa's chamber. She stood naked, scratched and bitten, pale, holding her shroud in one hand to cover herself. She looked exhausted, hollow-eyed. Her red hair was unkempt. It looked like she had been outside in a hurricane. Patty sighed and looked confused when she saw the trio.

The vampiress appeared suddenly behind Patty, and wrapped

her arms around her. "You're going the wrong way, my dear," the vampiress said, just above a whisper into Patty's ear. Then she licked the ear with her sticky tongue. The vampiress inclined her head to Patty's thin shoulder, inserted fangs, and made a new wound. Patty grimaced; her knees buckled. The vampiress caught Patty and supported her while she drank from the wound. The vampiress's lips made a popping sound when she released the bite. The vampire's foul tongue swirled to catch the overflow from her mouth. Then she licked the remainder of the blood from Patty's shoulder.

"Rest now, Patty. There will be much to do tomorrow. The brothers will get you food."

Patty staggered to her usual resting spot and flopped on the floor, pulled the shroud around her, and fell asleep instantly. The vampiress, also naked, looked at the group.

"Come to me, Bo."

"No. No more," Bo said. He averted his eyes. Refused to look at the vampiress.

"My little rabbit has become defiant in front of his friends." She thought a moment. Tapped her finger against her temple. "How do they say it? You are trying to grow a pair. Or should I say another pair. I would like that." Her face became stern. "Come to me," she demanded.

Bo hesitated. Rocked on his heels.

"Follow me, Bo," the vampiress said, this time louder. She turned and walked into the next room.

Lisa and Jimmy caught Bo's hands. He stopped. Opened his mouth, but no words came out. He looked dazed, shook off their grips and followed Eva. Lisa and Jimmy remained on the bed and hugged as Bo left the room.

The vampiress paused by her casket, turned to face Bo. "Undress for me, little rabbit. It has been a while."

"I don't want to," Bo said, but he had started to undress. Eva watched approvingly.

"You said not tonight," Bo moaned. Tears flowed.

"I changed my mind, little rabbit. You smell wonderful, Bo. Tell me, what is today's date?"

"The twenty-first," Bo answered, as if in a trance.

"You know that which was supposed to be a secret. Too much information is not good for little rabbits. They get themselves into trouble."

Bo had stripped. She held out her hand. Bo took it. The vampiress smiled. "Climb in, little rabbit. Excellent. Now once more you are obedient. Patty was entertaining, but not as much as you are. While we play and I sample your sweet blood, you will tell me the other forbidden things you know." Bo was on his back in the casket. He tried to talk, to scream, but couldn't make a sound. Eva looked down on him and smiled. "If you are very good, you will survive this day, my little rabbit. Perhaps."

CHAPTER THIRTY-FIVE

It was mid-morning and Goldenrod meandered through the headstones. Occasionally she kicked a pinecone out of her way. She carried a clipboard with a tablet attached in one hand. Over her shoulder was a large bag that held a 9mm pistol, extra clips, several wooden stakes, and a mallet. She paused often. Checked her surroundings through dark glasses. She feigned interest in the name on a stone, scribbled on her tablet. She raised her pen to her mouth, was thoughtful, wrote more notes, checked her surroundings again for Shadows, swept her eyes over the distant gravestones, and moved on. A light coat was warm enough to ward off the spring chill. Sunglasses allowed her to keep an eye on a Shadow she spotted concealed in the bushes about fifty yards ahead. From the Shadow photos captured by the Brethren in recent months, Gold knew immediately the Shadow was Johnson.

Johnson had been pressed back to duty before he wanted to return. His buttock wounds were mostly healed but still sore. He spent the winter months inside the old house. Now he carried a cushion with camouflage cover while hiding in the bushes. Sitting and standing were both fine. Getting to either position was still painful. He packed a .38 Special with three rounds. Gold could tell Johnson watched her. He apparently did not think Gold had seen him yet, because he stuffed a cupcake in his mouth, then slurped coffee.

Since the raid, Johnson was somewhat of a hero among the Shadows. His participation in the raid, his wounds, and his claims to have taken out a half-dozen Brethren made him a celebrity. No one seemed to notice he shot more rounds than his weapon held and lost the gun in the melee. The pastry and java had been gifts this morning. He complained to Fagan about returning to outside work. Let someone else do it, Johnson said, bolder than he had ever been, a Shadow with less seniority but who still could be trusted. Fagan was quick to point out that the Shadow numbers were low, and recruiting new members was underway again, despite Fagan's reluctance. More Shadows, even inexperienced ones, made the vampire horde feel more secure. Johnson wanted to know why he could not do interviews from a chair inside a safe location, and introduce potential Shadows to the world of the undead. After all, he was familiar with the losers who filled the Shadow ranks, people like he was. He knew where they hung out. They were the same places he had frequented. Fagan smiled but his eyes were hard, and he said Johnson was needed outside. Johnson relented, bowed to his master, and took his coffee and cake with him.

Gold smiled. *Shadows*, she thought. *How do the vamps expect to survive, flourish in the modern world, when they have such inept servants? That's what you'd expect to see in an old Hammer movie. The fiends were already superior. Did they need to be reminded of their power?*

Gold swiveled her head from side to side slowly, thoughtfully, as if confirming directions, while she checked the location of two well-hidden trail cameras still in place. They would have to be collected before the attack. After Gold was in the first camera's view, she bent over, pointed her ass at the tree where it was strapped. Gold liked a good joke. She knew the Brethren would get a kick out of her antics. When she came into view of the second camera, she turned away from the Shadow, toward the camera and made a face. She continued on a diagonal away from Johnson. She saw his head rise from the bushes. He was still watching her, apparently still interested. Gold stopped with her back toward Johnson, wrote on her tablet, then bent over, and showed him her ass this time, a fully clothed moon, as if she had found something in the tall grass. She let him get a good look before she straightened. Johnson was more visible now. She moved again, this time toward Johnson, with her head down, as if scanning the names on the tombstones. Meanwhile, she kept an eye on the Shadow through the tops of her glasses.

Her progress was painfully slow. She stopped often. Sometimes touched the tombstone tops. Let her fingers run over the tops. Contemplated for a moment. Wrote more on her tablet. He might think she offered brief prayers for the dead. Gold would also leave the path, walk down a row, then come back and go in the other direction. She would have appeared to any casual observer that she had all day to complete whatever quest she was on.

By the time she closed to within twenty yards, Johnson was in the open. His breakfast refuse was on the ground behind him. He wiped his hands on his thighs. He seemed nervous. Gold smiled to herself. *Like taking candy from a baby.*

"Hello, there," Gold called. She smiled, waved, and walked directly toward the Shadow. "What are you doing out here?"

Johnson paused. She could see he didn't know what to say.

"Bird watching?" Gold offered.

"How did you know?" Johnson said. He blushed.

She walked up close to him, and noticed the key ring on his belt. "Lucky guess. But there isn't much else alive to look at out here." Gold eyed the Shadow's coffee cup, balled up paper napkin and wrapper, which started to roll away in the breeze. "Don't you hate litterbugs?" she said, pointing at the wrapper and napkin scudding across the grass.

Johnson turned to the cup, bending, grimacing, to retrieve it. Then he chased down the wrapper and napkin, which separated in the breeze. It took several painful tries to snag everything. He returned to Gold with a limp. "I always pick up other people's trash and dump it in one of the cans. Problem is most of them are overflowing. The shit gets blown out again." Johnson smiled back at her. "But I try to do my part."

"This stuff looks rather new. Just discarded," Gold said.

Johnson jammed the napkin and wrapper inside the coffee cup, crushed the cup, and shoved it into a pocket.

"I like that you're conscientious," Gold said. "It looks like it's painful for you to bend. Back problem?"

"Freak accident. Long story."

"I'm sorry to hear that."

"I'm recovering, though."

"Good. See any interesting birds this morning?"

"Actually, I just got here myself—a few minutes ago. And...why are you here?"

"Research," Gold said.

"Genealogy?"

Gold smiled. "Vampires."

Johnson coughed. Took a step back. "There's no such thing."

Gold laughed. "I know that. It's for a friend who's writing a novel about vampires." Gold touched Johnson's arm, and let her fingers glide over the back of his hand.

Surely that gave him an erection, Gold thought.

"How far along is *he*?" Johnson's face looked glum.

"*She*," Gold said. "My friend is a she. An old high school classmate. It's her first book. I said I'd help. Said I'd find some interesting names among the tombstones and real dates for the deaths. My friend is into realism."

Johnson's eyes brightened. He looked eager. "Maybe I can help you."

"I'd love that," Gold said. She took his hand. His fingers were sticky from the cake. "It's creepy out here alone, even during the day."

"But it's quiet. That's what I like."

The pop-pop-pop of gunfire sounded in the distance.

"So much for quiet," Gold said. "Maybe somebody'll be digging more graves in here."

They laughed. "It's part of the landscape now."

"I'm also researching a story about a ghost that haunts the cemetery. Walks back and forth between two graves."

"I've seen her," Johnson said. He laughed nervously.

"Seen? You can't be serious." Gold took both his hands. "I love the paranormal. That's why I volunteered for this project."

Johnson pulled a hand free and placed it over his heart. "I've seen her all right. Sometimes I'm here late. Until I walk out it's dark or almost dark. I can show you her grave."

"Why would you stay so late? Owls?

"I like to..."

"Wait for the birds to roost for the night?" Gold offered.

"Yeah. That's it."

"Will you show me now?"

Johnson looked back at where his cushion lay. He glanced up and down the path. "I can spare a little time, but I can't stay long."

"You've saved the day, Mr.--I don't know your name."

"Everybody calls me Johnson."

"I like that name," Gold said. "Johnson. Is it because your... well, is Johnson a name you picked up in the locker room at school?"

Johnson blushed again. This time a deeper red. Looked at the ground. Kicked at the dirt. "Naw. It's not that." He looked up suddenly. "But it could be, you know. Johnson is my real name—John Johnson."

"Has a certain ring," Gold said. "Well, Johnson, let's go look at that grave."

Johnson grabbed her hand. Stopped her. "What's your name?"

"Gold. Kelly Gold," she answered. "Most people call me Gold-enrod, though."

"Because?" Johnson giggled.

"My hair's blond. At least some of it is, if you know what I mean."

Johnson smiled, swallowed hard, and pointed across the cemetery. He said the haunted grave wasn't far. There was no direct, easy path to the grave of Minnie Barnes. Tree limbs lay in the grass or hung low. Protruding roots were trip hazards. Old tombstones leaned or were toppled. The ground was uneven. Ahead, a tabby cat sprang from the grass and crossed in front of them. Three kittens followed.

They finally reached Minnie Barnes's grave, shaded and cooler than the surrounding area. The grass was still wet. Gold dutifully copied information from the tombstone, even the little poem at the bottom. Gold reached into her pocket, and pulled out two small white stones. She gave one to Johnson. She told him to place his stone alongside hers on the top of the tombstone.

"It lets people know two visitors were here to pay their respect," Gold said. "Don't you think that's nice? It's a Jewish custom. They will know she isn't forgotten while she rests in peace."

"That's the thing. She don't rest in peace. I've seen her floating from here to a grave over there." Johnson pointed. "It's creepy. She's in a cloud of mist. They say it was her boyfriend in life. Her husband is buried here beside her."

"A little hanky-panky from long ago."

Johnson smiled and led the way several rows over to Herbert Filmore's grave. They stood and stared down for a moment. "Does he rise?" Gold asked.

"I don't think he's home," Johnson said. "Never heard anything about him. But *she* walks back and forth all night, so they say, looking for him, I guess. I never spent the whole night in this spot, but I've seen her a few times. I leave when I see her. It's too creepy."

"Before we go, help me find two stones to leave here on his grave like we did for Minnie," Gold said. They searched. Their hands disappeared in the high grass. At one point they touched, and Johnson giggled. Finally, each came up with a stone, placed it on top of Herbert's stone. Again, Gold copied information from the stone.

"I gotta get going," Johnson said. "I hope..."

"Let me give you my number."

Johnson's eyes grew wide. "That'd be great." He smiled. Chocolate cake was stuck between his teeth.

Gold wrote a telephone number on the bottom of her tablet's page, then ripped it across, and gave Johnson the paper scrap. Then she wrote down his number. Johnson was giddy.

"Don't call me for a few days, wait till the weekend," Gold said, "I'm in the process of getting a new phone and it's been a nightmare. The first phone they gave me didn't work. Of course, they lost my contacts and all my apps. Right now, the phone I have doesn't work at all. Can you imagine how distressed I am?"

Johnson smiled. "I know what that's like. I'm always having phone trouble. It's not like you can live without a phone. Right?"

They took another route back to the point where they met. When they encountered a fallen tree, Gold took Johnson's sticky hand to step over it, bumped into him—they giggled—and Gold lifted the keyring off his belt, and secured it in her own pocket without a sound.

Now we have a way in.

CHAPTER THIRTY-SIX

Bo woke. He was naked and alone in the casket. Although *she* had gone, the stench of death remained. He never would get accustomed to her smell. He groaned, pushed open the casket cover. Suddenly it was pulled from his hand and opened. Kazmer was there with his meaty hand on the lid. Bo felt weak. The strength he had regained was gone. There was a new wound on the inside of his right arm near the elbow. The teeth marks already looked infected. His legs felt like he had run a marathon. His thighs were bruised. His shoulder was sore. Kazmer offered a hand to help Bo sit up. Bo's head swam. He pulled his hand free from Kazmer's big mitt and cradled his head. He had lost much blood to the vampire, more than at any one time before.

Bo looked up at the brother and shook his head.

Kazmer grunted.

Bo peeled off a slab of the vampiress's thick, dried, viscous spit from his cheek like it was a piece of latex and flicked it away. Kazmer looked around, pulled a newspaper from inside his hoodie, and handed it to Bo.

"Cover yourself," Kazmer said. "I will get clean clothes and take you for a shower. Can you walk?"

Bo nodded yes. He stood with difficulty and climbed from the casket, staggered a bit, eventually covered his genitals with the folded paper, although he had long ago shed any sense of modesty. "I have such a headache. What did she do to me? What time is it, Kazmer?"

"Watch is broken," Kazmer answered, out of habit. Then he thought. "Just before sundown."

"Too early for her to hunt," Bo said. "I feel so strange. It seems like my head was turned inside out."

"You can never tell with vampires. Their power over humans is great. And you cannot predict *her* moves. I am not sure, but it looked like the mistress went to Fagan. She was here one moment and gone the next." Kazmer snapped his thick fingers.

PERSIMMON CALLED the Brethren to order. Several new members had arrived from out of town, Willow, Oak, Sweet Corn, Daisy, and Guacamole. They were introduced. Some had served together in the past during other campaigns against the undead. Guacamole was a legend among the Brethren, known on both sides of the Atlantic. Guacamole was black, a Brit, special services background. She was tall and lean, wore dreadlocks, was a junk food addict, and had a penchant for gummy worms. She was also an expert in hand-to-hand combat, a marksman with the crossbow. Del Hatch took an immediate shine to her.

"Unfortunately, we have decided to call off the hunt for Jimmy Young," Persimmon said.

The Brethren mumbled.

"It's too dangerous. We know the vamps are recruiting new Shadows and that the Shadows are patrolling, looking for us. Del's been tracking Jimmy on foot..."

"Del could track a cricket across the United States," Mad Maggie interrupted, nodding her frizzy head, "with his eyes closed."

"Thank you, Maggie."

"Don't forget the *Mad*," Overboard George added. He smiled at Maggie, then at Persimmon. "She prefers her full name pronounced."

"It goes with *my* territory," Mad Maggie chimed.

The group laughed. Persimmon let it go. She knew when a light touch was needed. "We all know Del is an expert tracker. Give him a tin cup and a penknife, and he could survive a month in the jungle, the desert, even the Himalayas."

"That doesn't mean I'd want to," Del called from the back with a wave of his hand. "Take her word for it."

The Brethren laughed again. Even Persimmon giggled.

"Del set up a grid around the mortuary, our former base. He crossed and recrossed each section. There was no sign of Jimmy. Not a shoe print, not a personal item, not a thread of clothing. Del spent so much time in the field a few of the residents began to think he was a neighbor. Isn't that right?"

Del smiled. Nodded his head in the affirmative. Guacamole smiled and crossed the floor toward him.

Persimmon continued. "After all this time, Jimmy would have turned up—one way or another. He would never leave Lisa. Therefore, we must conclude the vamps got Jimmy or he...was lost in the fire and not ID'd. It's too dangerous to send Del out all day, every day, even though he would go. Shadows have cruised through this neighborhood already. That's why we installed the window bars on the inside, and hung heavy drapes to hide the bars from the exterior. To throw Shadows or anybody off."

"How about the good news you promised," Old Harriet called from the back. "Did you get another cake?"

"No cake. Not today," Persimmon said, between giggles. "I will let our friend and fellow Brethren Goldenrod explain the good news."

Gold walked to the front of the living room, turned to the group, and smiled broadly. "Well, I was in the cemetery below the vamp house, found a spot where a ghost rises at night, and walks back and forth between her grave and her old boyfriend's. The husband, who's planted next to the bitch, doesn't seem to mind because, apparently, he stays put, or has gone off to bigger and better things."

Some Brethren grinned, perhaps thinking she opened with a joke.

"You might ask, how does old Gold find a ghost in such a big cemetery?" She stopped and scanned her audience. "The Shadow knows, as they said on the old radio show. A very friendly, dopey, dumb Shadow, not even very cute, who probably thought he had just found his first girlfriend. And to top it off, he was a litterbug."

The group booed, hissed. One man called, "Dumb Shadow."

Gold held up her hands to quiet the Brethren. They complied. They looked expectantly at her. Old Harriet enjoyed herself— swung her legs—so much she almost fell off the bar stool where she was perched.

"In spite of his many flaws, this Shadow did have one thing going for him," Gold continued. She held up a closed hand. "He had keys to the mausoleum and the old house on the hill." Murmurs rippled through the Brethren. "What's best of all he didn't realize I stole them from him. Took them right off his belt." Gold opened her hand, and let the keys dangle from her thumb. "He's probably hunting for them even as we speak, crawling through the cemetery on his hands and knees, a flashlight between his teeth."

The Brethren erupted in applause, surged forward to congratulate Gold, and surrounded her. They hugged her, kissed her, and slapped her back. Then the kitchen door blew open. Del Hatch and Guacamole carried in a large cake with candles burning. The smell of brewing coffee wafted in. The group cheered again. The icing on the cake read, *Happy Birthday — Again! Old Harriet*

Old Harriet sat on her stool and cried, pulling at the ends of her wiry hair. "They did get a second cake. I can't believe it. Another party for me."

* * *

THE VAMPIRESS WAS STILL NAKED. She approached Fagan's vault and stared down two Shadows on guard. They withdrew and backed away quickly. One managed to blurt out, "He has not yet risen, mistress." Their heads were lowered. "He doesn't like to be disturbed."

"Out!" she bellowed. The Shadows fled and she hissed after them.

Eva was about to rake her claws across Fagan's casket lid when it sprang open. He leaped from the box, hit the floor, and immediately dropped to a crouch as if expecting an attack. He hissed in return. His bloodshot eyes looked like daggers. Eva relaxed. Straightened. Drew in her claws and fangs. Fagan remained cautious and rose slowly. His mouth retained remnants of last night's victim.

"We have trouble," Eva said. "My little rabbit has been meeting the Brethren leader during his trips to the laundromat. The Brethren are preparing to attack."

"When?"

"I don't know. A date has not been set."

"Where did you get this information?"

"Bo told me." The vampiress raised her head as if she were suddenly proud of her news.

"I will tear your pet apart," Fagan said. "He will scream in agony for days until he dies."

Eva stared at the vampire leader. Her face was cold. "I think not." She ran her finger along the edge of the casket lid. "I have already punished him, and there is more to learn."

"How?"

"I read his mind today. It was the first time in a while. We pleasured each other and then I opened his thoughts."

Fagan grimaced. "Really? Fucking a human more than *once*. I can understand your pleasure if you plan to drain him after the act. But a relationship? That's disgusting."

"Of course he is not the Lothario you are, Fagan. Who is?" Eva smiled. "Still, he amuses me. He will do whatever I command."

"Don't I do that? As many times as you like it?" Fagan looked over her body. The skin was tight, alabaster white. She licked her lips. "I insist Bo be executed at once," Fagan said

"No," Eva hissed. "Granted, he has betrayed me."

"Us. The colony."

"He has betrayed *us*. His days might be numbered. I might save him for the black mass. Imagine the infant and an adult male virgin."

Fagan's eyes closed. His tongue swirled. After a pause, he said, "Very well. But no more trips to the laundromat. What if he escapes?"

Eva told Fagan Bo had been sick. How she allowed him medicine and rest from her carnal pleasures and bloodletting. His will had grown stronger. Now, however, he was back under her control. His mind was again an open channel to her.

"Do you have any idea what an adolescent boy—hardly just a man—thinks? His dreams of being a big-league baseball player, a golfer, a champion at every sport—even things he never played. Skiing? He doesn't like the cold. Did you know he had the—what is it?—the *hots* for Lisa on the East Coast but was afraid to approach her. He went to the After Dark, where she worked, and saw her often, but never had the courage to talk to her. Was relieved when she wasn't there. I could continue ad nauseum. Every foolish flight of schoolboy fantasy. I'm exhausted delving into his mind."

Fagan smirked at her rant. "What would you expect from a human?"

"Another thing that is dark about Bo. He has terrible hate for the homeless, the drug users. He blames them for selling illegal drugs to his brother, who died from an overdose. He and his friends walked the city, fortified with alcohol from After Dark, and beat the homeless at night. To the homeless Bo and his friends were known as *The Beaters*." She paused. Stared at Fagan. "Bo must continue to go to the laundromat."

"He might give away our numbers."

"He already has."

Fagan shook with rage. Clenched his hands until his palms bled.

Eva raised a finger to Fagan's mouth, caught his swirling tongue, wiped the sticky secretion from it, and licked the goo off her finger with her own tongue. She had caught his attention again. "I will get the Brethren numbers and their plan of attack from Jimmy Young. A day in my casket should do it." Eva smiled at Fagan. "Best of all, Bo will return from the laundromat one day with the exact day and time of the Brethren attack. That way, he and Lisa—even Jimmy—will be prepared. They will hide away from the fighting, a place where the Brethren can find them."

"How would the Brethren know..."

"They have a map of our fortress."

Fagan shook with rage again.

"When the Brethren come, we will be waiting. We will not be cornered, they will. Now, let's pleasure each other before we hunt."

CHAPTER THIRTY-SEVEN

Bo was still weak when he returned to the laundromat with the vampiress's blood-spattered clothes. She had been especially sloppy the last few nights. She must have gorged herself, then regurgitated the excess. Johnson was with him again but remained outside, seated on the sidewalk on his camouflaged cushion. He wanted to give Bo as much time alone with Persimmon as possible, according to the vampiress's instructions. Miraculously, Johnson had managed to borrow another Shadow's keys and make copies to replace the ones Gold had stolen, even the large keys to the mausoleum gate and exterior door. No one was the wiser. The telephone number Gold gave him still didn't work. He waited patiently, expecting it to return to service. He never dreamed he was the victim of a scam. Neither did he tell other Shadows about Gold. Relationships outside the colony were forbidden. However, a hot chick like Gold would be worth the risk. After all, he was too smart to get caught. His new keyring had a gold-colored fob.

Bo scooped the bloody laundry into the washers, wondering who had been murdered violently to sustain the vampire. He had no sooner started the washers than a black SUV stopped outside the laundromat, Persimmon slid from the passenger seat and grabbed a hamper from the back. The vehicle roared off while Persimmon lugged in the clothing. She carried the hamper halfway up the aisle, dropped it to the floor, rummaged through the clothes on top, as if she were separating them, and kept an eye on the front window, where the crown of Johnson's head was visible. The Shadow's smokes and lighter rested on the windowsill.

Persimmon approached. She kept about ten feet away from Bo while she folded and refolded a pair of black jeans.

"You want some help?" Bo said.

"I'm done doing laundry." She blew a strand of hair off her forehead. Seemed exasperated. "Do you know what day it is?"

"Wash day."

"It's Monday." She seemed perturbed.

"I know that."

"You look like shit."

"The vampire drained me. Messed with my head. But thanks for the compliment. You look gorgeous."

"I'm worried about you, Bo."

"I think my days are numbered. And do you know what? I don't care. It can't come soon enough. I think Lisa's time is limited, too. She's getting cramps. They're painful. She tries to hide them, but she won't be able to hide a baby. The mistress didn't touch me for a while. A few nights ago *she* drank more of my blood than she ever did. I thought I was dead. She knows that Kazmer gets me the newspaper. I've been helping him with English for something to do."

"She should punish him. It's not your fault."

"She will. She won't abuse the brothers physically. They are too loyal. She will withhold pay. That hurts *them* more than a beating."

Persimmon paused. Looked at Bo. Checked Johnson outside. "It's funny he hasn't come in. He doesn't like to see you with someone. It's like...he's doing it on purpose."

"Johnson was wounded in the raid. Shot in the ass. He's still sore. Managed to fire a few shots, and helped drag out some of the other Shadows before he got nailed. Now he's a big hero."

"He's not even looking over his shoulder."

Bo shrugged. "How soon?"

"Soon." Persimmon paused. Stared at him. Bo looked expectant. "Friday at daybreak. We'll hit them with everything we have."

"How many?"

Lisa stared again.

"What?" Bo said.

"We're waiting for reinforcements. We still have to figure a way in. We don't have that yet."

"Can't you attack sooner?"

"No." Persimmon's voice had a sound of finality. "Everything hinges on Friday at daybreak."

"I hope we can hang on."

"You will. Don't tell anyone. Not even Lisa. Find a safe place to hide. We'll need to know where you will be, though. To get you out."

"I think the safest place is the vampiress's crypt. It's high on the main vault wall. A ramp leads there. There's a curtain on the opening. You can't miss it."

"Will she be there?"

"I don't know. Sometimes, when she hunts with Fagan, she stays the day in his casket. Sometimes, I don't see her for what I think are a few days. But time is always screwed up in there. It's like being in a time warp. At least with the newspapers, I get an idea of a day passing."

"Vampire sex. I've heard about it. The damage they do to each other heals almost immediately."

"Someday, you'll have to tell me about it. I never remember a thing. My damage doesn't heal immediately." He paused a moment. "The brothers will be there. They never leave our sides, unless it's for a food run. It doesn't matter who goes for food. One is always with us."

"But they are human. We don't expect a problem from the Shadows." Persimmon smiled. "Poor Bo." She stared again at him. "At least you don't look like Moe Howard anymore."

"That's another reason you must hurry. Kazmer has been talking about haircuts again."

Persimmon laughed. Then became serious. "*She* will not be easy to kill. A direct hit in the heart will kill her, but it might take a while. She can still do damage before she erupts in flame. The fire will be hot. That heat will do damage. You don't want to be near her when she dies. Personally, I've never killed one so old, so strong. Guacamole has, though. In the Balkans. An ancient male. She said his flesh was so hard it resembled a statue's. Almost like marble. You need a direct hit, or the bolts ricochet off. He exploded like a bomb. His burning flesh was like shrapnel. We're lucky we have Guacamole in this campaign."

Bo looked worried. "Make sure you stay safe. I'd feel better if I knew how many Brethren will attack."

"Why do you keep asking me that? We don't have a number yet. We need drivers, runners to supply ammo, and people to care for the wounded. There surely will be wounded...and dead. We *always* attend to our dead."

Bo shook his shaggy head. "Something in my mind wants to know how many will be in the attack. I can't explain it. If I had a number, I feel it would give me some peace."

"Feel peace in the fact that you, Lisa, and Jimmy will soon be free. Just wait and don't give the day away."

"Johnson is stirring."

Persimmon returned to her hamper. Lifted it with a groan and moved toward the front door. When she passed Bo, she whispered, "You know the plan. Friday at daybreak."

"Everything you got."

CHAPTER THIRTY-EIGHT

It was just after sundown Monday evening. Bo knew it because the vampiress appeared at his side suddenly in a blur. Scared him. His heart pounded. She smiled. "My little rabbit is touchy this evening. I thought you would be happy to see me. Your heart is ready to explode."

"That's because you almost drank all the blood it pumps."

"Nonsense." She stroked his hair. "Your body is already replacing it. If I wanted to scare you, you would be dead. Come to my casket. I have a present. We have plans for tonight."

There was a faint grunt from the exterior vault.

"My, what big ears you have, Kazmer."

Eva smiled at the sound of Kazmer fleeing to the shelf outside her crypt.

"No. I won't. I can't take it anymore," Bo said.

"You can take much more. I will tell you when it's over. Now, follow me."

The vampiress turned and walked from Lisa's room. Lisa sat on the bed, stunned. Jimmy sat beside her. Patty cowered in the corner, where she spent most of her time. Patty remembered what the vampiress did to her inside the casket and now battled multiple infections.

Bo followed Eva to her casket. She lifted out a pile of new clothes. "Tonight, we will go to a movie. Undress. Put these on."

"No," Bo said.

"Obey!"

Bo's mouth grew slack. His eyes glazed over. He began to undress. After he was naked, Bo reached for the new clothes. She pulled them back, set them inside the casket. "First, you will hold me, Bo. I miss your warm body."

Bo stepped toward her. She embraced him and pulled him close. "That is better. I can tell even you are excited."

"You're making me do it."

"My little rabbit. You will always love me. I will always love you. However, Fagan does not like you. He wants to murder you."

Bo's mouth opened, but no words came out. Finally, he blurted, "Let him."

"Fagan may think he leads this colony. In truth, I lead it, and despite what I tell him, nothing will happen to you, my little rabbit." She grabbed his hair, pushed his head to the side, and exposed his neck. She drew closer. Sniffed. Almost purred. Bo's mind went blank. He was powerless to resist. Her lips brushed his neck. Her mouth opened; her fangs extended. Gently, she brushed the fangs across his neck, so lightly they didn't make a mark. When the teeth found his pounding vein, she stopped. Moaned with pleasure. She retracted the teeth, and let her parted lips rest on the vein. She could smell the blood rushing under the skin. Feel its heat. She held Bo in this position for minutes. When his knees buckled, she supported him. Then she moved her mouth to his ear. Licked it. Wanted to bite off a piece. Instead, she whispered:

"Tell me, my little rabbit, when is it they attack us?"

As if in a trance, Bo whispered back, as if it were a secret to be shared only with the vampiress, "Friday at daybreak."

"Are you sure?"

"Yes."

"What a good little rabbit. And how many of your friends will come calling?" Her voice rose expectantly.

"I don't know. Couldn't find out."

"Are you holding back something, Bo? If you are, I will hurt you."

Tears welled in Bo's eyes and ran down his cheeks. "Please don't hurt me."

The vampiress squeezed Bo. He found it difficult to breathe. "Then tell me how many of your friends will be here for breakfast? So we have enough...Danish to go around."

Bo answered in a mechanical voice. "Persimmon said she doesn't know how many want Danish. They need drivers, runners, and nurses to care for the wounded. More Brethren are expected. Please don't hurt me again."

"I would not hurt a good little rabbit. A rabbit that is so beautiful and helpful. Your friends' numbers must be depleted, as we thought. We will be ready for them."

"Where is their new hideout?"

"I don't know. It is a secret."

"Obviously." Her voice rose. "They are doing a good job keeping it hidden. That's how the accursed Brethren survive."

Eva sniffed his face, his breath. Smiled. She parted Bo's lips with her tongue, slipped it into his mouth, and planted her lips on his. The tongue, with its pasty secretion, extended to the back of his mouth and entered his throat. Bo gagged and couldn't breathe. Just as Bo was about to pass out, Eva withdrew her tongue. Bo coughed. Gagged more.

"My little rabbit. Bo, you will be the first human to be a legend in vampire history. You will wake now, feel refreshed. Remember nothing you told me. Look forward to seeing a movie with me."

Eva released her squeeze. Bo's head lolled. He shook his head and woke. He coughed. Spat out some of the vampiress's goo. Stuck out his tongue. Made a face at the secretion's awful taste. He spat again and again until the goo was gone. "Yaack!"

Bo looked at the vampiress. "What movie did you say we're seeing?"

She lifted out the stack of new clothes again. "That is for you to select, my little rabbit, when we arrive at... what is it called?...the multiplex. We have lots to do tonight. Get dressed. *We* will stop to eat. Then we will go to the cinema. What a night it will be. I have promised you a movie night for so long and we never managed to go. Tonight is different. A real date night. I will give you money to make it appear you are treating me. You will buy popcorn and Coca-Cola. Then we will—how do you say it? Smooch—and cuddle in the theater. In the dark. All eyes will be on us. The beautiful lovers."

After Bo was dressed, he looked over himself and then the vampiress. "We're dressed alike. The Bobbsey Twins?"

"Isn't it wonderful?" The vampiress clapped her hands. "It was Kazmer's idea. He said this way, in a crowd, you won't lose me, and I won't lose you." She laughed. "I think it might be a good thing that you are helping Kazmer with his English. He has fallen behind Lazlo in so many things."

"Yeah, no wonder. He's too busy killing people."

"Bo, you are so funny. I think Kazmer enjoys killing people. They are, after all, only people."

In the next dug-out room, Lisa and Jimmy listened, hidden by the heavy curtain. They hugged. "The rescue will be Friday," Lisa whispered. "I hope little Jimmy can wait."

"He—or she—must. Otherwise, things will be very complicated."

"Now the vampires will know," Lisa said.

"Don't worry. I think the Brethren can take care of themselves. They'll have Del Hatch."

THE VAMPIRESS RESTED her chin on folded hands, smiling, while Bo demolished a double hamburger with bacon and cheese, french fries, and a tall, local IPA.

Bo relished the IPA and asked for another. "The last beer I had was at After Dark," he said in a flurry of excitement. "I asked Kazmer to get me some, but he refused."

"Kazmer takes most orders well. Not all, though."

"Come to think of it, this is the last meal I had out since I was with...TJ and Ridge."

"They are?"

"Were my friends. You killed them in After Dark. I found their shredded clothes in the basement."

"Well, a girl has to eat." Eva stared at Bo a moment, then ordered him another beer. Bo drank it slowly, his excitement gone, eyes on the placemat.

"Poor little Bo. Your mood changes so suddenly. Don't be sad. I have a feeling this will be a great night."

Outside the restaurant, the vampiress said they would walk to the movie complex. Leave the Shadows' car Bo drove in the mall parking lot. It was already early spring. The night was cool, nothing like East Coast weather, where it still dipped below freezing. They walked hand in hand. Eva smiled. Looked often at Bo. Giggled.

"If I were human, we would do this often. Walk and talk, I think, the way couples do in movies. And if you were a vampire—"

"I'd never want to be a vampire," Bo said, glumly.

A tall, thin black man approached. Ill-dressed, he carried his worldly possessions in a cluster of plastic bags. He stopped and smiled. "Now there's a nice couple. Look absolutely royal. Even dressed alike. Just come out of that nice restaurant down the street. I saw you. Had a good meal, I'll bet. Probably left no tip. You look like the type." He pulled his shirt up, revealing a handgun stuck in his belt. "I'll just collect that tip and return it to the waiter down there."

"We don't want any trouble, mister," Eva said. She showed

mock horror in her face. She turned to Bo and whispered, "It looks like *my* dinner has arrived. Delivery."

"So young, too, a real sweet couple," the man said. He showed them the gun again and waved them behind high shrubs. "First your money, then you" — he pointed to Eva— "get undressed."

They were behind the bushes, hidden from the street. "Park your ass on the grass, son," the man said to Bo. Bo raised his hands and dropped to the ground. "I see you won't be any trouble. Sit and watch. Learn a few things while I fuck your girlfriend. Then you'll know what to listen for when she enjoys it."

In a blur, Eva stripped and stood naked before the man. He took a step back. Released a long, low whistle. Removed the pistol slowly with his right hand. Pulled down his fly. Bo closed his eyes.

"Assume the position, bitch."

Eva giggled. "Is that all there is? What a disappointment. Well then, have your fun. I won't even feel you inside me. My Bo is a real man. Show the man what you have. I can see a bulge in your pants from over here."

Bo opened his eyes. He expected to see the man killed in an instant. The thief still held the gun in his right hand. He had pulled out his dick with the left. Regardless of what size it had been, it was flaccid now. The man sneered.

"Stroke it up, *little* man. I'm sure you get lots of practice. Let me see how you handle it. If you can handle me."

The man raised the gun at the vampiress, slowly. He pulled back the hammer.

Eva raised her hands to her face. "Now I am frightened. Please, mister. Don't shoot me."

"Cunt."

The vampiress giggled, threw back her head, and laughed at the man.

Bo edged away from the duo, moving slowly, crab-like, hoping they wouldn't notice. His eyes darted back and forth between the standoff and the street, now visible in the distance. After he moved out of their sight, he would spring up and sprint around the bushes, find safety in the crowd, where neither would dare follow. Bo continued his crab walk. His breath came in shallow gulps. He figured he was almost out of their line of sight. His hamstrings burned. His shoulders ached, unaccustomed to supporting his weight. He hoped his knees wouldn't buckle when he fled. He flicked his eyes one more time at the duo. They stared each other down.

The vampiress leaned toward the man. "Well, what are you going to do, shoot me?"

Bo scrambled to his feet. Ran for freedom. There was a smile on his face. For the first time in months, Bo felt liberated. He jumped and ran. Pumped his arms and legs as fast as they could go. He rounded the bushes. His feet hit the sidewalk. Strolling couples looked surprised at his sudden appearance. For a fleeting instant, he thought of Lisa and Jimmy still captive in the colony, but his only concern now was getting away. Bo looked over his shoulder. No one followed. He was at the entrance to the mall. Slow-moving traffic was heavy. He zigzagged between cars. Although he hadn't run far, he was already winded. His chest ached. His throat was raw. He jumped to the sidewalk and ran down along the storefronts.

Garish store lights illuminated the sidewalks in front of them. Two cars flew up the lanes between rows of parked cars and screeched to a stop. Two men exited each car, trained pistols on one another, and opened fire, spraying bullets everywhere. The four continued to fire, two on two. Shoppers screamed. Bolted in all directions. Some fell. The four emptied their guns, reloaded, and fired again. One shooter finally went down. His partner fled to the waiting car. The other two fired more shots at the car as it peeled out. The remaining gunmen returned to their vehicle and sped off after the first. The shootout was over in seconds. Most of it was captured on security cameras. The gunfight erupted so fast no one had a chance to pull out a cell phone. Five people lay dead, including two children. Seven others were wounded, rolled in agony, spilling blood, including Bo. A bullet in the thigh, another in the chest.

Sirens sounded immediately. The crowd, which had run in terror, surged back to see the carnage now that the gunfire had stopped, and the shooters had fled. One security camera video that would be played on local news over and over in the coming days showed a man in a Hawaiian shirt bending over a dead guy as if comforting him. He lifted his wallet from a rear pocket, palmed it, and walked from the scene. Other people gave medical attention to the wounded. Friends and relatives, sat with the injured and dead, wailing while they waited for ambulances to arrive.

Bo grimaced. His thigh ached where a bullet shattered his femur. His chest seeped blood. His left lung filled with blood. It was difficult to breathe. His eyes filled with tears. He stared at the neon signs above him. Their light made him look pale, already dead.

The vampiress arrived in a blur, following the scent of Bo's spilled blood. Her mouth was smeared with blood. She appeared so fast some people did a double take. A few made a face as if wondering how they missed her a split second before when no one had been there at this wounded man's side. Because there was so much good security footage, including images of the gunmen and the thief, Eva's arrival was chalked up to a glitch. It was assumed the blood splatter on her came from the shooting victim. Apparently, no one noticed her sudden disappearance with Bo a moment later. Only his sweet blood remained on the sidewalk among the blackened coin-shaped remnants of spat-out chewing gum.

Eva blurred back to the colony. She arrived as other vampires exited to hunt. Therefore, the doors were open, and she blurred through. She stopped a moment inside the main vault, holding Bo in her arms. Other vampires sensed the dripping virgin blood, gathered with their tongues swirling. The vampiress let out an incredible howl, so loud that handfuls of dirt fell here and there from the domed ceiling, temporarily scattering the circling bats. The vampires retreated. The bats exited the vault to the exterior. Eva blurred again to her vault. She held Bo effortlessly in her arms, watching his pain-racked face. As she lowered Bo into her casket he opened his eyes and shook his head. "Not in there," he whispered and choked on blood in his throat.

Lisa, Jimmy, and Patty had heard the commotion and were in the doorway to Lisa's room. "In here," Lisa said. "Put him on the bed."

Eva lowered Bo gently on the bed.

"What happened?" Jimmy said. His eyes were wide. "Did you...shoot him?"

Eva sent Jimmy a look of disgust and turned to Lisa. "We went to the mall to see a movie. People drove up, started shooting."

"Fucking gangbangers," Patty said. She looked around the room. "Even this place is safer than the streets."

Bo regained consciousness again. He looked toward Lisa. "This is it, guys. No rescue for me. Just as well."

Lisa shot a glance at Jimmy.

"It's all right. She knows." He coughed again. Blood bubbled on his parted lips.

"You told *her*?" Jimmy said.

"She pulled it from my brain."

"There must be something you can do," Lisa told the vampire.

"Nothing. Humans are so frail. This," Eva said, spreading her arms over Bo, "is more than anyone can do." She looked at Lisa, who detected sadness and pity in her voice. "I doubt your best doctors could save him, even if he were already at the hospital. I will miss you, my little rabbit, and your pounding little heart, which now barely beats."

Lazlo and Kazmer arrived, panting. Stood behind the vampiress.

Bo turned his head, smiled at Kazmer. Moaned in pain. Choked again. A pink froth covered his lips. Kazmer dropped to his knees. Sobbed. Lazlo placed a hand on his shoulder. "You should go out on the ledge, my brudder. This will be difficult for you."

"What about Bo?" Kazmer said. Tears streamed down his cheeks. "Bo was the only person who *ever* was nice to me. Liked me. Helped me." Kazmer stood, pulled from his hoodie the sling Bo had made for him when his arm was injured, pressed it to his face, kissed it, and applied it gently to Bo's chest wound, held it in place.

Bo managed to smile through the pain. "That feels better," Bo whispered. "Thank you, Kaz."

"I got the books you recommended," Kazmer said. He knelt next to Bo.

"Don't forget to read them," Bo whispered.

"I will read every word, my friend. I will read them out loud, as if you was in the room with me."

Bo closed his eyes and smiled again. "Thanks for being a good friend, Kaz."

"We made a good team."

Bo smiled and kept his eyes closed.

Kazmer lowered his head to Bo's chest. Listened to the shallow breathing. He turned his head toward the vampiress. "I want you to turn him. Do it before it's too late."

"He'll no longer be my little pet," Eva said. "He won't even be a virgin. His blood will..." It was like she hadn't considered turning Bo. She looked confused. "I don't know."

"I will serve him," Kazmer said. "My brother will serve you. I will serve you and Bo. You will see. It will work."

Eva sat on the edge of the bed beside Bo. She stroked his head. Placed a palm on his cheek. "You grow cold, little rabbit."

"I am cold," Bo said. His voice whispered.

"The grave beckons. A deep, untroubled sleep awaits for the innocent," Eva said. She felt for his pulse.

"Please," Kazmer implored.

"Please turn him," Patty said. "There's not much time. I'll serve, too."

"Let him go," Jimmy said. "Don't make him a vampire."

Lisa cried. "Not a vampire."

The loud voices roused Bo. He opened his eyes. "Please, not a vampire. Never. Let me die. I'm not afraid."

Eva looked between the two factions. Then at Bo. He seemed smaller. Paler. Long pauses came between shallow breaths. Lisa's bed was soaked with Bo's blood.

"I feel responsible for all this sadness—just to go to a movie." The vampiress seemed to sulk. Then she looked up suddenly, brightly. "What fun we shall make when you are whole, Bo. Wait and see." Her fangs extended. She bit her arm. A thick, viscous, black blood oozed.

Lisa and Jimmy started toward the bed. Eva hissed, and they retreated a few steps. Patty cried. Before the vampire disease could heal the two puncture wounds, Eva placed the wounds between Bo's bloody lips. She kneaded her arm to force out more blood into Bo's mouth. Some of her blood dribbled from the corner of his lips. When his mouth filled, Bo coughed and swallowed on reflex. With his remaining strength, Bo sucked on the vampiress's arm. Kazmer and Patty smiled as if watching an infant take its first mouthfuls of mother's milk. Lisa and Jimmy stood horrified. Lazlo showed no emotion. Closed his eyes to two slits.

Finally, Eva pulled her arm away from Bo's mouth. He smacked his lips a few times and fell silent. "He's not breathing," Lisa said. "I think he's dead."

Bo's body stiffened. Shook. Everyone stepped away except Eva and Lazlo.

"The transformation has begun," Eva said. "We will need..."

Kazmer had gone from the room unnoticed. Now he was back suddenly with a pick raised over his head, ready to swing. "A chamber for Bo," he finished the vampiress's sentence. He crossed the room dug the pick into the wall. He pulled out the pick with a large clump of dirt. He swung again and again into the soft earth. Lazlo joined him and shoveled the excavated dirt away from the ever-widening hole in the wall. Kazmer worked furiously. Lazlo could hardly keep up. Everyone stayed clear of the swinging pick, the slashing shovel. Kazmer only stopped to wipe sweat from his eyes. He breathed heavily.

"Take a break, my brudder," Lazlo said. "Rome wasn't built in a minute. We will go out for a smoke. I will roll today."

Kazmer grunted, then remained silent. He renewed his efforts, swinging harder, faster. Dirt crumbled from his onslaught, spilled into the room, covered his legs to the knees, and raised so much dust that Lisa, Jimmy, and Patty retreated to the next room, and covered their faces with towels. Meanwhile, the vampiress watched approvingly. After he was satisfied with the digging, Kazmer descended to the main vault floor and returned with armloads of wood left over from the black mass altar construction. He lined the niche he had dug with wood to prevent it from collapsing on Bo's body. Then he turned to the vampire, his face expectant and streaked with dirt and sweat and tears.

"Excellent work, Kazmer." The vampiress smiled at the brothers.

"We were miners in Europe," Lazlo said.

"I remember when the vampires took you from the mines to serve them."

"Of course, mistress," Lazlo said. "For that kindness, we will be forever grateful."

"Especially now that you have turned Bo," Kazmer said.

Eva called Kazmer to her side. Together, they undressed Bo, lifted him gingerly into the niche, and laid him on his back. They covered his body with the bloody blanket from Lisa's bed.

"We should have new blanket for Bo," Kazmer said. He looked at the vampiress.

"This one will do," Eva said. "I was thrown into a swamp sank among the reeds. Coughed out a little frog when I woke." She paused for a moment as if thinking back hundreds of years. "And look how I turned out."

Kazmer dared to look his mistress in the eye, nodded his head in agreement, and smiled.

"Can...may I look at him one more time, mistress?"

"If you must. It will be only four days until he emerges. Maybe five, possibly six. He was wounded rather severely. He will come out when he is ready, and he will remember you, Kazmer. Even though he is dead, he will know what you did for him."

Kazmer lifted the blanket off Bo's face, and touched his forehead. Using the rest of the wood and some of the dirt, Kazmer and Lazlo sealed up the niche. When they were finished the niche was undetectable on the wall.

LATER, Kazmer and Lazlo sat on the bench above the main vault floor. They smoked their rank, hand-rolled cigarettes, spit loose tobacco from their lips, now and then examined their still-dirty hands. Occasionally, one or both sighed. They also looked up to watch small amounts of dirt fall from the ceiling.

After a long silence, Lazlo said, "I knew this day would come, my brudder."

Kazmer grunted. "Tuesday?"

"No, my brudder. The day we might be separated. Go our different ways in life. You with one vampire. Me with another."

"I think we will always be together," Kazmer said with a weak smile. "That is the way it should be. That is why we have our apartment. Our collection of nice things to look at. I'm thinking we should have kept Bart's jacket."

"What if Bo decides to go to a different colony? Or go alone in the world? Where would that leave us?"

"I still think Bo will stay with the mistress. She will want it so. I think they will be in love."

Lazlo shook his head. "Vampires don't love. They can't love. Not even the way a brudder loves a brudder. When we are vampires, we will no longer love each other. That is the way it is."

Kazmer looked at the ceiling and remained silent.

INSIDE THE NICHE, the disease that corrupts all vampire bodies, and refuses to let them decay, crept through Bo Bentwood. The disease entered every cell, and changed even the DNA. His body pushed out the two gangbanger bullets. His flesh produced a secretion that covered him completely and then hardened into a chrysalis he would eventually break through when the transformation was complete. Its abominable smell went unnoticed inside the sealed niche. No longer needed, his heart and lungs withered. The heart became a smaller target. The shattered femur and broken ribs healed, pulled together by strong fibers and a thick mucus produced in great quantities. Meanwhile, his bones and muscles grew hard and strong. His brain became that of a predator. He would emerge from the chrysalis cunning, with heightened senses, able to think better and move faster. Above all, he would have an insatiable thirst for blood that would never be quenched, no matter what quantities he drank. That thirst would occupy, and control every waking moment. Fresh blood would keep the transformed dead cells nourished, maintain the disease in his body, and extend his life for as long as there was fresh blood.

CHAPTER THIRTY-NINE

"You turned Bo?" Fagan demanded when he appeared after hunting at the river. Bo was already entombed in the crypt wall, sealed in for the transformation. "How dare you?"

"There was no time. Bo was dying. Would you deny me this little favor?"

"Your Bo has caused nothing but trouble since his arrival. Lisa, too, and now her man is among us. Everyone needs an escort. Special food. Special treatment. You use the resources of our colony, especially now that we are diminished in numbers. Lisa needs a handmaid around the clock. Such things do not occur in the vampire world. Everyone is on edge. To make matters worse, the Brethren are at our doors."

"You won't complain, Fagan, when the black mass is concluded, when you add the strength of many to your arms. When your senses increase manifold. You will be like one of the ancients. Then you will thank me. Praise me. *Your* colony will be a legend among vampire lore, even in Europe and Asia. You will see, Fagan."

"I hope you are right. And the Brethren?"

"Merely a bump in the road, as they say. They attack on Friday; Bo has told me this."

"Then we will be waiting."

"We will be waiting, starting tomorrow, just in case the Brethren change *their* plans. They are crafty. I have fought them through the centuries."

"Tell me what happened tonight," Fagan said.

Lisa laid out the night's events and seemed to relish the recent memories of Bo.

"Now, there is still darkness. Will you join me? I want revenge on those who shot Bo. I will hunt them down and slaughter them."

"I have already fed at the river." Fagan sniffed the air in front of the vampiress. Looked at her full cheeks. "You have fed, too. Why kill again? Possibly call attention to us? The humans have cameras everywhere. We don't always recognize these cameras. Bo is turned. Saved from the mortal death. There is no need for vengeance. These so-called gangbangers with their proclivity for gun violence might be dead before dawn. They are bound to die from bullet wounds or drug overdoses. You don't need to hurry the process. They don't even make good cattle."

"I want their hot blood to run down my throat. Only then will this thirst be slaked."

"That is your misfortune, despite your age and great powers. Your thirst, any vampire's, will never be quenched. That is what drives us."

"Then I'll go alone. Be prepared for the Brethren. When I return, I will share a plan I have."

Eva blurred to the spot where she killed the robber. Police and firetrucks still lined the curb. Investigators combed the area, shining their flashlights back and forth on the grass, searching for evidence. *Fools. The vampire treads lightly. Leaves no traces,* she thought.

What will the crime lab do with my fingerprints? DNA? What is the expression? They will scratch their heads until they are raw.

Eva stood on the sidewalk across the street from the investigation among rubberneckers. Several had cell phones out to record developments. Some texted wildly to share their news. A burned-out streetlight that flickered occasionally kept her mostly in the dark, but a young man beside her stopped his video.

He turned to Lisa. "That should be enough for WKR-TV. Excuse me. Is that blood on your clothes?"

The young man was of average height. Had dark hair. A nice smile. *Everyone has nice smiles, today,* Eva thought. *Not like years ago when teeth were the first to rot, and rotted out of their heads, except for the peasants, who ate fodder like the animals they tended. The peasants had strong teeth.*

"It is blood. I helped someone who was shot," she said, returning the smile. "It's dry now." She brushed her fingers over the stains.

"I'm John Bargain from Bargain Videos. I'm a vlogger, a blogger, and do paranormal research, plus, videos for local television stations. You've probably heard of me."

Eva raised an eyebrow.

"You must be new to the city. That's what I do," Bargain said, smiling. "I'd like to interview you."

"On what subject?"

"The shooting, of course."

"I think not. Especially now."

"It'll be great and really help me. Just some remarks on the shooting. What you saw. What you did. Who you helped. It's all legit. I promise. Do I look like a pervert? Please."

The vampiress chuckled. "I don't know. Perhaps you are a pervert. How would I know?"

"You have a nice laugh."

"And you remind me of someone I know. Knew."

"I hope that's a good thing."

"It is." Eva leaned closer. Sniffed the young man. "You remind me of someone I knew long ago. Ages ago.

"Hey, what's up with the sniff test?" Bargain stepped back. Looked suddenly defensive. "I'm clean. Showered this morning. You couldn't have known him that long ago. After all, you're not that old."

"You're not a virgin."

"If you want a virgin, I'll be a virgin for you, if you go on camera. I can be a hell of an actor."

She smiled. "I like you, John Bargain. Better than the person you reminded me of so long ago." She stepped toward Bargain. He dropped his cell phone with gimble to his side. "I'll help you with information, John Bargain, but no interview for television. I will tell you I helped several people at the mall. Where the shooting was." She pointed in the direction of police cars and two firetrucks, while a lone ambulance pulled slowly from the scene. "One young man I saw was shot in the chest."

"Did he die?" Bargain was excited.

"No. He was taken away."

"Ambulance?"

Eva smiled. "You could say that. It seemed he was gone in a flash."

Bargain was fidgety. "Was there blood on the ground?"

"An enormous amount. More than…"

"Thanks, lady. Did you get the guy's name?"

"Unfortunately, no."

"I know a cop over there," Bargain said. He raised his phone and jogged toward the police cruisers. He turned his head and called back, "I hope you get those stains out."

Eva sighed and watched the young man run away. *Indeed. Perhaps I will let you interview you from my crypt, John Bargain. Someday.* Then a familiar scent caught her attention. *A shooter. Here in the crowd. Close. How I wanted to terrify these gangbangers!*

What I could do to them in the basement at After Dark. Let them watch while I tortured one at a time.

Eva meandered through the crowd. She clenched and unclenched her hands. Noticing the dried blood on her shirt and pants, a few people stared after Eva. She sniffed as she walked. It might have been mistaken for sobs. She smelled gunpowder and fear. Ahead, a young man, short and thin in oversized clothes, leaned against a light pole. He wore a baseball cap with a flattened bill at an odd angle. A doo rag protruded from under the hat. Gold necklaces festooned his neck. His arms and face were covered with tattoos. He watched the cops with a smirk.

Eva walked back and forth on the sidewalk a few times until she caught his attention. She moved into the bushes, turned, and waited. The young man checked his surroundings and followed.

PARTIALLY HIDDEN BY A NEARBY TREE, John Bargain emptied his bladder and looked skyward with relief. He was about to drain the excess urine in a last sprinkle when Eva entered the brush nearby. He ducked behind the tree. She spun and stood. A young Latino followed in a moment. It appeared Eva waited for him. Bargain gave it a shake, zipped up, and crouched.

Here I am with my cock in my hand, Bargain thought. *My camera's in my hip pocket. This might be interesting if I could only record it. What was I thinking? Should have waited with her instead of running to the police, who didn't give me anything.*

"What up," Eva said, cocking her head. Her voice sounded hollow. "Isn't that what you *men* say?"

"Hey, bitch. You making fun of me? I don't like it."

"I don't have to. You make fun of yourself. You're pathetic."

The gangbanger pulled a pistol from under his voluminous shirt. Smiled.

Bargain sucked in air and tried to reach for his phone without causing any attention, or any noise.

"I like a man with a big gun," Eva crooned. "Do you hit where you aim?"

"I hit all right."

"Did you shoot someone tonight? A gringo?"

"Maybe. I shoot a lot of people. Anyone I want. Maybe you."

"You're afraid, *Mojon*. I smell your fear."

"Cunt!"

He fired three shots. One hit Eva in the stomach. She stepped toward him. He fired three more times. All hit the vampiress at point-blank range. She blurred. Appeared behind the young man. Locked him in an embrace. Squeezed him so he couldn't make a sound. Licked the side of his head. Raked her thumb claw across his neck, leaving a deep gash that spurted blood. The man coughed and expired. Eva let him crumple to the ground.

The shots raised a commotion. People screamed. Footsteps ran. Most fled from the area. A few converged on the bushes. They were cops. Eva licked blood from her thumb. Her wounds were already closed. Bargain dropped his phone. Fumbled to retrieve it. He looked up. Eva smiled.

"Very nice," she said, nodding. She licked her lips. "Yes. I consent to an interview but on another night. I have others to murder tonight. I will not forget you, John Bargain." Then she was gone. Her laughter remained, hollow-sounding until it faded away after a second.

Bargain retrieved his phone and tore through the bushes to the relative safety of the parking lot. Winded and sweating, he stopped inside an amazed crowd that seemed happy to have witnessed yet another murder. He hoped he would not attract attention, but he already had his camera out and recorded the surroundings.

Eva blurred to the edge of the wood lot, slowed, and walked to the spot where Bo had lain wounded. She smelled his fresh blood on the sidewalk. Then turned her attention to the night. The air was still. The scent of cordite and sweat still hung low, just enough for only her to detect. Also, the smell of a car leaking motor oil. A car that was long past an oil change. She sniffed more and closed her eyes to determine the direction where the cars fled. Zeroed in on it. She stood as if frozen, calling her senses to play.

A hand touched her shoulder. It was a priest. "You're covered in blood. You're drenched," he said, pulling his hand away immediately. "Are you hurt?"

"My friend was shot," Eva said. She pouted.

"What's his condition?" The priest looked horrified. He was tall, lanky, and had a buzzed haircut.

"He'll be better in a few days."

"Thank God."

Eva smiled. "I must go to him."

"Of course. Do you need a ride? I could take you."

"Would you? I'd be very grateful. *Very* grateful."

The priest returned his hand to Eva's shoulder. Gave it a little squeeze. Guided her through the crowd, which seemed to open for them momentarily and close after they passed. Eva wondered whether it was the priest or her blood-covered clothes to which the crowd reacted. The people began to scatter. The priest continued to guide Eva. He dropped his hand to her waist.

"Over here," he said as they reached a car.

"This is a beautiful machine, Father, "Eva said. She ran her fingers over the highly buffed paint. "It shines."

The priest grinned. "It's not my cup of tea, you know. A bit ostentatious. But the parish insisted. They wanted me to have a *new* car. I never drove a *new* car until this came along. I'm really blessed. Such wonderful parishioners."

The priest held the door open for Eva, saw her in safely, and closed the door. He climbed in behind the wheel. There were sirens at the other end of the mall, and the crowd surged away toward them. "More trouble. What hospital did you say your friend was taken to?"

"I didn't say."

"Oh. Where are we going then?"

"Wherever you want to take me, Father."

The priest grinned again. "Well..."

"I know you're not a priest. You smell very unholy."

The priest swung at Eva's head. She ducked. He swung twice more. Missed both times. Eva clapped her hands and laughed. "You're not a boxer either, *Father*."

In a second, she opened his neck, clamped her mouth on the wound and sucked. She allowed the corpse to slump against the door after she was full and exited the car. She caught a whiff of dirty motor oil in the air. Just a few molecules. She turned her nose into the night sky. *That is the way. It's amazing that there are still perverts among humans. They would not eradicate rapists and pedophiles, but they would extinguish us. The longer I live the more I find few changes over the centuries.*

Eva blurred, then walked, then jogged, blurred short distances several more times to remain on the trail. She stopped on a back road. Saw a car down a bank into a tree. She blurred to the spot and noted the bullet holes. A young man shot through the head lay behind the steering wheel. She sniffed through the broken door window.

This is one of them. The one who shot Bo? Perhaps. What an end to a miserable life. Gunned down the same way you shot people. How many people? How many innocents? I don't care about humans. Still, the innocent should be able to live their lives until we need their blood.

A siren blared in the distance, coming closer. Eva blurred away, still on the dirty motor oil trail. After several starts and stops, the smell got stronger. At one point she had to retrace her steps. Then Eva found the car behind a dilapidated house, squalid even by medieval and vampire standards of cleanliness. She walked through the open back door and into the kitchen. Dirty dishes were stacked in the sink, oily frying pans and a pot sat on the stove, all with the remains of food. More crusty dishes sat on the table. The air was redolent with cooking grease. Four figures sat in the living room, illuminated by the television screen, two men and two women. Only one man watched the television intermittently with heavy eyes that opened and closed slowly. Eva stood in the doorway and watched them. He was barely awake on the sofa, where one of the women snoozed. The others slept in chairs. Eva sniffed. Drugs. She smelled the two shooters and the cordite that covered them. She walked behind the man who dozed off. His head jerked up to look at her. His face showed surprise and then horror when Eva opened his throat with her thumbnail. She let him lean to the side. His head hung over the sofa's side and dripped blood. Eva walked slowly around the room, noiselessly. She leaned over the other man, cupped her palm under his chin to prevent a scream, and slashed his throat. He gurgled and kicked for a moment before dying.

Next, she moved to a heavyset woman dressed in pajamas. She bent over the woman and detected drugs. Eva sighed. *What a pity. You prefer to be a junker. That is your doom.* She broke the woman's neck with an audible snap. Let her fall forward. The second woman stirred and woke slowly as if from a dream she didn't want to leave. Eva was at her chair in an instant. The woman blinked several times. Eva moved her face to within inches of the woman's. Their eyes locked. Eva smiled. The woman's face registered horror. Eva forced air from her dead lungs into the woman's face. The junkie coughed. Grimaced. She tried to scream, but Eva squeezed her throat with a hand. She suffocated her slowly in increments. The woman gagged. Her legs extended. Kicked. Her knees locked. Eva prepared to crush her throat, when the television caught her attention.

After a moment, Eva smiled. "I know this," the vampire chirped. "It's *Svengoolie*! How wonderful. I love *Svengoolie*." She looked toward the choking woman who was at the point of expiring. It was as if they were old friends. The woman no longer struggled. Her body relaxed. Eva released her grip. The woman gasped. Coughed. Tried to stand. Eva sat and pulled the woman onto her lap as if she were a child. Eva stroked her hair.

"Relax, little one."

The woman looked wide-eyed at Eva.

"We will watch *Svengoolie* together." Eva smiled. The woman cried. Struggled to free herself from the vampiress's grip. "What a shame your blood is tainted. Watch the television and we will see the end of the movie together. Then I will kill you."

The woman sobbed. During a commercial, Eva applied her hand to the woman's throat and strangled her slowly. Again and again, Eva suffocated her to the point of death and then released her. Let her recover. "The drugs have wasted your body. What a pity. You would be so much nicer to hold if you had more weight. What do they call it? To cuddle? You are thinner than Patty."

As the movie credits rolled, Eva killed the woman and dumped her body on the floor. Her revenge for the night was complete. It was near dawn, and she blurred back to the colony.

CHAPTER FORTY

The Brethren went on Wednesday instead of Friday. Persimmon didn't like the way Bo looked or talked when she saw him at the laundromat. His thoughts had been addled. He had difficulty articulating. The Shadow Johnson was too accommodating, staying outside, letting Bo and her talk as long as they wanted. *We could have sex on the folding table and Johnson wouldn't do a thing,* Persimmon thought. She believed the vampiress had tapped Bo's brain, put him under a spell to extract information the vampires needed to fight the Brethren. Persimmon had heard of such powers among the ancient vampires of Europe. Their powers were beyond imagination. Being able to see the future through their victims' minds was key to their survival. Once attack plans were learned, vampires could either move their crypts or attack first those who would destroy them.

Persimmon went over the plans one more time Wednesday morning. It was still dark outside the safe house. All the Brethren and the East Coasters were assembled. The mood was somber. Members looked around the room at one another, smiling, nodding, in the knowledge some of their number—their friends who shared other raids—might not return.

"One more thing before we leave," Persimmon said. She looked around at the faces. Some were battle-scarred from previous engagements with the undead. They all had checked their weapons. Knew where to get extra bolts. They looked resolute. "Even though we're hitting the vamps two days ahead of the original schedule, they still might be waiting for us in a half-assed way."

The group chuckled.

"They're always half-assed in my opinion," one member said.

"Even when she's asleep in her casket, the ancient one, Eva, might detect our approach. She didn't last centuries without a sixth sense that alerts her to danger. I don't know how it works. She might hear us, smell us, or just have a suspicion. The same suspicion one of us might get in a creepy place. The feeling might turn out to be real—there's a vamp hiding inside—or it might be a false alarm. Still, it's better to have that jumpy feeling—to be prepared. Eva might awake suddenly and raise an alarm. The vamps will be ready to go—no caffeine boost needed—but the Shadows will be groggy, need a little time to get up to speed. By that time, we should be on top of them. Remember, no matter what happens, stay in your squads. If you get lost, or your squad is decimated, join another squad. Don't try to go it alone. You won't make it.

"You know the drill: Del Hatch, Guacamole, Old Harriet and Mad Maggie, and their squads will take the house on the hill. Del has the door key. Overboard George and I will lead our group through the cemetery. George has keys for the mausoleum. Above all, complete silence once we start our approaches. Before we go, Oscar Meyer will lead us in prayer. Oscar."

Oscar Meyer, one of the last Brethren to arrive for the attack, was appointed chaplain, after Tomato's death. He had an avuncular smile as he reached the center of the room. That smile, however, belied the fact that no one—not even he—knew how many vampires he had slain. He paused, folded his hands, and lowered his head. "Dear God, as we go forth to fight evil, keep our members safe, give them the strength and accuracy to bring down our and your foes. In your name, we pray. Amen."

The group repeated, "Amen."

"Give 'em hell, ladies and gentlemen," Oscar added. He smiled and wiped the sweat from his bald head.

The Brethren dispersed into two groups, house and cemetery. There were several runners assigned to supply each main group with ammunition. Each group also had a triage to care for the wounded and handle the dead. Squads broke down further. They exited the home through the front and back in silence and retreated to their assigned vehicles scattered through the neighborhood that would drive them to the two destination points. Everyone would be expected to fight—runners, drivers, and nurses. Everyone carried weapons. One in each main group would tally the killed Shadows and vamps.

Only Persimmon and Guacamole carried radios. Everyone else would take hand signals from the two leaders. They would sweep through the colony before the fiends and their Shadows had time to organize. The squads would move through the colony, clearing the place room by room, chamber by chamber. All the Brethren were experienced fighters. There were no newbies. Shadows would be treated like vamps—no mercy. The first ranks would shoot either low or high to catch vamps trying to spring over the attackers to escape or jump among them to fight. While one row fired, the next aimed. By the time the third row fired, the first row had reloaded their crossbows. A fourth row waited to jump in line to replace fallen Brethren. There were also stake and machete-wielding fighters who would finish off wounded vamps on the ground. Mad Maggie carried two machetes. She had a third in her belt. Old Harriet armed herself with the legs from her chair on wheels, already hardened by the mortuary fire, each with sharp points whittled by Overboard George. To avoid suspicion, the Brethren left the ranch home at intervals of several minutes and cruised away quietly toward their separate destinations. All the vehicles had new mufflers.

The house attackers unloaded a block from the vamp lair above ground. Del Hatch cut a hole in the chain-link fence that surrounded the property. After everyone was inside the fence, the thirty fighters moved parallel to the fence toward the house. Thirty more Brethren would attack through the cemetery. As dawn approached, the black sky changed to a plum color. Now it was taking on an orange tint in the east. Del's group moved slowly, stayed low, and tried to be as quiet as possible. There was no talking. No radio cackle.

Del's BAR was strapped on his back. He carried a pouch with extra .30-06 clips and a half dozen stakes in a bandolero in front. A long, jungle knife with a serrated edge was on his hip. Finally, his group reached a jagged concrete path, sunken, cracked, and broken, that led to the front door. The sidewalk revealed more worn-down stones than concrete. Del nodded at Guacamole. She nodded back. Del duck-walked along the concrete walk toward the front door. Guacamole followed a few paces behind. After her came the Brethren at intervals, stooping or crawling. After every few steps Del paused, looked over his shoulder, then scanned the house for movement and signs the colony was alerted. Everything remained quiet. Finally, Del reached the three concrete steps to the wooden porch. The other Brethren fanned out on both sides and remained hidden in the high grass just below the porch.

Del knew the best plans often went south in the heat of battle. He was prepared. Old Harriet crawled to his side on her hands and knees. She apparently had the same thought. She carried a bundle of homemade torches. "These were supposed to be for After Dark," she whispered.

Del nodded. Smiled. Slowly, he unzipped his jacket and

opened the flap. The inside was lined with hand grenades, each nestled in a little pocket. Old Harriet's eyes grew wide. Then she smiled and winked at Del.

THE REST of the Brethren were dropped off along the cemetery wall, jumped over it to avoid the path Shadows and vampires used to reach the mausoleum, and blended in among the tombstones. They waited in place a few minutes until the sky brightened. Full daybreak was minutes away. Surely all the vampires had returned by now. Finally, they moved ahead slowly, led by Persimmon and Overboard George, who both wore Del Hatch's Forward-Looking Infra-Red (FLIR) goggles, which would see the heat signature of anything living. Del used the goggles to look for evidence of Sasquatch at night. Had several pairs just in case. Overboard George shook his head, thought it was crazy to run around the woods at night looking for an eight-foot-tall monster. But that was Del. He figured his old Navy buddy knew what he was doing. The goggles wouldn't pick up vampires, but they would identify the Shadows in their hiding places, allowing the Brethren to pick them off, one by one, while they approached the mausoleum. Persimmon didn't want any gunfire before they got inside and the underground muffled the noise.

Persimmon spotted five Shadows in various poses, two in bushes, two behind obelisks, and one sitting at the base of a tree. Two appeared to be asleep. One stirred, as if ready to leave that position. To better blanket the cemetery for Brethren, it appeared none of the Shadows could see one another from their hiding positions. Persimmon gave hand signals, denoting the number and positions of the Shadows. She pointed to various Brethren to move forward and kill the vampire slaves. The Brethren crept forward among the gravestones as if they were a combat unit entering enemy territory. As they spotted their victims, the Brethren crawled forward. The two sleepers were the first and easiest kills. A hand over their mouths and the flash of razors across their throats. The Shadows gurgled. Their asses bounced on the ground a few times, and then they fell silent. The one who had stirred, apparently tired of sitting, stood and leaned against a tall obelisk. The Brethren approached from the back, grabbed the unsuspecting Shadow, slit her throat, and let her slide noiselessly down the stone to the ground, leaving a wide smear of blood on the granite. Across the way, there was a sudden "Humph," barely louder than a whisper, but audible in the early morning air. A fourth Shadow was now eliminated from the conflict by one of Bad Nelson's converted potato guns. The last of the Shadows, Johnson, had moved to the mausoleum side, where he sat on his cushion, hidden by the marble steps and their ornate, scrolled balusters that curled out at angles from the front. He looked at his cell phone screen, and Johnson's head was in the perfect position for Gold's gloved hand to stifle a moan, while the other, holding a razor, opened his throat in a cascade of hot blood.

The Brethren were soon on the mausoleum steps. The outer gate and door hung open. The inner sliding door also was open. The path to the house was visible, inclining upward, lighted by new flapping torches. A few bats flitted in and up the passage. Late arrivals. Overboard George removed his FLIR goggles, let them hang around his neck, and pocketed the mausoleum keys. He hoped Del Hatch would have a similar easy way in.

Del Hatch crawled up the three steps to the house porch, with its warped, wash-boarded wooden floor. The edge of the sun's disk had just risen over the horizon. "Night, Night, vampires," Del mouthed silently. He slid across the porch until he could sit next to the front door with his back against the peeling clapboard siding. Del took a deep breath, and smiled back at the waiting Brethren, who nodded back in unison, crossbows ready, as if they had rehearsed the action for a movie scene. Del pulled from the breast pocket of his jumpsuit the door key stolen from Johnson, and raised it over his head, as if he were a priest giving communion, elevating the host. He lowered the key and inserted it in the lock. The key entered the lock smoothly, noiselessly. He turned the key, but it didn't move. He jiggled the key slowly left and right. Still, it wouldn't turn in the lock. He backed it out a bit and pushed it in as far as it would go. No matter how he positioned the key, completely in or partially, it refused to turn in the lock.

Del frowned. He turned around, kneeled in front of the door, and used both hands to turn the key, risking the key might break off. It wouldn't turn. Del pulled out the key, examined it, and sprayed a shot of Sasquatch sex lure in the keyhole. It couldn't hurt and should lubricate the old mechanism, which might be rusted. He tried to insert the key upside down, but it wouldn't go in. He looked back at Guacamole. Shrugged his shoulders. Old Harriet slid across the porch to the door. She took the key from George. Dropped it. Picked it up and examined it, squinting through one eye. She spit on the key and then spit on the lock. She inserted the key. Smiled. Twisted the key. Still, it would not turn.

Guacamole's headset radio crackled. "We're in," Persimmon said. "Moving forward. No encounters yet."

Del mouthed a silent message to Guacamole.

"We're not," Guacamole hissed. "Key won't work. Del said to make your move. We're going to Plan B."

"Damn. We thought all the keys would work," Persimmon said. "There was no Plan B."

"That's what I thought," Guacamole radioed back. There was a slight, silent pause. "Looks like there's a Plan B now. Oh my God!"

"Mad Maggie okay?" Overboard George asked Persimmon, as they entered the passage between the mausoleum and the main vault. "Are they inside?"

"They're working on it, going to Plan B."

"I didn't know there was a Plan B. We went over this operation enough. Did I miss something?" Overboard George twisted his mouth.

"Del's making one."

"I just knew Del'd have a Plan B up his sleeve." Overboard George flashed a big smile. "He's always thinking. I told him to take care of Maggie for me."

"I'm sure he will."

Persimmon pulled out the map Bo had drawn of the colony complex, took Overboard George's arm, and let crossbow-wielding Brethren pass them. The only noise was the crunch of their boots on the dirt floor and their breathing. She spread out the map against the dirt wall under a smoking torch. "You see this place Bo has circled?" Persimmon said. "This is the choke point. We'll have to go through the main vault and up the passage to the house, push the vamps ahead of us. Stop there, and wait for Guacamole to push the rest of the vamps down to us. Then we'll squeeze them from both sides." She showed Overboard her clenched fist. "He made this little cross-section drawing, too."

"It looks like the ceiling is low," George said, stabbing the drawing with a thick finger. "Hope so. That way the vampires won't be able to fly over the top of us." George smiled. Hugged Persimmon. "It will be one hell of a trap."

Mad Maggie and Old Harriet capered in front of the house. They giggled like schoolgirls while they lighted the homemade torches and passed them around, keeping two for themselves.

"We'll burn the hair off their balls, if they have any, fucking vampires," Mad Maggie shouted with glee.

"Whoopie," Old Harriet added. She raised her torch and danced in a circle. "Killing vampires is the most fun I ever had."

Del Hatch looped a string of hand grenades over the doorknob on the front door. He unslung his BAR, turned to the Brethren, and motioned, pressing his palms down, for them to hit the dirt. "So much for being quiet." Del pulled a grenade pin, sprinted across the porch, and dropped over its edge.

The front door opened inward. Two Shadows took a step over the threshold, stood there a moment, and leveled their pistols at the outside. One looked down at the grenades and had just enough time to turn his head toward his friend and open his mouth before the blast blew off the door, turned them into hamburger. While Del Hatch picked up his BAR and scrambled to his feet, the Brethren streamed ahead and through the door silently. Some slipped on the gore-covered floor, but within seconds they were all inside.

THE BRETHREN MARCHED up the passage in step, the ends of their crossbows almost touching. They reached the main vault. Bats circled overhead. Persimmon gave hand signals to investigate the various vaults dug into the walls. The Brethren fanned out, splitting their numbers, moving cautiously around the main vault's perimeter toward the vaults.

"That's where Lisa is," Overboard George said, pointing to the curtained hole high in the vault. "Maybe Bo's up there, too, probably a Shadow or two. I'm going to free them."

"Not yet," Persimmon said. "They're safer up there until the action is over. Then you can have the honors. We'll pick them up on the way out."

"Maybe we should let her know we're here," Overboard George said. "Say a quick hello."

"Not yet. It's not safe. They might want to join us. We have to drive to that choke point."

Overboard George frowned and nodded in agreement.

Squads of Brethren entered the chambers dug into the main vault. They returned quickly with thumbs-down signals. The vaults were empty. The fighters reassembled in a column at the passage entrance to the house, where the large wooden door hung open. On Persimmon's signal, they started up the passage to the house.

"I don't like it," Persimmon told Overboard George. "It looks like the vamps cleared out those vaults. There might be a trap ahead. This is too easy."

"We'll be ready for it." Overboard George checked his stake gun. Felt for his extra bottle of gas.

The Brethren proceeded up the passage to the house and found a chamber cut in the wall. Two caskets were inside. Three Brethren lined up quickly along each casket like mourners paying their respects to the corpses of old friends, pointing their weapons down. Stake-wielding Brethren backed them up. An unarmed fighter crept up to each casket and grabbed the lids. Someone whispered, "Now."

The Brethren flung open the caskets. The vampires inside hissed, caught multiple bolts through the body, and shrieked in surprise. Other Brethren arrived. Shot in more bolts. Struck the writhing corpses again and again. The Brethren surrounded the caskets. The lids were torn off. Some Brethren shot bolts. Some chopped with machetes. Some were stabbed with long wooden stakes. An undead arm and foot went sailing. Blood splattered everywhere, covering the Brethren. Finally, the stabbing stakes found the vampire hearts and the fiends exploded in fire one by one burned to ash. While this group caught its breath, coughed on the undead's foul odors, cleaned the gore from weapons, wiped their goggles, and reloaded, another Brethren squad in formation surged by up the passage.

Overboard George and Persimmon brought up the rear. "You think the vampires heard all that screaming?" Overboard George whispered. "I think we're still in surprise mode."

There was an explosion from above. Dirt fell from the ceiling.

Persimmon looked up at the ceiling, then at George. "If they didn't hear us, I'm sure they heard *that*," she said. "So that was Del Hatch's Plan B."

"At least they're inside," George said. "Whatever works."

THE LOUNGING SHADOWS inside the large living room reached for guns. Some fled, but they were all cut down by bolts within seconds. The Brethren did not miss their targets and reloaded immediately. Few among the Shadows managed to get off shots. Del Hatch unleashed his BAR, shooting from the hip, sweeping the rifle across the room. The bane of the Wehrmacht during World War II, the rifle roared. Armor-piercing bullets destroyed everything in their paths. Shadows and furniture were shredded. Bullets exited the home through the walls. The smell of cordite and entrails filled the air. With the room cleared, the Brethren squads separated, and moved on, each with a room to clear based on Bo Bentwood's map. Meanwhile, Mad Maggie and Old Harriet used their torches and the dry grass outside to set the house's exterior ablaze. The dry siding caught quickly.

"No sirens yet," Old Harriet said. "Let's get inside and kill somebody."

The women ran inside. The Brethren had already dispersed throughout the home. The twang of crossbow fire was audible over and over in every direction. Del's BAR stopped long enough for him to slam in another clip. The Brethren's onslaught came fast and furiously. Occasionally, a gun fired in response. Never more than a single shot. The hiss and shrieks of surprised vampires came from the upper floors. Flashes of fire erupted from doorways. The first of the Brethren casualties was carried down the steps, and taken outside through the fire. Cars rolled up, medical attention administered, the victims loaded inside the vehicles, and just as quickly, the vehicles sped away.

A child vampire hit the living room floor. It howled and was missing its legs above the knees. The torso had multiple bolt wounds and it leaked viscous, foul-smelling black blood. It looked over its shoulder, saw the women, and dragged itself away across the floor, digging its claws into the floorboards for traction.

"Not so fast, honey," Mad Maggie called. She ran to the child and cut off an arm with her machete. The stump spouted more black blood. Then Mad Maggie severed the other arm. The vampire rolled away, but Old Harriet was there to stop the child with a foot, avoiding the snapping teeth, and the pinwheeling spouts of black blood, and drove one of the sharpened legs from the chair on wheels through the vampire's heart. The resulting flash singed Old Harriet's wild hair and burned the tip of her nose. Her beehived hair was half gone in an instant.

"Little fucker," Old Harriet cried. "That gives me an idea."

Piece by piece, Old Harriet pushed the shattered furniture into a pile under the front entrance, then threw a rug on top.

"That won't keep them in," Mad Maggie said, exasperated. "They can't go anywhere in the sunlight."

Old Harriet turned to Mad Maggie. "I'm not taking any chances. This will keep them inside." Old Harriet picked up her dropped torch and set the pile ablaze.

"Did you ever think we'd need a way out?" Mad Maggie shouted, above the fire's sudden and growing roar. She put her hands on her hips.

"We're pushing right through," Old Harriet said with a wink. "You'll see. Right to the bottom. There's no going back now."

"I think the whole place will burn down."

"I hope so," Old Harriet said. "It's a dump anyhow. Not even fit for the homeless. Stinks like a sewer."

They were alone in the room. Smoke started to rise from the new fire, drifted through the shattered opening to the exterior, curled in clouds across the ceiling. They turned. Fagan stood across from them. He was livid.

Persimmon and Overboard George had worked their way back near the column's front. One row of Brethren was ahead of them, crossbows leveled, moving forward.

"There should be a cavity on your left—a small one, Persimmon said, looking up from Bo's map.

"Got it," one of the fighters called.

The Brethren streamed in and ripped the casket lid off. It was empty. A vampire attached to the ceiling dropped into the middle of the squad, slashed, and bit at the Brethren. In the close quarters, the Brethren couldn't fire their crossbows for fear of hitting their brothers. They stabbed at the fiend with their long stakes. The vampire slashed through the fighters, knocking down crossbows, breaking stakes, opening large wounds, and shrieking all the while. More Brethren poured in and raised their weapons. Still, they couldn't fire. The vampire stayed among the fighters and refused to be pushed to the sides. Its arms and legs slashed, gashed, and mutilated the Brethren. The floor was wet from blood, the dirt churned into reddish mud. Persimmon shouldered her way to the opening.

"Down!" she commanded.

The Brethren dropped to a knee, exposing the vampire for a moment. Even before it could blur away, Persimmon unleashed a bolt through the vampire's heart. It combusted immediately, spreading gore and ash over everyone.

The Brethren reformed, breathless, and continued up the passage. The injured and dead were removed to the cemetery. The next two crypts were empty. The Brethren hacked apart the empty caskets. The third vault had a single vampire that started to blur in a leap over the fighters. Persimmon's bolt caught it and dropped it to the floor, where the Brethren fell on it with stakes and dispatched it quickly while the fiend howled in anger.

The group reformed. There were no more extra Brethren to fill gaps in the front line. The squads tightened and moved forward. After another empty chamber and a turn in the passage, Persimmon halted the group. They had reached the choke point where an immense rock too large to remove lowered the ceiling to about six feet high. The Brethren rested. Inspected their gear and called for more ammo. A few crossbows were damaged and needed to be replaced. Then, everyone waited, listened to the commotion upstairs, worried their friends were left to fight the bulk of the colony's undead.

THE BRETHREN SWEPT through the upstairs in the vampire house. They moved in lockstep, precision marching, their weapons ready to fire. Rooms were cluttered with old furniture. Some pieces were shrouded with sheets. The second floor looked like a hoarder's haven with stacks of old photos and oil paintings leaning against the walls, all with ornate frames. Teetering piles of books, magazines, and newspapers threatened to topple at any moment. Locked doors were battered in. Furniture covers were ripped off, filling the air with dust. Remaining Shadows, often hiding among the clutter, were darted immediately, their pleas for mercy ignored. One Shadow was shot through the neck in the shower, and slumped to the floor, spilling blood down the drain. With the rooms cleared, the second-floor Brethren squads converged into one group and paused at the attic steps.

Guacamole moved to the front. "This could be the vamps' last stand. Proceed with caution." She gave the nod to start the charge.

The stairs were narrow and curved. Only two fighters could climb abreast. The stairwell was so narrow, that the fighters had to hold their crossbows one over the other. This was not a new tactic. All the fighters had attacked in close quarters. The lower crossbow fired first and reloaded while the higher weapon fired. The second row had two Brethren with long stakes to impale the fiends. Every time a volley was fired, the squad stopped for a moment to reload.

The Brethren rounded spiraling stairs. A group of four Shadows stepped out and fired their guns into the tightly packed Brethren. Most Shadows had their eyes closed. One bullet hit its mark. Another round shattered a crossbow, sending its bolt askew. The other bullets slammed into the ceiling. The Brethren responded with bolts that downed the Shadows before they had time to get off second shots.

"Two vamps in the attic," Guacamole shouted. "They're blurring. Fill the exit."

The vampires banged around the attic. Their blurs were visible, but they were not. They caromed wildly, knocked over furniture, and toppled all manner of discarded items. Old crockery smashed. Mirrors broke. Wood splintered. The Brethren filled the stairwell and raised their crossbows and stakes. One vampire jumped through an attic window into the morning sunlight and incinerated immediately in a large flash as the fireball fell to the ground.

"Fire at will," Guacamole ordered. "Stake the fucker!"

The Brethren fired. One bolt caught the fast-moving vampire through the calf as it blurred above the opening. It fell to the floor. It had transformed into a reptilian-looking creature, gray and green, covered in scales. It stopped for a moment to break off the bolt and pull the dart through its leg. In that second a second bolt caught the creature in the stomach, A third hit in the shoulder. The vampire screamed at the Brethren. It blurred but was hit again. This time it fell on the Brethren in the stairwell and slashed its arms and legs with razor-sharp claws.

"Get rid of the thing before it explodes," Guacamole called.

The Brethren hoisted the creature in the air on their crossbows.

Their bolts penetrated the tough reptilian skin. The vampire shrieked in shock and flailed its arms and legs harmlessly. Its thick viscous blood poured over the Brethren. Some choked on the stench.

"Heave!" Guacamole shouted.

The Brethren shoved the vampire to the side, disengaged it from their bolt and stake points, and dumped it on the attic floor. As the creature writhed through the dust, the fighters unleashed another salvo into it. Then they ducked. One bolt hit the vampire's heart, and the creature exploded into a ball of flame. The fire, the intense heat, caught piles of books ablaze. The Brethren exited the attic, reformed in the second-floor hall, and started for the basement. The wounded and dead were carried outside, lowered through windows now that the house entrance was afire.

"I THINK your home's on fire, Squire," Old Harriet said, with glee.

She pointed to the blaze at the door.

"How dare you impudent women enter my refuge," Fagan howled. "Kill my people."

"That's the idea," Mad Maggie screamed back. "And you're next." She raised her two machetes. "I'll open you up like a piñata."

"Make your move, liver lips," Old Harriet added. "I don't got all day. Don't want to miss the fire."

"You'll see what awaits you and your Brethren. You are the ones trapped. We will wipe you out. Today. Now!"

A floorboard squeaked behind Fagan. The vampire flashed a look. It was Del Hatch with what Overboard George would have called a *shit-eating grin*. As the vampire flexed his knees to blur, Del unleashed a fresh clip from his BAR. Twenty rounds slammed through the vampire's body, shattering bones, and opening large holes that almost cut the torso in half. Fagan fell to the floor. He hissed. His black blood spread across a faded and dusty oriental rug. Fagan pulled himself backward. His tattered body began to heal immediately, sending out strands to reattach the severed flesh and pull organs back in place.

"Onesie, twosie," Mad Maggie screamed, while Del ejected the spent clip, and slammed in a new one. She stuck the point of one of her machetes in the floor.

Old Harriet pulled it out. "Threesie, foursie," she added, and raised the weapon.

Fagan hissed. Mad Maggie planted her blade into Fagan's groin. Old Harriet's swipe lopped off Fagan's right arm above the elbow. The vampire screamed. The stump beat on the floor like a drum. Mad Maggie swung again, cutting a large V-shaped wound into Fagan's crotch. Mad Maggie screamed. Old Harriet flailed away on the right leg. Three chops later, she severed it above the knee.

Fagan rolled over and tried to propel himself away from the women. With her extra machete, Mad Maggie impaled Fagan to the floor. His remaining arm and leg kicked the old dusty carpet and tore it to shreds. Mad Maggie and Old Harriet renewed their attacks on the vampire. Del Hatch watched with amusement. He slid the BAR's safety on. After the left arm and leg were severed, they hacked away at the torso with reckless abandon. What was left of Fagan flopped up and down on the floor. Finally, Old Harriet raised her hand. Both women were breathless and sweated. Their weapons were covered with black blood on the handles.

If left alone, Fagan would have healed eventually, and grown new arms and legs. His torso would have grown back. He would have been able to pull out the machete that pinned him to the floor like a displayed bug. Old Harriet retrieved her stake made from one of the chairs on wheels legs, pushed her tongue into the corner of her mouth, raised the stake over her head, aimed carefully, and impaled Fagan's dead heart. The vampire made a final gasp and burst into flames. A retreating Old Harriet caught some of the flash. Her hair singed again, and an ear and her nose caught heat and blistered immediately. Her beehive hairdo was reduced even more and leaned over her forehead. The flame caught the shredded carpet on fire. No one moved to put out the blaze as it spread across the room.

The Brethren who attacked the vampire house returned downstairs and avoided the fire from Fagan's demise. Runners brought in bolts replaced damaged crossbows, and passed out water. Guacamole faced Del Hatch. Both smiled.

"It looks like the ladies took out the head vamp," Del said. He spread his arms, calling attention to the fire. Mad Maggie and Old Harriet nodded eagerly. "They hacked him up like a country ham. Then Old Harriet gave him one through his dead ticker."

Old Harriet held up the remnants of her stake, now mostly charred.

"Excellent work, girls," Guacamole said, bowing to the women. "But there's more work to do." Then she turned to Del. "How is Mr. BAR"

"He's having one hell of a time," Del said.

"That's what I like to hear. Take care of yourself, Del."

"I always do. You, too."

The remaining fighters who attacked the vampire house reassembled into formation and descended into an empty, junk-filled basement and found the passage to the main vault open.

CHAPTER FORTY-ONE

The Brethren moved through the cluttered basement, sweeping their crossbows back and forth. The East Coasters did the same with their converted potato guns. Cobwebs dripped from the weapons. They spread out through the basement, overturning moldy mattresses and furniture in search of hidden enemies in the wan light. Dust rose in the air. A few Brethren coughed despite face masks they had donned. "The basement's clear," one among the group finally called.

The Brethren paused at the entrance to the passage through the hill to the main vault. "It looks like the vamps have gone down," Guacamole said. "Our people will be waiting at the choke point. We'll proceed to cut off any retreat."

Guacamole's headset crackled. "Where are you?" Persimmon said.

"Ready to come down the passage."

"We're at the choke point. Watch for vamps along the way. Bo's map shows several vaults off the passage."

"Roger that. See you in a few."

Guacamole turned to her troops. "Reform. Follow me."

Guacamole led down the passage. The Brethren followed two abreast down the narrow tunnel. First crossbows. Then long stakes. Their shoulders rubbed the sides. Dirt fell, raised more dust. They dipped their weapons to avoid striking the intermittent flapping torches, which emitted oily black smoke. The group reached the first vault off the passage. The two caskets inside were empty. No hangers on the ceiling. No vamps hiding in the clay walls. The group reformed and proceeded. Another vault was partially bricked off. Del Hatch and Guacamole pushed through and tumbled the bricks to the floor. Inside hanging were the three Shadows in the process of metamorphosing into vampires. The chrysalids hung from the ceiling, undulated as the things inside moved rhythmically.

Bad Nelson looked inside the vault. "They look ripe, ready to be picked," he whispered to Guacamole.

"Rotten is more like it. Ever see one?"

"Nope."

"Want the honor?"

"Sure do."

Guacamole stepped to the first chrysalis. She rubbed her gloved hand over the exterior. The thing inside responded. Moved toward the pressure, and pressed its face against the lining, revealing a malformed head with open fanged mouth. Guacamole palpated the chrysalis and moved her hand up along its length. She drew an imaginary X on the surface. "Hit it about here and back up fast. It's going to get messy."

Guacamole stepped back. Bad Nelson moved forward. He raised his stake gun, put the sight on the imaginary X Guacamole had drawn, looked at the snarling vampire face inside, returned his eyes to the stake gun sights, and fired. Whump. The stake shot across the vault and penetrated the chrysalis. The thing inside shimmied. The other chrysalids reacted similarly. Shook violently, as if the three hanging vampires were psychically connected. The bottom of the staked chrysalis split. A revolting, half-formed creature fell to the dirt floor. It looked up and melted into a putrid liquid that spread out and was partially absorbed by the dirt.

Bad Nelson reacted to the noxious odor and stepped back. Other Brethren filled the vault opening. Fired into the remaining two hanging vampires. Those chrysalids split open, spilling their half-turned creatures to the floor, where they immediately changed to viscous puddles that washed across the dirt.

Del Hatch moved in and rubbed shoulders with Guacamole. "A couple of real stinkers," he said.

Guacamole raised a hand to her nose and smiled back at him. "Reform," she choked. "One last vault before we reach the choke point. This might be where it gets hot."

"Funny we don't hear anything yet," Del said. "No fighting down the passage."

"I agree, but every vamp fight is different."

The Brethren moved forward. The passage twisted around a rock too large to remove or break up. Guacamole stopped and raised her arm. "The last vault's around this rock. Be ready."

Guacamole lowered her arm and continued. A white form flashed from the vault into the passage. Guacamole and two other Brethren fired their crossbows. The form tripped, bounced off the crumbling tunnel wall, and slipped around another turn. The bolts flew into the passage wall, over the form, bringing down more dirt. Footsteps receded in the distance.

"Easy, Brethren," Guacamole said, with her arm raised again. "It has nowhere to go, except to our friends or back to us. We're almost there. Get ready. It's going to get hot." On the radio to Persimmon, Guacamole said, "You got one coming."

"Something's coming," Persimmon whispered, from below the choke point. "I can hear it now. It's running." The Brethren were crowded into the passage with crossbows and stakes ready. "Sounds like only one. Might be more. Here we go."

Patty streaked into the opening in front of Persimmon and the Brethren. She wore only a burial shroud. She dropped to her knees, clasped her hands together, and begged for mercy. The Brethren trained their crossbows on her.

Guacamole arrived at the top of the choke point. Looked down at Patty. She raised her crossbow. "She's the one we saw."

"Wait," Persimmon said.

"She's a Shadow."

"I don't know," Persimmon said. "Look at her arms. Her eyes, how they're sunken. They've been feeding on her." Persimmon approached her. Lifted Patty to her feet. She raised Patty's arm to show the infected bite marks. Guacamole lowered her crossbow and entered the narrow space between the two groups. She brushed dirt from Patty's red hair, swung her face toward her, and used a thumb to peel back Patty's upper lip.

"Please help me," Patty implored. She clasped her hands again. Tears rolled down her cheeks.

Guacamole used the same thumb to catch tears and wipe a dirty smudge across Patty's face under her eye. "They didn't turn her. Are you a Shadow?" Guacamole leaned into Patty's face.

"No. They took me," Patty cried. "Off the street. They're drinking my blood."

"Who is?"

"The ancient one."

"Does she have a woman named Lisa, a guy named Bo?" Guacamole asked. She dropped her hand to Patty's shoulder and squeezed.

Patty winced.

"What about a guy named Jimmy?" Overboard George said from the front row of Brethren.

"She has all of them, only she turned Bo. He won't be ready for another couple of days."

"How do you know so much?" Persimmon wanted to know.

"I was with them," Patty said.

"Where?" Persimmon said.

"In her vault, the high chamber in the main dome."

"The one with the curtain?"

"That's it. I don't know where they put Bo, but Lisa and Jimmy are up there now, guarded by two big Shadows."

"The brothers Lazlo and Kazmer?" Persimmon said.

"That's them. Real mean. Stink like rancid tobacco, too," Patty said.

"European stock," Guacamole said. "They went off our radar some time back. We think Kazmer killed our man at After Dark. It was his M.O. Our guy was posing as a bartender. The brothers were captured on camera inside the bar the night he died."

"I wouldn't know about that," Patty said. "I just want to go home." She sobbed again. "*She* makes me wear this. Makes me do things inside her casket, with *her*. She drinks my blood and hurts me." Patty dropped to her knees again.

Persimmon cupped a gloved hand under Patty's chin. Raised her face. "I know you," Persimmon said. "You are a Shadow."

"No. I'm not."

Persimmon released Patty's face roughly. "You were with Bo sometimes at the laundromat. Sat outside on the phone and smoked while he did wash."

"It wasn't me. I don't even smoke."

"It was you. I'd never forget that red hair."

"Let me go."

"You will have the same fate as the rest of the vampire friend-lies," Persimmon said. "Archer one."

"Ready!"

Persimmon and Guacamole stepped away from Patty as she stood. "Go ahead. But you'll all die today," Patty hissed, twisting her mouth. "The hunters have become the hunted. Vampires will attack you from both sides." Patty touched her index fingers to the sides of her head. "They're waiting for her to give them the signal, through her *mind*. probably on their way now."

Persimmon nodded.

An archer released his bolt that caught her in the head. Patty slumped to the ground.

Persimmon looked at Guacamole. "How many did you stake on the way down?"

"Five, plus the three turning."

"We got five more on the way up," Persimmon said. "That leaves almost twenty vamps unaccounted for. Where could they be? How did we miss them?"

Old Harriet thrust her head between two Brethren and their crossbows. "Plus, we think we got the head vamp. Mad Maggie and me chopped him up after Del Hatch made Swiss cheese out of him with that BAR. Then he cooked in his own juices."

"Good work, ladies," Persimmon said. "I think we owe you another cake."

CHAPTER FORTY-TWO

Outside the vampire house, with dew still not burned off by the morning sun, large swatches of the tall grass moved toward the front porch, shimmied across the ground. The house was again silent, except for flames that licked up the siding and the remnants of the front door's threshold. In the distance, the first sirens wailed. Several of the few neighbors had congregated outside the fence. A young man snapped photos, found the hole in the fence Del Hatch had cut, and slipped inside. Took close-ups of the recently cut chain link He was the first to notice the moving turf. He took more photos. Switched to video.

You would think, the photographer mused, *that if grass could move, it would run away from fire and this old house. Not the other way around.*

The photographer was John Bargain, who spent much of the day and especially the night tooling around the city in search of breaking stories. He sold his videos and still shots to newspapers and television stations when he wasn't vlogging from inside cemeteries. His subject: the dead, either murderers or their victims, and hauntings. Therefore, he wasn't especially shocked by the sight of grass moving on its own. He had come to accept all things unusual. He made a decent living doing what he did. Some days he wondered, though.

This will make a hell of a vlog, but how do I explain it?

Bargain moved along after the last of the moving turf that crawled like a moving piece of carpet. He knew he better find a cause for its ability to slide along, or he wouldn't have much of a vlog—just another curious clip among unexplained things caught on his camera and relegated inside a computer folder. The naysayers would complain the video was faked. Police or firemen, whoever arrived first, would shoe him away before they began to string their yellow tape. The oblong pieces of turf, about the size of a large sleeping bag, Bargain thought, snaked up the wooden steps and across the porch. Just as the turf reached the door, something jumped through the air, landed on the threshold fire, and blurred away inside, too fast to identify. Bargain filmed this again and again. Soon the sod covered the threshold and suffocated the fire on the floor at the door.

Aided by the gimble on his cell phone, which kept the video steady, Bargain moved his phone from right hand to left seamlessly. *Only one way to find out*, he thought. Bargain crouched, ran after the last moving piece of turf outside, caught a back corner, and flipped over the large chunk of sod. There was a woman underneath, squirming snake-like across the ground. She turned her head to him immediately after being exposed, showed fangs, hissed. What he saw next happened so fast it was visible only by slowing down his video speed later, when he finally returned home and watched it on his computer. Her black eyes caught the sunlight. Bargain saw two tiny yellow orbs reflected in the black, dead orbs on her pale face. The face twisted. The pale skin reddened for an instant, then bubbled. She inhaled deeply as if to scream and burst into flames in front of him. The sudden conflagration blew by him. Black ashes and smoldering grass were all that was left of her. The ash that remained formed the outline of the woman's body. Among the cremains were two smoking shoes and some jewelry. Bargain videoed the remains, focused on the ashes and jewelry, the charred shoes, for a few seconds. He was already thinking of the eerie music available to him that he could add to the video. *This is going to be great!*

Bargain was speechless. He decided to say nothing but panned the camera to his astonished face. He would do a voice-over later. With his hand in frame, Bargain picked up and pocketed the jewelry. *Will be worth an epilogue, laid out on his desk,* he thought. *Some final thoughts to finish the piece.* Bargain turned to the last of the crawling sod, which had just reached the base of the front porch steps. He approached, still in his crouch, videoing the movement. *Have to prove this isn't faked,* he thought. He grabbed the back corner nearest to him, gripped hard to fling over the turf when a pale, long-clawed hand reached out and seized his wrist. Bargain cried out in surprise and pain. He tried to pull free, but the talons dug into his wrist. The pain was incredible. He dropped to his knees and rode the slow-moving turf up the steps like it was a flying carpet preparing to take off. His camera was on. The moving turf was visible. The hideous hand clasped on his wrist. The long talons drew blood. Sweat covered Bargain. He tugged and tugged against the pale hand, but it was much stronger.

Refusing to stop his video, Bargain bent over and bit the fingers that held him. The flesh tasted putrid. Shreds came off in his mouth. There was a cry from under the grass. Bargain released his bite. He spit again and again but couldn't get rid of the awful taste. Then he transferred the gimble to his mouth, and closed his teeth on it, causing the video to change from portrait to landscape. The turf snaked across the sunlit porch. He seized the middle of the turf with his free hand and rolled off the grass, bringing the sod with him. The thing underneath shrieked. Exploded in flames. The hand let go as it incinerated, burning Bargain's wrist. His second encounter with the undead had videoed a small red ant that zigzagged through the turf that covered his face. Bargain threw off the sod. A black outline of smoldering ash was all that remained of the thing under the turf. A few hot coals lingered before burning out.

The first vehicle on scene was an ambulance. It was followed by a police cruiser and a moment later the first fire truck. Bargain had just regained his feet, and staggered a bit to catch his balance. He noticed a signet ring among the ashes. He bent over and added the ring to the pocket that contained the other jewelry. He was still filming. Rather than face the ire of the city officials, Bargain went inside the house through the halo of fire at the door and around the pile of furniture ablaze inside.

Bargain spoke for the first time. The camera pointed at his flushed, dirty face. Then he held up his injured and burned wrist. "You saw what I saw. What do you think? I'm saying vampires, but you know the drill. They don't exist. However, what else blows into flames in sunlight, burns to ashes in seconds, and leaves nothing left? We've all seen the movies. Bela Lugosi, Christopher Lee. They always manage to come back when the next movie in the series comes out. But these guys today, outside, and at least one was a gal, there's no way they're coming back. No way. You saw it here on Bargain Videos, all that's left is dust. I breathed in some of that shit, too. Any of you cut-throat lawyers out there watching who think I have a case, for some future health problem I'll probably contract, let me know at bargainvideos.com. What are my chances for a huge settlement?"

Bargain swiveled the camera around the burning interior. "It's starting to cook now. I'll have to find another way out because the police and firemen are closing in. I want to follow those things that were under the grass, anyway." Bargain passed a wide staircase. "Don't want to go upstairs, folks. That's where people in movies make their mistakes. Ever notice that? No matter where they are—a haunted house, a factory, or some other sort of place, they always take the high road, and that does them in because there's never a way to get back down. They're stuck up there until they get murdered, which usually doesn't take long and involves a fall from a great height. I personally don't like heights. Not to mention this place is on fire!

"Now that we have that cleared up, I see dirt on the floor. It's a trail of dirt that came off—dare I say it—the vampires as they left their dirt shrouds behind. I'll follow it and hope to hit—no pun intended— pay dirt."

Bargain walked quickly down a long hall, videoing a trail of dirt, occasionally panning back to his ever-reddening face. He coughed. "I'm hoping there's a back way out because it's getting smoky in here. Don't know how much longer I can take it. I might have to bail, even if it's toward the police. Sounds like the firemen have reached the front door. No return there or I'll probably go to jail for trespassing. Who knows? They might think I set the fire. However, the vamps had to go somewhere. We're in the kitchen now, as you can see. Here's a rather new-looking stove and sink and a fridge with a sign. FOR LISA ONLY. Lisa must be lucky to have a fridge all to herself. Why not? Vamps don't eat nothin'."

Bargain made a face at the camera and continued. "I'm still following dirt on the floor. Not as much now, though. Don't have to be Daniel Boone to follow it, even though the whole place is a pigsty. It looks like the back door is boarded shut. The windows, too. No escape there. Here's another door that leads down, probably to a basement. The dirt trail follows down. So do I. But before I get too far gone down these steps, the second mistake people in movies make is going to the basement. That's a big no-no. The best thing is turn around and go out the way you came in. If you can. But here I go anyway. What more can I do wrong today? At least I didn't go upstairs."

Bargain paused a moment, bent over, and picked up something. "My hand hurts like hell where that creature grabbed me. I can hardly grip this wood—looks like a stake. Very sharp. I'm taking it with me. Just the thing for vamps. I wish I had more of these things."

Lisa and Jimmy sat on the narrow bed in the vault that had become known as her room. They held hands. Looked glum. They could see Eva in the next room. The curtain that separated the two rooms had been torn down. While Kazmer waited with the couple, Lazlo had lain on the shelf outside, hidden from the main vault floor, and reported in a whisper that the Brethren had entered the main vault below and moved up the passage to the house. Eva stood as if she were a statue, unmoving, along with ten vampires ready to follow the Brethren up the passage, to force them into a fight from two sides. Some vampires would fall, Eva knew, some already had, but the Brethren would eventually exhaust their ammunition, tire as humans do. Then their age-old foe would be slaughtered, first tortured, then drained of their lifeblood. It had been nearly two centuries since she faced a squad of Brethren. Most of this colony would be destroyed. That was a fact she was willing to accept. After the last Brethren was dead and Bo fell from his chrysalis, a newly minted vampire, she and Bo would vivisect Lisa, take her child for themselves, and drain its blood. Jimmy would be Bo's first victim. She had everything planned. After becoming a vampire, even as a new vampire, Bo would feel nothing for the couple. They were merely food like the double cheeseburgers he had liked so much.

Lazlo crawled into the vampiress's crypt, stood, and brushed off the dirt from his clothes. "Mistress, excuse me." He waited a moment until the vampire's eyes locked on his. He lowered his head. "All the Brethren are in the passage. They have taken some of our members."

"I know, Lazlo. It was necessary that they kill some of us. To give them hope. Fagan and I placed the least among us in places where they would be found. Also, I placed those I mistrusted."

"Yes, mistress. I understand."

"Do you, Lazlo? Really understand?"

"No, madam." Lazlo bowed. "Will Fagan lead us?"

"Fagan is gone."

"Yes, mistress? I am sorry."

"Join your brother. Keep Lisa safe."

"Yes, mistress."

Lazlo walked into Lisa's room and joined Kazmer on the floor below the walled-up niche where Bo transformed into a vampire. His chrysalis undulated. The vampire disease ravaged what was left of Bo's body. It created a new shell of a body, perfect, without a blemish. It would emerge with enhanced senses, superhuman strength, and a raging, unquenchable thirst for human blood.

Eva stepped into Lisa's room. The couple recoiled. The brothers bowed their heads.

"You look well, Lisa," the vampiress said. She smiled. "I hear your heart and the baby's. How wonderful. Two hearts. Two people, but really one being for now. We go to fight your friends. The brothers will keep you safe."

"Is Patty staying with us?" Lisa said.

Eva looked at Lisa coldly. "The Brethren have killed Patty. I sensed it." She pointed to her forehead. "Shot her through the head with a crossbow, their preferred instrument dealing death."

Lisa caught her breath.

"In the end, Patty was not loyal. She did not make a good Shadow."

"Are there any good Shadows?" Jimmy said.

Eva Blurred to Jimmy and lifted him by the neck until his feet dangled and he choked. "You talk much for one who knows so little," Eva said, smiling at him. Lisa stood, grabbed the vampire's arm tugged on it but the arm did not move.

"Leave him alone!" Lisa cried.

The vampiress looked at Lisa and released Jimmy. He fell to the bed, choked more, and massaged his neck. Then the vampiress was gone. The other vampires followed.

Lazlo went outside on the shelf. He returned in a moment. "All the masters are inside the passage. Get your tools ready, my brudder. We will have many graves to fill today."

Kazmer grunted.

CHAPTER FORTY-THREE

Patty's dying words were the hunters have become the hunted. The Shadows, ill-equipped and trained to face any opposition, had been either killed or dropped their weapons and fled. All that remained were the undead with their forces divided into approximately two groups of ten on both sides of the Brethren. *Not the best situation to be in, but certainly not the worst,* Persimmon thought. She looked at Guacamole.

"Been in tighter spots," Guacamole said. "Faced more vamps, too. You just have to stake them one at a time."

"And you're here to talk about it.," Persimmon added. "When was the last time you were resupplied?" she asked Guacamole.

"Not since we left the house and went into the passage. Ammo check," she called back to her squad. Some Brethren had a full complement of twenty-five bolts, others fewer, depending on how much action they saw upstairs. Not all Brethren had to fire their crossbows. Persimmon's group had about the same. Those at the rear of the action had not fired their weapons, holding defensive positions. The Brethren traded places. Those who hadn't fired moved to the front. All were expert marksmen and unafraid, had fought vampires before. Some kneeled. Some stood. Long stakes were planted in the dirt on a diagonal to catch blurring vampires who launched themselves at the defenders. Other points were stuck in the ground perpendicular, in the event a vampire was able to jump over the Brethren to land in the middle of their group.

Patty's body was passed through the Brethren, her mouth agape, her eyes staring, a bolt impaled through her forehead. She was dropped lengthwise across the passage in front of the defenders, her shroud hiked up above her knees. The bolt in Patty's head was removed with some difficulty, a little wiggling was required, wiped clean on her shroud hem, and returned to the arsenal.

The Brethren shuffled into position under the low rock. Back against back, shoulder against shoulder. The long stakes were all deployed again. The formation was developed by the Crusaders, effective against vampires and humans. The East Coasters were sprinkled among the Brethren, their converted potato guns primed and ready. Del Hatch was among the front fighters. His BAR leveled for action. He placed a stack of clips in front of him. More were in his pockets. Persimmon placed Overboard George and Bad Nelson two rows back facing opposite directions. Mad Maggie and Old Harriet were in the middle, side-by-side, facing opposite directions, each holding two machetes. Old Harriet had her last leg from the chair on wheels tied over her back. The point sharpened by Overboard George was aimed at the ceiling.

Old Harriet spit on her palms. Her mouth was dry, and nothing came out. "Give me some spit," she said to Mad Maggie. Mad Maggie smiled and spit twice, once each in Old Harriet's palms. Then she spit on her own hands.

"Be ready when they come over the top," Mad Maggie said. "I'm aiming for the groin. OG says there's nothing a vampire likes better than to screw. I'm going to put them out of commission, male or female, in the event they might escape."

"*Famous Monsters of Filmland?*" Old Harriet whispered.

"No. FM is more of a family magazine to have such stuff."

Old Harriet pushed at the remainder of her beehive hairdo. "Then it must be a class operation if you ask me."

Mad Maggie nodded.

"If you chop off some junk and they escape, those parts will grow back," Old Harriet said. "Better just go for the hearts."

"Remember them Whistlers at After Dark. All deformed vampires," Mad Maggie whispered, with an air of authority. "Maybe the junk on one of these vamps will grow back deformed. Won't work. That's what I'm thinking."

"Possible. That's a pleasant thought, though," Old Harriet said, wrinkling her forehead. "I'm thinking about another birthday cake." Old Harriet scratched her diminutive nose. "Itchy. I think *they* are close."

"Rather have it sooner than later."

JOHN BARGAIN SQUEEZED the wooden stake he had picked up with his injured hand, wincing in pain. His camera video continued. "Guys, I hope you can see this," Bargain whispered. He panned from the passage to his begrimed face. "The light's kinda low. There's torches stuck in the walls here and there. Just like in a Vincent Price movie. Some are already burned out. Some just about out. Some were knocked on the floor. The ones still burning are real stinkers. Even the air smells like something is dead down here the farther I go. Burns my nose. Is that a sign of vampires? Leave me your thoughts in the comments. This isn't a live stream, so I can't read what you have to say now. I wouldn't be able to anyway. I can't take my eyes away from what lurks ahead. Could be a vamp standing there. Anyway, I don't think I'd have a signal down here, underground. In the meantime, don't forget to subscribe to my channel, leave some comments below, and ring that bell so you get my latest updates. With material like this, you won't want to miss a thing."

Bargain continued, after a pause. "Holy shit!" he hissed. "There's a room dug into the passage here. Plus, I hear some noise below in the passage. Sound seems to travel along the walls. Acoustics. Might be a nice place for a concert, if it were bigger and didn't stink as much. The air moves too, sounds like a sigh, now and then. Very creepy. I'm taking one of these torches to explore this room. Make enough light so you all can see better."

The video showed Bargain's arm and hand pulling a torch from its holder. The flame flapped, and released a trail of black smoke. "Oh, that hurts. You can see where my wrist is already bruised and burned. Proof I'm not a vamp. That asshole vamp would have to grab my right hand. I'll need some first aid when I get out of here. If there's a nurse watching, give me some advice. I don't have insurance and can't go to the ER. Leave a number, too. I'll ask you out. Ha. Ha. Just kidding. But I will ask you out. Dutch treat, of course. Not that I'm a tightwad. It can take a while to get paid in this racket. I don't always have extra money for a date night unless I go out alone. That's no fun, so I sit at home.

"Okay. I'm entering the room. You can't see it, but I have the stake under my arm just in case. The last thing I'm going to do is drop my phone. Holy shit! Guys, there are two coffins in here. The one is on its side. The other is on a stand. I hope you can see this. Thank God they're empty. It looks like this one has blood on it. Oh, this is too gross. I might hurl. I don't know what's going on with this torch. Suddenly it's dripping little flames that sizzle when they hit the floor. Ouch! The little fucker burned me. That's all I need. And on my good arm, too."

Bargain panned his camera around the room, up at the ceiling, back to his nervously smiling face, and toward the floor.

"Oh boy. Look at this. It's a pile of ashes. Black ashes. And three of these stakes. These look like darts, the kind shot from crossbows. The ashes looked like the stuff outside when I pulled the rug out from under those *things*. Actually, I pulled the turf off their tops and they exploded in the sunlight. Love happy endings. This one might have been staked."

Bargain picked through the ashes with the tip of one of the bolts, spreading them across the floor. "Ah, hah! Typical MO. Some empty shoes, all curled up, burned inside and out. And what is this? More jewelry. Two rings, a bracelet, and a necklace. Jackpot! Looks like old stuff. Antiques, maybe. Pawn shop here I come. Anybody know an honest pawn dealer? Leave me info in the comments. I'm liable to have quite a stash by the end of the day. There's also a couple of melted plastic things, probably were buttons. I'm not taking shit like that, unless it proves to be too cool to leave behind."

THE DIRT-COVERED vampires crept down the passage from the house, two-by-two, almost silently. Some swirled their tongues. Others moved their jaws and ground their teeth in anticipation. The last fiend in the column stopped and said to the next undead, "I hear someone behind us."

"I hear it, too."

"Whoever it is carries one of the wall torches. He's talking to someone, but I detect only one human. He is not one of us."

"I agree."

"I'll go back to see."

The second vampire shrugged. "Don't bother. It's one of our Shadows, scared shitless. He is talking to himself. Trying to find courage. Let's catch up. We will soon have gallons of blood to drink."

THE BRETHREN WAITED, breathing heavily. Even in the dank cool air, redolent of death, they sweated and kept their lips moistened.

EVA LED ten vampires up the passage from the main vault. She wore her blood-splattered cowgirl outfit, sans hat. They moved almost silently. The only noise came from their swirling tongues. The vampiress had fed well the night before. She had drained two illegal immigrants, eviscerated them with her hardened thumb claw, and let them float down the river like she was launching two skiffs.

The bodies soon sank in the darkness under the fast-swirling current. While she had drained one, the second lay nearby paralyzed with fear, too scared to run, too scared to scream for help. How she had laughed. It had amused her so much. Although she had looked forward to draining the Brethren today, gorging herself again, another plan occurred to her, and she smiled.

BARGAIN TURNED the camera back to his face. "Okay. I have somewhat of a dilemma. I just sat down on one of the coffins, caskets, whatever, although there is a difference, just like graveyard and cemetery, careful to avoid the blood. That's scary enough, but I need a breather, and my hand's killing me. Okay. Some of you might think I'm a pussy, but my wrist really hurts. Might be broken. So, you might say I shouldn't collect this jewelry. Let me know in the comments. I'm sure you will, no matter what I say. You know I read all your opinions. Honest. No matter how long it takes. Should I leave this jewelry, which looks mostly antique and valuable, in the dirt here underground, to lay forever? I know it belonged to *someone.* It was personal property. Why cause confusion to a future archaeologist? Oh, shit! Did you hear that. I know you didn't feel it, but some dirt fell from the ceiling and covered my head."

With the camera on him, Bargain shook his head, spit, and wiped his lips clean. "Not much. Just enough to dirty my hair.

Should have worn my Dodgers hat. I hope this fucking place doesn't decide to cave in on me. Then the confused archaeologist will find me and my cell phone in a thousand years. You know, like the dead in Pompeii found with valuables. Okay again. Back to the jewelry. Oh, by the way, there is definitely noise coming from down the tunnel. I hear it. Could be vamps. Who knows? So, what I'm going to do is wait here for a time before I move ahead. There's a twist in the passage ahead, and I don't want to walk around a corner and into the arms of Count Dracula. I can't go back, because the house is probably, as they say, fully involved with flames and has enough smoke up there to gag a maggot. The only way is forward. I'll have to bide some time. Wait for whoever it is to move on. Wait until it's safe, if there is such a thing in this place.

"Back to the jewelry issue. Again. By now, you must think I don't want to talk about it. But, here goes: Rather than see the jewelry go to waste, and rot down here, even though it wouldn't rot in the true sense of the word, like a body, if I take it and use it, or sell it, obviously I won't use women's jewelry, unless I can give some to a nice nurse who fixes my arm and becomes my girlfriend, a pretty young nurse, because I'm not a bad catch myself, as you can see in my videos. Maybe I should have my teeth cleaned, though. Any hygienists out there who could sneak me into their office on a Sunday, when nobody's there? The dentist will be out playing golf and won't care. I'd even be glad to accept some complimentary tubes of toothpaste, floss, and toothbrushes.

"Anyway, that jewelry will have some purpose, what it was meant for. The jewelry I sell will help me financially, because everybody says, 'You must go abroad. Do some videos from the continent. Soak up some culture. Eat all the good food. See the sights. So that's my idea now. Sell most of the jewelry, Keep a ring or two for myself. I'll have them blessed or something first, in case they're haunted or cursed—don't want a ring attached to a ghost. Suppose I wear a cursed ring and then can't take it off. I'll save some pretty pieces to give to a nurse who wants to fix my wrist and maybe be my girlfriend. Those pieces will be blessed, too. And I'll be blessed to have a nurse as a girlfriend. I'm talking a lot about nurses, I'm sure you can tell, but my wrist hurts like hell. It was squeezed by a vamp and then burned when the vamp went up in flames. I'm not a pervert. You all know that. We did the *pervert* video some months back. If you think I'm a pervert because I like nurses, please go back and revisit that video. I like everybody, really. I'll put the link below if I ever get out of this shit hole."

Bargain took a deep breath and exhaled. "Guys, I'm telling you this while I sit on a coffin in an underground vamp lair. I just realized how stupid it was to come down here. I should be more worried about getting out of here in one piece than about vamp jewelry. You agree? Sure you do. I should have let the cops outside the house possibly arrest me, maybe charge me with *wrongfully entering* and arson. I might be sitting in the back of an ambulance, drinking a Gatorade and having my wrist treated by a female EMT. Anyway, my phone battery is low. I have to shut down. I'll fire up when something happens, and I catch my second wind."

WHILE THE VAMPIRES from the lower side prepared to attack, Eva made her way through their ranks to the back.

"You know what to do. Slaughter the Brethren. Gorge yourselves on their hot blood."

She had fought the Brethren in Europe and knew, although they were human, their tactics were cunning. The colony would be almost decimated by the time the last Brethren was killed. She would not risk the chance of a stray bolt catching her heart. Then there would be no black mass. She would return to her crypt, open up Lisa as she had done to the feckless immigrants, remove the live baby and drain its blood. After Lisa and Jimmy saw their child murdered in front of them, she would drain their bodies of blood. All those who opposed her at After Dark would be dead within the hour, including the foolish junkers who fought with the Brethren. Her strength would be as great as any vampire in the world. She blurred to her lair, where the brothers Lazlo and Kazmer stood guard.

For their final preparation, the Brethren pushed from the interior of their ranks toward both front rows, a number of ornate jars containing blood. Just as the vampires had friends in high places, so did the Brethren. It was nun's blood, donated by virgins around the world for the fight against evil. They opened the jars, spilled a couple into shallow trenches in front of and behind the Brethren, and let the others stand, so the odor of the special blood circulated both up and down the passage. Within a minute, the Brethren heard the vampire's murmuring, moaning with pleasure. The first vampire attacked from the lower side, intoxicated by the blood, propelling itself foolishly against the fixed stakes. It was hacked to death immediately and burst into flame after one strike split its shriveled heart. The Brethren shielded their eyes against the burst of fire, braced themselves against the noxious smell of burning vampire flesh. Another attacked from above was darted immediately and burst into flame.

Eva, or even Fagan, might have maintained order among the vampire ranks. Led a marshaled engagement with the Brethren, but left to their own, intoxicated by the perfume of virgin blood, the vampires attacked without regard for their own safety, and the undead were cut down mercilessly. They sensed only their raging thirsts.

The Brethren remained in position. Fired their bolts with precision. There were no orders shouted, no cries for help. The Brethren remained stoic as they fired and reloaded, jabbed with their long stakes, and slashed with the machetes. Even though they might not see a blurring vampire, they predicted where it would be in the next instant and shot there. They all had practiced the routine countless times. Strikes slowed down the beasts, and brought them from the blur long enough for others to fire more bolts into them or stab them with long stakes. Where spent bolts were within arm's reach, they were retrieved and placed ready to shoot again. As one crossbow fired, another took its place while the first was reloaded. The vampires shrieked when hit, and vomited black blood at their adversaries. Everyone was soon covered in viscous, foul-smelling syrupy goo, with the consistency of used motor oil. The walls and Brethren were slick with it.

Even when multiple vampires charged at once, they became easy targets, tended to carom off one another, giddy with the scent of virgin blood. The vampire disease demanded to be slaked. The crossbows twanged. The converted potato guns whumped. The long stakes stabbed through the air. Machete blades rose, their blades flashing in the torchlight, and fell. Salvo after salvo fired into the vampire horde. Del Hatch's BAR roared. The 30.06 shells flew from the gun and scattered. In the confined space, the noise was ear-splitting. Del filled the vampires with holes, making them easy to stake.

Dirt fell from the ceiling. The vampires lost limbs and heads. Decapitated heads sometimes rolled among the Brethren before they burst into flames. The Brethren shuffled their feet through the dirt to put out little fires. They patted down neighbors whose clothing was suddenly alight on the greasy vampire blood. The Brethren soon had singed hair and burns and wiped vampire blood from their faces on their sleeves. A few vampires on both sides managed to make it to the little trenches and slurped a mouthful of virgin blood and gravel before being hacked apart. Several vampires invaded the Brethren's front ranks, spun in a blurred frenzy, slashed with their claws, and opened necks, arms, and abdomens before they were staked. The dead and wounded were pulled to the center. Mad Maggie and Old Harriet became nurses. As the triage grew, Brethren filled in the openings in the ranks. Gold was lashed across her cheek and down her chin with a vampire's dying hand. She refused treatment and remained in her position.

As the numbers on both sides dwindled, the Brethren were about to exhaust their ammunition. "Out!" came the call time after time. "No more gas!" Bad Nelson yelled. He dropped his PVC-pipe gun and stood with his last stake raised ready to strike.

"Me, too! Out of everything!" Overboard George yelled, despite the fact that there was no need to raise his voice because everyone, vampires included, was quiet in the sudden face off and the Brethren's numbers had been cut in half. Old Harriet unslung her stake from the chair on wheels leg and passed it to him. George nodded with a smile.

"Let's see how sharp a point you made," Old Harriet said. What was left of her beehive hairdo was plastered to her head, covered with black vampire blood.

Overboard George was even with her now. "You look twenty years younger, Old Harriet."

"Watch what you say, or I'll take my stake back. If you think I'm easy, I'm not."

Persimmon, who had burns on her hand and cheek and was covered with vampire blood, looked in both directions. The vampires had withdrawn a few paces. There were three on the down side. Four on the top. They waited, appeared still to be intoxicated by the virgin blood, rocked back and forth, and had no thoughts of fleeing. Smoke from the house fire finally trailed down along the passage ceiling, hardly detectable. Smelled like a camp-fire. There were shouts above. Apparently, firemen were in the basement, putting out the blaze amid all the combustible junk. It was a matter of time before they found the downward passage.

"Bolts?" Persimmon said.

Various Brethren sounded off. One, One, Two, One, One, One.

Dell Hatch said, "One clip, 20 rounds."

"Let's see that monster do some damage," Guacamole said.

Del winked at her.

"It's time to overdose the fuckers. Flypaper!" Persimmon shouted. "Make your last shots count."

Guacamole stepped in front of the upside Brethren, picked up the last jar of virgin blood still standing, and poured it over her head.

"*Noooooo!*" Del Hatch screamed.

BARGAIN WAS JOLTED to his feet. He turned on his camera, and pointed it at his astonished face. Eyes were wide. "Fucking me OW, guys! That's gunfire coming from down the tunnel. Sounds like a cannon. A fucking bullet just whizzed up the shaft here right outside the door. I kid you not. I can see it put a big divot in the wall outside. There's dirt falling everywhere. I'm afraid to move. This whole place might cave in. Holy shit! An arrow just whizzed by. I think it was an arrow. Too small to be a vampire. Maybe too short to be an arrow. Maybe from a crossbow. It's like World War III. BANG! BANG! BANG! THWANG! THWANG! THWANG! THUMP! THUMP! THUMP! Oh my GOD! I gotta get out of here. I'm shitting my pants. I kid you not.

"You can hear it. This might be the last Bargain Video, one way or another, even if I survive this massacre. Can you hear it? I know you can. The most ungodly screams I've ever heard. It's more than I can imagine. They're not human. They're otherworldly. Ear-splitting. Hollow sounding. Like you screamed in a barrel. Got to be vamps dying—I hope. Sounds like a battle of good against evil. I ask you—who will prevail? Will there be more jewelry? Can I get to it first? Where's the closest pawn shop?

"I'd try to get it on camera. Peek around the corner. But I'm too far away. Plus, I'm shitting my pants. I think I already told you that. Two more bullets just went by and an arrow. I kid you not. I wouldn't stick my little toe out in that tunnel for a million bucks. Maybe a million. Can you live without a little toe? Walk without a limp? This dirt is incredible. I'm filthy now. Will I ever be clean again? The fight goes on. It's raining dirt everywhere. Now there's a fucking crack in the ceiling. I'm showing it to you. I got to get out of here."

Bargain exited the room. He pressed himself against the wall. Dirt spilled over his shoulders and covered his head. He spit out loose gravel and moved slowly sideways down the passage. "Oh, fuck! I forgot my torch. I'll have to go back. It's really dark down here."

Bargain started to retrace his steps. There was a loud *whomp*. The ground shook. Even with the gimble, the video shook. More dirt fell.

"Holy shit, guys! That room where I was just collapsed. The ceiling caved in. Look. You can see dirt spilling out into the tunnel. Now I'm really fucked. I gotta continue down. There's dust from the walls and smoke from the fire above. Okay. Going back down. It seems like the bullets and arrows whiz up the tunnel's other side. That's good for me. I hope the vamps don't beat a hasty retreat. Note to self: next time wear a turtleneck, no matter how hot it is. One, you keep dirt from spilling down your neck, like it is now. Glad my shirt isn't tucked in. I might weigh about twenty pounds more just from dirt. Two, the turtleneck might give you two extra seconds against a vamp before he tears you apart. What am I saying? There won't be another time. Hope I can die of fright before I'm turned into a vamp. Maybe catch one of those bullets and die instantly." Bargain made a face at the camera. Twisted his mouth. "No, dear friends. I am not suicidal. Remember? We did a video on suicide last summer. I had a friend. You know. Go watch it. You'll see me cry. Genuinely. I'll put a link below if I live to do it. You might see me cry again.

"Again, you nurses out there. I might need more treatment than a wrist bandage and *a lot* of TLC. Maybe a transfusion. Just so you know. You nurses might find me in intensive care. Maybe the psych ward, if I survive. There I go again on nurses. I am not nurse compulsive. Truth be known, I am compulsive about everything. But when you're about to be extinguished you think of recovering from your injuries instead of dying from them. So, that's why I'm fixated on nurses right now. Tomorrow—if I should live so long—I'll fixate on something else. Maybe strippers. Any strippers out there who want to give me some TLC and strip for me? My apartment doesn't have a pole, but we can work something out. Maybe you can swing on the plumbing. OH MY GOD! I have to get out of this fucking place."

ALL THE VAMPIRES SHRIEKED. They shook in place when the sudden, strong smell of virgin blood reached their senses. They tasted blood on the air, through their swirling tongues, through their pallid skin. And they were enraged by the wasted blood.

Del Hatch opened up and shot one round at a time. The .30-06 caliber bullets blasted holes through the vampires. More dirt fell from the ceiling. Still, the fiends shrieked, oblivious to the wounds. Twang! Twang! Twang! The Brethren released their final bolts into the shimmering vampires. They were easy marks and exploded into huge fireballs.

The last vampire on the lower side disappeared in a flash of fire. One remained on the upper side. Guacamole took two steps forward. Out of ammunition, certain Brethren pulled throwing axes from their belts and got ready to throw.

"I'm out," Del Hatch sobbed. The Brethren had exhausted all their bolts. None were near enough to snatch off the ground. The East Coasters stood weaponless. The ground was littered with empty propane canisters. Mad Maggie and Old Harriet whimpered and held each other. Both were covered in vampire blood.

Guacamole was covered in virgin blood. It dripped off her, and the metallic scent of it filled the air stronger than ever. She stood, motionless. Closed her eyes. Lowered her head. The vampire seemed torn between fleeing and attacking. It was agitated, and pivoted its head from Guacamole, an escape route up the passage and back to the blood-covered woman. Apparently, it could not control its raging thirst, the allure of the sight and smell of virgin blood. Brethren with long stakes surrounded Guacamole. Pointed their staffs in an age-old, often-practiced pattern. Del Hatch moved forward. He held the BAR by the barrel like a club. Tears filled his eyes.

The vampire threw back its head, and roared in rage. The Brethren unleashed their axes. One cleaved the vampire's forehead. Another opened its chest. The thing staggered. That was all the time the Brethren needed to fall on it with their long stakes, stabbing again in swift, short strokes. The vampire shrieked. One jab pierced the side of a knee. It collapsed on the other knee. The vampire's head lolled. The Brethren stabbed, searching for the heart.

"Out of my way, everybody!" Old Harriet cried. "This mother fucker is mine! The Brethren pulled back a step, kept their stakes ready. Old Harriet raced forward. Struck the vampire through the heart with the leg from her chair on wheels. The thing exploded, and Old Harriet was thrown back. She immediately scrambled to her feet and broke into a dance.

THE BRETHREN FELL QUIET. There was a noise in the passage. They turned toward the up side. Pointed their stakes in anticipation.

BARGAIN WAS JUST above the choke point. He stopped for a moment.

"It's eerily quiet below. It's more than eerie. It's totally quiet.

For a split second, I heard a cheer. I think the battle is over. I hope the vamps are dead. I'm almost out of battery, so I might cut out at any moment. Haven't seen a single outlet down here in this godforsaken shit hole. After all, they have torches. I'll keep recording as long as I can. You'll want to see all the grisly details. Okay. There's more of these little arrows. Some are broken. Some partially burned, it appears. Who knows? Maybe shish kebab. See for yourself. I can tell you one thing. There's no fucking buffet down here. Yes, I'm looking for jewelry. It's pretty dark. There's more of the arrows. Some broken. Some stuck in the walls, some in the ceiling, as you can now see. It looks like a fucking porcupine! And there's a ring. A nice one, too, the ladies will be interested to see. Do I sound like I'm on a shopping network? There's more down here. Ash piles, too. Vamp jewelry. That means dead vamps, so I don't feel any remorse taking it."

Bargain got on his hands and knees, and started to crawl, focusing the camera either on himself or the ground ahead. He stopped to pocket more jewelry.

"One thing is strange. I haven't seen any watches. Some bracelets, but no watches. Dah! Of course. Why would a vampire wear a watch? All it—he or she—needs to know is it day or night? My bad on that one. Don't castrate me in the comments."

"This place stinks like a whore's...you finish it. My God. There is blood everywhere. Black blood. Never seen or smelled anything like it. Gag a maggot! More jewelry. Mother of God! Oh, A fucking body! She's dead. Shot through the head. I was so fixated picking up jewelry in the ashes that I almost touched her hand. I'm going to video her right after I vomit. I can always edit it out later—probably will, too. There might be a relative who watches this. This is it, guys. I'm really going to hurl this time. If I bent over, I could probably see right through her head. This is worse than the accident on the interstate I sold to the news hounds. She was a pretty little thing in her own way. Nice red hair. I would have asked her out. She might have been a nurse.

"Don't even think necrophilia. Don't go there. I'll delete any necro comments. You know me. I don't like to delete, even when people are critical, but necro is just too much. Besides, I did a video on necro last year after many, many requests for the subject. It wasn't *my* idea. It was you, my listeners. What's she wearing? What is it? A shroud. Nothing else. She's not—wasn't—a vamp, because she would have exploded. She *was* just a regular person. Looks like she picked the wrong side. That dress, that shroud, is really pulled up. 'Nice gams,' as the German soldier said in *Saving Private Ryan*, one of my favorite movies, even though it takes about eight hours to watch with all the commercials stuffed in on TV. What a shame.

"All this dirt keeps falling. Soon she'll be buried. Wait a minute. I want to snag a little more jewelry. Another man's ring— what they call a cat's eye. And a woman's necklace. Look how fine the chain is. Must have taken forever to make under a microscope. Time enough for a vamp. The necklace is partially under the girl's leg. I'm going to pull it out. I might almost have to touch this corpse if I want to get the chain. She's going to be buried in a cave-in anyway. I want the stuff. It will all be blessed. I'll spring for a mass for her, too. It won't hurt, even if she's not Catholic. Here goes. I'm going for that necklace. My hand's shaking so much. It's the one with the injured wrist. I hope I don't have a permanent palsy.

"Oh my God! I touched her. I didn't mean to. That's how my hand is shaking, from the injured wrist. Okay. Here's the necklace. Rather nice. Looks like real gold. Whoever's thinking that now that I've touched a corpse, I might pull up that shroud another inch to see her...you know. I'm not doing it. That might be pornography. I could get kicked off my platform. Two things I won't tolerate. Necro and porno. I never tolerated vampires, either, until today, unless it's Bela or Christopher with the pointed teeth. Still, I like a woman who shaves her...you know. But I won't look. Some mysteries are better left unsolved. Add perversion to the two things already mentioned that I won't tolerate. No pervs, no porn, no necro.

"Oh, shit. My battery light on the camera is blinking. You know what that means. I'm about to get cut off. Not like when a rich uncle cuts you out of his will because you're a real jerk off, but like when your phone battery dies. I'll try to give you one last shot down the rest of the tunnel. And...there are people here. All covered with blood. Some are standing. Some are dead. Some are wounded. They're all—in one state or another, except for the dead —looking at me. Guys. Bargain Videos signing off. Peace. Out."

Guacamole took John Bargain's cell phone with her bloodied hand.

Bargain scrambled back until he was against the wall next to Patty's body. He pointed. "You know, that might be considered theft."

Guacamole waved her hand. "I have witnesses that say you abused a corpse."

"That's not true."

"The witnesses are reliable. Are you?"

"I want my phone back. I'm a vlogger. It's my livelihood."

"You'll get it back, after I see what you recorded. I might do some selective editing."

"I'm also a freelance photographer. A journalist and member of the Fourth Estate."

"How interesting."

"Hey, are you a Brit? I love the Brits. My mom was a Brit. Still is. I for one could go for a spot of tea about now. Wash down the dust and all that. I'm what they call parched. What do you say we get out of here—you, me, and my phone. Any chance you're a nurse, too? What do you say *we*—as my Uncle Lou used to say—blow this garage."

"Somehow, I don't believe you," Guacamole said. The remaining Brethren tittered.

"That's my problem," Bargain countered. "I'm not very believable and most people find I leave a bad first impression."

"Now, that I believe." Guacamole pulled Bargain to his feet.

Persimmon stepped up. Brushed dirt from Bargain's shoulders. Looked him over.

"Are you the leader?" Bargain asked Persimmon.

"Why do you ask?"

"You look the type."

"You're really a freelance news photographer?"

"It pays the bills. Plus, I have a kind of paranormal channel on YouTube."

"Do you have any family?"

"None to speak of."

"A significant other?"

"No. But I'm available. Are you a nurse, by chance?"

"Interesting. I might have a job for you. We'll talk about that later."

* * *

EVA STOOD PATIENTLY FACING the door to her crypt. Her hands squeezed into fists. Her black blood dripped to the dirt from her self-inflicted wounds. She took a step. Stopped. Took another step. Turned to Lazlo. "I smell virgin's blood. Not one but the blood of many." She seemed ready to swoon. Righted herself.

"It was a Brethren trick," Lazlo said from the dirt floor.

Kazmer grunted in agreement.

"The fools!" The vampiress screamed. She shuffled forward a few steps. Raised her arms. "No! No! No!" Then she swore an oath in an ancient, foreign language. The brothers nodded. The vampiress turned toward the bed. Lisa and Jimmy saw her expression and recoiled. "The colony is destroyed. All gone."

Lisa and Jimmy stirred on the bed. She turned at them and hissed. "The Brethren's numbers have been decimated, too, but some remain." She turned to the brothers. "Watch *them* while I kill the rest."

She blurred down the exterior ramp to the passage entrance and paused a moment.

———

Persimmon turned to the remaining Brethren. Even those standing were weary and showed signs of wounds, leaning on their empty crossbows. "Did anyone stake the ancient one? It would have made a terrific bang. Smelled like the gates of hell."

"*Not I! Not I! Not I!*" the Brethren answered.

"She must be in her crypt with Lisa," Overboard George said. "Is it time to save the rest of our people?"

"Now's the time."

Bargain interrupted. "We all ought to get out of here. I heard firemen in the house's basement." He pointed up the passage. "There's tons of shit up there, probably on fire, but eventually they're going to make their way down here. There were cops outside, too. They'll be right on their heels. Look. The smoke's almost gone."

"Will you help us?"

"I got nothing better to do and a phone with a dead battery. Actually, it's a phone you have now."

Guacamole rested her hand on his shoulder. Squeezed it. "What happened to your wrist?"

"Vamps outside. Smoked two of them. They were hidden under the sod."

Guacamole said, "I'll make it feel better later. You killed vampires. You're one of us now."

Persimmon said, "Anyone who can help the wounded, stay behind, if you are wounded yourself. I want everybody else outside in the sun. Get our rides ready. We don't want to meet the authorities. I want every able-bodied on me. Pick up all the bolts you can. Machetes and axes. Leave the dead Shadow. That will slow down the firemen. The cops, too. Nothing's burning down here."

"Not yet," Del Hatch said, almost to himself, and smiled. He helped pass out the collected bolts.

"Formation!" Persimmon called.

The able-bodied Brethren formed their ranks, crouched, and moved down the passage two abreast, crossbows raised. Persimmon took the lead in the first row next to Guacamole. They scooped up spent bolts as they went, passed them around, and loaded their weapons. Now, each had a few more shots.

"This one will be a tough nut to crack," Persimmon said, looking at her friend for a moment.

"I cracked tougher. More of them, too," Guacamole said, returning her stare.

"I don't doubt it."

THE VAMPIRESS STEPPED into the passage.

All her senses were on high alert. She heard the Brethren's' boots crunching down the passage. How many were there? Seven? Eight? Ten? She couldn't tell. They stepped in time.

The scent of virgin blood was strong, like a perfume, intoxicating in the narrow confines of the passage. Her thirst raged. Consumed her. She wanted the blood, even if she had to suck it from the soil. She knew the Brethren had spilled the blood to intensify its aroma. She wanted to charge up the passage, through the approaching Brethren, slash them to pieces, to get to the blood. She didn't care how many bolts, bullets, ax strikes they landed, she would reach the spot where the blood was poured, grovel on the ground to sop it up. Her swirling tongue ached. Her throat throbbed. Every fiber in her body shrieked for this nourishment.

She sensed the blood came from multiple virgins; she could not detect how many. She knew the blood traveled toward her. Yes, they had spilled some virgin blood in the passage, but they wore it, too. She could lick their skin, rip off their clothes, and suck it from the fabrics, even though it would never slake her thirst. There would never be enough. She leaned forward, prepared to blur and caught herself. She squeezed her hands until they bled and bellowed. She took one huge draft of blood-scented air and was gone.

"That's our girl," Persimmon said. "She's cruisin' for a bruisin.'"

The Brethren continued down the passage. Del Hatch brought up the rear, a long stake in one hand, a throwing ax in the other. Overboard George, who stayed with the wounded, shouldered the BAR. George was the only person Del trusted with the gun.

The Brethren breathed heavily. Del was tired. The Brethren were tired. Still, they marched on. He transferred the ax to the hand that held the long stake, and felt the chest of his jumpsuit. Ten grenades were left, plus a package of plastic explosives. *It's about time I shed a little weight.*

Eva returned to her crypt. She squeezed her fists. Her hands bled again. Healed. Bled again. She shook with rage.

The brothers pulled out two old Enfield rifles. "We will kill them, mistress, with our rifles," Lazlo said. "We can stay hidden on the platform outside, where they can't see us. My brudder and me—"

Kazmer interrupted. "They stopped shooting. They must be out of ammunition. For us, it will be like shooting fish in a bucket."

Laszlo smiled. "Already you know the English expressions, my brudder. I will take away the bridge to...stop them."

"Hinder," Kazmer said.

"First, make me a hole in the wall near Bo," Eva said. "I want to be there when he emerges. Then cover the hole, so no one will see it. Let me know when the Brethren are dead."

The brothers grabbed their picks and dug into the wall. When they had a spot large enough for the vampiress, she crawled in, and the brothers sealed it. Then they crawled out on the ledge, where they lay flat, their Enfields aimed at the floor below. Each had extra clips at his side.

THE BRETHREN REACHED the entrance to the main vault, stepped out cautiously, and reformed. The vault was quiet. Despite the daylight outside, even the bats had fled. Persimmon walked out near the main vault's center. She kept her crossbow raised, swept back and forth, waiting for the vampiress to move. Persimmon moved to the ceremonial altar. Inspected its top, the channels and depressions designed to catch and hold blood.

A shot rang out. Lazlo's bullet missed Persimmon, hit the ornate altar, and splintered off a corner. Persimmon dove behind the altar just as Kazmer pulled the trigger. His bullet hit the spot Persimmon just vacated.

The Brethren answered with several bolts that sailed over the brothers' heads.

"Save them!" Guacamole called. "Damn it. I told her not to go out there."

"She drew their fire so we'd know where they are," Del Hatch said. "Now we got to find a way to get her back and I might know how to do it."

"How?" Guacamole said.

"Trust me."

Del put his jumpsuit against the wall and slid, where the brothers couldn't see him without exposing themselves, toward an area under the shelf. He pulled out three grenades, wired them together, and hung them on a piece of root, one of several that protruded from the wall. Although there was an empty ground-level crypt under the shelf, Del didn't trust it. He pulled a pin and sprinted back to the Brethren. The grenades exploded. Part of the vault roof collapsed. The shelf crumbled and the brothers fell head over heels down the incline to the floor. Kazmer scrambled into the crypt with his rifle. Lazlo was left exposed, dazed by the fall. The Brethren pumped three bolts into his chest in a tight grouping, killing him instantly. Del Hatch ran back toward the crypt, tugged out another grenade from inside his jumpsuit, pulled the pin and lobbed it into the opening. It exploded, dropping more material, sealing off the crypt.

Del returned to the main dome floor. "Hey, anybody home up there!" he called, with his hands cupped around his mouth. "No need to worry. The two big uglies are dead."

Lisa and Jimmy appeared at the crypt opening and teetered on the edge. "How do you expect us to get down? You destroyed the path," Lisa called.

"What about the vampires?"

"They're all dead, really dead," Del called back. "Except for the female."

"She's buried up here, in the wall, with Bo."

"Those vamps, with their claws, can tunnel like an earthworm," Persimmon said, joining Del Hatch. I don't know that we'll find her."

"That doesn't answer my original question," Lisa said. "How do we get down? Don't say you're going to use more dynamite."

"Just a couple grenades. That's all," Del replied.

Persimmon looked over their predicament. After a moment, she called, "Pull that curtain off. Slide down like a carnival ride. Make it snappy. We got firemen coming down that chute."

Persimmon pointed to the passage. "We have rides out in the cemetery." She pointed to the exit door.

The Brethren started to carry the wounded and dead through the vault, headed for the exit. A few limped behind. Bargain ran up. Was breathless. "They're in the tunnel. They found the girl's body and called for police. They stopped for a minute until the police get through the house, but then they'll start moving, be here in a minute or two."

Persimmon waved to Jimmy and Lisa. Jimmy tore down the thick curtain and spread it on the ground near the edge of the drop. He helped Lisa sit on the material, sat behind her as if they were on a sleigh, folded the carpet over their legs, and pushed off. Lisa screamed. They sailed down the inclined wall, bumping all the way, and skidded to a stop partway out on the vault floor. Del Hatch helped Lisa to her feet.

She said, "You must be..."

"Del Hatch, at your service." He winked.

"We never met, but I feel I know you."

"I get that a lot," Del said and smiled. "Maybe you've seen me on television."

The Brethren led Lisa and Jimmy to the exit. Outside, vehicles waited. The wounded and dead were already loaded.

"Hey kid, come here a minute," Del Hatch told Bargain. John trotted to the man.

"Are you the guy who shot up all the vamps?"

"Sure am. Del Hatch at your service."

"That was fucking cool."

"I know it was. Now, take a couple of these and follow me." Del pulled out the remainder of his grenades, gave some to Bargain, and ran to the base of the crypt. He handed Bargain wire. "String these together. When one blows, they all blow. Del dug dog-style into the loose dirt with his jungle knife. Pressed the grenades and the plastic explosive into the depression. "Now see this grenade on the end. You pull the pin..."

"Me?

"Sure. I figure you're fast enough. Faster than I am, anyway. Pull the pin and run like hell for the outside."

"Me?"

"You'll be fast enough. Faster than you've ever been. I'll be waiting on the other side."

"I snuck up the tunnel a bit. Heard them talking. The firemen got tired of waiting for the police. The fire's out. They carried the girl's body back to the house. They were afraid the tunnel would collapse; the way dirt was falling. They're probably on the street by now. What kind of damage are we talking about? From your blast?"

Del scratched his chin. "Oh, I don't know. Just run as fast as you can. That's my advice."

"Advice? You don't know?"

"Sure, I know. Run as fast as you can. That charge is going to bring this whole darn place down. Make you feel better? Maybe what's left of the house, too. It's not an exact science, at least with me it isn't. That plastique is going to make a hell of a bang." Del moved away, backward, said with a smile, an index finger in the air. "Remember—pull the pin and run like hell."

"What if I trip?"

"Don't."

Bargain approached the explosives. He looked back. Del was near the exit. He grinned, nodded, and mouthed, *"Do it."*

Bargain fingered a grenade pin. He stood sideways as if the extra half step it would give him might save his life. He looked back. Del Hatch grinned. Nodded to him again. Bargain closed his eyes. Tightened his grip on the pin. Opened them. Overboard George was at the door with the BAR. Del flashed a stop sign. Overboard whispered to Del. Del pursed his lips. Nodded his head at whatever Overboard George told him. Del waved Bargain to join him. Overboard George passed Del the rifle while Bargain jogged across the floor.

"George found me a bullet," Del said, with a smile. "I'll detonate it from here. No. Over there under the big arch of that door. It'll give me a few extra yards. You and George get down to the mausoleum and stay out of my way. Go on. I'll be coming like sixty."

"Do you want me to take the shot?" Overboard George said.

"Not a chance," Del Hatch said.

Overboard George and Bargain retreated to the safety of the cemetery grounds and their waiting ride. All that remained was for Del Hatch to join them.

"That old fool," George said. "He's liable to blow up half the city. There might be a gas line buried in that hill. Do you think he cares? He's crazier than a bed bug. Running around looking for Sasquatches, keeping explosives on his person, carrying that relic of a heavy gun."

They waited in Del Hatch's SUV. The engine idled. It was parked to roar away from the cemetery. The AC blasted. They watched the mausoleum door. Traded glances. Looked back through the cemetery.

A large boom shook the ground and rocked the SUV. Smoke exploded from the mausoleum entrance. Del Hatch followed, covered in dirt, rifle in hand, pumping his arms. He ran across the cemetery lawn, leaped through the stone wall's open gate, and jumped into the SUV's back seat. The door was already open. They roared off, spinning the tires, just ahead of the landslide that followed. It covered the old mausoleum and several others along the row. The husk of the charred vampire house teetered, collapsed, and slid down the embankment, too, starting another fire. On the top, water geysers shot in the air from the house's guts. Electric sparks showered the rubble. Auto horns blared. An electric transformer on a pole up the street exploded as the SUV whizzed by the scene while the firemen rolled up their hoses.

John Bargain watched out the car window.

Del Hatch was giddy as he tried to catch his breath.

<hr>

JOHN BARGAIN WANTED to relax on the ride to wherever the Brethren were taking him but couldn't. At least he felt safe. His wrist throbbed. He was covered with dirt and blood, most of which he hoped wasn't his own. The only person he knew in the vehicle was Del Hatch, who rode shotgun; a man whom he had met only an hour ago, a man who just blew up a house and half a hillside. A man who might still carry explosives. How could he feel safe? Everyone was silent. The hulking Brethren next to him snoozed.

Bargain thought it might be a good time to find a real job. A good job, in fact, a position, a career, with a steady income that would allow him to save and invest money for retirement, instead of living accident to accident, crime scene to crime scene. A job with benefits. One in which an office romance was possible. One for which he dressed nicely and didn't get dirty. After all, he had a college education.

Finally, a job that would prohibit cell phone use. He had had enough of that. His mind wandered as he watched the landscape whiz past. He returned his gaze inside the vehicle. His wrist the vampire grabbed was bruised and swollen. His body was sore from over-exertion. His mind paused as he contemplated his wrist and then the back of Del Hatch's head. He thought *I wonder whether Del Hatch will give me an interview.* And finally: *How long will it take the Brethren to find another vampire colony?*

WHAT'S NEXT?

The After Dark Series concludes with *The Reluctant Vampire*, the third novel in the trilogy, as newly minted vampire Bo Bentwood looks for love, struggles with his vow never to take a human life, and avoids the Brethren and their crossbow arrows on a trip back to his Midwest hometown with trusty servant Kazmer Savoy.

About the Author

Dean Alan Conrad is a former newspaper reporter and columnist. He is a graduate of the Pennsylvania State University with a degree in English. He lives in Pennsylvania and always has been interested in everything spooky.